OF JUDGEMENT FALLEN

Steven Veerapen was born in Glasgow to a Scottish mother and a Mauritian father and raised in Paisley. Pursuing an interest in the sixteenth century, he was awarded a first-class Honours degree in English, focusing his dissertation on representations of Henry VIII's six wives. He has received a Master's in Renaissance studies, and a PhD investigating Elizabethan slander. Visit: www.stevenveerapen.com.

OF JUDGEMENT FALLEN

AN ANTHONY BLANKE
TUDOR MYSTERY

STEVEN VEERAPEN

Polygon

First published in paperback in Great Britain
in 2023 by Polygon,
an imprint of Birlinn Ltd

Birlinn Ltd
West Newington House
10 Newington Road
Edinburgh
EH9 1QS

www.polygonbooks.co.uk

9 8 7 6 5 4 3 2 1

ISBN 978 1 84697 629 2
eBook ISBN 978 1 78885 561 7

Typeset in Dante by The Foundry, Edinburgh
Printed and bound in Great Britain by Clays Ltd, Elcograf S.p.A.

DRAMATIS PERSONAE

THE ROYALS AND THEIR HOUSEHOLD
Henry VIII, King of England
Catherine of Aragon, his wife
Dr Mordaunt, their physician
William Rowlett, his assistant
Anne Boleyn, a lady of the Court

CARDINAL WOLSEY'S HOUSEHOLD
Cardinal Thomas Wolsey, Archbishop of York, Prince-
Bishop of Durham, and Lord Chancellor
Richard Audley, his principal secretary
Mr Deacon, his gentleman usher
Harry Gainsford, his gentleman
Lord Henry Percy, heir to the earldom of Northumberland,
his gentleman
Anthony Blanke, his trumpeter
Mark Byfield, his trumpeter

IN LONDON
Sir Thomas More, royal councillor
Alice More, his wife
Lancelot Cosyn, a scholar
Bess, his housekeeper
Rob, an apprentice

AT BLACKFRIARS
Brother Gervaise, a troublemaker
Brother Alfred, master of the dormitory

PROLOGUE

Lancelot Cosyn tried not to think about the men who hoped to see him dead. He shut them out of his mind, his knotty fingers working at his doublet. A flare of pain passed through his arthritic joints and he paused, praying silently that it would pass. He sang inside his head, in Latin, the lines he had sung more frequently with each passing year:

O Christ our Lord, who art the physician of salvation, grant unto all who are sick the aid of heavenly healing. Vouchsafe to deliver them from all sickness and infirmity, through Jesus Christ. Amen.

The mantra worked, as it always did, and he slid the last wooden button through its loop, before gathering his plain grey cloak around himself. When he was ready, he moved quietly through his empty house. The walls stood mute, shorn of their hangings, the cabinets which once nestled against them, the plate and candlesticks that had once made the house a home. Still, the lack of household stuff made it easier to move in the half-light.

He considered rousing Bess.

No.

Let her sleep on in peace, in silent dreams.

She would only try and dissuade him from doing what he must. Women were, by their nature, timid and fretful.

She knew nothing of his business. It was better that way. It was not a woman's part to know of men's dangerous courses.

The problem was that he himself felt unmanned – felt as though by going against the Church, against Godly order, he was stripping himself down to ugly, sinful flesh and bone.

No. No. No.

That was weakness, come to tempt him. He must be brave. He must be David, standing before Goliath. He must be Moses, confronting the Pharaoh. He must be Ptolemaeus, rejecting the cruel and unjust laws and chancellery of Rome.

Still, a bolt of fear shot through him as he felt his way down the stairs to the front door, his heart fluttering with every cautious step. At the bottom, he turned his head and looked back up the tunnel of darkness. Farewell, dear Bess, he thought. To himself, he mouthed, 'I shall not see your sweet face again for a long space, but all shall be worth it in the end.' Unlocking the door, he stepped out, blinking, and patted at his breast. The papers crinkled underneath his cloak.

He would be heard.

God would be listening, if no one else.

Reassured, Cosyn ignored the excited barking of Bess's little dog and marched through the plain yard, out of the crumbling gateway, and into the sinful city. Its morning sounds rose to meet him and there was a strange kind of beauty in them. From his left came the rise and fall of singing: men were setting up some pageant or other. He could see them – could see a great, tall wagon being dragged into place up by the tower of St Magnus. It was their boys – young pups indeed – who were singing, bawdy nonsense, some with armfuls of paper flowers, others with pails over one arm and brushes ready in little white paws.

He turned away from the preparations and, his head down, sipped air shallowly as the stink of the river thickened. The wharf was already busy – it was always busy – with the oaths and grunts of sailors. The big ships couldn't go much farther upriver, not past the nearby bridge, and so they unloaded their cargo at the warehouses just shy of it. The river itself spread behind their masts and sails, looking eternal, looking strong and grey.

Cosyn watched it awhile. Something like sadness came over him. It was more powerful than fear and more draining. He could turn back now and return to his empty house. He could let the world go on as it was, saying nothing, doing nothing, dying one day, peacefully in his bed, without ever having caused a ripple.

It would be easy.

It would be pleasant.

'Lookin' for something, sir?'

He jerked at the piping voice, wheeling, trying to look everywhere at once. 'What?' he croaked. He saw her – a thin, ragged girl. She wore no coif or apron. All she had on, in fact, was a dull, dun-brown dress – homespun woollen, patched, and too big for her – with the top cut away to reveal bosom. Or, he realised in horror, it might have revealed bosom had she had any. She was no woman – she was a child, little more than twelve, dressed like a doxy. All she lacked were the painted baubles the old trulls south of the river wore. Her youth, probably, would make up for that – the look of maidenhead would be jewel enough for some rough, base brutes. Cosyn stepped back, raising his scrawny arms protectively over his chest.

'Won't cost much, sir,' she said. 'They tells me 'ow much is fair. 'Ow much they want.'

Cosyn swayed a little on his feet. Pain flared again, in his stomach this time – the by-now familiar burning, which spread outwards, clutching at his belly. 'Be gone,' he said. 'Get you to. . .'

To where?

He didn't know.

In these evil days, he'd heard that hospitals and monasteries – even the great monasteries – were pleasure palaces for rich men and their friends. If they tended to the poor and fallen, it was only to encourage them in idle sloth and fecklessness.

The girl shrugged, already looking past him – looking down towards the wharf. Her eyes didn't light up at the sight of more likely custom amongst the mariners. Instead, he thought, they deadened a little more. He watched as, without a word, she trudged down towards the river. He could imagine her little feet under the skirts, wrapped in cloth probably – a child's feet, still small enough to be held in the palm of a hand.

A tear pricked at one eye and he let it fall.

She was a sign from God, he thought – God was urging him onwards, approving his plans, chiding him for doubting them.

He would go. He would do whatever he might to improve the world.

Embracing the pain in his middle, he turned from the wharf and began moving along the northern bank, past the skeletal cranes and weathered timber warehouses, each step drumming a tattoo, a call to arms, against the fallen state of the city.

Ahead, the bridge appeared: a jumble of houses and shops, spreading left across the river like a raised arm clad in velvets, bangles, and jewels. As he approached, he could see the water churning and rushing under its arches. Ignoring the rise of London on his right, Cosyn stepped across New Fish Street and swung left, taking the waterman's stairs down to the Thames.

It was early enough that few wherrymen were about, but those that were appeared unoccupied. They leaned against the sides of their crafts, chatting to one another. Ragged ends of conversation reached Cosyn.

'All night he was in the stew, dawn till dusk. Didn't think he had it in him. I says to meself, Andrew, I says, he's had it this time. Could barely see straight whens I dropped him at Church Lane, never mind the other.'

'Wouldn't mind seein' the wife's face when 'e got 'ome. ''Im all bitten by a Winchester goose.'

'Sour one, that.'

'Sourer still when 'is pox gets on 'er.'

'Good morrow,' said Cosyn.

Heads turned to him. He addressed himself to the boatman who'd called himself Andrew. 'I must go upriver.'

'How far, sir?'

'Richmond.'

Andrew's eyes lit up. 'That's a distance, sir. But I was intending to goes that way meself. Good business, being near m'lord cardinal.' Slyness crept over his features. 'I hears the king is off down to . . . where is it?'

'Portsmouth,' called the other boatman, creaking back on his bench.

'Portsmouth,' agreed Andrew. 'You have maybe some business with m'lord cardinal, is it, sir?'

'Yes,' said Cosyn, flatly, hoping to discourage any further questions. It would, indeed, be a long journey upriver, and he wished to drink it in. He wished to see the birds soar up from the reeds and have a look at the great palaces by the river as the morning sunlight glinted off their coloured windows. He wished to dangle his hand over the side of the wherry and feel the sudden, sharp ice of the water. 'The cardinal.'

A searing pain through his middle nearly folded him over.

'Here, sir, are you well? It's . . . it ain't the sweat, is it?' asked Andrew.

With grunting effort, Cosyn straightened. He forced brightness into his voice. 'Age only,' he said. 'And poor apothecaries.' He thought of the bottles hidden under his cloak. Not time for them yet. He would have a steadying drink and toss them in the river soon enough.

This seemed to relax the boatman, who stood easily. He stepped down the length of his wherry and held out a hand. Gratefully, Cosyn accepted, smiling his thanks as he stepped from the water-lapped steps onto the swaying boat. More gratefully, he sat.

'To the cardinal at Richmond, then,' said Andrew, half-asking, half-stating.

'Yes. To him.'

Cosyn settled himself as the boatman cried, 'For Richmond, Richmond ho!'

For the cardinal, Lancelot Cosyn thought.

For Wolsey.

As they cast off, gently bobbing until Andrew caught the water with his oar and began propelling the wherry smoothly, Cosyn kept his eyes on the innumerable spires and crosses that jutted upwards from the rickety, uneven city skyline. He could name almost all of them and he made a game of it as they sailed on: All Hallows the Less; All Hallows the Great; St Martin Vintry; St James Garlickhythe; St Nicholas Olave; St Mary Somerset.

It wasn't the structure of the Church, he thought, that was rotten – it wasn't its material things, its places of worship. It was the men who had come to squat within them. They were worldly men who cared more for their treasures and the affairs of the commonwealth than for spiritual cares.

Men like Cardinal Thomas Wolsey, Lord Chancellor, Prince-bishop, Archbishop: a clutch of titles and a range of interests, none of them pure, none of them holy or focused on ministering to anyone but Cardinal Thomas Wolsey.

And the king, a little nagging voice in his head reminded him.

The wherry rocked on.

'A fine place, is that one,' said Andrew, evidently having decided he'd rowed in silence long enough. Cosyn looked up. They were gliding past a wall of red, which rose almost directly from the river. 'King's palace at Bridewell.'

The king.

The king, thought Cosyn, was a virtuous man – a good, devoted son of Rome. But his virtue wouldn't last, not as long as he kept men like the great wether Wolsey around him. Such creatures as the proud cardinal bred corruption; they were parasites, feeding on the flesh of the great, and leaving it to rot, to turn black and festering, to stink. It had begun already – that noxious stink: the rottenness at the heart of the body politic had already sent its foul airs out into the city, spreading whoredom and drunkenness, leaving filthy words and images scrawled on tavern walls and in dirt, forcing children to sell themselves, encouraging bishops to gather rents from stews. There was an endpoint to it all, of course – an endpoint to God being snubbed and mocked: a final collapse in order and justice. If the king's reign had begun in hope and glory, justice and mercy, the cardinal had soured it. He *was* souring it. He was drowning it in courtly minions and flatterers and sycophants, in trulls and trull-keepers, in panders and heathens – some, Cosyn had heard, even plucked from the ends of the earth, from Africa and God-knew-where, and imported to make the ornamented court even more of a place of vanities and vices.

But not for long.

Beyond Bridewell, they passed the stout grey walls of the Blackfriars, where Wolsey's great parliament was to meet – to help the cardinal fund his war games, to keep the great brute bestride the whole of Europe. Foolishly, childishly, Cosyn peeped towards the edifice as they sailed by the gatehouse, as though his good friend therein might have happened to be at that moment standing there in his cope, waiting to salute him. But then they were past the priory, the boat rocking gently as it negotiated the white caps formed by the outflow of the Fleet.

Oh, well. Farewell, anyway, Brother Gervaise.

Cosyn settled again, closing his eyes. The sun had risen now and, though it gave off little warmth, it felt good to be bathed in its rays. It felt better, too, to know that soon he would make his stand; he would walk into the black heart of the English court and by God's grace he would be heard.

A sudden caw-caw-caw tore into the air.

Cosyn opened his eyes to see a flock of gulls taking flight, as though eager to be free of the fallen world.

I

Richmond Palace, Spring 1523

There is a thrill, an excitement, in doing something you know you shouldn't. We learn it as children – cursing, or stealing a spoonful of honey. And we learn as quickly to conceal our little sins – to find ways of swearing when there's no parent to hear or rolling our tongues around the spoons when older backs are turned. Probably, learning how to get away with being bad is one of the first things we set our little minds to after discovering what good and bad are.

I could hear that same tense, exhilarated excitement singing in the girl's laugh. In response, I drew deeper into the shadows behind the statue – a saint, whose carved, painted eyes looked up to the curved wooden ceiling of the recess. The little cubby, with its pious tenant and its listening interloper, lay only a foot away from the door from which the laughter drifted.

They hadn't closed it, I knew. That was a stupid, reckless move. It led into one of the royal staterooms and anyone might come upon them.

And anyone had.

A little thrill – of shame and excitement – ran through me.

How did I come to this?

It had been no accident, of course. I'd seen Lord Henry Percy, son of the earl of Northumberland – known as Hal, said with a smile by his friends and rolled eyes by the rest of us – whispering and looking handsome and soft and weak in the cardinal's rooms. There had been laughter amongst his little group too. And then, as he'd taken to doing these last weeks, he pulled down his feathered hat and slipped from the room, pushed on by hearty claps on the back – a change from his usual mooning about, sketching on boards and trying to appear uncaring of the world.

I'd followed.

People noticed when Percy crept out of Cardinal Wolsey's rooms. No one cared when I did the same. No one pays any attention to a menial groom of the great chamber. Probably they thought I'd been ordered to see that a grate was lit somewhere, or that carpets were being beaten clean. It's like being invisible. Though only a page in Wolsey's privy chamber, Percy would never be able to be invisible. The fool.

Me, I was no such fool. I'd kept my distance as I'd followed him out into the great gallery. His footsteps echoed on the polished wooden floorboards. He passed in and out of shafts of light permitted entry through tall, rectangular windows and the little circular ones above. The room was empty but for a pair of boys sprinkling fresh herbs on braziers of sea coal. Their work filled the air with spice, with a sharp tanging perfume. With the king on the road somewhere, Wolsey's people wanted to be near the cardinal, in the inner sanctum, not beyond it. Percy was running away from power. Just for a moment, he paused on the other side of the large room. I froze, expecting him to turn. And then I saw the reason why he'd halted.

Who are you?

A little man, muffled under grey robes and a grey cloak, had appeared before Percy. His head was bowed. I stepped closer, into the large room, but their voices, even in the echoing gallery, were distant. The two chamber boys had turned to look too, though without much interest.

At length, Percy's voice rose and he half-turned, giving me his profile. I froze, caught now in the middle of the hall, my throat drying. But my prey was gesturing to his left, directing the little visitor.

Waiting chamber.

Meekly, the guest became a shuffling blur of grey. Old, I thought – wrapped up against the imaginary cold as old men will, even on mild days. Percy had successfully blocked him from entering the gallery, whoever he was. When the old man had disappeared, the younger man only gave himself a nod, twirled the red feather in his hat so that it curled, and passed out of the doorway. My own footsteps, as I followed, did not echo.

When I reached the door myself, polished wood turning to tiles under my feet, I glanced to the left. I could see into the waiting chamber, where the grey man was standing, only his lined face visible amidst the grey. Sweat stood out on it. A petitioner, I thought – some man of the city or Church come to beg Wolsey for some favour or other. Next to him, seated beside a blazing, applewood-filled fireplace, was a younger man, lengths of red cloth spread out over his arm like a carver's towels.

One of the ushers, I knew, would be along to convey these waiting fellows to the cardinal, when His Grace deigned to see them. They were none of my business.

Still, the intense old man held my interest for a moment. Dark circles hung under his pouched, sunken eyes.

Is he trembling?

I rolled my tongue in my cheek, before blinking. I was wasting time, finding excuses not to do what I'd been bidden. Percy was still on the move.

Turning away from the waiting chamber's open doorway, I crept onwards, through the narrow, panelled hallway, and followed the earl's son through a chain of reception halls – all the cardinal's, all lined with glinting tapestries and carpeted in red. Even the light turned colourful, falling in as it did through dyed Flemish glass, as I reached the staircase leading downwards. Unless he had ducked into a side room, this was where my quarry had gone: the ground floor, where the lower servants toiled behind screens: the boot-cleaners and the old seamstresses, and the men who held offices of the household and kept their ledgers and accounts hidden there.

Where are you going?

I knew. Or I thought I knew. And so I wasn't surprised when Percy left Wolsey's suite of lodgings and I passed out after him, blinking into a morning of fitful grey clouds pierced with darts of sunshine. Across the cobbled Great Court ahead, the wardrobe building rose like a cliff of red brick and glass. Its projecting, octagonal turrets were each surmounted with onion-shaped, gilded cupolas. The royal pennants hung limp, as if they knew their master was from home.

They'll stiffen at the sight of him, no doubt.

I shuddered.

There was the bobbing feather.

All alone.

Fool!

I had at the least expected Percy to have employed a menial – one of the low fellows he insisted do his duties for him as a page – to keep watch.

But no. He was bearing right, towards the wall of sparkling white brick that marked the inner palace – a quadrangle of staterooms which stood around the Middle Court.

I wonder why. . .

There was no need for secrecy in the Great Court. People stood around everywhere, men stripped down to their shirts, straining as they heaved coffers off of carts, women in coifs and mobcaps sloshing the cobbles with water. The clerks of the market, their staves of office held like batons against their shoulders, led little clusters of servants carrying linen-draped baskets of fresh goods. Ladders had been set up against the side of the cardinal's block, some of them with linen-aproned men at the tops, bringing the lead-paned windows to a sheen. Great wagonloads of bushels of apples stood about, their loads ready to be peeled and stewed and made fit to sweeten fish. Snatches of song rose and fell from those who hadn't yet tired of their labour, accompanied by the ubiquitous pipe players; it was still only late morning. Here and there, soot-faced children shuffled, their pails of night soil mercifully covered with slats. I stood back from one and watched for a moment as others did the same. And then I was off again, sidling round a horse still tethered to its cart, making for the huge, semi-circular gateway cut into the white stone.

'Cardinal's business,' I said, putting my chest out to let the porter see my livery. I had a brief impression of green and white: a yeoman of the guard, lounging in the little gatehouse by a fire, his boots up to it.

'Anuvver?' The question drifted after me.

I might have been lost, had it not been for Percy taking another moment to preen. This he did before a tall window on the left-hand block. And then he was off again, passing through an open doorway. His gait had shifted: he kept one hand loosely on his hip and let his hips swing. Like a rakehell, I thought – as though he were a man of France and not from nobility that might as well have been Scottish.

There were fewer people about in the smaller, more intimate Middle Court – only a couple of older women, dressed as though they might have been nuns. My heart skipped at the sight of them, as it always did at the sight of habits.

Fool.

I shook it away. They were only a pair of the queen's old Spanish ladies, and they turned their backs, making – fittingly – for the colonnaded cloisters on one side of the courtyard. I moved ahead, towards the wing Percy had entered, and paused in the shadows of the doorway myself, listening.

His Grace seeks to see how the queen does.

That sounded a reasonable enough excuse if I were challenged.

His Grace my lord cardinal wishes to know if the queen seeks music.

Better.

There were no sounds from within. I lingered for a moment, enjoying the coolness, the feeling of being between something and nothing. And then I lifted my chin and stepped into the building.

Carpeted flooring ran off in either direction – not red, but a deep purple, with Tudor roses woven into it. The walls were whitewashed, with doorways set at intervals, and between each were cut deep recesses with their painted saints – some with votive offerings lit to them. The buttery smell of the candles competed with the sweetness of perfume – damask-rose powder, I thought – which lingered in the air. These, I knew, were the royal staterooms, but they might well have been a great priest's house.

It was then that I first heard the laughter, high and clear and musical.

It is her.

I had a fair memory, for sounds and voices especially. When you made your way in the world with music and wrote little, you had need of one.

And then an accompanying giggle – Percy's giggle – harsher.

Moving towards it on tiptoe, the smell of roses growing stronger, I folded myself in behind one of the statues – the one nearest the door.

And so, like a filthy, grubbing spy, I found myself eavesdropping.

The rumours about Percy had been floating around for weeks – months. I wasn't one for rumours, really – but it was my duty to listen out for them, to smell the stink of them and see if it led to shit or sugared almonds. I'd once been in Wolsey's service as a musician – or, more honestly, as a trumpet blaster, announcing him as he processed into dinner or out to Mass. But I'd given that up, and only gone back into service reluctantly.

Back. . .

I shook out my sleeve, the cuff of which dangled over discoloured skin.

I had agreed to return to the cardinal's service on the condition that I might be allowed to dress as I pleased, however disorderly I might look, and that I not be put on display as a novelty. Wolsey, of course, had conditions of his own. His words floated into my memory, in his rich, University-accented voice.

'I have no need for a man who wishes to do as he pleases. But a young man who might serve me in other ways . . . a man who has learnt discretion . . . yes . . . your sharp ears and eyes I understand well . . . yes . . . you might yet do me some good service. . .'

And so I'd become a spy – a pair of ears and eyes, rooting out troubles: rumours of theft or loss; rumours of disloyalty or complaint; rumours of slack service. You found them all in a great household, and someone had to dig them out.

Someone had *to*.

If it weren't me, it would be someone else. It might be someone harder, someone who would cause real trouble.

I could feel my father, dead for three years now, shaking his head.

Excuses.

Well, I had to make my way in the world.

Voices now.

Hers.

Growing louder, bolder.

I couldn't see her, of course, but I remembered her well enough, Mistress Anne. Her dark, almost black eyes – I could envision them crinkling in laughter. She would be wearing a hood in the French style, her head cocked on one side, looking up at Percy, holding his gaze for just long enough.

'He will make some trouble,' she said. I tried not to breathe. It was hard to tell if she meant it as a statement or a question.

'He won't, at that,' said Percy. I frowned.

'My father,' she said, and I imagined those slanting eyes looking away from him now, looking off into the distance of whichever chamber they were in, 'says he has power beyond the earthly world. Nothing will topple him. Nor overtop his will in anything.'

'When it's done . . . when it's done. . . there'll be nothing he can do, when it's done. . .'

'A fine word, *when*. Then let it be done.'

My heart skipped a beat.

There was a shifting sound, as though someone had moved towards someone, followed by the rapid creaking of shoe leather and slithering of lacy skirts. And then the lady's fluting laughter rose again. 'No, and no – for shame! Only when it is done, then it will be done.' There was refusal in her voice – steel beneath the mockery. I froze as the whisper of skirts came nearer the doorway. My mouth dried.

'But . . . I love you,' said Percy.

She didn't laugh. The air stilled. Time seemed to spin out. I wondered what she was doing – standing with her long-fingered hand on the door, perhaps, her head bent down, wondering if he was speaking the truth. There was, I thought, a sincerity in his words.

I love you.

He repeated them, and this time they rang false. I wondered if she heard that, the sharp thing that she was. I hoped she did. 'If you are – if we are . . . silent a little while. Then . . . in a little while. . .' His tone was wheedling.

I drew my breath, as quietly as I could. I could picture him, reaching out to pat her sleeve. From what I knew of the lady, if a man dared enjoin her to silence, she would likely commit herself to wagging her tongue with abandon for the rest of her life. Yet, for a long moment, stillness reigned. I could hear only my own breath whistling in and out.

'Sing for me a while,' she said. Her voice was all air now, as though the breath was being torn from her.

You haven't heard him sing, I thought.

He began, in a high, affected voice, his accent as deep as a Morpeth mud pile: 'For I love you so much . . . tru-u-lee . . . God might sooner dry up the deep-est sea, and ho-old back its waves . . . than I could constrain my-y-self . . . from loo-ving you-ou.'

Jesus, Percy.

His warbling continued, without music as accompaniment or music in his voice. And still a little stab of jealousy needled me. Mistress Anne Boleyn had become a darling of the court – everyone knew who she was. I had spoken to her a year before, a couple of times. Since then, she had risen in prominence, becoming dazzling, becoming a name spoken of in the cardinal's rooms. I had never had a word with her again, not even when our household was lodged with the queen's – and she had never looked at me. Not that I'd expected her to; her father was a man high in favour.

Still, I'd heard from my friends that Lord Hal had set his cap at her, and without Wolsey's knowledge.

And now I had proof. I eased myself out from beside the saint, making him rock on his mount, making the staff he held tilt at a crazy angle. Still, his painted gaze wouldn't deign look down at me, as though I were shameful, as though he disapproved.

Why are you doing this?

My father's voice, his Spanish patois thick in it, rang in my head. My answering thought came quickly enough: Wolsey set me to discover where friend Percy was creeping off to.

Don't do this.

The scent of Anne's perfume had become cloying. It stung. I sipped at the air, padding over the carpet and down the hallway. More laughter . . . her voice singing, far more sweetly than his. A few notes played on a lute – played well – joined it. It would be she who was playing, not him.

I turned to the doorway into the Middle Court and stepped out, gulping now at the fresher, cooler air. The nun-ladies had disappeared into the shadows of the cloistered wall over to my left. There would be chapels there, no doubt, where they could thumb their beads.

Looking out into the empty courtyard, I spotted a small water pump: a carved mastiff, painted in brown and gilt, with the pump held in its clawed paws. A large stone basin sat in front. I skipped towards it.

After a glance around the yard – definitely empty, save for the rustle of leaves as the light breeze passed through ornamental trees – I looked into the basin's depths. My reflection wobbled back at me. My collar was high, to hide the burn scars on my neck. Angrily, I thrust my hands into the water, enjoying the stinging cold, and began scrubbing at them aggressively, clawing at the skin, at one tawny hand and one discoloured, livid-looking one. I felt dirty, like one of the night-soil urchins. They, at least, had the benefit of honest filth.

I'd tell Wolsey nothing – something – something of no consequence. Percy had been going to look at books? No, a keeper of the books might give me the lie.

I shook my hand – my good hand, as I thought of it – dry, patting it on my crimson doublet.

He had been going to walk outside, to take his ease. That might work.

My bad hand got an unceremonious drubbing, as I dried it roughly.

'You!'

I jumped, spinning, my backside hitting the lip of the basin.

Shit!

'M-m-my lord!'

Percy was standing in front of me, looking down. He was a broad, handsome man, about my own age, but with golden-brown hair and regular, neat features. No broad lips or thick nose on him – and pale blue eyes rather than dark brown. His skin, as white as the Host, was, I saw, flushed with rose. It was as though her perfume had infected him. More likely, I thought, that he'd been frustrated, maybe infuriated, by her refusal. I hoped, anyway.

'Why are you here?' he asked. His eyes were on my livery rather than my face. He was not known as a man of intelligence, but neither could he be so stupid as not to guess my mission.

I swallowed, keeping my eyes on the satin front of his scarlet doublet, on the polished gold buttons he'd had sewn on. When I spoke, I was pleased at the steadiness in my voice. 'His Grace has commanded that I see . . . Her Majesty . . . if

Her Majesty wishes music.' Inspiration struck. 'Ahead of the Maundy.'

I glanced up as fine lines appeared on his forehead. I could almost see the mind beyond searching, groping. Queen Catherine was due to hold the Maundy service the following day. Wolsey had been busy vetting the poor women whose feet would be washed.

'Maundy,' he repeated, dumbly, like a child.

I nodded.

His eyes rose, travelling up my collar, seeming to see behind it. Few men knew how I'd come by my wounds. My friends knew well enough to let rumours of vicious fights circulate, to toughen me, so that none in the household dared mock.

I could almost see the idea of challenge rise and retreat on Percy's face. He was no friend of mine, nor ever had been, but nor was he an enemy. He stepped back, his lips drawing tight, his high cheekbones sharpening. 'Go to, then.' The north stretched out his vowels. 'Now that you are cleansed. Go to and see the queen.'

Shit, I thought again.

He assumed his courtier's stance for a moment and then began striding away from me, towards the gatehouse that led back into the busy Great Court. Was Anne Boleyn watching from a window? I wondered. Had she seen me? The urge to turn and search the polished glass for a long, oval face came to me. I wrestled it down.

Gnawing on the inside of my cheek, I made a sham of washing again, before beginning an ambling tour of the yard, wondering vaguely how much time I ought to waste to make my lie appear more plausible. When I judged it had been long enough, the sun had broken through the restraining clouds and I stepped back through the gatehouse and into the sprawling expanse of life beyond.

The salty sting of fish was heavy in the air. It would soon be time enough for another Lenten dinner. The night-soil children were gone, presumably taking their loads down to the river. The ladders had been moved along, the window washers leaving gleaming panes in their wake. I retraced my steps back into the cardinal's apartments, upstairs, and along the hallways towards the gallery. The door to the waiting chamber was now closed. I ignored it and hurried into the long gallery. Here, trestle tables were already being draped with woollen carpets – cheap stuff, for the lowest of the household to dine. Beyond, I entered the presence chamber, and was assaulted by the combined chatter of dozens of voices rising to the painted wooden ceiling.

The room was as long as the gallery, but the press of men made it feel smaller. Nearest me, the lower chamberers were at work setting up their dining tables, laying out canvas cloths. Beyond them was the table I might eat at – in the middle, as fitted a groom – already spread with linen, the bumps and folds being pressed out. Farthest away from me, and closest to the door to Wolsey's privy chambers, a fine table had already been laid with damask. There, the gentlemen and higher would take their meal.

I strode through the room, keeping my head high as I passed through the lower hall, lowering it a little as I reached the middle of the room. I jumped again as I felt a tug at my elbow.

'What d'ye find?'

'Mark!' I said, my head snapping up. Turning, I saw that

it was my friend, Mark Byfield: a trumpeter my own age in Wolsey's service. His eyes were wide and eager; as always, there was an open, honest grin on his face. I'd told him everything of my mission. 'Later,' I said. The truth of Percy's assignation would be safe with him, I thought. Or, at least, he'd spread rumours of trysts with Mistress Anne no more than anyone else would. 'Later.'

His brow knotted in disappointed. 'Ay, then, later. You can tell me what the dirty beasts was up to.' He chanced a look over my shoulder, up the hall, before smacking his lips a few times and setting his spoon and knife on the table with muted thuds.

I gave him a weak smile before lowering my chin to my chest and passing on through the knots of laughing, snorting gentlemen. If Percy had returned from Anne, I didn't see him – though by rights he ought to have been seeing that the cardinal's eating knives were gleaming before going into the privy chamber. Nastily, I thought that he might have found somewhere private to relieve the tension that his would-be lover had caused; and I found myself having to stifle a fit of the giggles.

'And why do you laugh?'

I let my eyes roll up. I'd reached the tall door to the privy lodgings. Standing beside it, a stave in his hand, was Deacon, one of Wolsey's ushers – a lithe, unctuous little man only a few years older than I was, young enough to remain beardless. 'I'm. . .'

not laughing

'. . .sorry, sir.'

'Compose yourself, man.' Deacon had a light voice – fluttering, like a moth's wing – but he knew how to use it to good effect. 'His Grace is finishing with the master draper.' With a note of disapproval, he added, 'And he has been waiting for you.'

'Yes,' I said, my heart already sinking.

Deacon said nothing else to me. He turned to the door, lifted his chin, cleared his throat, and pushed it open without knocking.

'The cardinal's lower groom of the great chamber, to see His Grace my lord cardinal.'

His words were perfunctory.

An inferior person of no certain station, he might have said.

He took his usual neat, fussy steps ahead of me and, my cap already in my hand and potential lies still shuffling in my mind, I followed.

2

The privy chamber was a large, airy room, dominated by its own low dining table – this one spread already with snowy white silk and satin cloths, all edged with golden tassels. Wolsey, customarily, ate privately, so that he might continue working. Already, the table was laden with papers; even the silver salt cellar had been pressed into use as a paperweight.

There were several men in the room. Wolsey, dressed in a scarlet surplice over white robes, was hunched forward on a throne set on a dais on the other side of the table. At his side, bent at the waist, was his secretary, Richard Audley. And on his knees at the edge of the dais was a man I'd seen earlier, in the waiting chamber. Now, his bolts of cloth were not draped over his arm but laid out at Wolsey's feet, like strips of bloody bandage. Windows stood open on either side of the room, giving plenty of light. Deacon hadn't moved far; he was standing by the door beside me, waiting to draw it closed as I stepped forward. Unsure what to do, I moved to stand beside the dining table, my shoes sending up little puffs of lavender scent from the rushes. Behind me, a gentle click sealed me in, and I hung there, between the busy world outside and the great man at work.

'I perceive,' said Wolsey, barely glancing up at me as I bent my head, '. . .I . . . perceive . . . yes . . . that this bears a richer colour. Ay, richer.' One of his white slippers jerked out from beneath his robes, nudging the edge of a piece of cloth. 'This is our choice. Yes.'

'Very good, Your Grace,' said the bending draper. 'It is,' he coughed, a hand bunched at his lips, 'more . . . in terms of . . . when it comes to how much. . .'

'Expensive, master draper,' barked Wolsey, making the man's back quake. 'Say what you mean, man. It is the more expensive. Do you think that His Majesty is a penny pincher? Do you?' The draper began stammering, and Wolsey silenced him with a wave of a broad hand. 'The best is what the king will have for his lords. The eyes of all England, yes – all – fall on his parliaments. The best.'

'As Your Grace wishes,' said the draper, a little too eagerly. He began rolling up his wares.

'Leave them. Leave them. We will have those, too,' said Wolsey. 'A fine gift from you. In . . . ah . . . acknowledgement of the favour we show you. In accepting your suit for our commission.'

'I . . . I . . .' began the draper, his hands still hovering over the cloths. 'But. . .'

'His Grace,' said Audley, straightening and fanning his forked beard with neat fingers, 'thanks you for your gift. You may go.'

With a grunt – of frustration or effort – the draper hauled himself to his feet. He crushed his hat between his hands – clean hands, I noticed – and mumbled something. And then he bowed and began backing from the dais. 'Oh!' With a bump, he hit the table and spun. 'Oh – oh – I – meant no—'

'Good day, master draper,' said Wolsey, a smile touching the side of his thin lips.

'Good – yes – good day, Your Grace. And thank you – I thank you.' He began to move towards me, before looking up in alarm. Rather than going around me, he turned and went to the other end of the table, passing it at that end and making for the door.

I didn't turn to see Deacon release him. Instead, I looked up under lowered lashes at Wolsey.

There was a story I'd heard recently about the cardinal, although I never discovered the truth of it. It involved a dyer in the city who'd been arrested and interrogated – by whom I didn't know – for having said, in a tavern, 'How high will that poxed priest climb?' According to the rumours, the fellow had been released but had since found it difficult to get powders and dyes, impossible to get orders, and suddenly was walking unaccompanied to his parish church. Wilder tales said that he'd gone mad at the loss to his business and ended up in the Bedlam – that I didn't credit. The rest, however, seemed likely enough.

Wolsey had recently added to his titles the prince-bishopric of Durham, the bull confirming it being despatched from Rome. When the king had ridden south on business, he'd left the privy seal at Richmond with the cardinal – his lord high chancellor, papal legate for life, and archbishop of York, primate of England. He knew his power, too – it was here, in the privy chamber. His throne had a wooden back a good two yards higher than his head, on which was hung a cloth depicting his heraldic banner; it showed a griffin rampant carrying the lord chancellor's mace, underneath the stitched arms of the see of York impaling his personal arms – and all this beneath a depiction of a round cardinal's hat. Yes, Wolsey knew his power, and he disliked anyone – high or low – questioning it.

Yet, to look at him, he was no more or less than a well-favoured man in his fifties, his hair grey beneath a scarlet skullcap. His skin was perhaps a little grey too, but his cheekbones still stood out proud – as proud, almost, as his strong, jutting chin. His rich robes, too, gave him a commanding, top-heavy bulk, their innumerable ripples sloping and curving to the floor. I fixed my gaze on them, holding my cap to my stomach in imitation of the departed draper.

'Yes,' he rumbled, at length. I took this as leave to look up, but he was frowning at Audley, who had bent to whisper to him. Suddenly, Deacon coughed, making the two men look over me, past me. 'Well, Mr Deacon?'

'Begging your most excellent Grace's pardon,' piped the little man.

Ugh.

It was always a wonder to me that a man of wit like Wolsey could revel in too-obvious flattery. 'It is . . . now that the draper is gone – we have still the old gentleman, Mr. . .' I thought I heard papers shuffle. 'Ah, Mr Cosyn. I left him in the waiting chamber, begging my good lord's time.'

'Lancelot Cosyn,' barked Wolsey. The animation lifted my eyes to him. The cardinal had one defect – a slightly lazy eyelid. It jerked now, twitching in anger. 'That . . . that old creature. *Cosyn* would dare speak with *us*!'

This, I supposed, was the old fellow in grey. When I had spotted him on my way after Percy, I'd thought he looked frightened, nervous. I could see why, now.

'Shall I send him away, Your Grace?'

'Yes,' boomed Wolsey. And then, again, Audley bent to

him, whispering. Wolsey's lips puckered into a little moue, but he appeared content to listen. I knew the quiet, suspicious secretary well enough. He was a canny creature, for all he was officious and cold. The cardinal's cheeks drew in and stayed there for a beat, before he blew out a disgruntled breath. 'No, no. We shall listen to the foul-mouthed goat. Yes.' Animation crept in again, accompanied by a look of sly, almost childish delight. 'Yes, by the Mass, yes. We shall see him defend himself to us. Here, in our own chamber, in all our . . . yes, we shall see then what he has to say for himself.'

I felt myself start to vanish, caught in the presence of this angry king who was no king, in his court which was really no court at all, without King Henry present.

'As Your Grace wishes,' said Deacon. 'I am at your feet, my lord.' He proved this with a deep bow. 'I shall bring him unto your most serene and princely presence.'

'No! We will attend to our dinner first.' Wolsey hunched forward on his throne, arranging his robes with prissy gestures of his strong, grey-haired hands. 'See to our table, Mr Deacon. And see to the tables for our people. And then when we have finished our meal . . . yes. Then you might bring this . . . this *Cosyn* . . . to us. When it suits *us* to hear him.'

'As Your Grace wishes,' Deacon repeated, his tone unchanged. Behind me, I heard soft clatters and movements as he began preparing the table, moving gold and silver plates and cutlery from the huge wooden sideboards which lined the sides of the room.

'In the meantime,' said Wolsey, finally looking at me and – for effect, I thought – stifling a yawn with a hand, 'we shall hear from our young groom. Come forward, Anthony, my friend. We find with each year our eyes. . .' He made a dismissive gesture at the side of his head. I stepped towards the dais, my head down. 'Now . . . yes . . . you have watched the earl's boy? You have found where he goes when he leaves us?'

I took a breath, keeping my own eyes fixed on the white-and-scarlet bumps of his knees. 'I . . . followed him. As Your Grace asked.'

'And?'

'He – it was – this morning. Earlier today, I mean. . .' I commenced to give a rambling, invented version of my trip out, mentioning seeing the old man – this Cosyn – arrive, mentioning the weather and the people out at work, and ending with my losing Percy somewhere towards the front of the palace. 'I suspect he goes to . . . like as to . . . be away. Taking walks. By the river, perhaps, to take the air,' I added, pathetically.

I looked up. I was in the strange position of not knowing fully what I'd just said. I knew it was a tissue of half-truths and nonsense, but I couldn't have repeated it. The words had just spilled and every thought in my head, suddenly, seemed to be competing to be the most irrelevant. I tried to summon up a hard, serious glare, and felt a smile tugging at my lips.

Goddammit.

Wolsey stared at me, unblinking, his expression dead, as though he were daring me to meet the challenge of his gaze. I failed, my eyes darting again to his knees.

Say something!

'Perhaps,' I swallowed, 'I might try again. Some other time, maybe tomorrow, or if he leaves again – I'm not sure. . .'

Wolsey made a sucking sound, before putting an elbow

to an armrest of his throne and leaning heavily on it. 'Anthony, Anthony,' he began, his voice somewhere between tired and disappointed. 'Look at me,' he said. I did, meeting an expression that matched the voice. 'Commonly,' he adjusted his position with another grunt, 'commonly, in our experience, you tell a tale . . . in a manner straightly. Without these . . . these digressions. Fancies. Yes. That makes us doubtful. Doubtful of so senseless and sleeveless a tale. You understand? I begin to doubt. And when I begin to doubt my people. . .'

'I perceive the fellow lies,' said Audley, without expression. *You old bastard.*

I opened my mouth to speak and was saved by Deacon, at my back.

'The table is prepared for your delectation, most illustrious Grace. I shall see to those outside and send forth your dinner. And . . . Mr Cosyn, I shall tell him he must wait on Your Grace.'

Wolsey frowned, looking over my shoulder and giving the usher an irritated flick of his hand. As the door clicked open behind me, though, he called over towards it, 'See if the wretched old goat will take something. Some small beer, perhaps – no better.'

'As Your Grace wishes and commands.'

The door snicked shut.

Silence stretched in the privy chamber again, as both Wolsey and Audley looked at me. I felt myself shrinking into my clothes, into my livery. It struck me that I might rightly be stripped of it for lying and cast back out of service.

Would that be so bad?

I didn't know. I had a strange, strained relationship with

the cardinal's service, loving the people and the feel of life, of action and business – and despising myself for what I was called upon to do. If there was a thing that meant disliking something and needing it, that, perhaps, was my feeling. Besides, my place in the household was more position than occupation. That was the way of it in courtly service: it outfitted a man for nothing but courtly service.

'We have some small knowledge of young Percy,' said Wolsey, wrenching me from my thoughts. I looked up. 'Yes. And without your . . . tales of him walking up and walking down. Walking abroad to *take the air.*'

I frowned.

Then why send me out spying?

Wolsey supplied the answer. 'We have some knowledge of what, if not with whom. That, I'm afraid, you shall have to discover.' He smiled without humour and then let it fade. 'When the coming parliament is concluded, we shall have to apply ourselves seriously to any. . .' His eyes rose to the ceiling, which was made up of a network of octagonal wooden frames, with heraldic devices painted on the recesses within. 'Any breaches,' he concluded. 'Of proper conduct, you understand. Of proper behaviour.' His tongue wetted his lips and he looked back down towards me. 'For the present, the matter of the parliament is our chiefest concern.' He gave a little laugh and his foot darted out towards the half-rolled cloths the draper had left. 'Woolsacks!' he barked.

'Your Grace?' I asked.

His laugh came again, warmer and more genuine. 'Woolsacks! We are required to judge the right shade of red for the linings of the woolsacks to be sat upon. At the parliament. Woolsacks!' He seemed to find the world hilarious, and I found myself joining in, more as a means of releasing my own tension. At length, he began wiping water from his grey-blue eyes and shaking his head. 'My God, the things. . . The lining of woolsacks. From that, to the lodgings of the lords. To the reviewing of bills. To the precedence of the Commons. To the selection of a speaker. Woolsacks.' This time, the word seemed to hold more wonder than mirth, and he shook his head. 'For the moment . . . yes . . . keep watching Percy. We have others doing the same. His . . . *privy* business – it will not remain so. Nothing ever does. Never.' He lifted a finger and tapped the side of his head. 'Regard this – look. Every grey hair – each one – born not of age, no – born of some young fool in my charge who thinks he might be the first to keep a great secret to himself. Every one, born of damned young pups who give us trouble.' His finger fell, flexing irritably, to his lap. 'Two weeks. We have scarce two weeks until the parliament commences. And when this matter of woolsacks and lords and subsidies – when all is concluded – then, shall our noble friend learn how to conduct himself in a great household. Young *Hal* shall keep, I fancy. I—'

Before he could say anything else, the door behind me opened, and this time I turned. Deacon had transformed the dining table into a snowy kingdom in miniature, with golden mountain peaks and perfect round lakes of burnished silver. In strode several men, their liveries spotless: the cardinal's server and carver and cupbearer and. . .

Mark!

He held his trumpet in both hands. I smiled at him, but he had the wit not to return it. He was working. Instead, he took up a position beside the door, from where he could announce the approach of each course. The sound, I knew, would be deafening in the privy chamber, but Wolsey would hardly be a prince-bishop, lord high chancellor, or archbishop without it. The three gentlemen servers – one with a Holland towel round his neck, the second with one over his arm and neck, and the third with only his arm draped – bowed in unison, before moving to stand behind the table. There they remained, facing Wolsey over it, their heads bowed. I looked back towards the cardinal myself.

'I think,' he said, 'it is time for us to eat. Anthony, you may—'

'Stop!'

The cry tore through the room, drawing everyone's attention.

'What the good year!' boomed Wolsey, half-rising from his throne. 'Deacon?'

It was the little usher indeed. He half-fell into the privy chamber, only belatedly remembering to remove his cap. His hair, which he kept combed back and wetted to a rigid flatness, tumbled down over his brow. One hand remained on the lintel, so that he spun in an arc, bent over, nearly colliding with Mark as he tried to catch his breath. 'You – Your Grace – there is – please –' Mark side-stepped, just as Deacon was gathering himself up.

'Well, man – spit it out,' said Wolsey. He didn't shout – his voice had become measured, with a lacing of warning. 'You men,' he said, standing fully and looking over the table, 'will leave us for a moment.' He seemed to have forgotten I was there, off to the side and seemingly invisible. Without protest, the servers and Mark backed from the room, letting only flashes of curiosity colour their faces.

When they'd gone, the still-wheezing Deacon threw the door shut behind them with a bang.

'Cosyn,' said Wolsey. 'It is Mr Cosyn, is it not?'

'You must . . .' Deacon began shaking his head, at first in wonder and then furiously. His face had drained of colour, making him look younger, somehow, lost. All traces of his usual flattery had melted away. He clapped a hand over his neat little mouth and, for a moment, looked as though he were going to vomit. And then, with another shake of his head, a shake of denial, he said, 'Please come, please come quickly, Your Grace. Cosyn! Ay, Cosyn!' He seemed to embrace the word. 'The old man – he – he – by the Mass, he has been murdered.'

And this time he leant over and began retching violently.

3

I knew what was coming before it came.

'Walk with us, Anthony.'

Death seemed to haunt the court. Most of the time it visited in all innocence – a sudden sickness, requiring us to flee to another house, or a fall into the river, or honest old age. But I'd seen it arrive on the wings of violence, too – too often, and more than anyone would ever be allowed to speak about.

Wolsey pushed himself up from his chair in a whirl of scarlet, wobbled slightly on his feet, and then stepped around the bolts of cloth. He was a man of movement; one arm immediately began striking against his side – it was as though he had been sitting too long and his limbs now rebelled, cried out for hard use. Audley followed him, his dark brows folded together.

'Come, Mr Deacon,' said Wolsey, his voice gentle. 'Come, now.' He ignored the table and its plate and went to the usher, who had vomited on the rushes. 'Be at peace. What did you see?'

'Unhhhh. . .' Deacon straightened, just as I rounded the table myself, to stand behind the twin towers of Wolsey and Audley. 'Unhhh.' The fellow's eyes widened. 'Y-your Grace.' His mouth began working stupidly, trying to form letters, words, failing. And then his eyes fell to the floor and nearly popped. 'Oh . . . oh . . . Your Grace . . . see what I've . . . I . . . my . . .'

'Be still, Mr Deacon. It is no matter.' Wolsey's voice was soft, as though he were trying to persuade a child to cease wailing. 'No matter at all. It will be cleaned.'

Ay, by Deacon himself!

'But I—'

'You say Mr Cosyn is . . . dead?'

Panic again gripped the usher. 'Slain! Slain, Your Grace – most foully, oh, horribly!'

'Take us there,' said Wolsey. The cardinal straightened, brushing down the front of his robes with great sweeping gestures, fixing his skullcap, and then settling a hand on Deacon's shoulder. 'Be of stout cheer. We will attend to this matter ourselves. Let no man beyond see your . . . let no man see. . .'

'Let no man think aught is amiss,' finished Audley. He hadn't moved, hadn't offered the usher a word of comfort. Instead, his arms were locked by his sides.

As if they all wouldn't have seen the man tearing through the chamber already!

'Yes. Yes, quite,' said Wolsey. He turned, giving me his profile. One eye was narrowed. 'Come,' he said.

Given something to do, Deacon appeared to rally. He gave one horrified look at the mess he'd made on the rushes and then began gnawing on the inside of his cheeks, blinking rapidly as though to squeeze out the image of whatever he'd seen. Yet he managed to move towards the door. With a hand on the ring, he turned, gave one hard nod to the air, and pulled it open.

Diffuse chatter invaded the privy chamber.

'Well, then,' said Wolsey, just loud enough for us to hear him. 'Let us see this . . . this.' His head high and one arm swinging merrily, he strode out into the great chamber, followed by Audley. Deacon hung back, his head bowed, as I fled after them.

The moment Wolsey appeared, the chorus of voices fell silent. Hats and caps were swiftly removed. One man fell to his knee, prompting a mass dip. As I passed through the doorway, I noticed the three gentlemen servants, their towels still in place, kneeling with their backs to the wall of the privy chamber. Mark, too, was down, his trumpet sitting on its bell before him. But he was looking up, looking at me, with plain curiosity on his face. I gave him a quick shrug, my teeth sinking into my lower lip, before hurrying after Wolsey, with Deacon at my heels.

The cardinal processed down the chamber, past the tables with their various classes of cloth, men shuffling out of his way. I noticed, as he passed, that quite a few faces turned upwards, trying to read his expression. All wore differing shades of Mark's narrow-eyed interest. Thankfully, theirs was fixed on Wolsey, so that I could pass unobserved – a creature of no particular interest when the cardinal was in plain sight.

The trim Mr Cavendish, another of the gentleman ushers, stood at the door to the gallery. He opened it, and we all moved out into the reek of fish and sauce. The menial table had been set up, but it hadn't been laid. Instead, the various servants charged with carrying the food up from the kitchens stood against the walls, with platters and trays weighting down their arms, waiting to be called in to serve Wolsey first, and then down through the ranks. Rather than kneel, this long chain of men simply bent their heads as he swept past.

As I walked, my heart began to speed.

Death.

Murder.

Again, I thought of the sights I'd seen in the past, and my mind rejected them. Those images came to me sometimes, in the way the mind likes to torture, and I'd always found the best way to take charge was to think of something else. The stench in the air made it impossible: a parade of broken bodies bleeding onto cobbles and bruised, strangled throats moved through my thoughts, making my stomach join my heart in skipping madly. This darkness seemed to communicate itself to Deacon. Behind me, I heard him make muted swallowing sounds.

The door was mercifully closed – by yet another usher – behind us, and we were free of the fishy tang and the gallery of watchful, excited faces. Wolsey continued his stately march, his hand still drumming against the side of his robed leg. At the door of the waiting chamber on the left, he drew up. Audley reached out to grasp the ring, and the cardinal stayed him with a hand. 'No, Mr Audley. This is properly Mr Deacon's work.'

Cruel, I thought, as I heard the usher gulp. *Cruel to make him do it.*

Then, immediately, I saw Wolsey's motive. Deacon stepped around me, seemingly changed. He was a man of occupation, a fellow of propriety. His job had either become his nature, or his nature had fitted him out for it. All traces of queasiness seemed to disappear as he stepped forward lightly, his back snapping straight. Wolsey knew his man.

Bizarrely, the fellow announced – to no one, I assumed, but a corpse – 'His Grace, my most excellent and mighty lord cardinal and chancellor of England and his secretary, Mr Audley.' And then he threw open the door, stepping aside to let us enter. As Wolsey and Audley did, he remained standing there, his chin high. I hadn't warranted an announcement, but I followed anyway, slipping into the room I'd only seen earlier from outside.

The smell.

It was sharp, invasive. My gorge rose to meet it, bile seeking to embrace. . .

. . .*roasting pork? Ash? Burnt wool?*

'Sweet Jesu,' said Wolsey, by the sound of it through clenched teeth. Ahead of me, his wandering arm made a huge sign of the cross. 'Sweet Jesu.'

The smell forced my hand over my mouth. I couldn't see the body – Audley and Wolsey blocked it from view. The room wasn't large, but it was well appointed. Wainscoting rose to waist height around the walls, with plain whitewash above, save for where the diamond-paned windows admitted light. An Irish rug covered most of the floorboards, and small stools lined the walls. A fire still burned merrily in the grate, its flames dancing and leaping. I felt my head swim a little.

'He lives!' Audley's voice made me jump. 'Your Grace, he lives!'

Audley's narrow form, directly in front of me, dipped suddenly. Wolsey stepped back, away, as if to give the man air.

And then I saw him.

Cosyn was indeed the old fellow in grey I'd seen shown into the chamber earlier. He lay on his back, with small pools of blood warmed to tackiness beneath him by the heat of the fire. Blackness had spread in circles around the midsection of his grey smock. His thick woollen cloak was gone, and his skeletal wrists were raised, claw-like, before him.

'He lives. . .'?

My eyes travelled sideways, to his face.

Jesus Christ!

I couldn't make sense of it at first.

From the tip of his beaky nose upwards, the man was colourless. But his lower face – his lower face was a bloodied, blackened confusion. His mouth was either open or covered in some dark liquid, mingled with blood, as though he'd vomited up something black.

I couldn't look any longer and squeezed my eyes shut.

Still, as though stamped there by the power of the firelight, the shape of his head remained before my closed eyes.

'My God,' I heard Wolsey say. 'A physician. Fetch a physician, Mr Audley – now.'

'The men outside. . .' began the secretary.

'Mr Deacon?'

'Yes, Your Grace?'

'See to their dinner. All must appear as usual – see it served to the gentlemen and on, and on. All must appear as usual. There must be no panic. No. . .' I opened my eyes to see Wolsey waggling his fingers in a vague gesture, 'whispering, you understand. Yes. See to it.'

'As Your Grace wishes and commands.' He bowed low, tilting his head as he did.

I heard him fleeing the heat of the room, just as crystals of sweat began to form on my brow. 'Yes. And the physician, Mr Audley. I think . . . ugh . . . old Mordaunt did not travel with the king. Not at *his* infirm age.' His tone soured a little at the name. 'See to it. You are right. I think he breathes a little yet.'

Audley didn't answer but bowed and hurried from the chamber.

'Alive,' I said. Against my will, I looked down at the body, at the bloodstained midsection and the bone-white wrists. But not the face. 'Still alive.'

'Just,' said Wolsey, his voice low. 'I should not think. . . He will not last.'

His cloak. . .

'His cloak,' I said.

'What?'

'I saw him when I passed this way. He was wearing a cloak.' I turned from the body, towards the feet, and saw it, saw something, heaped in a bundle in the corner of the room.

Yes!

It was lying in a little dejected mound: a small pile of dark grey wool. And something was weighting it down. 'What is this?' asked Wolsey.

'I. . .' Crossing to the cast-off cloak, I bent, frowning. It lay against the foot of the wainscoting. 'It's. . .' I reached out and grasped at the thing – long and thin, with one end thicker. A handle: it had a thick, wooden handle. I cursed my own stupidity as my palm closed around it. It was still warm. I'd seen them a thousand times, in every house and inn and palace I'd ever been.

'It's a poker,' I said. I lifted it and turned, already looking past the body, past Wolsey, to the flames. And then I dropped the thing, hearing it thud on the rug. 'My God!'

Wolsey didn't chastise me. Instead, I saw my own horror

reflected on his face. We both turned our attention to the fallen man.

Someone, I realised, had stabbed the old fellow repeatedly with it and then . . . and then. . .

My mind refused to accept it.

I blinked, forcing myself to look at the stricken man's ruined, lined face. Sure enough, his eyelids, parchment thin, still flickered, their spidery blue veins stark against the whiteness.

Swallowing once, I said, 'They . . . before they struck him about the middle – probably before, or he'd have screamed – they put the thing . . . put it burning hot . . . into his mouth. Down his throat.'

Again, my head swam. My own tongue stilled, as though horrified by even the thought of invasion, of assault, by a hot poker.

'Sweet Jesu,' said Wolsey again, and again he crossed himself. We stood awhile, listening to our own breathing. 'To silence him. Ay, to silence the man indeed.'

As if in response, the fellow on the floor let forth a rattling gush of air. Wolsey and I hopped away, as though he were infectious, our hands rising. But Cosyn did no more. Only his eyelids began fluttering more rapidly, letting blood-flecked pale blue scan the ceiling dumbly.

'Should . . . we move him?' I asked.

Before Wolsey could respond, a new voice crackled into the chamber.

'What is this, at the dinnertime?' A tall, thin man of about sixty stood in the doorway. A curtain of grey hair hung from a physician's cap with ear-flaps. Peering around behind him was a younger fellow, plucking at a gingery beard.

'Good morrow, Dr Mordaunt,' said Wolsey.

The tall man gave a sharp bow from the waist. When he rose, the nostrils on his strong nose flaring, his face registered. I'd seen the old physician occasionally at court – he was one of King Henry's doctors. The king had a whole team of them: I'd often thought he must have England's most loquacious urine to warrant such an army. Yet I'd never known this Mordaunt to attend on Wolsey, who preferred to keep his illnesses hidden in case they fanned rumours. His own physician had, in fact, been disgraced for taking bribes, and since then the cardinal preferred to ignore piss-prophets, as he called them, entirely; I'd known him to work at his desk despite a fever, until his gentlemen had had to lift him from it and carry him to bed. 'No mediciners,' was all he'd been able to repeat. 'None! I am well!'

'Mmph,' said Mordaunt. He stepped into the room. 'My assistant, William Rowlet.' The younger man – in his thirties, I guessed – slid off his cap, craning his head at the same time. He was neat, I noticed – his features were too small for his face, giving him a pinched look, but his doublet was plain, its points regular, his hair was combed, and his red beard trimmed to perfection. 'We were told that there is a wounded man. . .' His voice fell away on the last word. Wolsey and I had stepped aside, giving both new arrivals a view of the dying Cosyn. The old physician seemed to forget the cardinal entirely, leaving his cap on as he stumbled forward, Rowlet at his heels. Audley came in behind them, his hands clasped behind his back, and softly clicked the door shut, just as Mordaunt slipped down to what I imagined must be bony old knees.

'Why, it is Lancelot Cosyn!' The physician turned a shocked face up to Wolsey.

'We are aware, sir.'

'But. . .' The shock faded to something I couldn't read. *Accusation?*

'Some wicked villain,' said Wolsey, 'some lewd and evil person has come into our chambers from the outside. And done the creature to death. With a fire poker. He was found thus by our usher. He breathes yet. We hope you might restore him. Restore his speech and let him tell the truth of what was done here.'

'I am no surgeon, I. . .' If doubt wasn't plain enough in Mordaunt's voice, it was apparent on his face. Yet he bent again to the fallen man and began placing his hands about him. His face crumpled. 'Dear Rowlet, would you be so good as to. . .' He tutted, before letting forth a stream of Latin. His assistant answered in kind. Mordaunt, I noticed, was trembling – whether due to his age or shock, I couldn't say. His head threatened to fall, and the smaller man took a grip of his arm, squeezing and saying, quite clearly, *'Crudelius est quam mori semper timere mortem.'* I understood the *'mortem'*. The rest seemed to strengthen the physician, and together the pair began examining the body.

Almost immediately, the younger, Rowlet, gasped, 'Jesu, by *Jesu*, sir! Yet, the manner – how could. . .'

It is an awkward thing for laymen when physicians attend to a patient. My own father, in his last days, had seen no physician, but my stepmother had called in an apothecary – useless, she decided – and a cunning woman to see to him at the last. When both expert people had been at their labour, turning deep dishes of his piss to the light, sniffing it, pressing on various parts of his body and having him cough and spit, my stepmother and I had done nothing but put our backs to the wall. I'd only been called down from court to witness those last days – the extent of his illness had been kept from me. Still, I felt useless, stupid, unable to cry or offer anything other than my being there. We defer to the mediciners. My stepmother, God love her, later told me she'd felt the same. We expect them to carry the burden of doing something, she said, so we feel we've done something in calling them in.

Wolsey retreated to the door, where Audley began a whispered conference. With my head bent, I stepped around the pile of cloak and went to the window. The diamond panes glittered in the sunlight. Below, I could see the tops of caps and bonnets moving about and could hear – just – distant singing. The chill of the glass radiated outwards. My breath replied in a fog. For no reason, I put a finger up and wiped, flesh whitening around the nail as I pressed and squeaked.

'I regret . . . I regret the man is dead,' said Mordaunt. His voice turned me to him. 'You agree, Rowlet?'

'Dead,' grunted the assistant, hauling himself to his feet. His face had whitened, his little eyes, nose, and mouth resembling a bunched fist in the middle of it. 'Murdered most foully.' His statement dared argument.

The low hum of Audley's voice ceased. Wolsey turned, frowning. 'What?'

'He had lost much blood,' began Rowlet.

Mordaunt cut in, his tone now curt – the voice of a man at his profession. 'It seems that he was stabbed. I count three wounds in his middle portion. Not deep. And a burning of the interior of the mouth. Done by an inexpert hand. Unpractised. Do you agree, Rowlet?'

The assistant, to my disgust, touched the wounds, sliding in a finger to measure the depth. 'Yes, sir. I should say more for. . .' He blanched again. 'Almost as though it were done more for sport than quick release. Shallow.' He removed his fingers, frowned at the stains, and with deft little strokes began wiping them on the dead man's clothes.

'Mm. I agree. We shall raise you up from the barbarous arts yet, good William.' Mordaunt's voice lost its perfunctory, official tone. 'God help him,' he said, blessing himself. 'But enough to draw blood from such an aged body.' The old physician had found the poker where I'd dropped it, and he confirmed my own disgusted suspicions. 'This, I think, did the wickedness. It was. . .' He jabbed the thing in the air, in Wolsey's direction. The effort made him wobble on his knees. 'Thrust, I think, in his mouth. The pain must have been great. Even had he lived, he could never have spoken of what had happened, not to any man. His tongue – his throat – both seared cruelly.'

'It was meant to silence him,' I volunteered.

Mordaunt appeared to notice me for the first time. His pale, nearly colourless eyes narrowed under thick, grey brows. 'Who are you? Rowlet, who is he?'

'I—'

'He is a lower groom of my outer chamber,' said Wolsey. 'Well trusted.'

'He . . . was here?' asked Rowlet. The fellow clutched briefly at Mordaunt's sleeve. 'When this man was . . . attacked?'

I felt my colour rise, my cheeks darken. Not replying to his assistant, Mordaunt was looking up at me, the old goat, as though I were the man's murderer, as though I were stamped with guilt. 'He was alone with poor Cosyn?' he asked.

'No,' said Wolsey. 'He was with us, in our private rooms. Our usher came to fetch the old man to us and found him thus. What does this signify?'

'I cannot say,' said Mordaunt. 'His Majesty's coroner must—'

'His Majesty is not at court,' snapped Wolsey. 'The coroner must. . .' He frowned down at Audley, who looked a little lost for words.

'Court is where the king is,' said the secretary, his voice free of expression. 'The king is not here. His coroner need not—'

'The queen's majesty is here,' said Mordaunt, putting his knobbly hand in Rowlet's as the assistant helped him rise. He grunted with the effort still. I half-stepped forward to offer him my own hand too. My shoes caught up in the cloak. It rustled at my feet.

Rustling wool?

But Mordaunt managed well enough. He stood, one hand on his hip. Yet the effort seemed to cost him, and he grimaced, letting go of Rowlet's hand and kneading his stomach with a fist. 'It is not . . . it is not right . . . this is plain murder done within the king's own house.'

'Who would wish to come in from the outside,' asked Wolsey, his voice rich in innocence, 'and slay the poor fellow?'

'There's something here,' I said.

'Who? The man was – I regret the man was – hot against your own—'

'There's something here!'

Mordaunt stopped talking. He and the other three men turned to me, as I bent to the cloak. I lifted the thing. It was cheap, and it had been torn a little, as though someone had ripped it from Cosyn's body.

There!

From its folds fell a piece of paper. It went whispering to a bare patch of floorboard by the wall.

'What is that?' asked Audley.

Before he could leave Wolsey and cross to me, I snatched it up and let my eyes rove it.

I couldn't read it fully; Audley was before me, snatching it out of my hand. About all I managed to make of the weak, spidery script was

dico vobis nisi granum frumenti cadens in terram mortuum fuerit

'What is it?' asked Mordaunt. He tilted his head back and peered through lowered lids. 'Rowlet, what have they found?'

Audley's cheeks drew in and he read the thing silently. 'A petition. Of the usual style from Mr Cosyn. Railing. Demanding. It appears it was this he wished to deliver in coming here today.'

'That is evidence of some wicked crime,' said Mordaunt. 'It must be delivered up to the king's coroner. The knight marshal at least.' Something lit up his face. 'Or More. Is More here, Rowlet?'

'I believe so,' supplied the assistant.

'Yes! More hasn't gone with the king – he knows the ruffians of London and their filthy habits. Their tricks. This evidence must be delivered up to proper men.'

'And it will be, when we speak to His Majesty. Until then, Dr Mordaunt, we trust you shall say nothing to no man.

No, nor your servant,' said Wolsey. Rowlet drew himself up to his meagre height, the redness of his cheeks deepening again over the whiskers. There, I thought, was the threat the cardinal always managed to make sound soft, a dagger wrapped in velvet.

Mordaunt appeared to hear it too. He frowned, gave one last look down at the corpse – no longer Cosyn now, but a thing, an object – and shrugged. 'As you wish, my lord cardinal. As you wish. Yet I think. . .' Whatever he thought he elected to keep to himself. He raised his head, finally remembered his cap, and removed it for just as long as his bow lasted. 'Come, dear Rowlet. We shall think on this further.' The assistant darted ahead of him, opening the door and holding it. Together, the physician and his man departed with a bang.

'They shall not remain quiet,' said Wolsey, clucking his tongue. 'Such men never do. I shall speak to the king before *he* might, of course.'

I bowed my head. I knew the cardinal could and would cover up crimes. He would bury anything that he thought might excite or trouble or otherwise engage the king's mind in ways he, Wolsey, couldn't measure and guide. I'd seen him cover up the deaths of his people and of strangers. But the murder of his enemy within spitting distance of the court? Even his smooth charm might make that difficult. And whoever this murderer was, he knew well enough to do his grisly business somewhere that couldn't but gain attention, that couldn't but rise in screams and cries to the king's ears.

'Read, Your Grace,' said Audley, moving towards the cardinal with the piece of paper.

Wolsey read it aloud, mumbling. '"We write of these our

own wicked times, when sin is grown like a foul infection, spreading as it were from the inside to the outer parts, until it infects the whole of this our said commonwealth." Bah!' He almost scrunched the paper. The rest he read in halting sentences, adding his own commentary here and there: 'The fellow writes as though he were running out of breath;' . . . 'and this from a trained man of rhetoric;' . . . 'he quotes the Scriptures to *us*?' . . . 'he dares speak of our just war with France as *my* policy?' . . . 'a wicked shedding of blood for vainglory!' . . . 'this creature sought to censure *us*?'

What Wolsey read went over my head. It appeared to be a mingle-mangle of Latin quotes and comparisons, of English fears and threats, and – and even I couldn't miss this – attacks on what Cosyn called 'the harlotry and bawdry and sundry spoliations into which canting priests and proud prelates have forced the Church of God'.

I shivered, as Wolsey finally did scrunch up the paper. From his position near the door, he launched the thing straight over the dead man and into the fire. I lost sight of it in the flames.

'And that for your proud prelates, Mr Cosyn,' he hissed. The anger passed in a flash. He fished a silken handkerchief from his sleeve and mopped his brow. The room was growing oppressively hot.

If only I could open a window. . .

'Fetch some trusted men to bear him away, Mr Audley. Harry Gainsford and yourself might do it.'

'Yes, Your Grace,' said Audley. He left the room again, leaving me and Wolsey with the body. A log crunched in the fire, as though disapproving of the vicious, seditious words that had been offered it.

Wolsey took a long, deep breath. 'This news will travel,' he said, more to himself than to me. 'Ay, it will.' He blinked slowly, his handsome features contorting, as though his eyes were stinging. 'We will have the blame of this.' He looked at me. 'Yes. You understand, lad, that this . . . this Cosyn . . . a university man. A man of the new learning. We were friends once, in our fashion. We might have been friends still. I might have seen him into good work. In the beginning of schools, in the devising of . . . of education. And yet he turned. Ay, turned, into this new brand of creature. A headful of anger and tongue aflame, always aflame. "Canting priests and proud prelates." He would have the Church altered, he said. Made purer. As though we were corrupted creatures and he a breath of divine air.' He turned to the dead man and looked over him, to where he'd thrown the paper. 'Was this why you came to me? To condemn, condemn, condemn, you foolish old . . . you foolish. . .'

I stepped back towards the wall.

Tears had started up in Wolsey's eyes. His handkerchief appeared again and he dabbed at his face, sniffing. 'We were once friends,' he said. 'And might have been . . . still.'

I kept my gaze fixed on the cloak at my feet, shame and embarrassment filling me. My mouth worked stupidly. Absurdly, I blamed the cardinal, blamed him for putting me in front of his embarrassing, awkward tears.

'It is well,' he said. I looked up. A tired smile was pasted on his face. 'We are past all griefs.' And he seemed to be. Whatever strange burst of sadness . . . *or regret* . . . had taken him had released its grip.

He cleared his throat and straightened up. Another tear rolled down his cheek. He raised his handkerchief again but stilled his hand in mid-air. His eyes narrowed. 'No. Let them see our grief. Let no man say we are stone-hearted. Let no man say that we are not sorry that there should be unhap and . . . ah . . . ill fortune in our house.' The little piece of silk went back up his sleeve and he shook out his arm, becoming Wolsey again. 'One of our chiefest delators murdered,' he announced, 'in our own house. It looks poorly on us. It cannot be allowed to stand.'

'I . . .'

He looked at me sharply. 'You. Yes, Anthony Blanke, you. What are your thoughts?'

I shan't lie and say I had none. In truth, given I had experience of matters of murder in the cardinal's household, I found that my mind was already working on possibilities. I licked my lips. 'It would be an easy matter for a man – or a woman – to come in from the Great Court. Up to the waiting chamber. You can move without let or check. I did it myself this morning – both ways.' And then I jerked my head towards the window. 'And the window. I saw ladders there this morning, Your Grace. A man might have come in whilst affecting to wash them and got him.' I found this unlikely – but I had noticed the new gleam on the diamond panes.

The alternative, of course, was that someone within the household had done it. That possibility I kept to myself. He would know it, as well as I did.

Wolsey's face split in a grin, odd as it seemed in the hot room still tenanted by a corpse. My own lip twitched in response. 'You are a good man, my boy. A fine thing to be growing expert in, this thinking of how murders are come by.' His smile faded. 'I regret it. I regret the man's death. Yet I . . . I would ask you, again, to put yourself in yoke. Use those sharp eyes and ears of yours. Think on your windows and your entrances and exits, lad, and see what you might discover of this. Discover, yes. Go where you must.' He turned his hand in the air. 'Wherever you must . . . as shall seem to the purpose. Discover or cause to be discovered the truth of this matter. Yes. You know how to keep matters close.'

'Yes, Your Grace,' I said, already moving towards the door, hoping to follow Audley's example by fleeing on demand.

'And do so quickly,' he said. 'With speed; with haste. The thing touches us too near to grow stale . . . for its stink to reach too many noses. Go to, before that physician can make trouble. Before the king and his creatures can put their own men in harness.'

'As Your Grace wishes.' I stepped towards the door.

'And,' he said, putting a restraining hand on my sleeve, 'let us hope you do a more . . . ah, a more creditable job of work than you did in chasing the Percy lad this morning. Yes.' A little humour danced in his voice – but not much.

Saying nothing, I left the room, and the heat, and the body, and stepped into the low reek of fish and the distant thrum of chattering voices and slurps and belches.

4

I was sorry to miss dinner. Not because I was hungry – the sight of the dead man's mouth had robbed me of that – but because I'd heard it said often enough that true Englishmen had larger stomachs than other men, and I was loath to appear anything other than true. Rather than eating, I became a murderer.

I followed the path I'd taken out of Wolsey's apartments earlier that morning. Now, though, I had just killed a man. I was creeping out, avoiding detection, wary of all who might catch a glimpse of me.

As I proceeded downstairs, I was met only with busy servants bringing up the middle courses of dinner: the smaller, baked fish, swimming now in rich sauces. They wouldn't have been there when Cosyn was murdered.

So who would have been?

Down and out I went, into the ordinary press of the courtyard. The creature could, as I'd known, have easily slipped into and out of the apartments – into and out of the waiting chamber. I pursed my lips, looking down at myself.

Am I covered in blood?

No. The old man had been stabbed, he'd bled, but there was no great gout of the stuff. Raising my head, I looked around. Ahead and to my right was the gateway to the kitchens, on the same side as the entrance to the private Middle Court.

People were about, as they always were, carrying things, their heads either down or bent to one another. All were lower servants; it was the dinner hour – the better sort were at table.

No one is looking at me.

That would usually be a good thing. Now, it irritated me. No one would have been looking at the murderer when he fled either.

Where would I go?

Escape seemed the obvious answer. If I'd murdered a man, my heart would have been racing. If I'd done so horribly, surely my head would have been full of it. Maybe I'd even carry the reek of singed flesh on me. I'd want out – out.

I raised my head, feeling my own heart begin to speed as though I really had done something. Affecting an air of calm.

No running – running gets you noticed, criticised – it frightens people and makes them think something bad is happening.

I strolled out into the courtyard. The wagons of apples were long gone, off to be sauced. Across the way, the window-washing ladders had been set up now against the wardrobe building. I'd been serious when I'd told Wolsey it was unlikely that the killer had used the window. But I had nothing else.

Think on your windows and your entrances and exits, lad, and see what you might discover of this.

I set out across the cobbles, nodding occasionally at men and women whose faces I knew. Some nodded back; others were too intent on their bundles of laundry or their leather wallets of coins or papers.

The wardrobe was a barn of a building, on two floors

and, like the outer walls of Richmond, of red brick rather than the gleaming white of the staterooms and inner royal apartments. I ambled along, clinging to its side, until I came to a ladder. Looking up, I saw that the window washer was at work, balancing monkey-like, a pail over one arm up to his shoulder and a wet rag in his other hand. This he was applying to one of the upper windows in neat, circular motions.

'Good morrow,' I called up.

No response.

I chewed on my cheek for a second. And then I began to climb.

'Hey, now, what's this? Get out of it!' The man – he was old, perhaps past forty – turned to look down. A few spatters of water hit my arm, my cap. 'Get out of it!'

I retreated the two rungs I'd gained and stood back.

The fellow slid down faster than I'd have thought possible, this time spilling nothing, and hopped off the ladder lithely. His face was more curious than annoyed. That curiosity deepened as he took in my livery. And then it immediately faded to neutrality. 'His Grace ain't happy with them windows?'

Thrown, I licked my lips, instinctively looking back over the heads populating the courtyard. The sun made white rectangles of the windows of Wolsey's lodgings. 'No, I . . . no. I mean, yes, the cardinal's happy. With the windows, I mean.'

Skilfully done.

I blinked. Stupid of me not to have thought through some artifice, some pretence. Swallowing, I forced what authority I could muster into my voice. 'His Grace is looking for a man. A man who came to . . . petition him. This morning.' I adjusted my cap and tried a weary sigh. 'The man left without giving his name. But he was in the waiting chamber. And then he left.'

I was losing the fellow. Bafflement had overcome him. Why, I imagined him wondering, was this odd young court-toy bothering him with nonsense about some wandering petitioner?

He slid the pail off his arm and set it to the cobbles; he stayed bent and wrung out his rag over it. 'A man?'

'Just so,' I said. 'And we saw that you had done a fine job of washing the windows there. Did you see the fellow? When you were at your labour? Or perhaps even after, when he left? Whether he went . . . where he went. . .' I let the sentence wither. Which, I thought, was all it deserved.

To my surprise, the window-washer straightened, putting his arms to the small of his back. One thick eyebrow rose. 'Yes, bully. I saw yon man.'

'What?' My mouth fell open. I'd been expecting . . . I don't know what I'd been expecting.

Nothing?

'Saw him, I did. When I was at the window. Man who was waiting then come out.'

'But – when – what – who was he?' Excitement stuttered. I almost reached out to take him by the shoulder. As if he anticipated this, he took a step back.

'Steady, now. You'll find him. Ay, I saw the man. Waiting in there. . .' He put a hand to his chin. Enjoying his moment, I thought, enjoying delaying me as I was delaying him. 'Came rushing out later. I was filling me bucket again. Got to fill it, see, fresh, else you just put the dirt from the clean window onto the next, see?'

I don't care!

'Did he leave?' I asked, forcing calm into my voice.

Again, the fellow gave his chin a rub, furrowing his brow. Then he brightened. 'Maybe gone by now.' He shrugged. 'Can't say. But he came tearing out of Wols – out of the cardinal's rooms. Then he went over yonder.' He lifted an arm and pointed over my shoulder and to the left. I twisted, following his finger towards the kitchen gate. 'Reckon he'll have wanted himself a drink, a bite.' He shrugged again. 'Didn't see him no more.'

Yes!

I didn't wait. Thanking him over my shoulder, I clattered away, heading for the kitchens, not bothering to nod at anyone.

I knew I'd be unwelcome and didn't care. I'd been in great kitchens before – foul collections of buildings, made fouler by Lent. The kitchens at Richmond were separate, mostly whitewashed structures, standing apart from the staterooms around the Middle Court. Giant's thumbprints of soot smudged their sides. No porters stood at the narrow gateway that led to them. After passing through it, I found myself standing amidst the shouts and laughter of men in stained white aprons, and boys stripped to the waist, lounging about to cool off. This, I supposed, was their period of rest. The dinnertime cooking had been done; their work was now the charge of those who carried it up to the households. Still, the reek of it hung in the air – honey mixed with fish mixed with vinegar mixed with stewed fruit.

I turned on the spot, taking in the low, slate-roofed great kitchen, and the satellites that hung around it – butteries, larders, the pastry, the coalhouse. Shaking my head, I began asking around – the same question: 'Have you seen a man lately come from the cardinal's household?'

Once again, I seemed to be in luck.

'Ay,' said a red-faced, round-cheeked man in white. 'Your master riddin us o' the brute?'

'Yes,' I said, 'yes, yes. Where is he?'

'In yonder.' Another pointing finger directed me to a little wooden hut near the squat bulk of the pastry. 'Get him to fuck, will ye? Comin' 'ere, makin' demands, I dunno.'

My heart rose.

The last time I'd been engaged in finding a murderer, the creature had led me a merry, dangerous dance. This was easy.

Too easy.

No – this was how it should be. Commonly, when I'd heard of murders in the city, the monsters had been clapped in irons and made ready for the gallows before the body had even been embalmed. If a woman was slain, her husband was easily enough found to be the culprit. If a neighbour bashed another over the head, he was taken up as soon as it was known the pair had been feuding.

This was how it should be.

And perhaps there was even a certain genius spirit to it. If the creature had fled and his wicked deed been quickly discovered, as it had been, he'd have been easily overtaken on the road back to London or on the river. But to hide in plain sight, to do the act and then remain, blending in. . .

I kept my eyes on the little hut. But to the cook, I said, out of the corner of my mouth, 'See that he remains there. Just for a – for a minute. I have to fetch someone.'

Ignoring his grumbles, I darted away, out of the kitchen

block and back into the courtyard. Hooking right, casting repeated glances over my shoulder, I clung to the wall of white brick until I came to the gateway to the Middle Court. At the gatehouse, I beat on the door, crying, 'Quickly! His Grace's business! A man is to be taken up!'

'What's that?' The porter stuck his head out. I repeated my plea. Looking over his shoulder, he murmured something. Laughter followed. I gave the wall of the gatehouse another whack.

'I'm coming, I'm coming.' From behind the porter emerged a scrawny guardsman in royal white and green, a Tudor rose at his breast. The best of the guards, I supposed, would have gone with the king on his business; this was one of the dregs.

Better than nothing.

'Come,' I said. 'Quickly. Cardinal's business. We must make an arrest.'

'An arrest?' The fellow scratched at an eyebrow. 'That's the king's knight marshal's business.'

I hopped from one foot to the other. 'Come!' I could think of nothing else. 'Please,' I added, pathetically. 'The cardinal demands it!'

My new friend gave an amused look to the porter, who shrugged, returning it. 'Ay, well. Let's see, then. Thief, is it? Sharp gambler?'

I didn't answer. Instead, I turned my back and slid back along the building towards the kitchen, leaving him to follow me.

When we'd gained the kitchen block, I turned to him. My palms felt wet. I rubbed one on my livery. The other I folded deeper into its trailing cuff. 'In the little wooden building.

Report of a man the cardinal seeks. He's done . . . a bad man. Take him up.'

He didn't know, I told myself. The yeoman didn't know, didn't understand. That was why he showed no excitement, no concern. Yet, to his credit, he nodded. His cheeks tautened. 'As you like it,' he said. 'If His Grace'll answer to it. Well, come then, lad.'

Whatever training the fellow had undertaken took over. Suddenly, I was the bystander. I'd found the fellow, but actually taking him up was someone else's job. God knew, I'd suffered enough in the past trying to seek out wicked men on my own. I thus hung back a step, watching the embroidered vines on his back as the guardsman marched – a good, stately gait, he managed – over to the low wooden shack.

With one sharp rap, he beat on the door. The whole wall quivered. 'We enter,' he said, 'in the name of the king.' And then, without waiting for a response, he stepped back and kicked the door in. It fell easily, as though it were made of parchment, and he slid inside.

I gave a quick look around. The cooks and their boys had all ranged themselves against the walls of the other buildings. Wide, laughing eyes were on us. I shrank a little into my livery. But just a little.

I stepped into the shack.

★ ★ ★

Jesus Christ.

I could say nothing. My voice died somewhere in my throat, died of thirst and shame and embarrassment.

Confusion reigned in the dim single room. It was a

refreshment room of some sort, with one wall covered in shelves containing stoppered hide bottles. There was nothing expensive, nothing that would furnish a table. Probably it was where the cooks came to have a drink and a bite of their own, out of the sun or the cold, out of the stink.

'You are arrested, sirrah!' the yeoman of the guard barked. I stood, rooted the spot, staring dumbly. 'This your man?'

'What? I. . .'

The rangy guardsman was leaning over a fellow sprawled on a bench. On the floor at his feet were several empty wineskins.

''rest . . . 'rest me?' Hiccoughing, the draper raised an arm over his head. His eyes were wide, shining even in the dimness. He cowered under the sudden, shouting assault. 'This . . . is s-some jape. For . . . the cardinal. Doesn't wish . . . t'pay.'

Of course, it was the draper. I'd forgotten the fellow's existence, forgot that he'd been in the waiting chamber with the dead man. The sight of the body had driven woolsacks and waiting men out of my mind.

'This man is drunk,' said the guardsman. He straightened, turning on me with a look of distaste. 'This is who your cardinal would have me take up? What charge – drunkenness?'

'It's not him,' I said. My voice came out in a shrunken croak. I could feel the heat in my cheeks, as though we were in the kitchen proper. The urge to run away, to flee the room like a naughty child, washed over me.

You fucking idiot.

'Drunkenness, is it?' pressed the yeoman. I sucked in my cheeks.

Stop pressing the matter!

Closing my eyes, I said, 'No . . . no charge. It's not the man. It's the wrong man.' I forced myself to look, not at the unfortunate draper, who had begun whimpering, but at the guard. 'I was . . . misled.' As quickly, I looked at the packed earth floor. 'This isn't the man His Grace seeks. I was misled.'

The guardsman was my friend no more. He stepped away from the draper and his fixed his gaze on me. 'What is this? Some jape, indeed?'

'No. No. I. . .'

Don't say misled!

'. . . was misled. A mistake. The cardinal seeks a man, another man – I'll report – I'll tell His Grace the other man is – he's. . .'

The guardsman spat on the floor, before raking me with his eyes. 'No, boy. *I'll* report. Ay, report these games. If your master seeks to arrest some fellow, he might send to us some better man. Not some . . . what are you?'

'A lower groom.'

A smirk crossed his face. 'Not some lower groom.' He looked down again at the draper. 'And you, you lousy, filthy beast. Get the fuck out of this house. Get you gone. We want no drunkenness near Her Majesty.' In response, the draper fell off the bench, crushing the empty wineskins.

'Didn't,' he spluttered, 'didn't mean harm, no harm. Just a drink, to toast His Grace's – his good custom. 's all. I go – I go.'

The guardsman tutted, before pushing past me. 'Some better man,' he sniffed. As he ducked out of the doorway, his voice boomed, 'Get back to work, slaves!'

Left with the drunken draper, I began fumbling for

apologies, letting them fall on him like hailstones. He didn't seem to care. Probably, he thought that he'd simply been given a deliberate fright for gorging himself on the king's bounty. Eventually, I offered him my hand and he took it, using it to haul himself to his feet. He swayed there a moment, his eyes trying to focus on me, his lips framing thanks.

Might as well try to make good on this. . .

Before he could speak, I said, 'Mr . . . Mr . . .' I didn't know his name. 'Sir, do you recall waiting in His Grace's chamber? Waiting to be called in to show him your cloths?'

His gaze sharpened. 'Said he would pay. For the best, the cardinal did.'

'And so he will.' I kept my voice steady. 'When you were waiting for your audience – this morning – there was another man there. Do you recall? Sir, do you recall?'

'Another. . .' He screwed an eye closed. 'Man. Yes. Waiting.' He sniffed deeply and his eyelids flickered.

'Yes. Good, sir. Thank you. One Mr Cosyn. An older gentleman. In grey.'

'Holy-looking man. Monk, was he?'

I didn't know how to answer that, so I said, 'Did he – did anyone else come in? When you waited?'

'Else?'

'Another man – a third man?'

His eyes rose to the ceiling. Shafts of light speared in through breaks in it, catching bits of dust in their swirling dance. 'Another . . . the usher? Just the usher. To fetch me along to Wolsey.'

'No,' I said, ignoring the irreverence. 'Not him.'

'No one else. Me, the monk, and the usher came to fetch me up.' As he spoke, his voice seemed to grow stronger. Fear and the wine retreated. 'That's all.'

'And the old man – the man who looked like a monk – did you speak with him?'

'Me? No, no. I tried, lad. Said, "How fare you?" Waste. Didn't look like the kind to give good custom. All grey. Strange. Strange old dog. Kept looking up, looking at the door. Waiting to be taken to Wolsey, eh?' He bent his head and mimed what I assumed were Cosyn's glances – up, down, up, down, up. 'Frightened, he was. Scared of his audience with old Wolsey.' The colour drained from his face. 'Your master – the cardinal – His Grace, I mean. No offence, lad.' I shook this away with my head.

Scared of his audience?

'Anything else you recall, sir? Anything he said or did?'

'No. Just sat there, looking up at the door. Frightened, like. Maybe wasn't used to meetings with men as great as your good master.' It suddenly seemed to dawn on the fellow that these questions were unusual. His eyes widened. 'Has he done something, the old monk? Made some ruffle?'

'No,' I said. 'Nothing like that. Just left before his audience. That's all.'

This appeared to satisfy him. 'Frightened off, then. You . . . ah . . . there will be no trouble with His Grace? I only came to toast his custom, lad. No offence.' He looked at the floor. 'I came seeking a little good cheer. They showed me in here. The wine . . . French, is it? It was new to me. I meant no offence to the cardinal or his house.'

'It's the king's house,' I said. It came out more sharply than I meant. 'Perhaps . . . it would be better if you took your leave.' This I managed more gently.

'Yes, lad – sir – and thank your master again. A fine, great man, is His Grace, and he'll have the best for his parliament. The king's parliament. As he wishes.'

'Thank you,' I said, my voice shrinking again. 'And good morrow to you.' I gave him a little bow, turned, and then passed out of the shack and back into the press of laughing, jeering kitchen folk, keeping my head down as I wound my way back to the cardinal's apartments. Cosyn's murderer, I thought, could be well on his way to London – or anywhere else – by now.

Of course, I thought: nothing was ever that easy.

5

The sudden crash shook me, lifting me nearly out of my shoes.

Some nervous, light-sounding murmuring and whispers followed.

The click and spark of rushlight tapers sounded over them, and gradually the hall began to return to life, as the ringing cymbals were passed over to a waiting servant.

It was early: we'd just finished listening to Lauds in the hall – the chapel was being prepared for the day's celebrations – sung by one of Wolsey's chaplains in total darkness. It was a thing I'd never understood. During the Triduum the Lauds service had to be said in a complete absence of light. We fear blackness; we fear what we can't see and what we don't often see. And when we can't see anything, the chaplain's unannounced crashing of the cymbals is all the more sudden, shocking. That, I knew at least, was meant to remind us of the horrors of Christ's death and the dreadful rolling of the rock over his tomb.

I was still thinking about death, but not, God forgive me, Christ's.

After my unsuccessful attempt to have the poor draper taken up for murder, I'd found the rest of Wednesday equally bootless. And my enthusiasm had flagged, as I'd listlessly moved around the courtyards, asking the same questions and receiving the same answers. Cosyn had been seen going up to Wolsey's apartments; the draper had been seen, whether on his trip up or down; I'd been seen, some wags noted; and sundry lordlings and divers servants had been seen. But a murderer creeping from the place must have been wearing a blind cloak, or else been one of those noted (and I had the grace to exclude myself, being relatively sure I hadn't done it). Cosyn's death had become known about in the cardinal's household; some knew his name, others only that an old fellow had fallen ill and dropped dead whilst waiting for an audience. As far as I could tell, Wolsey had managed to cover up the exact circumstances of the death, because he was Cardinal Wolsey, and he could do anything he wished.

Except pick a useful sniffer-out of murderers.

As the rushlight tapers were put to torches, the big room – free now of dining tables, stools, and cutlery – took on its familiar guise of carved ceiling and covered floor. At my side, Mark's round, soft face split in a grin.

'Always makes me jump, does that,' he said, not troubling to lower his voice. Others took it as a sign that we could all speak freely – the crash and the relighting marked the end of the Tenebrae Lauds service. The rest of the cardinal's men began to form into their usual knots: lordlings with lordlings, gentlemen with gentlemen, lower chamberers with lower chamberers, and Mark and I, in the middle, with each other. I'd told him everything the previous night.

'I suppose we'd better—'

A burst of laughter cut across us and we turned as one. An upper groom – not much better than we were – was looking at me, miming drinking, his hand cupped to his mouth. He swayed, affected a swoon, and gained some more laughter.

I cursed myself for a fool.

Word had got round that I'd attempted to have a man arrested for drunkenness. Since then, I'd been getting jeered as a doddle-pate and a milksop. Mark smiled again – but this time at the fake drunkard. It graduated to a grin, as he raised his middle finger and jabbed it in the air. Some oohs rose from the laughing grooms, but it was none of it too mean-spirited or passionate. Most in the household liked a bit of raillery without taking it far enough to attract the attention of Deacon or any of the other officers.

'Shouldn't rise to it,' I said, shaking my head and giving a watery smile and the palms of my hands to the japester. Everyone, I knew, enjoyed a laugh when a fellow made a fool of himself, and it was always better for the fool to laugh too.

'It was me finger rose to it,' he said, mildly. 'If anyone's goin' to be havin' a laugh at my boy, it's goin' to be me.' His smile faded. 'Them lot don't know what's up.' He managed to lower his voice. 'Don't know nothin' about what happened. Not really.' He tapped his nose conspiratorially.

I licked my lips. Mark liked to know what was going on – he had a big mouth, but he knew when to keep it closed. 'Right, well,' he said, stifling a yawn. 'Work, then. Jesus, it's cold. Them candles being out don't half steal away the heat.' He shuffled over to his pile on the floor, which lay hard by mine. Our little beds – if that's not too fine a word for broadcloth filled with inferior feathers – had been cleared away as soon as we'd risen. But our trumpets stood polished and ready, next to our good shoes. Mark leant for his instrument, picking it up easily and brushing away some loose rushes from the bell. I followed him, reaching down for mine. My hand closed around its familiar – too familiar

– cold smoothness. It was the thing my father had gifted me, music. When I blew it, I felt too much like him. Its sound was his sound, its notes his notes.

But, I supposed, every man grew to hate anything that meant work. We're all, at root, idle. And there were plenty out in the wide world who would give up their ploughs or their pails to have a skill which put them in a great household, with a bed and a roof and a table to eat at.

No, what bothered me now wasn't work, and it wasn't the memory of my father, and it wasn't even the feeling that I was neither one thing nor another. It was that, when I was still called upon to play, I'd be required to be seen, with my charred hand and neck.

'Hurry up,' said Mark, snapping me out of my self-pity. He rolled his eyes. 'What, you reckon any man'll be looking at a trumpet? They're looking to what the trumpet . . . uh . . . announces.' His teeth showed in a grin. 'And the ladies, too. Ay, they ain't looking at what *makes* the sound. No one's wantin' to look at *us*. Soft bastard.'

He was right. Of course he was right.

'Well, come on then,' I said. I hefted the trumpet and let its bell tap against my side. 'Better be—'

'Ho, here's trouble,' said Mark. He was looking up-hall. I followed his gaze and smiled, my free hand reaching up for my cap.

'Good morrow,' said Harry Gainsford, striding towards us.

'How do?' asked Mark.

'Mm,' said Harry. 'Yes. Good morrow.'

Though a gentleman, Harry was one of my best friends. 'Harry,' I said. He stood tall, his hands on his hips, before us.

I lowered my voice. 'You've heard?' He inclined his head, and I exhaled relief. Harry worked for Richard Audley, Wolsey's irritating secretary.

'I've heard all. And . . . about . . . the draper.' He drew in his cheeks and then blew out a breath, giving me a hard nod. 'Not your fault. No. A simple enough error, of no import.' His chiselled face carried a look of absolute authority; you always believed what Harry said – his good looks and firm voice encouraged you to.

'Why you sniffing our foul airs, Mr Gainsford?' asked Mark. He'd taken his cap off – without much ceremony – and was twisting it in his hands, his face mild. His voice, when he spoke, was all honey. 'Can we do something for you, master?'

'What?' asked Harry. 'I. . .'

'He's jesting,' I said, letting my instrument clump to the floor. Harry, I knew, had trouble with levity. Jokes were like a language he hadn't mastered. That made him, I thought – but had never said – a perfect disciple of old Audley. 'What news?'

'Ah,' said Harry, still frowning at Mark, 'yes. Mr Audley thinks you might do His Grace some service after the Maundy.' He whispered, 'Poor Mr Cosyn . . . he had a house near the sign of the Bottle at Botolph's Wharf. Near the bridge. He was unmarried, I understand, but it is meet that his household be informed of his . . . passing away. Of age, you understand – of advanced age.' He cleared his throat. 'The cardinal, tell them, will see that the defunct is returned to his parish for good Christian burial. Out of his own privy purse, tell them.'

How magnanimous!

And then I thought: the *defunct*?

I nodded, and Harry brightened a little, his face loosening. 'Good man. And . . . ah . . . it might be good that you are . . . away from the household for a spell. It shall give the lustier fellows time to . . . forget . . . the error. About the draper.'

'Let them find some new poor bastard to laugh at,' said Mark, cheerfully. 'Ay, and he's right at that. You know how it is. Someone'll piss their bed or fall down the stairs or fart during Mass. You'll be old news, boy o' mine.'

'Quite,' said Harry. He reached out and tapped my shoulder.

'Oh, yes – some coins to speed you on your way.' He fished at his belt and extracted a stringed brown purse, handing it over. I took it, smiling my thanks. 'Well,' he said, 'I must be off. His Grace wishes to make sure all is in readiness for the Maundy.' His chest rose. 'Her Majesty Queen Catherine is placing her especial faith in His Grace. We would not wish to appear slack.' A little shyness crept over his face, making him look younger. 'Though I think it would take less time to clean the stables of Augeas than it does for the queen's ladies to have their hair pinned up . . . you know, in . . . readiness. For the Maundy.' I forced a smile. Laughter I couldn't muster. Mark managed neither. Sternness returned to Harry's brow. 'Look sharp now.' He gave us a brief up-tilt of his chin, before turning and showing us a scarlet-liveried back.

'We,' echoed Mark. 'What's this "we?" "Look sharp,"' he mimicked. 'Was that meant to be a jest? Where the hell's Augeas?'

'Harry's a good man,' I said.

'I know, I know. Wet, though. Wetter'n a dog in a rainstorm. Here, how much did he give you? Enough for a bed in London and a wench to warm it, I hope. Sign of the

Bottle – that sounds like a place you'd have good cheer.'

I tutted but said nothing. Already, in my mind, I was escaping Richmond, travelling down the Thames – and locating the dead man's house. Unmarried . . . no wife – I'd be intruding on no grief, save for that of a lot of servants who found themselves masterless. If Cosyn was – had been – a decent man, he'd have made some provision for them to be taken in elsewhere. My stepmother always said you could measure the goodliness – or was it the Godliness? – of a great man by how much he thought of those beneath him. It was the same with women, according to the second Mrs Blanke – she loved Queen Catherine precisely because of how much the queen saw dished out to the destitute.

Queen Catherine.

Maundy.

'Let's get this done,' I said, my hands already fiddling with the strings of the purse. When it was hanging at my belt, I lifted my trumpet again.

★ ★ ★

The Middle Court, so empty when I'd visited the previous day, was now an ant's nest. Carts stood about, overloaded with twigs, looking in the morning brightness like the massed bones of men, dyed brown. From the Great Orchard, I supposed, which lay beyond the kitchens. Probably boys had worked through the night, by torchlight, snapping and cracking away. The twigs would be scattered about the altar in the royal chapel after the Maundy, to remind the queen and her ladies of Christ's scourging.

The mastiff-borne water pump was almost hidden. A knot

of people stood around it, alongside filled barrels. They were women, I saw, in plain white shifts and homespun. Some of them were whispering together. Others were looking up at the soaring whitewashed brick and glass of the staterooms, up to the gleaming slate roof and the gilded vanes. All of them were barefoot, the soft whites of their feet reddened from walking on the cobbles.

'Fancy a night with one of them?' asked Mark, at my elbow. I gave him a half-smile. The poor women were present to have their feet washed by the queen. But, naturally, no one expected Queen Catherine to touch soiled feet; the women would have been scrubbed down before being allowed into the courtyard and were likely awaiting a secondary soaking before being allowed indoors. Mark set off ahead of me, his trumpet swinging, gawping openly at the poor women as he circled around them. I followed, and together we passed through the buzz of chatter from dozens of court officials: ushers, chamberlains, secretaries, chaplains.

Is someone here a murderer?

I knew it was possible. Such things had happened before. Men would murder or set others to murder if they might gain by it. The problem was that they didn't like to be caught in their plots; they'd lay false trails, let others take the blame.

A pretty big problem.

Perhaps, I thought, when I knew more of the – *defunct* – unfortunate Mr Cosyn, I might be able to trace his path to death.

A tall figure caught my eye, moving just shy of a trio of clerks. It was the physician, Mordaunt, his face pinched and his back bent. Supporting him was a man I knew by sight – Cardinal Wolsey's friend, Sir Thomas More. Mordaunt's words of the day before cut through my memory.

Or More. More hasn't gone with the king – he knows the ruffians of London and their filthy habits. Their tricks.

I'd never spoken with the lawyer, or writer, or scholar, or counsellor, or whatever the fellow was, but I'd seen him coming and going from Wolsey's chambers often enough. He looked as he always did – short, heavy through the shoulders, a little unkempt. His chin hadn't seen a razor, at least not closely, in a few days. Though his clothes were well cut, he wore them heavily; it looked as though they'd been made for another man.

I locked eyes with the physician just as he looked at me. His mouth twitched and he leant more heavily on More. The scholar's eyes landed on me too. They were soft, like a tame dog's, and the side of his lip rose. He looked as though he might move towards me and Mark, but Mordaunt jerked on his arm, winced, and began leading him on. They passed us, in a babble of the physician's cryptic Latin. Once they had gone on, moving towards the cloisters, More cast me one last look over his padded shoulder, more interested and kindly than suspicious. And then he was gone into the shadows, he and Mordaunt, where I could see the assistant Rowlet was waiting for them.

'They talkin' about us?' asked Mark. 'Looked like they was talkin' about us.'

'Maybe,' I said. I coughed, my eyes tracing the grey stone arches under which they'd disappeared, the shadowy spaces in which they were now. 'Who knows. Old men. Come.'

On the right, on the opposite side of the cloistered wing of the building, the doors of the great hall stood open. Perfume and the soft rise and fall of choral music spilled out.

A face appeared in the doorway, flushed. Deacon, the gentleman usher who had found Cosyn's body. 'Trumpets!' he announced, more to himself than to us. He twisted his head and hissed into the hall, 'Trumpets!' Returning to us, he said, 'His Grace is with Her Majesty. Quickly, now, trumpets, come!' He clapped his hands together and then disappeared back into the building.

Well, he, I thought, had got over his shock.

'Trumpets,' Mark bleated. 'How comes this, then – sailors ain't called *ships* and – and – wheelwrights ain't called *wheels*. Come on, then,' he sighed. 'We'll blast them dirty-foot wenches inwards, when they're fit for it.'

There was no porch – just a marble step up into the stone arch of the doorway. I stepped up after him. Just beyond the doors, the thick wall was flanked with recesses where we would stand, blocking no one's passage but stinging their ears with our treble-blasts. Just so, we could see and announce those coming in by the main entrance. And, more importantly, we really wouldn't be seen. Absently, I shrank my neck into my upturned collar.

'Looks ready,' said Mark. He'd ignored his recess and taken a couple of steps into the hall. I joined him. The room was large, like any of its type. The wooden ceiling high overhead was carved in a honeycomb of hexagons, each painted with arms. Banners hung down at intervals, from our lower end onwards, all displaying the arms of England. Arrases glinting with gold and silver thread lined the walls and, at intervals between them, silver platters had been fixed, with projecting lips for candles to sit before them. The reflected light cast a cheerful, glittering glow back into the vast hall. Both the cardinal's and the queen's choristers were already at work, singing high in the gallery above our end.

Directly before us was an empty space, strewn with rushes. Meadowsweet sang up from them, spicy and sweet. Two long benches stood in the centre of the hall, their lengths running up towards the high royal dais at the far end. Dotted along each bench were stools, for the poor women to put their feet up. Deacon and Cavendish, his fellow usher, were attending to these; Deacon evidently found one not evenly spaced from its fellow and, as I watched, he bent and adjusted it by what looked like a half-inch.

'To our places?' I asked.

Before Mark could answer, a blast of trumpets issued from somewhere at the top of the hall.

'Shit!' Mark's eyes widened.

We edged back a few steps, as women poured into the room from a hidden entrance at the upper end, which let out onto the dais. Somewhere there, I knew, connected to the smaller quadrangle of royal apartments attached to the staterooms. My heart skipped a beat.

The queen's ladies.

They were a plain-faced lot, many of them aged, some stout. They came in a cluster, like a sudden opening of leaves. Each of them had on a spotless linen apron, over dull mauve and claret corsets, gowns, and sleeves, with plain white or cream kirtles.

Except one.

'It's herself,' said Mark, loudly, so as to be heard over the music falling on us.

'It is,' I said, barely above a whisper.

Mistress Anne Boleyn, whom I couldn't call a friend, but I could say I knew, gave her face to the voice I'd overheard the day before. It was a long, oval face, sallow and thin. Her prominent cheekbones made shadowy recesses in her cheeks. Her wide mouth and full lips were upturned in a smile. Her expression, I thought, was amused – always a little amused, though you never knew by what. Unlike the matrons, she was wearing the colour they called Judas – a sickening shade, I always found, of yellow. Rather than the boxy gables of the older ladies – which I'd seen her in only rarely – she had on a curved hood in the French style. Her corset was square cut, low – it would have given a man a hint of her cleavage, if she'd had much of one. She held her posy of violets just below the line of it, showing off long, slender fingers.

'The Mistress Anne,' said Mark. This time, he did lower his voice. He had danced with her once at a masque – it had all been part of a guise, a piece of flummery – and had never quite got over it. She, of course, had never looked at him since, and privately I suspected that she'd been disgusted at finding herself made a fool of, dancing with a trumpet.

The ladies soared down the hall. They would be near us, by us, waiting to receive the poor women and give their feet yet another preliminary wash. The smell of them, like amber, washed over us, as they formed ranks, the oldest matrons nearest the ends of the benches, and the youngest ladies nearest us. There followed a procession of clerics: the queen's chamberlain, under almoner, and grand almoner, the usual flurry of chaplains in black, swinging censers and filling the air with a stronger, heavier musk.

To hell with it.

I dropped my trumpet in its recess by the doorway and hopped forward just as the ladies reached us.

The young women let out a burst of murmurs; the old

dames either didn't hear over the music or had the breeding not to turn. 'Mistress,' I hissed. Anne Boleyn stood amongst a number of her fellow demoiselles, some of whom had copied her in wearing French hoods with trailing, gauzy veils – the kind of pretty fancies that Queen Catherine only wore when entertaining Frenchmen.

A pair of dark eyes lifted, alert, bright, under needlepoint lashes. One inky eyebrow rose. I had no idea if she'd remember me. I thought she would. I hoped. Her gaze, open and bemused, betrayed nothing. Only her lips parted slightly, a little pink tongue darting over them and retreating.

'His Grace seeks to know your secret,' I said.

Her expression changed. Her head tilted downwards, but her eyes swivelled up, tracing me. Something pulsed deep in her long throat. And then she shifted, giving a brief glance up the hall. Her cheeks tautened in something like annoyance. I saw no fear of the cardinal discovering her secret, no terror of being punished for whatever she was plotting with Percy – love? Secret marriage? – but only a flash of irritation. And then she was looking at me again. Her mouth moved in what might have been mute thanks, before blankness overtook her expression, as though a hand had wiped feeling from her face.

I suddenly realised that the other young women were staring at me, some with pudgy white hands held before their mouths. Whispering behind them, probably, laughing at me with one another.

No matter. I'd made up – somewhat – for my spiery. I'd warned her, and she could warn Percy.

I melted back, my head bowed. I'd forgotten to remove

my cap in addressing her. I reached up stupidly for it as I reached my place, facing Mark.

'What the hell was that?' he shouted across the doorway.

I raised my hand to make a throat-cutting gesture. Before I could, the trumpets from the top of the hall blasted again.

My recess, on the left-hand side of the doorway, gave me a view straight up the room, if I craned my neck to the left.

Wolsey stepped out onto the dais and began making signs of the cross.

Another blast.

The ladies fell to their knees. The ushers and other men about the hall had melted away. Even the choir above stopped, letting silence fill the air.

Queen Catherine appeared on the dais, wearing all white, her corset and bodice lined with snowy fur and her headdress bordered in shimmering pearls. Only a huge, jewelled crucifix added a splash of golden and red colour. She was a tiny woman, made tinier still by the cardinal, though her gown and her history – I knew of the weight of sadness of many lost babies which hung about her belly – made her almost as wide as she was tall. Yet she didn't move in the way stout little men and women often move, like a bowling ball rolled over a green. She stepped with care, her face set in a smile, her strong, rounded lower jaw jutting. It was a small face, again made smaller by the pearled gable hood, from which peeked some of her famous red-blonde hair. Age hadn't dimmed Queen Catherine. It made her something else, something between things – she was as small and doll-like as a child, and yet as grave as an old matron; she was both, and neither. I liked her, almost as much as my stepmother did.

And this was Queen Catherine's day.

With the King away, this was to be her day.

She dipped, falling on her knees at the cardinal's feet as he spoke over her – blessings, I supposed.

A shriek tore in from outside.

Another followed, splitting the air, animal in its intensity. *Murder?*

Cheering rose, drawing out my relief. It caught mid-sigh. A lump rose in my throat.

The queen turned, puzzlement on her face. Even Wolsey had broken off his prayers and was frowning down the hall towards us.

I looked at Mark; he was already half out of his recess, staring out of the doorway. With the muttering of the young women at my back, I joined him. 'Jesus,' he cried, his face breaking into a grin. 'It's himself. It's the king come home!'

I felt the colour drain from my cheeks.

Looking out into the courtyard, the scene spread before me, like an unrolled painted cloth.

King Henry was in a gold-and-white coat, astride a gilt-caparisoned white courser, his big, powerful legs seeming almost to hold the beast in place, to stop it from flying up into the air. Ahead of him, people – the poor women included – had scattered, leaving a sea of cobbles as his stage. At his back, a dozen or so well-dressed, mounted attendants were arrayed in a rainbow, a semicircle of cloth-of-silver coats, violet doublets, forest-green hose, pink silken hats, white feathers. If the cobbles had become his playing place, they had become his canvas backdrop.

Still, the cheering went on, from all of those whom Henry had intruded upon. A broad smile showed off his good, white teeth. He bowed in his saddle, and then drew up his reins in one hand and his crop in the other. Looking around the crowd, he grinned more deeply, before his face straightened. 'Holla!' he cried, in a tremulous voice. 'Holla, boy!' And then, somehow, the horse was leaping, its front legs up off the ground, and twisting in the air. The king went with it, up, up, round, now his back to us, now his side. Sparks flew up from the cobbles and then, before they'd faded, the beast thundered back down, facing the way it had been.

A collective intake of breath drew the air from the yard, drew it away from the king. And then another great cheer went up. The king's small eyes roved the crowd, drinking their applause, and seemed to fix on me. I felt, for a moment, that he had performed the feat of horsemanship only for me – but, then, his gaze moved on, likely giving the same feeling to everyone.

'Mother of God,' said Mark, his voice close to my ear. 'Thought he should take off, there. Fly up, fly away.'

If only.

Suddenly, rain began pelting. I saw it first misting the cobbles, and then looked up. Henry had swept off his hat and was looking up himself. His attention fell again upon his audience, the lake of caps and bonnets spread before me. And then he laughed. As his red hair darkened to brown, he roared his amusement. It was a high sound, I thought, more like a woman's than a big-chested man's. In one quick movement, he whipped his hat into the crowd. A huddle of women fell upon it, and his laughter shrilled, screeching even over the hiss and tick-tack-tack of the downpour.

The king drew rein again, turning more easily back to his fellows. Together, they departed the Middle Court, presumably going off to stable their horses. But his spell remained. Folk surged into the yard, as though eager to stand where he'd just been, where he'd done his trick.

'What a man,' said Mark. 'Never . . . never. A merrier king was there never.'

I considered this.

And I thought: what a brute this king is.

I turned from the doorway, intent on getting back to my recess. Only then did I realise that a crowd had filled the space behind me: chaplains, the ushers, and, of course, the young ladies, Anne amongst them.

But this was Queen Catherine's day.

Of course, she'd be delighted that her husband had returned. Everyone said that she loved him beyond all earthly things – that she smiled more when he was by her side and hated to be apart from him. And yet . . . and yet. . .

A thing I had long suspected about King Henry was that he couldn't bear his wife to be loved. He couldn't bear anyone to be loved. It was as though there was only so much adoration in the world, and every bit of it that went to another was a bit being taken away from him. You saw it, when you were at court, though no one ever commented on it. You saw it in his dancing, and his capering, and in the constant rumours of spies he set out to find out who was swearing loyalty to whom, who was wearing what, who was eating off of what, and what they were eating. I don't say he was a bad man, but, as my father had once warned me, he was a king – and all kings were more children than men, and prey to the same thirst for affection and reckless vainglory. It was better not to be directly in their sight or their path – or even to be on the periphery of it, because that's where their listening men lurked. No, I didn't hate King Henry – you couldn't *hate* him

– but I didn't feel the love of him that I should, that others – *true Englishmen* – seemed to feel.

Still, I'd wit enough to bury my misgivings deep enough that no one might suspect them. And I'd thought the Maundy was safe enough. Wolsey hadn't expected him back; probably, the cardinal had thought that his king would hunt his way home, tarrying in fields and lodges, surrounded by friends and good fires and rain-washed trees and dead things, until he was absolutely required. The queen mustn't have expected him back either. Not today – not on her day.

And yet King Henry had evidently planned it – the suit, the great white courser, the elegant leap. He hadn't ridden through the night – that much was clear from his clean clothes. Instead, he must have slept somewhere nearby and timed his return to rob the queen of her moment in the sun. Even the poor women would get little delight from having their feet washed by their sovereign lady – not when King Henry had just performed for them, thrown them his hat; they might even be invited to watch him creep to the cross on the morrow.

Those in the hall seemed to lose interest, now that the king had gone. They resumed their places, but the big room itself reverberated with excited chatter, when before there had only been serenity. I leant over and looked towards the dais. Sure enough, little Queen Catherine was smiling like a child given a big spoonful of honey. Wolsey, however, looked as though he'd been struck. He was standing at the edge of the dais, leaning down on one knee, in conference with a group of his secretaries, Audley at their head.

I crossed the empty doorway to Mark's recess. He'd resumed his place, but now his face was shining with eagerness. I sometimes wished I was like him. It was an English enough thing to love the king. But you can't unthink what you've thought, any more than you can unsee what you've seen.

'See my trumpet back upstairs later, will you?'

'Did you see him turn? The size of that horse, and he mastered it.'

'Mark! My trumpet. See it gets upstairs later.'

His gaze turned from wonder to confusion. 'What?'

'I'm going. Going to London, as I was bid. See the dead man's household. See what I can turn up.'

'Lond . . . but – after the Maundy, I thought. You're goin' after the Maundy.'

I shrugged and looked out again into the now-grey morning. The rain had slowed from a fizz to a patter. 'The Maundy's done,' I said, 'for me.'

Amid his protests, his questions, I stepped out and began forcing my way through the wet, whistling, jabbering crowd.

6

I shivered at the sight of the body, its head bent to its chest, the wound gaping in its side. The hair was matted, clinging wetly, bound by its jagged diadem. A strip of linen was knotted around the waist.

It stood on a wagon on the corner, the effigy of Christ, where Thames Street met Botolph Lane. Behind me, the blocky tower of St Magnus the Martyr was still ringing out, a tinny dong-ding-ding-dong clamour which rose to meet similar tolling from elsewhere in the city.

Traditionally, the mercers' wagons were reserved for Corpus Christi plays. They'd be wheeled out and decorated with Biblical scenes. I remembered being led past them as a child – my father and stepmother had both taken me to see them. It was how children – well, those of us who would get no Church Latin – learned about the history told in the Bible. They'd be carpeted with fresh and paper flowers, the wagons, and statues and effigies would be set up on them – brightly painted, colourful things, dressed in real clothes and given real jewellery. I'd cried once at the sight of one: a female figure with blank eyes, decked out in strange dress – the queen of Sheba, probably. My stepmother still told people about what a fool I'd made of myself – and I'd often looked to see if the damned thing reappeared again over the years, so that I might laugh at it. More recently – I couldn't say when – the wagons had begun to appear more regularly, for all festivals and holy days. Christ – with a wax head, real hair, and a finely carved wooden torso – had evidently been brought out ahead of Good Friday. He – *it?* He had been set up with His straw-filled linen arms outstretched against what appeared to be the crossed planks of well-weathered ship's timbers, as though He'd been shipped directly from Jerusalem and crucified by overeager sailors. It was a strange effigy – discomfiting, I thought, being made of such different parts all stitched and fixed together. But it was something. There would be no Eucharist for people to bow to on the day itself. Folk needed something to see.

Someone pushed past me, barrelling into my shoulder. It was a woman, an old woman, her mob cap askew. She went to the edge of the tall wagon and threw herself onto the straw and muck and spittle of the street, coming down heavily on her knees. Then she threw back her head and began wailing, keening like an animal. With both hands she began scooping up ordure and smearing it on her face, before tearing at her cap until it fell off and starting on her hair. She kept up the wail, kept up the crying out for Christ.

I looked down at the broken paving stones, still streaked with rainwater. The rain had been off a good while, but I could still hear the patter of it from countless unseen eaves. Some of it still dripped from the edges of the wagon, between the big spokes of its wheels; the wilted flowers glistened with it. My eyes rose again to the effigy. I wondered, dimly, if it had hurt God to see His son done up like that, or if it was like a parent watching a child be hit with a switch by a schoolmaster, or having a bad tooth pulled – not pleasant but all for the good. And Christ Jesus – did He mind very much sacrificing himself to bloody death, without His father plucking him out of pain?

I shook away the thought. I was just looking for things to think about rather than getting on with doing what I must. Around me, some of the others who'd stopped to look at the great wagon – well-dressed men and city wives in box hoods – began murmuring approval and nodding. Some were already unstringing their purses, either to throw money up onto the wagon or to give it to the grieving woman.

It was growing dark. I detached myself from the crowd, eager to be away from the lamentation. Thames Street ran on ahead, all the way to the Tower. Botolph Lane, however, cut through it, worming its way down to the river and Botolph's Wharf.

Poor Mr Cosyn . . . he had a house near the sign of the Bottle at Botolph's Wharf.

Harry's words had banged around in my head all the way downriver. There'd been no difficulty in getting a wherry – the waters at Richmond had been thick with them. They came, the wherrymen, wherever the king was, like flies to . . . like flies. As soon as King Henry appeared, there would be messages going out to every palace and great house on the river.

Turning right, I began picking my way down Botolph Lane. It was narrower than Thames Street, and the shadows thickened, lurking under every overhanging gallery and roof. The cries of the old woman, mercifully, stilled.

Would I, I wondered, receive a similar response from the servants of the late Cosyn? If so, I'd no idea what I might do. One never knew how deeply servants' loyalties lay, as I knew well enough. Still, I shivered again. It was only April; chilly breezes still prowled, especially in the wake of rain. The ground sloped as it ran towards the river. The central sewer channel ran fast, as though eager to spill its filth into the waiting water. Although I'd alighted on the other side of the bridge, my shoes – foolishly, I'd stormed off from Richmond still in my fair court clothes and livery – were already crusty with muck. Fingers of dirt, brown and grey, danced up my hose. But the badge was visible, and if I turned around the embroidered 'TC' for Thomas Cardinalis was plain enough. That usually encouraged people to rein themselves in. In the palaces, heavy rain washed everything clean; in the city, it churned everything to muck. People always stood a little straighter when a little of the glimmering palace came to town – even scraps of it like me.

I gained the area of the wharf easily enough. The sky above was a moody, heavy grey, like wet wool. It must, I thought, be after five, though the competing bells and the nothing-of-a-sky made it hard to be exact. The thick ribbon of the Thames presented a duller steel. A ship sat out at the wharf – a big thing, a merchant vessel. Without its sails, it presented only a gruesome forest of masts and a spiderweb of rigging, made more sinister still by the bent arms of cranes standing around it. Beyond that, beyond even the river, smudges of smoke rose; Southwark appeared only to be a small cluster of greys and whites, surrounded by the rolling, dull green of the washed-out countryside surrounding it.

The buildings grew more ungainly the closer I came to the throat-stinging stench of the riverbank: windowless warehouses replaced stacked lodgings and narrow, wooden-shuttered houses. The number of people dwindled; merchants were hurrying home, their caps pulled low as though they hadn't realised the rain had stopped. I caught one by the sleeve. After a sour glance, he directed me to the tavern known by the sign of the Bottle. I thanked his back as he hurried up towards Thames Street. Drawing my collar up and pulling my own little crimson cap low, I put the river on my right, swinging left.

Sure enough, on the corner, facing the river, was the tavern. A projecting sign proclaimed it: a tilted bottle had been burned into a thick chunk of cracked and weathered oak and hung out on a pole. Burn marks I assumed to signify droplets fell from the bottle's neck. It was a sign promising plenty, plenty enough to afford spillage.

Light spilled, too, from shutters above, though it was soon assaulted and pushed back by the coming twilight. It was a dull building, its plain wattle-and-daub frontage only made lively by a covered wooden gallery, on which stood a few boisterous drinkers and pissers. Someone in there, I knew – the tapster, most likely, or keeper of the place – would know where the Cosyn house was. Taverns were mines of information.

And you're a miner?

I silenced the nagging voice. Doubt. It came at me in another form.

It's a foolish thing, I own, but I always felt suddenly very conscious of myself when meeting strangers – even when considering meeting them. I found myself imagining the impressions they might form of me.

What is this?

A cardinal's man.

A burnt creature, damaged.

A trickster.

Strange.

Dangerous.

Unclean.

I frowned inwardly, knowing myself an idiot, and looked down at my hand. It looked pale in the darkness. A fair cardinal's man: I'd take that. I drew in my cheeks, affecting a serious air, and clambered up the wooden steps to the gallery, straightening my cap with one hand.

'What have we 'ere?'

I didn't hear it at first; I was scanning the lime-washed wall of the tavern, seeking the door. The question came again, followed by thick chuckling.

'What?' I asked, and then froze.

Here's a breed of creature, I thought, that I'd no reason to love. A group of apprentices – aged about sixteen, by the spotty, oily look of them – were stationed on the gallery. The tallest had spoken. I regretted engaging. I put out my chest a little and let my tumbling steps do the talking, my eyes returning to the door.

''ere, you ain't getting by us, friend,' snapped the prentice.

Shit, and slide in it!

'Let me pass,' I said. My voice came out higher than I'd have wished.

Laughter met it.

''ark at it,' said the leader. ''Ark at the queen come calling!'

'What is 'e, Rob?' asked one of the younger ones.

'A cardinal's man,' I said. 'Get out of my way.'

The lead rascal – Rob – ignored me. But I heard something sharpen in his voice when he spoke. ''Ere, and you're right at that – what is 'e at all?'

Before I could take another step, the little group of ruffians had surrounded me. I counted them – one, two . . . five. Five louts, probably drunken. I was, of course, within earshot of any number of people inside the Bottle. I had only to scream.

But I won't give them the satisfaction.

I raised my chin. 'Get out of it,' I said. 'You lowly . . .' I cast around. 'Knaves.'

A collective hiss ran through them.

'I know what 'e is,' piped one – the youngest, by the look of him, with a mop of straw hair tumbling out from under a flat bonnet. ''E's a dirty great Turk, 'e is.'

My eyes widened. Heat washed up my neck, and with it came an urge to retreat into and under my livery, to hide every inch of me, to run.

These low creatures – to have such power over me!

I spluttered, my tongue working stupidly in a drying mouth.

But I look as white in the gloaming as you do! My hand, see? Don't I? Don't I?

'A fucking Turk!' roared Rob. He had a wooden tankard in one hand. With a snap of his arm, he hurled it at the side of the building. It clattered to the wooden planking. 'Fuck if 'e ain't a Turk! Me old man said they was coming to take up our roads. Slay us in our beds! Fucking Turks!'

Roads?

'I'm not a damned Turk,' I said, conscious of my accent – good London, with a little glister of court. 'I'm an Englishman.' I felt lowly myself, saying such words to such creatures – defending myself to them. A quivering had overtaken me, born of a strange coupling of fear and fury.

I might have saved my breath. The rabble had started prattling amongst themselves. They fell back a little, at least, as though I was diseased, unclean. 'Right, right,' chattered the young one. 'My master says the same – the Turks is coming over our roads – beasts, blackened brutes in wild weeds, 'e said. Like to roast us on spits, 'e said.'

I raised my fist in a nothing gesture – I'd no skill in fighting and certainly not against a team of riffraff-recreants.

Run.

Fight.

Speak.

Shout!

'To hell with you!' I snapped. 'Scum of all scum!'

Still they were chattering: 'creeping up our roads' . . . 'wild Turks' . . . 'beasts' . . . 'dirty, savage brutes, me master said.'

And then it hit me.

The god-damned idiots – the thick-headed, stupid, custard-brained dolts.

Roads?

Rhodes!

For months, all the talk at court had been that the Great Turk and his army were invading – had invaded – somewhere called Rhodes. I'd no idea where that was, but it certainly wasn't London's roads. The news must have trickled down, been mingle-mangled in the empty heads of these louts, who wanted nothing more than to have someone to throw stones at. I could have them taken up for spreading false news, if I wished, could have them whipped from Charing Cross to the pillory at Cheapside – and I'd do it, too, I'd report, I'd lead the constable to them.

Damn them!

'The fuck d'you just call us, Turk?'

I swallowed. I was shaking badly now. Rob had stepped

forward, letting his friends form a mass behind him. 'I called you scum,' I said. 'Because that's what I think of you.'

'You dirty fucking foreign Turkish bastard son-of-a-leper.'

His toes met mine. He was taller than me, but not by much.

Another wave of anger washed over me.

I'll show you a goddamn Turk!

I wanted to fight with him. I'd be pummelled – possibly to death – but I wished to roll about, digging out his eyeballs, tearing flesh from his throat, until we tumbled down the stairs and were drawing blood, letting it wash into the street mud, into the sewer, into the Thames.

We remained, almost nose to nose, both quivering.

Behind him, the catcalls started.

'Do 'im, Rob!'

'Kill 'im!'

'Yeah, cut 'im open to the cods, Rob!'

Rob let his sour breath wash over my face. There was cheese in it, curdled in ale. 'Reckon you should thank me for cutting you up,' he said. 'If'n it was me – if I'd a drop of Turk blood in me – I'd thank whoever cut me open to be rid of it.'

No.

I took a step back. 'I would kill *you*,' I said. 'But I wouldn't stain my livery. You're fitter for the gallows.'

I swear that that might well have been the last thing I ever said. The whole pack of them ranged together again. They were drunk – as drunk as only young men with only a few years of strong drinking to fire and glaze their bellies can really get – and that spelled danger.

It was a blast of light saved me.

It washed over us all, making us blink. Rob put a hand

up to shield his face, making me jump. Noise came on its beams – a rich boom of laughter and chatter and song. Then it dimmed suddenly.

'What's all this, then, eh?' It was a fat man, a dirty apron straining over his gut. His petulant tone shifted. 'What the . . . you little rats!' He was looking down at the bare planking, where Rob's discarded tankard lay. 'Throwing my good – you bring my stuff back and don't be throwing it at my house.' He bent, awkwardly, to retrieve the thing. As he rose, he seemed to sense the atmosphere. His large, jolly face hardened. 'Now, then. Now. What's this – trouble, lads?'

'A rotten Turk crept among us,' squeaked the young prentice. 'Rob was going to kill 'im and save the king the trouble, like.'

'What?' The tavern-keeper squinted, scanning the boys and finally coming to rest on me. Or rather, I should say, my livery. His eyes widened. His mouth began working dumbly. Eventually, he managed, 'You lot, get the hell out of it. Go on, now – I know your masters. You, give me back my cups.' Like children, the prentices who had tankards handed them over, until the big man had three cradled under his arm. 'Go on, now, Robert Barnwell, I know your master. Get on home and we'll hear no more about this . . . get on home, now.'

The prentices, chastised, filed past me, most of them clinging to the low railing by the steps, as if they couldn't get far enough from me. Rob came last. As he passed, he hissed something that might have been 'foreign shit'. Then, showing off – I hoped – he added, more loudly, 'I'll cut Turkey man from cods to chops and see what colour his blood runs. Next time, he's dead.' I half-turned, watching him and his cackling mob disappear on the waterfront.

Off to whichever rat's nest they crawled from.

Turning to my new host, I held up my hand, pale palm outwards. 'I'm not a—'

'A cardinal's man, is it, truly?' Before I could answer, he said, 'Please, please, come – come. I don't usually let such low creatures – I didn't let them in the house, you see – only outside to pass the time. Your master won't find none like that in the house. Come, come.' Bowing, scraping, he folded his way back into the Bottle.

God, I thought – the fellow thought I might've been looking for lodgings for the cardinal himself. Wolsey, I knew, would sooner have had his head shaved with a frame saw than set foot in such a place as a Thameside inn-house – but the innkeeper wouldn't know that.

'Thank you,' was all I said. I followed him.

I blinked again, as my eyes adjusted to the light cast up by dozens of tallow candles, some affixed to the walls in iron brackets, others on tin dishes about the scattered boards. The air was thick with the reek of them, souring further as it took in the sting of ale and the flatness of sawdust. Someone in the crowd was playing a shawm – or using one, at least; its notes were flat. Thick-bearded men were everywhere, most standing but some seated on stools, hunched over boards heaving with either dug-out trenchers or cards and dice. The tavern-keeper was wobbling through them, sharing the odd word over his shoulder with a fellow who was dicing or who had to pull out of his way. I followed in his wake, my head bent. My heart, I realised, had only just begun to slow.

Around me, voices chimed, this time more pleasantly.

'I win! Another game, sirrah!'

'. . . not be had for money!'

'Always the same in this city.'

'. . . will shake hands on it on the morrow, so I hear.'

At the far side of the square-shaped room was a long bar. The tavern-keeper didn't disappear behind it; instead, he set down his tankards. A woman on the other side – she might have been his sister, by the look of her, though more likely was his wife – took them and bent, presumably to dunk them in her hidden barrel of water.

'We've few rooms,' wheezed the big fellow, as I reached him. 'Yet we'll find one for cardinal's men.' I tried to speak, and again he cut me off. 'It's this talk of the meeting – this parliament. You've all these. . .' he gestured, surreptitiously, around the room. 'From the arse-end of nowhere. Men of men, you know.' He lowered his voice and gave me a wink. 'Servants of parliament men.' Joviality returned, and loudness with it. 'But if His Grace's men need rooms, we'll find them. Ay, that we will.'

I shuffled my thoughts, my tongue wetting my lips. 'That's kind of you. Good of you, sir.' He beamed at the title, and I inclined my head an inch. His palms rose and he opened his mouth. It was my turn to cut him off. 'And perhaps His Grace will have need of you. Perhaps. But I've come looking for someone – for someone's house.' I cleared my throat quickly. 'Lancelot Cosyn. Do you know of him?'

'Know of him? A fine scholar, Mr Cosyn, fine man. He—'

'Do you know where. . .'

he lives

'. . . where his house is?'

'Know where his house is? Certainly I know. A fine house, it is.' He gave me a sharp look. His nostrils flared. 'Not dead, is he?'

'What? I . . . Why should you ask that?'

He shrugged, hooking his thumbs behind the flap of his apron. 'Said to the wife, I said – last time he was here – I said, he looks a sick man. Old, you know. Nothing much left in him. You see the old boys on their last legs, in a house like this. You can tell when you'll lose a good customer, when the illness takes them and shakes them and . . . starts to drain 'em. A long one, I mean. Not the sweat, or the like.' He gave himself a shudder. Thankfully, he seemed to have talked himself out of his question.

'I've just been asked to visit his home.' I forced brightness into my voice, feeling none. 'To see him, if he's at home. Could you tell me where the house is, please?'

My host directed me to the place, a stone's throw away, before insisting on giving me a free tankard of small beer – which I took – and giving me a history of the house. It wasn't until I was on my last sip, my upper lip still frothy with it, that he clasped both hands over his stomach and sighed. 'Ay, a fine man, Mr Cosyn. Haven't seen him in a week or so.' Nor will you, I thought. 'That's how come I reckoned. . .' He blessed himself, before suddenly eyeing me sidelong, his brow furrowing. 'Not good friends with your master, though, I thought. . .' The prospect of news, of scandal, animated him. 'What is it – is the old fellow to be arrested?'

'What? No, I. . .'

'Didn't like the look of his friends, I said that to Mildred, I did.'

Friends?

'What is this?' I asked.

'I said to Mildred, I said, I don't like the look of those creatures with Mr Cosyn. Mildred!' The woman, fatigued-looking, rose behind the bar as though by magic. I set my tankard down on it, but she didn't reach for it. Instead, she pouted at her husband. 'Mildred, did I not say I didn't like the look of Mr Cosyn's friends?'

'You did, Will,' she sighed. And then she looked at me and shrugged. 'So he said.'

I shook my head a little, again trying to get my thoughts in order. 'Wait.' I held up a hand. 'Mr Cosyn, you say, drank here?'

'Oh yes,' said my host. 'Often, often. Drank light, Mr Cosyn. Didn't have a brewhouse at home, nor a cook. Just him, day servants, and. . .' he shrugged. 'His woman. A strange thing, if you ask me, but then, a man's business is his own. And mayhap she is just a good, honest servant. A man without a wife needs a woman to tend his house. But, well . . . I don't say anything about that.' He smiled.

Right, I thought. So Cosyn had a woman. That would make my job a little more unpleasant later.

But who were these friends?

I asked him just that.

'Can't say,' he said. 'Don't know them. Didn't know the faces. Commonly he'd come in with a friar – some kind of monk.'

'Of what order?' He gave me a blank look. 'Austin Friars? Crutched? Greyfriars? White?' I could have named a dozen more.

'Black cope, as I recall. Might have been a clerk, of course, or a secretary. Was he here that last night?' he asked himself. 'I can't recall. He's been in often, has Mr Cosyn. But that last night. . .' He jutted his chin towards the left side of the room, where a small door was set. 'Private room. Over there. For business and such. Suppers. Mr Cosyn was in there . . . oh, a few weeks back now, I think. Mildred?'

'A few weeks,' she said, addressing my empty tankard.

'How many men?' I asked.

'Oh, now you're asking, son.' He put one sausage of a finger up to his chin. 'Two. No, more'n two, by my reckoning. Three? Four?'

For Christ's sake!

'Mildred?'

'Oh,' she said. 'Three or four.'

I let my eyes rove the room. Just drinkers, gamblers, men in from outside. The dead man had been a patron and had met with an unknown number of unknown men some time ago.

Helpful.

It really wasn't. Any man was allowed to have friends, and to meet with them too, if he chose to. 'These fellows,' I asked. 'Could you describe them?'

He did. Or he tried. They were old and young, shiftless and well-dressed, and, come to think of it, wasn't it just one man? It was only one man he remembered saying he didn't like the look of. Or possibly two. Or three. Mildred concurred with everything.

I hate people, I thought, wonderingly. I really bloody *hate* people.

'Thank you. You've been very helpful,' I lied. 'I wish to visit his house now. Thank you.'

'Oh, you're off, then, son? Mildred – give the feller something.'

Christ, not a bribe!

But she bent down and reappeared with a little crust of

bread, an end of cheese, and a little slip of dried fish. Her fingers darting expertly, she folded the whole lot into a piece of cloth. I tried to protest, but she only smiled, shaking her head and pushing the package towards me. I felt myself shrink a little in taking it, regretting my hard thoughts towards the couple. 'Let me show you out,' her husband said.

'No, there's no need – you've alr—'

But he was off, waddling through the crowd, cutting through the chatter like a great bowling ball, men falling like pins to let him pass. I followed, sliding the package of food under my doublet, where it left a little bulge. Over his shoulder, this time, he spoke only at me. 'You tell His Grace that my house is his house. Any time, we'll have a room ready. And, you know, tell him that old Cosyn he's a good man, for all he's a fire-mouth. He doesn't mean any harm, I'm sure. And we don't allow him to do any of that preaching in here.'

Preaching?

We were at the door. He pushed it open and made an effort to stand back. Still, I had to bend and squeeze my way past him. 'Dirty night,' he said.

I looked out. Full dark had fallen, shroud-like. A mist of fine rain blew towards us. 'Isn't it.'

'Now if he's from home, don't you let that old dame frighten you. Just between you, me, and the river, she's an odd one.'

The door banged closed before I could ask what he meant. I turned and stared at it for a few seconds. The voices, the song, had been muted. And then I wheeled, looking out again over the gallery's railing. I could just about make out the blackness of the great ship at anchor.

Closer to, I thought I saw another dark shape shift – someone was watching from the riverside. A mariner, perhaps, or some merchant engaged in a late bit of business.

Or the prentices, I thought. Perhaps they didn't go home as they were bid. Perhaps Rob didn't, anyway.

Blackened brutes.

One hand curled into a fist.

Good, I thought. They say you become slower to anger with each passing year – that the blood cools. You don't. You just become less certain about being able to do anything about it. But I would if I had to.

I stepped away from the Bottle, and down from the gallery, keeping my eyes peeled on where I thought I'd seen movement.

Nothing.

Or, at the time, I fooled myself into thinking it nothing.

After a few beats, I scurried off into the night, and into the warren of houses where the Cosyn place – *she's an odd one?* – stood.

7

Some houses look like they were built to collapse. The home of the late Lancelot Cosyn was one of them.

It stood in the corner of a square of buildings thrown up around a plain, featureless yard. I'd entered through an archway facing the river, turning my head every few seconds to see if I'd been imagining Rob the prentice – or anyone – following me. If they were, they were being subtle, and I doubted any of those louts had a subtle bone in them.

But someone else *was subtle.*

I sniffed away the thought, breathing in the rancid air. Then I kneaded one hand with the other. I'd been followed before, and never saw the attacker coming. If I didn't see a pursuer coming when there was one, it stood to reason that if I thought I was being followed, if I feared I was being followed, then I likely wasn't. If I had instincts, I didn't trust them.

Fear conquered, I strode through the yard as if it were my own. That one, I thought, looking into the corner where the tavern-keeper had directed me. A light was burning in an upper window – a single candle. That's where—

'Yip!'

'Jesus!' I cried.

A mangy-looking dog had slunk out of a dark corner –

a little sackcloth of bones. 'Damn it,' I said, half laughing. 'Dog!'

Living at the court, I was used to dogs. Wolsey had tried occasionally to limit their numbers, to allow only ladies' little lap-curs passage – but still every great man brought a dozen, and his attendants gave them the run of every palace. It made you like the stupid things, when, in the city, you knew them to be pests. I bent down, sliding out the cloth parcel of bread, cheese, and fish. 'Here you go, fool,' I said, tipping out the contents as its inky, liquid eyes gleamed.

The dog needed no further invitation. Its snout dipped and it set to, its tail wagging. I touched it behind the ears, but it had lost interest in me. It was hard to tell, but in the gloom its fur appeared the same colour as the back of my hand, the poor little. . .

. . . *mongrel?*

'Who goes there?'

I nearly tumbled forward, crushing the brute.

A high, clear woman's voice had boomed down from above. I regained my balance, one palm sinking into the packed earth. 'Ah?' was all I managed.

'Stop, thief!' she called.

My heart thudded. I scrambled up, clutching at my piece of cloth, trying to wipe my grubby hand and think and speak and stand. 'I'm no thief,' I cried. 'I . . . are you . . . is this the house of Mr Lancelot Cosyn?'

I was up. I looked towards the source of the voice, but it had been everywhere, bouncing off every wall in the enclosed space. The light was more useful. I fixed on it. There, at the upper window, was a blur of white, ghostly. My eyes adjusted, trying to make sense of it.

A woman in white – a nightdress, probably. White cap. White hair.

'It is,' she said. 'Who goes there, at this time?'

My hand clean – more or less – I took off my cap. 'Anthony Blanke. I come from the court of His Grace Cardinal Thomas Wolsey, archbishop of York and primate of England, lord chancellor of England, and—'

'I know who *he* is,' she shouted. 'Cease crying out upon Mr Cosyn's house.'

Me *crying out*?

'Might I speak with you plain, mistress? Might I come in?'

She didn't answer right away. Nor did she leave the window. Instead, there fell a strange, awkward silence. All I could hear was the sound of the dog still lapping and snuffling, and the distant sounds of the retiring city – the odd bell, the odd halloo, the odd grating sound of a cartwheel turning, or a door clipping shut.

Eventually, she relented. 'Wait. If it please you.'

I did. And as I did, I tried to straighten myself. I moved towards what I assumed was the door to Cosyn's lodging. The house itself seemed to have been added to close off the quadrangle, hastily and without care. The ground floor looked steady enough, in keeping with the rest of the buildings. Everything above, however, leant out into the yard drunkenly. If it had been made of anything other than wattle-and-daub – a sickly dark grey now – it would've been top-heavy and fallen over. I felt it leering over me as I stood waiting.

Shuffling sounds came from within, followed by the heavy click of a key turning. The door scraped open.

'Yes?'

I swallowed. The woman was as tall as I was, and well into her sixties, if I was any judge. A fresh tallow candle was clutched at her stomach, throwing light over a lined, austere face. She'd thrown a dark, furred cloak over her shoulders, but a nightcap was still perched on her head, its strings tied under her chin. 'Mistress . . . ?'

'Cotes. Bess Cotes. I am not married.'

I didn't ask, I thought. She had a clipped way of speaking, and London hung heavy on her vowels – decent London. 'Mistress Cotes, then. I wonder if we might—'

'Come. Briefly. It is late. The master is from home.' She turned. Under her cap, long white hair had been braided in a knot and hung down. She jerked upwards, and then again. The house, it seemed, was all on the crooked first floor. The ground floor must have belonged to some other tenant, accessed by some other means.

I stepped after her, drawing the door closed behind me. As I climbed, I felt the weight of the place. The walls on either side were undressed. It was, if possible, chillier within than without. The top of the stairs opened into a broad, rectangular . . . nothing.

My hands clutched at each elbow.

In another house – in a home – the chamber might have been a fair reception room, where servants could serve guests little cakes and spiced ale whilst they waited to be called into some more intimate chamber to meet with the master.

But this is no home.

It was an exercise in negativity. Here were no painted cloths – only lighter patches on otherwise grey walls. No furniture – save one board balanced on a barrel. No items of homeliness, such as chests and coffers. No dishes of food –

only, on the board, a single eating knife and spoon. No stools or chairs, no carpets or rugs, nothing, nothing, nothing.

Did he live like this?

'Well, sirrah?'

Shit.

I slid off my cap again, just for something to do. She had moved to stand by the plain board, and she set down the candle, not taking her eyes from me. 'I have come from His Grace's household at Richmond,' I started. And then I gnawed a little on the inside of my cheek. I'd brought similar bad news to a household once before, and I'd had time to prepare. But I had prepared, on the journey downriver, for a household of servants, not this hard old wench. She seemed to misunderstand my pause.

'I regret we have nothing to offer you,' she said, gesturing around the house. 'We are . . . there is no . . .'

I shook her words away, swallowing. 'You work for Lancelot Cosyn, mistress?' She just stared at me, unblinking. There was something odd in the gaze, something . . . I couldn't say what. I cleared my throat. 'I regret to bring news that Mr Cosyn has died. Has gone to the waiting arms of the Lord.'

Gone to the waiting arms of the Lord?

I blinked, hard. Where had I picked *that* up?

'Dead?' she asked. Her voice, so powerful before, was barely a whisper.

'I regret so, mistress. He departed. . .'

Softly and gently, as rain falleth from the clouds.

'Suddenly,' I said. 'In His Grace's own house.' Harry's words came back. 'The cardinal will see to all matters – the . . . the burial. The return to the parish, and. . .'

She had said nothing, but one hand went to the perfect, polished square of the board and she clutched at its edge. The thing wobbled on its barrel, the fat candle and its flame shifting. I lunged towards it, but she was too fast, righting the makeshift table herself.

The movement had shifted something between us.

She turned her gaze on me, her face waxy in the candlelight. 'How, suddenly?'

'I . . .' hadn't prepared for that question. It wasn't, I'd imagined, for servants to go enquiring what had passed in a cardinal's household. She wasn't the dead fellow's wife. Yet she seemed shrewd. 'I cannot say. He was found dead.'

'His illness?'

'What illness?' I asked. That was the second time I'd heard of Cosyn being sick. 'What illness, Mistress Cotes?'

'Not his illness, then,' she said, more to herself than to me. She stepped back from me, looking at the bare floorboards as though seeking answers to something in them. I could sense her mind turning, working, though not to any purpose I understood. 'He went to your master,' she said, enunciating carefully. 'He went to Wolsey. To remonstrate with him.' She spat the word, before looking up. 'Did the old wether listen?'

The old wether?

This was getting out of hand. Who was she to demand answers of anyone? Cosyn's aged whore? I felt my jaw clench. 'He did not speak with my lord cardinal, mistress. He was . . . dead . . . before he had an audience.'

Emotion had begun to crack through. But I couldn't read it: it was somewhere between sorrow, disappointment, and something like exhaustion. When she spoke, it was the exhaustion that won out, weighting down every syllable. She swayed a little on her feet, staring somewhere above me. 'He went. . .' she said, at length, 'he went to speak the truth. Our men of faith are more affected . . . to worldly achievement than achieving knowledge. He went to list his sins and the deformities of the Church. And now. . .' She focused on me. 'You say he is dead?'

'I . . . he. . .'

'If it was not his illness, I ask you: was he slain?' Her voice was quite calm, as though this were a reasonable question.

'What?' I wasn't angry – I was shocked.

'I ask again, sirrah. Did you and yours mean to silence my good master?'

'No,' I said, stepping towards her, my hands up. She jerked back. Her cloak had come loose on one side, exposing a white-gowned shoulder. My head shook from side to side, my mouth working dumbly. I couldn't lie to her outright.

Could I?

'You see?' she said, with a mirthless smile. 'You deny nothing. My master was murdered. Is it so? Do you confess it?'

I reached out for her, as though I could calm her. 'I confess to nothing. . .'

'Stay back. I will have none of your false words – not in this house. The great wether has willed it, and it is done. My poor master gone to speak and silenced. Ay, silenced. I can perceive how matters run well enough.'

A sly one, I thought. A skip away from wilder accusations.

'You are not his wife,' I said, trying to force authority into my voice. 'Mistress, you have no right to speak . . . like this. Constrain yourself.'

This seem to rile her. She drew herself up, clutching the

collar of her nightgown with a bony fist. 'Me? I have no right? Am I not an Englishwoman? I know the law. I know it well enough.' She began sliding away from me, and again I was stepping after her. Anyone might have thought we were engaged in some elaborate, courtly dance.

The 'Je T'accuse . . .'!

It seemed, I thought wildly, that she was giving a performance fit for a revel.

'All is in hand,' I said, trying to soothe now.

'And a creature is sent to bear the news?' She gave a sharp little croak of laughter. 'A minion? Keep away.' Her back bumped against a wall of the room, and she began sliding along it, making in the direction of the little window embrasure, her hands raised. 'It shall not stand. He has friends, my master. True friends. Educated men. Friars. Friends at court, ay – Sir Thomas – good Sir Thomas More.' Her voice rose, as though she wished people outside, if there were any, to hear. 'We shall all of us see that such a cry is raised as your wicked master cannot shout above it.'

The name stopped me, even as the image of the man came into my head.

'More,' I echoed.

If she heard, she gave no sign of it. 'The rule of law holds in this realm, no matter who wears the feathers of the chancellor. The king should have heard if my master was murdered.' She swallowed. 'Has His Majesty heard?' I said nothing, unable to meet her eye. She raised a finger, pointing at me. 'You.' Bizarrely, a smile spread across her narrow face. She still had good teeth, nearly a full set. 'I heard you. I did – outside. In our yard. You cry out against the Lord. You, minion of the great wether – you take the Lord's name in vain. This is the state of our Mother Church, which my master spoke against often. You, young peacock, are the stuff of it.'

'You can't slander His Grace!' I managed. Strange – I didn't love Wolsey, but the old rogue seemed to bring loyalty to my lips readily enough.

'Oh. I see your eyes begin to open. You master will prove a nine days' wonder. Soon the eyes of the world will open to him. You will be discovered, you and your creatures. Murdering a good man for speaking against the pomp of prelates. Your wicked master will be – will be disgarnished and utterly cast down.' She said this with a show of firmness, which seemed to me more hope than belief.

'I have brought my news,' I snapped, eager to be gone before I cursed more roundly. 'And now, mistress, I will go.'

'Yes, run – go – out into the night.' Her strange calmness seemed to be running thin; her voice began to crack. 'Run back to the devil and you tell him that Lancelot Cosyn will have justice. I have seen it – I have seen the old wether brought low – in chains, ay. Get out. He will bury nothing. He will fall into his own pit. He will not see the top of May hill. All will be discovered, and he will go in chains, tell him, to the devil, his master. And his minions with him.'

Prophecy! I thought. She had taken on the ramblings of a seeress. That was the kind of talk best turned away from – part religious, part curse, part madness: a concoction only far cleverer or far stupider men than me dared drink. I wasted no more words. Instead, I took once last look around the barren room. And then I turned and made for the low lintel that opened onto the stairs.

As I was halfway down, I heard the crying begin and

I paused, unsure whether to go back and try to calm her, to talk her out of whatever she intended – to make a fuss, I guessed.

To hell with her.

I clattered down the last few steps. What could an old woman – a servant – do to make a fuss against Wolsey? If she wrote to these friends of her master. . .

Didn't like the look of his friends!

. . .then the cardinal would buy their silence. Or have the whole affair huddled up – whichever was easiest.

Whatever justice she imagined, I thought, almost laughing as I yanked open the door – a release of the tension, I suppose – would begin and end with me. And it was me she thought part of the murder – the doer of it, probably. That was a lark! An old saying my stepmother still used came back to me and only made my unwanted smile deepen: 'There is too much law in the world and too little justice or judgement.'

I pulled the door to the crooked Cosyn house closed behind me and passed out into the yard, sucking at the evening air. It was wet. I was thirsty. Thirsty and excited and annoyed. It was only then that I realised I was trembling. The old woman's words – her threats and accusations and pert boldness – had set me astir.

But she's old.

And weak.

And a woman.

Not even a married one.

What, really, could she do to harm anyone? To make any ruffle?

Gradually, my heart began to slow. So, I thought, Cosyn was ill, of what I didn't know. He'd decided to make some great argument against Wolsey. Before he could do it, his killer had chosen to silence him. Yet what he had planned to say didn't seem much: a litany of complaints against the cardinal, which Wolsey and Audley had glanced over and consigned to the flames. Cosyn also had friends – Sir Thomas More and, apparently, wandering friars amongst them. I thought it unlikely that whoever he had met in the Bottle was anyone great. Sir Thomas More was easily recognised – certainly by a man as attuned to gossip as the tavern-keeper at the Bottle appeared to be. This friar – if he was a friar, and not a secretary or a clerk or a judge in his black robes – might or might not have been with him, though.

I had a lot of notes, I supposed, though none of them made a tune. Rather, all I could hear was a jarring, discordant racket: the sound of a woman yelling when she should be crying and the wailing sobs of another woman crying for the saviour. I lifted a hand to my brow and was surprised to find it slick, despite the nip in the air.

I passed out, earning not a bark from the dog, but a near-trip as it danced around my feet. 'Sorry, cur,' I said, bending to give its ears a scratch. 'I've nothing else for you.'

Leaving the courtyard, I passed out into Botolph's Wharf, where the wind blew cold and stinging off the river. I would, as I'd decided, lodge at my stepmother's on Shoemaker Row in Aldgate; and I should make it there before there was trouble at the gates.

Home again, home again, market is done.

As I began trundling up Botolph Lane, my eyes on the ground to avoid standing in anything too unpleasant, I froze.

'Yip. Yip-yip-yip.'

I recognised the bark.

Probably the mad old witch locking her door.

I waited for a beat, but my little friend seemed to have fallen silent. I shook my head, and continued onwards, passing the wagon-bound Christ without looking at Him or considering His sacrifice.

8

You'll laugh, or shake your head, but I knew every apothecary east of St Paul's. The memory of the night I'd been attacked in the streets of London still haunted me; nearly a year later, I still twitched and turned in my sleep at the thought of a dark creature emerging ahead of me with a flaming torch. I could recall being cocooned in linens afterwards; I could remember the intense itch and flaking skin, and that there had been pain too powerful to even imagine clearly. And there was the scarring, of course, the result of the burns he'd inflicted.

In the weeks and months following my brush with the flames, I'd trawled every apothecary in the city in search of something that would cause the marks on my neck, chest, and arm to fade.

I'd learnt quickly enough which were trustworthy and which would try and sell you watered-down louse-slime mixed with crushed beetles (which, incidentally, did nothing and stank). I'd even been given a garlic bulb and advised to crush and rub it onto my skin, leaving it there a night and then washing in vinegar. I'd got as far as testing a patch of my arm with the garlic, and even that had made people avoid me for a couple of days. It hadn't worked. Nor had letting a fellow – an expert fellow, so I'd been told – in Bow Lane cut a twig from one of his bushes, shape it into a cross, and bless every patch of scarred skin when the moon was full. By so doing, he said, the flesh would have healed perfectly by the next full moon. But the worst – the most memorable of all – was the poultice I'd purchased made of grease, honey, spiderwebs, ground crabs, and clay. This, supposedly sovereign against open wounds, would – the apothecary promised me – also reduce the appearance of burn marks if slathered on and bound tight with bandages. All it had done was leave imprinted on my mind – and for a full week my body – a stench so foul I could still retch at the throat-tearing pinch of it.

Fraud.

More than ever, I was coming to believe that time, prayer, and turning your mind away from bodily infirmities and blights was the surest remedy against both. In time, in fact, I hoped to have leave and money to go to Bury and pray before the coals that burnt St Laurence. All that really stopped me from doing so was the fear that it might not work, and even that last hope for a remedy would then be lost.

I turned away from the memories – and the fancies – and tried to focus my mind.

Cosyn had been a sick man – of what, I didn't know. It stood to reason then that he'd have been no stranger to an apothecary and the nearest to his house stood on Love Lane, which snaked its way off Thames Street. Its proprietor was a decent enough man, who, as I recalled, had told me straight that scars faded, but never went away fully – they were like bad memories. It hadn't been his fault that it wasn't what I'd wanted to hear.

It was Monday before I thought the shop would be open. Besides, I'd found much ado at my stepmother's house. Once she'd squeezed every detail of Queen Catherine's dress out of me – 'The king,' she said quite openly, 'was a young pup for intruding on her Maundy.' – she'd set me to work. She took in men looking for lodgings, feeding them with her good ale, home-brewed, and she, like the keeper of the Bottle, had found the house in demand for the servants of men flooding London ahead of the parliament.

Two weeks or so, Wolsey had said. There was still time.

One of the benefits of courtly service was that you could lie down and sleep anywhere, whether under the clouds and stars or on a lumpy bed in a hall full of snoring men. Thus, I had no problem sleeping in the little kitchen outhouse in her yard. It had the boon of being always warm from the oven, at any rate.

Another benefit was that the body woke early, in expectation of Mass and work. The sky was thus still pearly as I strode across Fenchurch Street, heading vaguely riverward. Jauntiness livened my step. It came in waves, being away from court – a kind of loosening, of not having to think about the hundred daily things, of the constant listening for the time as it counted towards the cardinal's next movement from room to room. As much as I enjoyed the bustle of court living, sometimes I liked to be well away from it – sometimes. I supposed now and again that if a surgeon cut me open, he'd find my heart double-chambered, black and white, all at odds and divided against itself.

But I didn't wish to think of things being cut open. The day was fresh, just beginning to open itself up.

Nor did it seem to be only my mood that had lifted. Outside St Gabriel Fenchurch, a troop of giggling women were leading young men by ropes, their hands bound before them. They, too, were laughing.

Hock Monday.

It was a game of sorts, which had leached in from the provinces. Women would capture their sweethearts and hold them hostage until they or their families paid the Church for their release. I remembered it from my youth, though no girl had ever sought to capture me. I and some city wives and maids stood back as the girls, their laughter matched by folk out on their overhead galleries, moved on with their captives towards St Gabriel's, where they could call out for the ransom money.

When I'd skipped over the sewer and found the narrow opening of Rodd Lane, I heard them at my back.

'Jack Abell – Jack Garnis – Edward Cheyne – oo'll redeem 'em?'

More laughter, even from the lads.

I went on my way, the world darkening around me. As in most of London, the moment you stepped off a main thoroughfare, the roofs closed over your head, as though giant birds were bent in conversation above you. I let out a sigh of relief when I reached Tower Street, but from there it was only a hop to the right and a hook to the left, past the standing cross of St Andrew Hubbard, before I hit Love Lane.

The buildings on either side of the little passage were fine, with lime-washed fronts. I'd heard – though I couldn't say for certain – that they were used as stews for the better sort: merchants up from Thames Street and, at present, probably parliament-men looking to enjoy the delights of the city without risking returning to their wives and children with poxed, seeping yard-shafts.

A good place for an apothecary.

The shop was small, looking as though it had been crammed in under the red-tile eaves at the butt end of a tenement building. It did, however, boast a pair of shutters cut high in its plaster wall; both, I noted with relief, were open, some fresh flowers hanging out. I took a look up and down the lane. It was quiet enough – just a few servants tossing out soil-pots and what looked like a mariner skidding his way south.

I wasn't afraid of being followed. I'd had no sense of it at all since Thursday. It was rather that one didn't just walk into an apothecary. If you happened to be seen, and if you happened to be known, there was always the danger that talk would get around and folk would avoid you. You might have some infectious disease; you might be starting the sweat; or – grinning wags would say – you might've been spending your time and wages in one of the bawdy houses and paying for it with a French itch.

Without lingering, I stepped into the shadows and pushed open the door.

My breath caught in my throat. Stepping into an apothecary was always a little like stepping into the spicery of a great kitchen. The tang of sage mingled with sweeter, spicier nips. It had always smelt like cleanliness, to me, like good health.

It took a moment for my eyes to adjust. The light falling in from above came grudgingly, as though the morning resented giving any away. And then I saw the fellow – a small man, in his forties – not behind his counter but before it, standing suspended in mid-air.

What . . .?

I realised what he was up to. He had out a rough hunk of

wood, like a large mounting block, and was standing on it to reach up to the raftered ceiling. From there hung his latest prize. No alligator or lizard, such as one usually finds; yes, I recalled – this fellow was proud of his stranger wonders. On my last visit, he'd had a stuffed sea pig up there – the kind of thing the king would have had served at a great feast – brought to something neither quite like life or death.

He twisted his head down to me. 'Good morrow, friend,' he said. I returned the greeting. 'You see? Come – come – look.'

I stepped over the polished floor to find him looking up at the thing, pride on his neat, bearded face. The knobs of his fists were pressing into his sides. Just beside his head, the hunched, rounded thing hung.

'What . . . is it?' Yet even as the question formed, the beast resolved itself. It was a tortoise of some kind – but far larger than any I'd ever heard of. The great domed carapace itself would have covered one of Wolsey's cook's great pies. Something – wire, I supposed – had been put through its body, so that the head emerged and jutted upwards. Its face was ancient and lined; it reminded me for a moment of the odd, ranting old drab, Mistress Cotes, with its shrivelled-looking, currant-like eyes.

'A tortoise,' said the apothecary. Barely swinging at all, the beast glowered over us, as though we were beneath its attention. 'You know old Tonbridge, over by St John the Evangelist?' Another apothecary, I thought; sure enough, I knew him. 'His old moth-eaten alligator still hangs. Skin worn right thin. He'll have nothing like this good old boy. Here, help me down, lad.'

As I gave him my arm and he hopped lightly to the ground,

I recalled his name. 'Master Hughes, you've a fine thing.'

He grinned again. And then the smile faded. 'Ah, young sir. I told you before – my answer won't change to suit the weather.'

I pouted. 'It's not about – that – I've come.'

'Oh.' He brightened and looked again up at his tortoise. 'Ah, well, then it's glad I am to see you. Ay, a fine thing, isn't it?'

I forced a smile into my own voice. 'The greatest I've ever seen. You didn't hunt the poor fellow yourself?'

'Me, sir?' He turned, looking affronted until he saw my own grin. 'Ah, but you jest. No, sir, not me. You wouldn't find such a beast anywhere in this realm, not for the king's money. That,' he jutted a finger in the air, 'is come from far-off lands of plenty and richness. They live to be a thousand, the old brutes. This old fellow would have been a babe in arms before King Arthur was a boy. We might learn much from them. They have nature's special protection.'

I'd been polite enough. Whilst he was still nodding sagely to himself, I said, 'I don't mean to trouble you, Master Hughes. I'm seeking news of a man you might have known. He lived nearby. One Lancelot Cosyn. An old gentle—'

He sucked air in over his teeth. 'Old Cosyn,' he said. His voice became conspiratorial. 'Not dead, is he?'

Oh, for f—

'Yes,' I said flatly. I slid off my cap. 'I'm afraid he is. He lies dead at Richmond. In the cardinal's court. His Grace has commanded I find what killed him.' That, in a sense, was true.

'Oh. Well. I wouldn't. . . You understand, it doesn't do to go discoursing on folks'. . . If word gets around that a man talks loose about a private gentleman's . . .'

'He's dead,' I said. And then, more gently, 'His Grace my lord cardinal is very – he's most eager to be assured of Mr Cosyn's condition.'

Silence fell between us for a few beats. Hughes appeared to be looking inwards rather than at me, his brow creased, like folded linen.

At length, he said, 'Well, it's not infectious, you can assure him. I mean – I'm no physician. No, nor even a man trained in the surgical skills.' I nodded slowly, prompting, as he began to tug at his beard. 'Reckon I can tell His Grace *why* the old one took what he did from me.'

'That would be well thought on, Master Hughes.'

He turned away from me entirely and began pushing the mounting block across the floor. It slid smoothly, as he headed for a corner of the little room. At the same time, he talked. 'Been coming here a long time, Mr Cosyn. Ink. Would come in himself for the best ink, until lately. Didn't make it up himself. Until these past months. Sent his woman in then. Don't know her name.'

'Mistress Cotes,' I said.

'That's it.' The block slid neatly into place under a low shelf. Still, Hughes kept his back to me. He drew himself up and immediately began sorting the items out on display: a motley collection of bleached skulls, most of them with curving, pointed horns, and large jars labelled 'dragone water' and 'treacle agaynst ye swet'. 'Mistress Cotes,' he said. 'Ay. Well, it was the same with his remedies. She came for them. Always paid, never credit.'

'Remedies for what?'

He paused. It seemed he was still wrestling with

whether or not he should release the information. I saw his shoulders slope. 'Pain,' he said. They rose again. 'Always the same – what he found worked. Decoction of willow bark, stewed in wine. Only . . . only the last. . .'

'Yes?'

'Mmph. The last time the woman came to draw his remedies, she asked for more. Much more. More than the usual.' He finally turned. 'Done me out of the last of my Rhenish in the making up of it. I thought . . .' His gaze shifted to the floor. 'Perhaps, you know, when the end comes, the pain is very bad. Even good men wish it dulled as much as can be. I supposed he was meeting his end and wished to go in what comfort he could.'

'He wished his pain dulled,' I echoed.

'So I thought. To prepare his passage to God.'

'Mm.' I bowed my head.

Or to ease his bouncing journey upriver for one last hurrah and harangue.

'And so,' he crossed himself, 'I thought the old man done.'

And right you are!

'Do you know – has Mr Cosyn any friends hereabouts? Men he might meet with at the sign of the Bottle?'

He looked up. 'Friends? No, I . . . He was a good customer. A known man, I'd say. Surely he had friends, but I . . . not known to me. Great men, I imagined. An educated gentleman like him – old.'

'Thank you,' I said. I hadn't held out much hope. 'Tell me, do you know what it is – was – that ailed him?'

'I can't say – I'm no physician. Only what he told me. I suspected . . . from what he said, I suspected some canker in the gut. It cost him much to walk abroad, at times. I've seen such things. They grow, they invade.'

'Can they be cured?'

He bristled. I realised, suddenly, that I was disparaging his profession. 'Not by any means known to me,' he sniffed. He began to move over towards the counter, sliding around behind it at the open end. Putting up a barrier between us, I thought. He'd not give me much more. 'When the things take hold, they can proceed slowly or quickly, by their own will. All that might be done is to . . . perhaps to slow the spread. Most gentlemen accept it. They seek only to dull the pain, as Mr Cosyn was wont.'

I considered this. 'You're telling me that the old fellow was dying a natural death?'

His eyes lit at the words. 'Yes, most natural. Nothing by my hand would have sped it. My remedies only provided . . . a certain relief. From the pain.'

I lifted my chin. 'His Grace will be pleased to hear it,' I said. A lightness came over me. The old man had been dying. His neighbours had known of it. His strange housekeeper – or whatever she was – had known of it.

But had his killer?

Probably not, or they might have saved themselves the trouble of skewering him like a pig. A dying man needed no jabs with a poker to prod him into the grave.

'I will . . . uh . . . make a record of all. To His Grace,' I said, giving another little bow. Hughes had the grace to return it. Idly, he began scraping at something on the scarred counter with a fingernail. I turned to leave.

'I suppose that house of his will go?'

I had my hand up to the door-ring when his voice caught me. 'Mm?'

'His house, down by the wharf. All those fine trappings of his. I was wondering only – what will become of all those fine things?' He glanced up, a little slyness on his face. 'To the cardinal, I suppose?'

My throat dried. 'I can't say.'

I slid back out into Love Lane. Shafts of heatless sunlight fell in between the rooftops, drying patches of muck whilst others remained slick. I stood for a beat in the shadow of the apothecary's roof, my mind turning.

In my mind, I saw that barren chamber. It had, evidently, not always been so undressed. The old fellow must have sold his goods, in anticipation of death. Or something else. . .

Well, where did the money he made from it all go?

The innkeeper's words sounded in my head, in his own boisterous voice.

Private room. Over there. For business and such. Suppers. Mr Cosyn was in there.

His friends, these mysterious folk whom the host of the tavern didn't like the look of – might they have been some fellows with whom he had business dealings? Some fellows to whom he had sold his worldly goods in anticipation of . . . well, whatever he had anticipated?

It worked. It was as good a notion as any other. And it was something to carry back to Wolsey, when I could be satisfied my stepmother didn't need me any more. I'd been too long away from the court – had, in fact, been enjoying a little holiday in the city, away from the dullness of routine and the collective wonder of King Henry creeping to the cross over flower petals and silk carpets. But Wolsey's patience was short, and the purse of monies he'd given me was tending that way too. I might eke out another few days and then it really would be time to return to life in whitewashed brick and glass.

I could refine my new theory before my return.

At least, I thought, as I struck out into the spotty sunlight, the palace appeared – if the city rumourmongers were any use – to have been quiet. All the talk I'd heard had been of the king, the war with France, and the depredations the parliament's outlanders were bringing to the city. I'd be returning to no fresh horrors.

9

Approached from the river, Richmond is a place designed to impress. It has an air of novelty about it. You see the towers and finials of the royal privy lodgings first: a tight, neat square of marble-white rising in stately lines above the treetops. As your wherry beat onwards, your eye drawn by the luminous brickwork, the glare of sun on glass, and the gleam of golden vanes, you see that the building isn't so blocky; the towers at each corner are angular, and along the front – along every side – are further projections, each with their own painted beasts bearing pennants.

'Rich-mond,' cried my wherryman, unnecessarily.

I said nothing, keeping my knees spread on the little bench at the head of the craft.

We weren't the only vessel plying the water. As the privy apartments slid by on our right – close to the riverbank, they loomed – we joined a number of other, mostly larger, craft. I settled in for a wait, as my wherryman drew up his oars. The boats around us were going our way – but I could tell from the look of them that they wouldn't be staying. Ahead, a break in the riverbank was surmounted by an ornamental water-gate, fashioned in Suffolk pink brick but so thickly painted in arms that you could barely see the plain colour. It led to the moat, which curved around the king's orchards, cut between the kitchens and Middle Court on one side and the royal apartments on the other, and made a sweeping return to the Thames. The plain barges behind which we waited were empty transport vessels.

Of course.

I smiled. In truth, part of the reason I'd tarried in London was to avoid this. Cardinal, king, and court would be moving eastward for the parliament. But their actual removal couldn't take place until their city palaces had been properly furnished. Now, with Wolsey still at Richmond, his stuff required removal. Carpets, bedcurtains, tapestries, would all be getting rolled up, packed up, and sent on their way. Candlesticks, copes, and vestments would require several barges. Papers, quills, and lesser seals would all precede him, along with their clerks. Servants would require passage: chamberers, lower domestics, laundrywomen, hound-masters and their boys, hawk-masters and their boys; stablemen; Wolsey even had boys, I knew, whose sole job it was to stuff cloves and perfumed rags into dried, sugared orange husks, and to hang them in discreet places, spending the rest of their time monitoring the chambers to ensure that no foul smell made an attack on their labour.

It was such princely living that made rich men detest my master. It was why poor men – and I'd count myself one of them, more or less – liked him. Commonly, it was said that Cardinal Wolsey wouldn't let a poor man go from his gates with an empty belly, nor masterless. If there was no work for you, he'd have someone find it, however foolish the job might seem to people who either couldn't afford or didn't need stuffed oranges hung from nails.

There was singing ahead of us, as the barge that had beaten our wherry to the gatehouse moved on. Taking up his oars again, my boatman lurched us onwards himself.

'Cease rowing!'

I frowned. 'Hell is it?' grumbled the wherryman. He drew us to a halt in the shadow of the gatehouse.

Between the devil and the deep blue Thames.

And then the crazed woman's rant returned: 'All will be discovered, and he will go in chains, tell him, to the devil, his master. And his minions with him.'

'State your business,' cried a haughty voice. I looked up towards it. On the right side of the gatehouse was a room, set into the lower leg of the arch. There was usually a guard stationed inside – a yeoman, in his white and green. I couldn't, in all the times I'd sailed in and out of Richmond in the cardinal's train, recall ever seeing one of them out of the little chamber. But there he was, on the projecting wooden platform, which hung a few feet over the water.

'I'm His Grace's – I'm Cardinal Wolsey's man,' I called over. I stood, wobbling, drawing a hiss from my wherryman, and then sat back down. 'Cardinal Wolsey,' I said. My voice bounced around weakly, but I fancied he'd seen my livery.

'Oh, and to fetch what *now*, for His *Grace*, precisely?' asked the fellow.

I felt an eyebrow shift.

Cheek!

No guard, no man, ever questioned Wolsey's business. 'To fetch *me* up to His Grace, if it please you,' I said. It came out sharp – but not as sharply as I felt it. 'I'm Anthony Blanke, His Grace's trumpet and a lower groom of his outer chamber. What is all this?'

The guard sniffed, and for a beat he said nothing. Then he gave a gap-toothed grin – a nasty one, I thought, full of malice. '*King's* orders,' he said. 'Stout searches to be made of all suspected persons. Whether coming or going.'

Suspected?

Of what?

'What would you have me do?' I asked. 'Strip down to my shirt and bare my backside for inspection?'

Behind me, the wherryman barked laughter. But the guard frowned suddenly, leering down over our boat. 'I need none of your lip, you . . . *cardinal's* man. The king is my master, and the king will have no suspected or lewd creature pass without check or let.' He went silent again, and I met his glare, matching it. Eventually, he looked away, hissing. Another vessel had drawn up into the mouth of the moat at our backs. Probably there were more to follow. 'By St . . . get you gone then, cardinal's *pup*. But your day's coming, I reckon.'

'What do you—'

But my wherryman jerked, retrieving his sweeps, making the boat bob. He hawked a gob of spittle into the water. It didn't sink at once, but floated there, like an oyster. And then he was propelling us onwards, out of the nothing-place, the gloomy border with its surly gatekeeper, and into the light. As the wherry sank into a sudden wash, that damned old woman's words laughed again in my head.

He will fall into his own pit. He will not see the top of May hill.

And his minions with him.

The moat stretched ahead, a crystal road sparkling merrily. On the right, the trees of the orchard sprang up. Birdsong filled the air – a pleasant, furiously cheerful chirping, carried on the scent of apples and freshly-cut spring grass. There, I knew, baskets were filled, and people gossiped that, from the windows of the privy lodgings which climbed above it, the king liked to watch maidens at work. Less scandalously, and more honestly, folk said that Queen Catherine enjoyed watching the little children servants at labour and would send down comfits from her own table to be distributed amongst them.

At the far edge of the orchard, the moat presented a hard shoulder, twisting to the right. Expertly, my wherryman rocked us around it, and on we went, the kitchen buildings rising on the left. My insides curled at the sight of them. My humiliation, at least, would have been forgotten thanks to whatever was going on.

But what was *going on?*

''Ere'll do, squire?'

'What? Oh. Yes, thank you.'

To my annoyance, he'd drawn up at the landing stage for the kitchens. The sun was high in the sky; and though April was closing the door on the wetness of March, there was still little real warmth. But dinner would be over, I judged, and Wolsey at work. I glanced ahead. The moat continued on, past the Middle Court and under the overhead covered bridge which connected the staterooms there to the privy lodgings. 'Here is fine,' I said, fumbling for my purse. As I paid him the fare, a couple of apron-clad boys clattered down the steps and began emptying pails of rubbish – peelings and the dregs of sauces, by the look of it – into the water.

''Ere,' snapped the wherryman, my coins still in his hand. 'Get out of it, the pair of you. Watch me boat!' They began laughing at him, thumbing their noses.

I took advantage of the altercation to step lightly from the wherry myself, hopping onto the rough stone steps, sliding past the cooks' boys, and darting up into the kitchen compound. Then, still conscious of my idiocy on my last visit, I lowered my head and kept it down; gravel and my own shoes were all I saw until I had gained the Great Court and crossed, amid a sudden explosion of chatter and neighing and barking, to Wolsey's lodgings.

What I noticed first was the silence.

Or, rather, it was more that the cheerful – the usual – conversation out in the sun became a low, hissing whisper as soon as I stood on the threshold. I looked up. Much of the ground floor service quarters were screened, as always, with painted wooden shutters. But from behind them, I could hear the assemblage of lower servants speaking to one another.

I thought of death.

The air in Wolsey's house, even below stairs, had that same, awful, quiet quality you find in a house of mourning. When my father had died, I'd heard it then: neighbours coming in, speaking with my stepmother, speaking to me, and never as they normally would, but always with caps off and voices reduced to something ghostly, as though death had visited their tongues, too. The atmosphere was made ghostlier still by not seeing the speakers, the whisperers. Nor could I even pluck anything clear out of that low, wordless, hiss, punctuated as it was by. . .

Sad silences?

Sobs?

I took off, biting at my lower lip, pounding up the stairs to the first floor. The hall outside the waiting chamber was empty. The door to that room was open, but I could see no one there. Usually, in the afternoons, it would fill with visitors come to petition the cardinal; often they spilled out into the hall and sometimes men lay down and slept, remaining for days, if Wolsey was busy with the king.

The gallery was a little livelier, with lower men clustered about in knots. Others were busily scrubbing down the bare walls. As at Cosyn's house, discoloured gaps had appeared where hangings had once stood. I marched on, twisting my head this way and that. Some gave me looks and then, as quickly, looked away, back to the walls or to their fellows. When I'd reached the far side of the long room, I knocked on the door. It was opened at once by Cavendish the usher.

I fought the urge to ask him what had happened. He was a fair man, but it wasn't my place to question him on anything. Instead, he gave me a nod, a tight smile, and drew open the door, jerking his chin at me to enter. I did, into an unearthly silence.

The outer hall was packed, I noticed at once, but strangely so. If we'd been on a sinking ship, which tumbled all men downwards, it would have been going down by the head; the majority were grouped at the top of the room, near the entrance to Wolsey's private chambers. It was a jumble, gentlemen mingling with middling men, middling men with the lower sort. But none seemed to be talking, not even in whispers. Cavendish seemed to spot this as I did. He tutted to himself before slamming the door behind me and marching towards the assembled men. But, I noticed, he didn't raise his voice, and he made no effort to break them all up and send them to their places.

Left alone, I stood, irresolute, looking around the big, half-empty room. It, too, had been largely stripped, so that it resembled the skeletal ribcage of some great beast. An empty, straw-like smell hung in the air.

I don't like this.

For lack of anything to do, I swallowed, and went off after the usher. As I reached the group, I scanned for faces. The knot was so thick it took me a moment. At length I spotted Mark and croaked his name.

He turned, annoyance plain on his brow, and then softened. But still, he held up a single finger to his lips, before turning sideways and edging his frame out of the crowd. As he approached me, he reached out and gripped my arm by the elbow.

'What's happened?' I whispered. 'Searches outside, and all this. Suspected persons, I . . . What's happened?'

Mark rolled his tongue in his cheek, glancing over his shoulder to the crowd. And then, still clutching my shirted arm, he pulled me away, over to the side of the room, where the crowd was far thinner. My eyes widened in further question. 'Well?'

'It's bad,' he said.

'What's bad?' I shook myself free of him. 'What's happened?'

He bit on his own lip, and then his mouth began to work silently. After a sniff, he whispered – a rare thing for Mark. 'His Grace ain't in favour. King Henry – the king's heard about you know what. They're all sayin' as how the king heard about an . . . what's it – an *unnatural* death. Under his roof. And how as the cardinal tried to cover it up, like. King won't see His Grace. Only writing to him from his rooms over yonder. Notes. They're sayin' as how big Henry's wantin' his own . . . uh . . . *investigation*.' He said the word as though he didn't really know what it would entail. Nor did I.

'I . . .' I looked towards the group of men outside the

door and shivered. No death, at least – that's what I'd been expecting to hear: that there had been some other murder. But the king taking an interest, the king beginning his own investigation – that would let me off the hook, I supposed. Or place me more firmly on it, given I'd been seeking things out thus far. I narrowed my eyes. 'What are they all doing,' I whispered, 'standing like a lot of shaved apes. Listening?'

Mark nodded. 'One of Henry's doctors is in there. Big tall man, thin as a needle. Needle-looking, too. Prickly.'

'Mordaunt?' I asked.

'Ay, I think so at that. Been in there a while. They're shoutin' at each other, the king's physician and the cardinal. Proper set to! You can hear, just about, if ye're close enough.'

Shit.

Before I could speak, another figure emerged from the group.

'Harry,' I cried, stupidly, drawing a dozen angry looks. He held up a hand and came towards us.

'Anthony, my friend,' he said. His voice was as expressionless as his face. 'Mr Audley has been worried.'

Sure he has, I thought.

'About me?'

'About your not coming swiftly back from London,' he hedged. Harry, I noticed, didn't trouble to lower his voice. Nor did the fellows at the door dare to cast him angry or even baleful looks. 'I think His Grace would wish you present.'

'But he's in with—'

'You were engaged in the matter. Mr Audley has been desirous of your presence. As has the cardinal. They hope, I think, that you might give them some proofs of . . . the matter.'

They want me to hand them a murderer, I thought – they want me to present them with a name to restore their credit with the king. And I'd spent day after day in London, helping my stepmother sweep floors and going out to buy her in cheese and eggs to feed her lodgers.

Goddammit.

Before I could protest, Harry turned on his heel and went to the crowd. He didn't raise his voice; he disappeared into the thick of it. I chanced a look at Mark.

Help me!

But it was no good. He only looked stricken and gave me another pat on the arm. He could tell by my face, I supposed, that I had nothing beyond some knowledge of Cosyn's failing health – though I'd worked it up into a fine theory on the journey west. Sadly, that theory would put no one on the gallows.

The lithe little usher, Deacon, strode through the gap Harry had left. He didn't cross to me, but shouted from the edge of the group, 'Anthony Blanke, step forward.'

I felt one last arm-squeeze from Mark, followed by a wave of warmth that brought sweat to my forehead. I stepped towards him. 'Mr Gainsford has announced your return,' he said. 'You will explain your absence to His Grace, my lord cardinal. He will not have disorderly slaves marching about the world.' This he barked out into the room. The words bounced around, climbing to the ceiling. Then he turned. 'Make way!' he shouted. 'Make way, you fellows, and do not crowd His Grace's chambers!'

Reluctantly, the men clustered outside the door began to drift away. Sullen, suspicious, resentful faces glared at me. Others preferred to tilt their heads, still hoping to catch snatches of whatever was being said inside. I passed Harry, who gave me something that might have been a smile. Closest to the door, I saw the tall figure of Lord Hal Percy, and dimly wondered if he'd broken off with Mistress Anne Boleyn. He was leaning against a wall of Wolsey's privy chamber, his ear almost to the plaster, some of the gentlemen who hung about him providing a little phalanx. As I approached, he glanced at me without recognition, before resuming his listening position, a smirk on his face. Sure enough, there were raised voices drifting out from within – I recognised the shriller, broken one as Mordaunt's.

Deacon paused just ahead of me, dwarfed by the door. With his wooden stave, he beat once, twice, three times. And then, with one curious little look at me – *Nervous?* – he pushed it open and stepped inside. Immediately the shouting within ceased. Dimly, I heard Mordaunt hiss something about 'intrusion'.

I stepped into whatever battle was going on, unprepared, wholly, to make any good account of myself.

10

I bowed, making a show of removing my cap. When I looked up, I tried to look at anything but the men in the room. Instead, I glanced at the table, laid out before Wolsey. It was not his usual dining table, covered and lain with plate – that must have gone east – but a small one stacked with dainties: a plate of pink cakes built up in a pyramid, a covered jug.

'Your servant and trumpet, Anthony Blanke, lately of London,' fluttered Deacon. His fluting voice forced me to look up properly. 'Come to speak with your most mighty and puissant Grace.' I sank to one knee.

'Get up,' said Wolsey.

I did, swallowing.

He was seated, as he always was when giving audiences, on the high-backed throne mounted on his dais, dressed today in a rich violet. Harry's master, Secretary Audley, was beside him – and for once the unflappable fellow was red in the face. On my level, in addition to Deacon, stood the crow-like Dr Mordaunt, just shy of the table of confections, entirely in severe black. One bony hand gripped the stem of a goblet. His knuckle was deathly white. Some of the wine within, I noticed, had spilled onto the plain carpet, leaving what looked like dark bloodstains. The goblet still shook, even as the fellow lifted it to his lips and sipped.

'This,' said Wolsey, before giving a discreet cough, 'this is my man. You will remember him.'

'A trumpet,' spat Mordaunt. He looked at me over the rim of his goblet, before setting it down, banging it against the plate of cakes. One of them rolled down the side of the pyramid, off the dish, and came to rest on the linen tablecloth. 'And His Majesty shall hear of that, too, mark you. A – a trumpet engaged in the discovery of a murderer. His Majesty shall see then how little you care to discover evil within your own house.'

Wolsey hunched forward in his seat, saying nothing.

I knew the look.

The old man was furious. Anger, with Wolsey, meant booming and railing, usually over some slight, imagined for effect or otherwise; it was a lion's roar. Fury, however, was something lower, sleeker, like a venomous adder gliding silently.

Mordaunt appeared to sense it too.

The two men glared at one another. Despite his pallor, a sheen of sweat blanketed the doctor's brow. His lank grey hair, hanging in its curtain below his cap, appeared wet with it. Wolsey, too, had high colour in his cheeks, so that I had the impression of having walked in to find two old dogs panting, having just wrestled and bit and clawed at one another.

I held my breath.

I'd seen Wolsey in conference with men before. There was a theatricality to it; they would each say what sounded like prepared lines, giving gestures – smiles, nods, raised hands or covered mouths – when required. This was different. This was disorderly and unexpected; it had sent both men into ill-humour.

'If you accuse our household,' said the cardinal, his voice low, 'then you accuse us. And if you accuse us, Mordaunt, it will go badly for you. We are not without friends. And His Majesty is chiefest amongst them.'

The physician spluttered, moving forward himself. If it hadn't been for the table, I thought he might have launched his bone-bag body directly at Wolsey. As it was, he gripped at the edges, and seemed almost to sway. 'You,' he gasped, 'seek to do a great evil. To make hidden a great evil. The king will not allow it. You might not hide behind His Majesty any longer, my lord.' His voice rose in a sudden blast, making me jump. 'It will not stand! I perceive – I perceive how you have caused to be silenced a good man. For having the will to challenge you! And His Majesty will see the. . .' Still gripping the table, he turned his beaky nose in my direction. His nostrils flared. '. . .the darkness. Ay, the darkness with which you surround yourself.' My mouth dried. I felt the others in the room looking at me and forced my gaze to the carpet. 'It will not stand, I say. His Majesty is the fount of all justice. You, Thomas Wolsey, are a usurper of his sacred powers. He will not allow it. He will have none of it – an overmighty creature putting the law out of all office and making himself a petty king. No. His Majesty will no longer be . . . bewitched . . . by your darkness.'

I looked up again. I couldn't not. The fellow before me had as good as called my master a witch. Wolsey, too, felt the slight. He rose from his throne, brushing off Audley's restraining hand.

'Get out,' he breathed. Then, louder but still not shouting, 'Get out, you foul-tongued piss-prophet. Run you to the king, ay – and he shall blast you for a slanderous heretic. God's death, get you gone from my chamber and my house before I set the dogs to tear you apart. Get out.'

Mordaunt drew himself, shakily, to his full height. With one hand, he drew a wavering sign of the cross in the air over the table. 'I go,' he said. 'And pray God that the world soon enough will see you for what you are.'

Wolsey remained standing, as the physician stalked towards the door. Deacon, I noticed, made no move to open it for him; Mordaunt clutched at the ring himself and pulled, leaving it open as he passed out into the hall. Whip-fast, the cardinal hissed at Deacon, 'Follow him – see where he goes.' The usher did as he was bid, sweeping a bow and muttering effusive promises before closing the door and leaving us.

'Wine,' said Wolsey, collapsing back and sinking into his cushion. Audley stepped down from the dais, moving towards the table. 'Not that piss-water. I won't touch the damned bitch-piss we served that wretch. I wouldn't throw that to the dogs. Have that stupid, doddy-pate lordling Percy bring the finest stuff this time. French. We would . . . we would be reminded what we *are* after that. . .' He hoisted himself up again, as though he couldn't decide what he wanted to do. 'After *that*. Find my chamberlain. Have him have the ushers chase the creatures from my door. Enjoin them to silence, by God. Our council – prepare our great council – a meeting – all must be seen to run smooth. Yes. Smooth. We will not have any man think us pierced by the sharp sword of the king's displeasure – and free to slander and harry us. By God's teeth, we are struck at by all sides. Must we have strong *chains* fitted to our doors to keep such men out?'

Audley, whose hands were still poised over the table,

folded them behind his back and turned, bowing to the dais and backing away. I'd no doubt he could make sense of the stream of orders. He straightened when he was halfway to the door and gave a cough. 'Your trumpet,' he said, looking at me, 'has he discovered anything?'

Why don't you ask me, *you old piss-pot?*

'We will speak with him directly,' snapped Wolsey. He stepped down from his dais and put his big hands to the small of his back, straightening it with a dull crack.

'Yes, sir,' said Audley. With one last, reluctant look at me, he went to the door and, without a sound, opened it and slipped out. It closed again, as silently.

'You have found me the creature who did this deed,' said Wolsey. His voice was flat, but it still carried more hope than conviction.

'I haven't . . . no, Your Grace. But I've found other thing—'

'God's bloody *death*,' he barked. In my mind's eye, I saw the crucified effigy again. The spray of rain which had reached Christ's face had made it look like He was weeping. Wolsey began moving around the room, leopard-like, the violet folds of his robes rippling like sinuous muscle. It was always his way. When custom or circumstance didn't require him to be still – enthroned or at a desk – he seemed unable to keep from moving, like an animal suddenly unloosed from its chains. His arms, especially, were great, swinging adjuncts to his speech, as though his words alone were never enough. One swung up as he rounded the table and pointed at the door. 'What are they saying out there, boy? What are their whispers? I perceive these are whispering times.'

'Uh. . .' I shifted my weight from one foot to the other.

Suddenly, I wished I had my trumpet, that I had anything to hold in front of me. 'I. . .'

'Speak, lad. Tell us the truth – we can bear it.'

'They're saying that you're – that Your Grace is . . . out of favour. With the king's Majesty.'

He paused. And then one hand shot out, a fist punching into the pile of rounded cakes. They flew everywhere; one, I noticed landed on the dais, rolling around the foot of his throne. 'God's bones! To be so slandered!' He seemed unaware of my presence for a beat, drumming his fingers on the table, before making another fist and pounding on it. Those sugary things that had survived the first assault tumbled about the linen, like frightened pink rabbits. 'That creature. That foul-mouthed, slanderous, seditious – that old *slave!*' He closed his mouth, and his eyes, and lifted both hands to his forehead. It still shone under his skullcap.

Alone with the – *old wether?* – cardinal, I thought. A position that any of those men outside would have given their right hands for. And yet, I wished I was somewhere – anywhere – else. This was a Wolsey I hadn't seen; it was, I felt, a Wolsey who wasn't quite sure what to do. And that was a frightening one indeed.

'Anthony,' he said. I looked up to find him staring down at me. Whatever had been going on in his mind appeared to have passed, or he'd mastered it. He seemed to be seeing me for the first time. 'Anthony Blanke. You . . . that – that *physician*. You recall him?'

'I do, Your Grace.'

'Yes. He attended upon the dead man. The dying man, as he was then.' I said nothing. He appeared to be thinking things through as he said them. 'The fellow – he – he came upon us today, of a sudden. He came into these our chambers prepared to cause a ruffle, to stir up some great fight. We have never – never have we seen the like of it. A king's physician speaking with so sharp and slanderous a tongue.' His pacing began again. I was relieved to see that it was statelier, more like his usual carriage. The fingers of his left hand waggled back and forth, as though he were testing invisible waters.

'Mordaunt,' he said. 'Nathaniel Mordaunt. Physician and scholar. Friend to the late Lancelot Cosyn. His fellow in blasphemy. Heresy. Rufflers, both.' He spat the words. 'He has ever been my enemy. And now, you see, he has told the king of what occurred in these lodgings. Ha! Did I not perceive such a man would talk?' He had reached the doorway into the outer chamber, but he only looked at it, before spinning in a circle and striding again into the centre of the room. 'All my enemies will now raise their heads. Ay, and their voices. Thinking . . . thinking that they have won His Majesty's love away from me. Vultures. They think the death of that wretched Cosyn has felled a lion, and now they might fill their bellies. Beasts and brutes. Beasts and brutes.' He shook his head, before turning again, and this time moving towards an arras. His privy rooms hadn't been stripped; the cardinal wouldn't spend a single evening without his comforts. Stopping before the silver- and gold-threaded image – of the triumphant Virtues, each dressed in red-and-gold or blue-and-gold – he lifted a hand and began to trace a finger down a burnished flagpole.

Abruptly, he swung round to me.

'You have been gone a spell. And you have discovered no man's name I might lay before the king as . . . as the very doer of this evil?' I stammered a response. 'A man,' he said over me, as though I hadn't spoken, 'has come into my house and – by crafty and – and cautelous means – has done murder. And you heard that wretched man. Because this slain creature was our enemy, he – and it shall not be him alone – seeks to lay this blood to *my* charge. What say you, Anthony Blanke? What say you to that? What have you discovered in finding the house of the late Cosyn?'

I kept my head up as I launched into recounting my activities, watching first his chest, then his arms, then his back, as he resumed his tour of the privy chamber. I worked backwards, beginning with my visit to the apothecary and the news that Cosyn had been buying up medicines – because he'd been dying.

Wolsey threw his head back and roared laughter, pausing in his tracks. He shook his head. 'By God, the old fool. No – no – his murderer, there's the fool. To kill a dying man.' He laughed again, but without much enthusiasm.

'I thought,' I chanced, 'it might signify. His killer mustn't have known him well. Or he'd have needed no poker. Time would have done the deed.'

Wolsey, who had reached another door – this one I assumed to his office or bedchamber – turned to me. He gave me an appraising look. 'Well said. Yes. Yes.' His brow smoothed. 'I always said, inferior men – I mean no insult – are better fitted to discover such things. But why now? Why at this time?'

I let my expression – blank, I imagined – speak for me.

'You understand a parliament has been called to sit,' he asked. I nodded. 'Yes. Good. Strangers coming to the court and city, men from the north and south and east and west. And then this. It is known we must ask this parliament to vote us money for our just wars against France, and then this.' He seemed to be talking to himself, his words lending clarity to his tumbling thoughts. It was remarkable, as though his mind had been laid open and the workings made visible, like a clock broken up so that the wheels and gears could be seen to lock together and turn. 'Some French agent, perhaps. Seeking to undo and unman us, yes. Yes. Some friend of the French, hoping that we and our parliament fail. A Frenchling would know nothing of old Cosyn's health. No, nor some outland creature from the provinces. And yet they would enterprise at murder if it pleased them.' He became aware of me again, as though I were a fly that had momentarily ceased to buzz. 'Pray forgive me. I think on, and on. You – *go* on. Yes. Other than the apothecary, what?'

'I found also that the old fellow's house had been emptied. He must have sold everything. Possibly to some . . . uh . . . low fellows . . . he met with at the sign of the Bottle.' Before Wolsey could speak I plunged on, eager to share my theory. 'I think, Your Grace – I think that perhaps, it might be that he expected not to return.' Wolsey frowned. 'I mean, sir, that he came to this house expecting – after he'd spoken with you. . .' I swallowed, shifting my gaze to the floor. 'Expecting to be arrested for what he planned to say.'

'And so he would have been. I would arrest yonder physician if the king – if. . .' The words died in mid-air. Wolsey took a deep breath. 'Well. Yes. So it would seem. The fellow took medicine to ease his passage to our house, where he intended to dispute with us. Slanderously dispute. Yes. In . . . preparation . . . he sold his earthly goods, knowing we should put him in ward as a seditious, heretical . . . a damned blaspheming. . .' He crossed himself. 'Well, this gives us the fellow's wanderings. And a window into his wandering mind. Yet,' he added, lifting a finger and rubbing at his temple, kneading some grey strands. 'Yet . . . it tells us nothing of who crept in here and – not knowing of his sickness – wished him dead before he might do aught. If they knew nothing of his . . . condition . . . did they know of his selling his goods? Did they think to kill him for it? There was no money upon him. Where is it?'

You've got me there.

'He lived with a woman,' I said. 'She spoke . . . words of prophecy. Saying you would suffer a great fall.' I cast my mind back. 'That Your Grace . . . uh . . . wouldn't see May hill.' I'd taken that to mean that this month would propel his – his whole household's – downfall before the end of April.

'A woman,' echoed Wolsey. 'By God. A married woman?'

'Unmarried. She was very clear there. One Mistress Cotes.'

Again, he gave that mirthless laugh. 'The foul old sow.' I didn't know if he meant Cotes or Cosyn. 'By God, we might have had him in our courts ecclesiastical for that alone, and thereby silenced him. We had no cause to. . .'

I chewed on my cheek. Wolsey launched himself away from the wall, back into the centre of the room. He went to the table, lifting the jug, sniffing it, and grimacing. 'Where is that blasted fool with my wine?' Tutting, murmuring, he lifted the jug and moved again towards the wall.

A large double window was set in it, just before the doorway into the northern range, where he kept his most private rooms. It would look down, I knew, on the Great

Court. Wolsey regarded it, and with his free hand he nudged the lead, which criss-crossed the coloured diamond panes. 'Open it, lad. Yes. Do.'

I nearly tripped over the carpet in my haste to be useful. Reaching the window, I saw that the glass was imperfect; it warped a little, bending the view outside. At its dead centre, the king's and queen's initials were intertwined. I found the catch and fiddled with it, cursing, all fingers and thumbs. Eventually, it clicked, and I pushed the two sides open and wide, splitting Henry from Catherine. Immediately, the world below and across came into view: the red wash of the wardrobe building, a lake of rippling grey, populated by feathers, the white rounds of caps and coifs, and squat wagons loaded with stuff to be taken east. The voices of dozens of people came in an indistinct murmur. Closer to, somewhere above, some cooing sounded – birds ruffled up by our intrusion.

'Step back, boy,' said Wolsey. And then, out the window, he cried, 'Holla! Garde a l'eau!' With a flick of his wrist, he upturned the jug, sending a column of – *bitch-piss* – wine downwards.

He continued looking out, his head twisting to the right, in the direction of the distant Middle Court and its white walls and towers. 'God damn him,' he breathed. 'God damn him.' I studied his profile. Wolsey had a strong face, the neat, regular handsomeness of youth replaced by something more dignified. I'd heard tales of ancient Rome, and its stream of emperors, their faces stamped on coins. In my imagination, those faces, worn to faintness by countless thumbs but retaining authority, retaining power, were the cardinal's.

And then it shifted.

His lips, a little mottled but still firm, opened. His eyes narrowed.

'What the – by the Mass – what is—'

I heard it before I looked: a change in the chorus of chatter and song that drifted up from the Great Court. It sharpened. Alarm screeched through it.

I stepped closer again, joining Wolsey, looking out, down. The heads were bobbing furiously, some darting forwards, others falling back towards the northern range. I looked right, deeper into the yard.

Wolsey was ahead of me, his mind faster. 'Is that Mordaunt? Is it him?'

I saw what he meant.

People were falling into a circle around a stick figure in black. I craned my neck farther.

Yes, it was Mordaunt.

He was . . . *running in circles?*

His hands were waving upwards, entreating and gesturing, like an unloosed and unmanned puppet.

Over the sound of the watchers, his voice rose in a wild scream, tearing up into the air. And then he fell to his knees. People drew back. Still in that position, one of those twig-like arms lifted and pointed.

At us.

11

'Go, boy,' hissed Wolsey. 'Go – discover what the madman is doing. Now!'

I forgot even to bow. He wouldn't have noticed anyway; he remained at the window, staring down at the spectacle.

I flew across the carpet and, as I reached the door, it fell open, nearly striking me in the face.

You!

Deacon the usher stood there, Cavendish and a couple of other ushers at his back, the chamberlain, and yet more officers lined up behind him. The little usher pushed past me, 'My lord' already framed in the pursing of his lips. I slipped out before the other men could block my passage.

The hall beyond had shifted. Order had been restored. I barrelled past the gentlemen, who were all watching the procession of officers. When I reached the middle of the room, Mark stepped in front of me.

'What's the hurry?' he asked. 'Should we be running?'

To my shame, I nearly pushed him down.

Another scream wafted into the room, this one loud enough not to require open windows. We turned as one to them. Every man in the hall, it seemed, looked eastward. 'Come on,' I said. 'Come!'

Mark needed no more encouragement. Together, we wound our way past thickets of men each moving towards the windows to see what was going on. As we reached the door on the far side, the sounds from outside grew louder – without permission, men were unclasping latches and leaning out.

The long gallery was the same. Everyone was already lining the wall, crowding the windows, pushing and jostling for a place. As we moved, Mark kept up his chatter. 'What is it – the king? Is the king at his tricks again?'

Shut up, shut up!

'I don't kn—'

We'd reached the hall that held the waiting chamber. Coming towards us, his face a mask of dislike, was Hal Percy. I pulled up short, Mark colliding with my back. In the lordling's hands was a fresh silver jug, with a silk handkerchief artfully draped over the top. 'Make way,' he snapped.

Mark and I hopped to either side of the hall, snatching at our caps. We had to stand and wait until he'd gone on into the long gallery; only in that pause did I feel my heart beating and the blood pounding and surging in my ears, in my jaw.

'He's in no hurry,' said Mark, when Percy had disappeared. 'Wonder how long before he's for the chop, if the king's displeas—'

'Come on,' I hissed.

Again, I began moving, almost falling out onto the staircase that led to the ground floor. I took the steps two at a time, my palm whispering over the balustrade. I'd reached the bottom when another cry froze me.

Mark!

I'd barely time to turn when he fell against my legs, sprawling, sending me to the ground with him.

Gasping for breath, the wind knocked out of me, I managed, 'J – Jesus . . . Mark . . . are . . . you hurt?'

We lay a moment on the bare wooden landing, wheezing. I groped around at him, my fingers fastening on his arm. 'Are you hurt?'

Mark took a deep breath. 'Fuck me,' he said. I managed a smile. Not hurt, then. 'Ain't fallen down stairs since I were in skirts. What the . . . what's this? Bloody tripped on this.'

Having gained his knees, he was fumbling around on the floor. He raised his hand. Between thumb and forefinger, he turned a little bottle, no bigger than a thumb itself. 'Here, this is a phial,' he said. 'Like what apothecaries use. Me old mam used to get them. Stuff in them cures the aches she got in her head. From us lot wagging our tongues, she said. Me, I used to have to run 'em back to the 'pothecary, the empties, before he could sue her for keeping 'em.'

I was still on the floor, a little dazed, staring at the thing. 'Phial,' I said. 'That tripped you?'

'Lying there, musta been. Dumped.'

'Can I. . .' I reached out, and Mark passed the thing to me. It was smooth, warm – and empty. I was still holding it when Mark had got to his feet and held out a hand to help me to mine. As I stood, I stowed the thing inside my doublet. The hard little round of it pressed into my chest – if not for my good Holland shirt, it would have touched the scarred skin.

Mordaunt. Still out there.

'Come,' I said.

We resumed our journey, passing through the empty ground floor. No words, no whispers, came from behind the screens. Everyone had gone out to see what was passing in the yard.

And what a crowd had gathered. Dozens, perhaps a hundred, men and women filled the space before us. A strange kind of silent watchfulness had fallen on them, punctuated only by shouted blessings.

'God save us!'

'God save *him*!'

'What is he doing?'

'The sickness!'

'Saints preserve us, it's the sweat! Run!'

'It's the wrath of God!'

'Madness – get back – get back!'

On the fringes of the crowd, I could see nothing. But every now and then, a guttural groan passed over the assembled heads. I exchanged a look with Mark. He wore the same worried, confused expression I imagined I must. 'Come,' I said.

Together, we began carving a path with our elbows, drawing oaths and curses. These I ignored and Mark returned with more colour. As we neared the clearing, the scene resolved itself.

Mordaunt was now on his side. Yeomen of the guard circled him, trying to block him from view. Some were holding back the crowd, but there was little need. Whatever was wrong with the old physician, no one would want to get too close. And something was very wrong. His long legs kicked out under his gown. One side of the black cloth had ridden up, exposing one of them, the hose half-fallen down. An arm, too, jerked convulsively.

But it was his face that drew my eye.

It was white, whiter than fresh snow. Just as white was the foamy spittle around his mouth. Both eyes were bulging, rolling. His whole body jerked, as though a puppet-master had tugged on invisible strings. And then his head snapped back. He vomited again. This time, no foam poured from his mouth, but a stream of redness.

Intermittent screams and cries rose from the crowd. I could feel it begin to melt backwards behind me.

'Sweet Jesus,' said Mark, close to my ear.

A foul smell filled the air, forcing people back still farther. Even the yeomen backed away from Mordaunt, whose cries became the piteous whines of a whipped mongrel. The twitching resumed, and he added to it by trying to roll from side to side.

'Make way,' shouted a voice on the opposite side of the crowd from us. As I looked up to them, I noticed that every window in the wardrobe was open, each filled with staring faces. Over at the staterooms, it was much the same story. 'Clear a path, won't you? Make way.'

The guards, plainly relieved, joined the thinning crowd as a pair of other physicians appeared, in blacks and greys, with the same flapped caps Mordaunt had worn. His own was off, lying dejected on the cobbles. The new fellows leant down, old dogs, both of them, frowning and shaking their heads at one another. One of them – a friend, I assumed – gripped the old man's hand.

'Better priests,' said Mark, 'than physicians. He's had it.'

I said nothing. I couldn't disagree. But my hand wandered up and made the sign of the cross. Others, I could see, were doing likewise.

Though we couldn't hear the learned men's murmured consultation, we didn't need to. Already, from those still standing around, the word 'poison' was being said openly.

Poison.

My hand scrabbled around at my chest. I felt the bump where the little bottle sat. It had fallen on its side. The sign of Bottle, I thought, and almost laughed. To prevent it, I bit my lower lip and looked around at the circle of people still standing close by. Honest, God-fearing folk had run off, to be as far away from potential disease as possible. Others still stood about, their eyes narrow and dancing. Yes, only the spies – *like me* – remained, each watching to give a report of what passed to whomever they served.

Presently, more guards appeared with a board, to carry the stricken man off somewhere. It would be somewhere outside the palace, I thought, some house where he might die well away from the king's Majesty. Everyone knew King Henry took an especial interest in sickness and unnatural death – but from the perspective of rooting it out, so that agents of it might never come near him.

We watched as Mordaunt was lifted, grunting, onto the board. Lengths of rope appeared, and the guards lashed him to it. Suddenly I felt exposed, as though I were standing there naked. The staring eyes from all those windows felt like a weight; they might have seen through my clothes, seen the phial nestled against my chest.

You will be discovered, you and your creatures. Run back to the devil!

The urge to heed Mistress Cotes was strong. I wanted to run, run far, far away, to the edge of the earth where accusations couldn't touch me, and accusing eyes couldn't see me.

But I could see.

In fact, I saw what might have happened, and I didn't like it.

Someone had poured a phial of poison into something Mordaunt would drink.

Mordaunt had drunk Wolsey's rotten wine.

That someone – that shady, faceless someone – had then fled, tossing the phial, not wishing to be found with it, as they escaped the cardinal's lodgings.

And Wolsey – Wolsey – had very definitely decided not to drink the stuff. Had poured it away, in fact, with his own hand.

A numbness fell over me: a cold, weightless, nothingness. *Did he know?*

The dying man certainly thought so. He had pointed up at us, one bony, accusing finger signalling, 'There – I have drunk of that fellow's wine and he has had it poisoned most foully; and I cry out for justice, justice, justice!'

I couldn't believe it. Cardinal Wolsey was many things – he was proud, and in love with luxury, and vain of his station – but he was not a murderer of men. As he'd said, he might have recovered the king's favour and simply had Mordaunt arrested – yes, and Cosyn too – on trumped up charges.

Could *I believe it?*

Was I being used, a weak tool for discovering a murderer because he didn't wish that murderer discovered? Because the creature was, perforce, his own agent – and I was simply to give cloak and colour to his pretence of seeking the truth?

'Well, that was disgusting,' said Mark. His voice carried a little humour, but I looked up and saw him ashen. The guards now had Mordaunt bound to his board. Between four of them, they lifted it easily. Someone had even provided a loose piece of canvas to hold him down. It covered him up to his twisting neck. The crowd parted fully as they bore him away, in the direction of the moat. I suspected a boat would already have been prepared to carry him off, to some grubbier shore. He likely wouldn't last the night, and better his ghost didn't return to Richmond to walk its leads and bother the ladies with rattling chains and cries for justice.

The physicians departed, their dark backs heading in the direction of the staterooms and royal apartments. I could imagine them on their knees before the king, crying that one of His Majesty's own physicians had been poisoned. And I could see Henry, his knuckles whitening on the edges of his throne, as he cried out in horror, his squealing, womanish voice rising to the rafters, his neat bow of a mouth drawing tight.

'Glad it ain't me cleaning that lot,' said Mark. He had the grace to bless himself. Mordaunt had left behind an effluence of blood and foam and shit – all the remnants of a body giving up its insides as it tried to expel the poison. No one seemed to be in a rush to fill the filthy space. The lower servants, I supposed, even the boys would be in hiding, lest it fall to them.

'Anthony!'

I pivoted. My own name had suddenly become an accusation, and I held my hands up to ward it off.

'Harry,' I breathed, relief colouring each syllable.

As I removed my cap, he drew up before us. His face was flushed. He must, I guessed, have been watching the grim interlude from upstairs. 'A terrible business,' he said. His tone was not Harry the friend, but Harry the servant to Master

Secretary Richard Audley. He ignored Mark entirely.

'Does His Grace require me?' I asked, dreading the answer.

'No.' He took a breath, glancing up once at the stateroom buildings before returning his attention to me. 'Mr Audley understands the king is most aggrieved to hear of these unnatural events.'

'No surprises there,' cut in Mark.

'Hm. Yes, quite. His Majesty has commanded Sir Thomas More to discover what all of this dark— this unnaturalness signifies.' Harry's chin rose, and he pointed over towards the northern range bounding the Great Court. 'Cardinal Wolsey wills that you visit Sir Thomas now. His Grace says to be plain and open in your dealings. All falls to his good friend Sir Thomas in the handling of this matter from this moment forward.'

Sir Thomas More.

A fellow who seemed to have been intruding on the business from the start.

Friend to Cosyn. Friend to Mordaunt. Friend to Wolsey. Friend to the king.

Harry's expression changed, shifting easily into the befuddled, gentle one I knew to be my own friend. He frowned, shaking his head a little. The curtness fell away from his voice. 'But . . . you see, after he said to be plain and open, he said, "Do you take my meaning, sir?"'

I closed my eyes for a beat. I understood well enough. 'Yes,' I said.

'Good. Excellent. Poor, poor Dr Mordaunt.' He accepted our bowed heads before turning on his heel and heading back towards Wolsey's lodgings.

I took one last look around the huge courtyard. People had taken, largely, to the corners. Only a few heads still peered down from the windows around and above. The excitement had faded from the air, though traces of the fear lingered.

'Workin' with More?' asked Mark. He gave a low whistle. 'Always heard he's a sharp man. Clever.' He jabbed the side of his head with a finger.

'Working for him, probably,' I said, absently. 'Mark . . . uh . . . the phial. Say nothing, would you? Not even in the cardinal's house. I don't . . . I don't yet know what it means.'

Mark pulled a face. 'Reckon I was born soft? I know how to keep me mouth shut.' He looked over towards the building. 'Only . . . you know what it means, don't you? If it were bad stuff in that phial . . . dropped in our house.'

'I know,' I said.

He gave me a clap on the shoulder, opened his mouth to speak, closed it, and then began moving heavily in the direction Harry had gone.

Breathing shallowly, blood and shit still needling my nostrils, I moved slowly towards the northern range, to bow before the genius of the famed lawyer, scholar and counsellor.

12

Sir Thomas More's chambers were nothing like Wolsey's.
Nor were they like those I'd seen in Cosyn's house – or
what had been left of them. They were, rather, something
in between barrenness and pomp. I was reminded, in fact, of
my stepmother's rooms in Shoemaker Row.

His lodgings in the northern range comprised only a
couple of chambers, one of which sat over the great gatehouse
that led out onto the road. As I'd approached, grooms and
servants had been hurrying in and out. Spies, I supposed –
messengers conveying in the latest news of what had just
occurred.

Waiting in the outer of his rooms, where I'd been told to
tarry by a white-faced servant, I realised that I hadn't quite
digested that news myself.

My heart thudded.

The image of the old physician, curled on his side, on his
back, on the board, bloody, foam-mouthed, eyes bulging – I
was giddy with it all, sick myself. I swayed on my feet.

'Cardinal's man?'

A head had popped out of the inner chamber: the same
servant who'd bid me wait. I tried, and failed, to raise a hand.

Unprepared.

I'd just *come*, I thought, blinking like a bumpkin – just
come on the orders Harry had conveyed. A smarter man

would have kept his counsel, at least long enough to think on what he'd just seen and try to make sense of it. A clever fellow might also have taken the time to prepare his approach and consider how to smooth his path.

'Come, sir,' hissed the servant, nodding his emphasis.

'Yes,' I said. 'Yes.'

The servant drew the door wide, and I stepped in. He moved to go around me and leave, and I dodged in the same direction. We tried again and did the same.

I laughed – a high, hysterical little sound that reminded me of the king. That brought on another wave and I was still grinning like a moon man when the unfortunate fellow managed to skirt past me and close the door.

More's inner chamber stood on the first floor, directly above what I assumed would be the guardhouse of the great gate. It wasn't a large space, but every inch of it seemed filled. A few books were stacked on their sides in open-fronted wooden cabinets, their gilt edging catching the light that fell in through oriel windows. But mostly there were leaves of papers, some stacked, some loose, some tied with string. Several small desks stood around, each of them tenanted with all the stuff of writing: quills, inkpots, pounce pots, more papers. The sharp reek of ink filled my nostrils. My mouth fell open to gasp at the air and I was still fishlike when I spotted that More wasn't alone.

You.

The great man was hunched on a bench in a window casement, looking muffled in his gown, a small book forgotten at his side. His hat was off, his hair still sticking up in the uneven tufts it had left. But in front of him, squatting on a low stool, was Mordaunt's assistant, the ginger-bearded fellow who'd attended on Cosyn's body.

What was his name?

Rowley, Rawley, Rallet.

His face was turned to me in profile. His cheeks were wet.
He let out a sniffle, causing More to lean forward and hand
him a handkerchief.

'What, sir? Oh. Oh, and I thank you.'

The fellow turned away from me.

Rowlet!

It was Rowlet – I'd put money on it.

'Oh, come in, lad,' said More. 'Fear not – we are not at
business.' A slight smile lifted his lips. 'I have long since had
my spring bleeding. Pardon Mr Rowlet's grief.' His attention
returned to his friend. 'We heard this wickedness as the great
noise reached us here.' His voice came in a gentle mumble. I
placed him in his forties. His hair, a rusty brown, was stained
with grey at the temples. An air of scruffiness seemed to
weight him down, as though wearing a fine, thick gown was
an imposition. 'Indeed, we have heard the news.' He looked
up, his brow darkening – more in confusion, I thought,
than anything. 'The cardinal.' It was somewhere between a
statement and a question. 'The cardinal's man,' he affirmed.
'His Grace has despatched you?'

Rowlet gave another deep sniff. Without looking at me,
he said, 'Yonder . . . yonder young imp was present at the
other . . . at the death of poor . . . poor. . .' His voice was
choked off by a fresh wave of tears as his mouth was muffled
by the handkerchief.

Was that accusation?

'Peace, my dear fellow. There is God's work to be done
in the discovery.' More's voice had a lulling quality. It was

like hearing a kindly mother speak. He looked again at me, the briefest feather of a glance, and then used his big hands to haul himself to his feet. He wasn't a tall man but the light from the window cast him in a glow, making him seem larger. He offered a hand to Rowlet. 'Please, my friend. No more tears. I suggest . . . you might return to your chambers. Rest awhile. Have faith. All will be taken in hand.'

Grudgingly, it seemed to me, the assistant took More's hand, gripped it, and rose from the stool. He embraced the scholar, who seemed startled but let him, squeezing his shoulders in return. And then Rowlet whispered something in his ear. Whatever it was, More seemed unsurprised, but he gave a slight nod.

They separated, and Rowlet turned. He took a few steps towards me, stumbling halfway and raising the handkerchief. 'Oh. Oh, my friend, your—'

'Keep it,' said More, shaking his head. A smile twitched on his lips. 'My wife sees my sleeves well stuffed with the things. I might knit together a bedsheet and have more spare.'

'Yes, Sir Thomas.' He folded the handkerchief into a neat little square and clutched it.

Rowlet brushed past me, a sidelong glance narrowing his deep-set eyes. I stood aside. At the same time, the door opened. The servant who'd admitted me leant in, holding up a paper. 'Message from His Majesty, Sir Thomas.' He looked at me and Rowlet doubtfully, before resting his gaze on his master.

'Oh?' said More. 'Another? Take it, Rowlet.'

The assistant did so.

And then he gave a sharp intake of breath. 'Poison, sir. As we thought. A crime unheard of in England. A subtle Italian evil, alien to English hearts. His Majesty says the French might stoop to—'

'Thank you, my friend,' said More. 'My letter, please. And then get you to your rest.' He laid emphasis on the last word. Just a little, but I heard it.

I waited again as Rowlet padded across the room, handed over the letter, remembered to bow, and then backed away. This time the look he gave was undisguised suspicion; his hand, gripping the handkerchief, was trembling white with it. He and the servant retreated, one of them closing the door behind me. More had resumed his place on the bench and was frowning down at the letter, his lips moving silently.

I waited, my eyes on a ratty looking carpet and my cap twisting in my hands.

Eventually, he coughed, drawing my attention.

Sir Thomas More's face was a study in neutrality. And then his head cocked to one side. I might have been a carved heraldic beast: interesting, well painted and gilded, worthy of a look but not particularly unusual in a palace.

'You are kin, I think, to the Moor – John? – the Moor who resided in London.'

My stomach descended an inch. 'My father, if it please you, sir.'

'Mm. I recall him. I never had the honour of meeting with him, I regret. But my work was heavy in the city. A man hears of . . .' He shrugged. The look – curiosity, I think it was – left his face. And then that little smile touched his lips again. 'A fine man, from what I can recall hearing. Gave no trouble to no man.'

'He was that.' I heard the words, as though someone else had spoken them. They tripped out neatly, like pretty maids

– 167 –

out to dance and make a show. I was better at talking about my father – or being talked at about him – than I'd once been. I no longer fluttered and stuttered, trying to drive him out of people's minds, to make them forget him and not see the him in me. 'A fine man.'

A pity I was such a rotten ingrate of a son.

Suddenly a real smile crept across the fellow's face, making him look ten years younger – more, in fact: making him look mischievous. 'Moor. I've been called a Moor myself. Wits – men who think themselves wits – make sport of my name. More, corrupted of Moors. But in the sun I rather turn red than dark. You know the duke of Suffolk?'

The king's great friend, I thought. I knew him to look at. A big, blustering, bearded creature. Women liked him, from what I'd heard. He had the kind of loud, smiling boldness that people – stupid people – mistook for charm. 'Yes,' was all I said. 'A fine man.'

'A man who thinks himself a wit,' said More. His eyes twinkled again. And then he shook his head mildly, the blankness returning. 'The cardinal sent you, Mr . . .?'

'Blanke,' I supplied.

'Yes, yes – I recall now. Blanke. Blanco. White. A groats-worth of wit at work again, I think.' I said nothing. 'The cardinal's man. I see he has engaged you in this business. Mr Rowlet has told me of the other.' His tongue seemed to play around his teeth. 'Death, I think, is an unkindly guest. He presumes much upon an invitation.' His gaze fell to his side, where the book sat. Brushing it with his fingers, he said, 'We were reading, Mr Rowlet and I, of it. He was good enough to fetch me this Italian book from the city. *The Art of War.* Necessary reading ahead of our parliament. We have been disputing it since the cock crowed.'

I thought of the fellow who'd just left.

The fellow who'd been, as I'd been, in residence at Richmond when two murders took place.

I tilted my head towards the door.

'Mr Rowlet was with you, Sir Thomas? All this day?'

More looked up sharply. 'What, lad? Was – he – oh. Oh.' He smiled again, amusement and interest flickering. 'Oh, I see. You've a mind.' He gripped the rough edges of his bench and leant forward. 'Yes, I'm afraid, dear Rowlet has been with me since quite, quite before – before this terrible . . . quite. He is a man much devoted to learning. Of a high, reasonable mind. In fact, he told me that he had failed in the night to dissuade Dr Mordaunt from going with a temerarious tongue to your master.'

Temerarious?

'Yes, sir,' was all I could think of.

I was still unwilling to let the accusatory little assistant off the hook. He might have hired someone to poison his master and made a show of grief to cover the crime.

'And so my lord cardinal has engaged you on the affair. Why?'

I gaped. 'I – well, I – was there. When Mr Cosyn was found.' I let my chest rise. 'I've found such wickedness out before.'

'What?'

Damn it.

In the past, Wolsey had managed to cover up misdeeds.

'Low fellows,' I said, not meeting his grey gaze. 'Brawling and such.'

'I see.'

– 169 –

More seemed to be waiting for something and appeared content to let time spin out until I offered it. 'His Grace has bid me assist you. He understands the king, sir, has asked you to . . . take this matter all in hand.' Nothing. 'And so, I put myself in your service. Until the truth of the matter comes to light.'

'Would that it would,' he said. 'And have you discovered much thus far, young fellow?'

I swallowed, looking at the book beside him. 'No, sir. Only that. . .' I tried to recall Wolsey's words, '. . .some fellow, by crafty and . . . cautelous . . . means has tried to blacken his name. His Grace suspects some Frenchman or agent of the French. Trying to prevent the parliament. To prevent the cardinal – the king, I mean – raising monies for the wars – the just wars – in France.'

More nodded sagely. 'Trust my lord cardinal to distrust the French, when it is in season. And you – your household – has turned up no French agents?'

'No, sir.' It took me a beat to realise he was jesting or coming close to it. His expression didn't change, nor his tone. I gave a short smile. 'No,' I repeated.

'Ah, well, that is a shame. His Majesty should like to know if there are roguish French at work. England would mislike it.' He shuddered deeply into his gown; I was reminded of a cat stretching in the sun. I considered what he'd said. When men spoke of what England liked and misliked, commonly they meant what their town or village or friends did. When the king stated what England would mislike, he meant – *himself* – England.

More went on, regarding the rumpled form of his gown. 'Tell me – do you think there are French spies at work?'

'No, sir.'

'Good. I have some little experience in these wicked matters. Of murder, I mean. From my work in the city. Do you know what I have found?' He paused, for form's sake. 'I have found,' he licked his lips, 'that in matters of murder, the creature is often one of the household.' He gave a sharp look up. 'Or close to it.'

I stiffened, meeting his stare with my own.

'Peace, lad. I say nothing against you.'

Not openly, perhaps.

He went on. 'I hardly think. . . I mean only to ask whether you have uncovered any suspected person in your own house.'

I felt the empty phial press against my chest. I'd almost forgotten it was there.

He can see it.

Surely, he can see it!

'No, sir,' I said. 'I have been away in the city. Discovering the late Mr Cosyn's. . .' I grasped around for the word, '. . .activities.' His slow nod encouraged me on. 'I found that he had sold his household stuff. Met with strangers in a tavern, possibly to . . . uh . . . conduct the business. And then he came to this place, and . . . here, he was. . .'

'Yes, yes. Mr Rowlet has told me. Poor old Cosyn. You know, I imagine, that he was an enemy to your master?' I said nothing. 'He was a man who spoke against my lord cardinal. As was Dr Mordaunt. He set out to do just that today, as Mr Rowlet protests. And both men slain going to or coming from your house.'

'Dr Mordaunt is not yet—'

More lifted the letter still in his hand. 'Poison. A strong

quantity of poison. Confirmed by His Majesty's other physicians. Or it shall be fully, when my friend is. . .' He let the letter fall. '. . .is opened up.' A cough. A wetness of his eyes. 'Administered, likely, in food or drink. A cursed spirit, I think, haunts this house.'

Maybe. But it's taken large possession of a man's frame.

'Yes, sir,' I said.

'Tell me, young man – did my friend take anything in your household?'

'Perhaps some wine.'

He gave me a sharp look, darting it up from under a furrowed brow. He had the flinty face, I thought, more of a grain merchant than a scholar. Perhaps that was a lawyerly face. It softened when it saw me staring back. 'Served by whose hand, do you know?'

I could see Mordaunt, not so long ago, grasping his goblet, spilling it. 'His own,' I said.

'He didn't bring the stuff to your master himself, though, I shouldn't think.' More settled back on his bench, locking his fingers over his stomach. He began rolling his thumbs, one round the other. I was being interrogated, I realised. It was a gentle sort of interrogation, like being mauled by a lapdog, but there were teeth there.

'I shouldn't think so.' The image of Henry Percy replaced Mordaunt. But I knew that he wouldn't have passed the jug over himself. I could trace its path in my mind, from his hand to an usher, from an usher to a cupbearer in the privy chamber. Perhaps Percy had stopped to speak with his friends and minions in the outer chamber. Besides, the page was a nobleman's son. More knew how households worked and who might speak out against whom. I could see that in the deepening wrinkles around his eyes.

'Tell me,' he said, 'are you all well-disposed in His Grace's house? Amongst yourselves. Happy, I mean.'

'Yes, sir.'

He seemed to consider this, his thumbs circling one another more furiously. They stopped. His hands parted. 'Well. Perhaps this whole sad matter is nothing to do with my lord cardinal.' He looked up at me. 'Perhaps dear Dr Mordaunt and old Cosyn . . . had some other enemy. Mr Cosyn was like Mr Rowlet – unmarried – devoted to study, as better men of learning than I am – no suspicion of love-born jealousy or greedy children. The sweat took Dr Mordaunt's wife and both living sons years ago. Poor fellow has been in agonies of mind and body since.'

I shivered. I didn't like to hear that sickness spoken of aloud. It hovered in filthy airs, and I'd a notion it could hear its name spoken and – folk said – took that as an invitation.

More went on. 'We can rule out family troubles and put aside private malice. Perhaps this wicked murderer, whatever moves him, sees the cardinal as a useful. . .' One hand made a vague gesture in the air.

A useful man who might take the blame, I thought. I gave a little shrug.

'Perhaps,' said More again. 'It is possible. Both men – good men – they were . . . loud in their condemnations. Of many things. Such men make enemies.' He gave his own shrug. 'Well. It will come to light.' When he stared at me, his face a mask again, there was dismissal. I stood irresolute. 'I think His Grace has put you under me. And I am already under His Majesty.' His smile reappeared. 'It is nothing difficult, my boy. I have been under-treasurer, under-sheriff . . . altogether more under than over, in my time. More lesser than more.'

I smiled – forced it – at his jest. And then I gave a stiff bow. 'I'm your servant.'

More waved a dismissive hand. 'His Majesty wishes to see me,' he said. 'Though I regret I will be leaving for home on the morrow.'

'You're leaving? . . . Sir?' I gawped.

'Mm. The king's captain of the yeoman can keep this house secure whilst our sovereign lord and lady are in residence. I see no need for an old lawyer and talker like myself to be still away from his family. I see no reason to alter my plans and disappoint my wife, just because of this sad . . . this sad alteration of the world.'

'But . . . to find the – the man who did this. . .'

'I can think,' said More, amusement dancing in his eyes, 'better at home than at court. And I might discover what I can in the city.'

Checking up on my story!

The old lawyer and talker gave a long yawn, stifling it with a hand. When he pulled it away, I saw that his own eyes had dampened. He made no effort to find another of his handkerchiefs. 'You might accompany me,' he said.

'Sir?'

'Pray do. I like my servants to be near me. I think His Grace can spare you. He has.'

I tried to think. I didn't want to go anywhere – I wanted to be here, to be thinking of something, to discover who had poisoned Mordaunt and stabbed Cosyn.

And then, again, I felt the little bump of the phial.

I needed no surgeons to open up the dead man. I had friends enough amongst London's apothecaries to tell me something of the stuff: to sniff at the bottle and perhaps even to tell me who might make up such brews and where; how long the evil liquid took to take hold.

'As you wish, Sir Thomas.'

'Thank you. Be ready at dawn. I should like to be home as early as I might. It serves to be on the river before the great exodus from this house starts.' His tongue flicked over his lips and his eyes fell to the letter, which he'd set down on top of his book. 'We might – on the journey – we might get to know one another a little better.' Looking back at me, he added, 'And perhaps to trust one another. If we are to work together. Good day to you, young Mr Blanke.'

This time my bow was a little looser, a little more natural. I backed towards the door, opening it as he began murmuring to himself. 'Hat, hat, where is my hat?'

'On that cabinet, sir,' I said, spotting the battered-looking thing, half-hidden by books.

'Mm? Oh. Oh. Bless you, young man. And get you gone.'

I darted downstairs, through a crowd of listening servants, and back out into the Great Court. The sky had grown overcast. People were still milling about, still keeping closer to the gatehouse than the far side, where Mordaunt had fallen. I slid sideways through them, jamming my cap back on my head. I wasn't surprised to see that a pair of boys had been found and were applying mops to the cobbles in slow, sullen jerks. I kept well clear, though. Some men were grunting and swearing as they fought to free a wagon, the wheel of which had become jammed between cobblestones. A bucket of fat from the kitchen was already being emptied, its contents applied with slick cloths by a sour-faced lad.

So much activity, I thought. Any man might move

through it all, confident of being unseen. And yet no one could be sure someone didn't happen to be watching from somewhere at any moment.

And where did *he slip, this murderer?*

I moved on, behind the wagon, intent on the idea that had occurred to me.

Rather than entering Wolsey's apartments, I went straight on, through the gateway into the kitchens. The scattered range of buildings rose to greet me, along with a sickly sweetness: the pastry, I assumed, its men at work for early evening banquets.

The cellars.

They stood beyond the pantry, edging the moat. In fact, the low building appeared to have been dug down into the riverbank. I kept my head up as I strode towards it, ignoring the buildings on either side of me.

I'd been laughed at the last time I came sniffing about the kitchens.

No one's laughing now.

It was true. Boys and men alike were keeping to themselves. Some of them had beads in their hands and were casting ominous looks either towards the Great Court – blocked though it was from view – or up into the cloudy sky.

I paused at the door of the lime-washed mound, which looked less like a building and more like an artificial hillock. No, I thought – like a great, scrubbed oven robbed of its surrounding kitchen. The door was open, a shallow flight of stone steps leading down into darkness.

'Good morrow,' I called. My voice disappeared into the gloom, weakening as it went. Only a strong smell called back:

a heavy sweetness, like the lees of a wineskin. I repeated my cry, deepening it.

'What ze bloody – what now?'

I stood back, crossing my hands over my chest, as a face resolved itself, followed by a trim little body clad in white. He had elfin ears – little pointed things that stuck up on either side of his bonnet – and his face registered irritation. 'Are you the yeoman of the cellar?' I asked.

'Do I bloody look like ze yeoman?'

You look like you've been dismissed from an enchanted forest.

'I am his groom. Jean.'

A Frenchman, I thought, from his name and his accent down to his truculence. He appeared to exaggerate the lilt rather than trying to stifle it, as some did.

Some French agent, perhaps. Seeking to undo and unman us, yes. Yes. Some friend of the French. . .

No. Only the stupidest murderer would so advertise his crime by doing it in the course of his duties. It would be like me expecting to get away with murder after leaving a corpse lying in Wolsey's outer chamber, its head broken and my own bloody trumpet lying beside it. I was letting suspicion take the reins, and it was a reckless driver, running over everything in its path. I knew better.

'What is it?' snapped the groom.

I took a breath. 'I'm His *Grace's* man. And now . . . uh . . . for Sir Thomas More.' If the steward's slave was impressed, he didn't show it. 'Has any other come here?'

The little man, who looked to be in his thirties, came no farther than the doorway, as though he were afraid of the light. He leant one arm against it. Insolence, I thought. Or irritation – they wore the same hat. I held my ground and repeated my question.

'These are ze cellars, boy. Men come and go and come, as it pleases their masters' thirst.'

'Who has come?' I asked, drawing only what looked like an annoyed murmur.

To hell with it.

'You're aware a man has been murdered. Possibly poisoned?' I put a hand on my hip. It worked, though; he stood a little straighter, looking over my shoulder, as if he expected a yeoman to come knocking, smashing up the bottles he kept down in the dark. 'Who has come to these cellars?'

The servant's cheek twitched. A scowl contorted his face. 'It's none of mine. I keep ze king's wines secure. If anything was done to any – it's none of mine. Someone took it from here.'

'Who?'

He shrugged. 'Ze northern princeling. Couple of times. Oui. Twice.'

Percy.

'And he said nothing?'

'Mmph. Just barked what he was sent for and took it. No thanks.'

Good.

'And ze other man asking questions,' he said, tilting his head back.

'What? Who?'

The servant was beardless, but he waggled his fingers at his chin. 'Some man. Red beard, like ze king. Come not long back, same as you, demanding to know who'd been here.

Claiming also ze king's great scholar's . . . ah . . . credit and authority.'

Rowlet.

I could hear More's instructions to him.

And then get you to your rest.

So much for trust between me and my new master. He'd set his little friend off on the same trail – investigating Wolsey's household because . . . because. . .

Because I wasn't Sir Thomas More's man under anything other than duress. And he'd use his trusted friends to investigate me as much as anyone else.

I was staring.

Clearing my throat, I squeaked, 'And? Did you tell him other than you told me?'

The little servant shrugged one shoulder. And then a nasty smile passed over his pixie face. 'Oh, yes, young sir. That I did.' His voice had taken on the tones of a stupid child. 'And ze other. I told him about ze other passing through before ze great hue and cry of murder and poison.'

I took a step towards him. 'What? Who else?'

'Passed through ze kitchens, you mean?'

'Yes!'

'Why, your good self, sir. Said I saw you come up from ze river. As I left ze cellars to go for a piss earlier. He asked me which of ze cardinal's men were about this great kitchen, and I told him ze northern page, and ze cardinal's parti-Moor – you – were about.'

I stepped back as quickly, my hand now pressed over my chest and its secret phial.

'Of course, if you'd got to me before he did . . .' He rubbed his fingers together. 'I might have . . . forgotten, you might say, that I'd seen you. But you did not do this. Is that all, sir?' he asked. I heard him chuckle in his throat as he retreated into his lair.

People love a murder. They'll protest to the heavens otherwise but show me a man who doesn't revel in illicit death and I'll show you a liar or a priest.

I could hear that buzzing, excited love in the hum of voices in the cardinal's outer chamber. It was early, before Lauds, the streaks of light in the sky outside barely making a dent in the dimness of the room. News had come in, in the way that it will, from nowhere and everywhere, that Mordaunt had expired in the night. To my annoyance, the official word from Wolsey's privy chamber was that the old man had drunk nothing that the cardinal knew of; wine had been provided; wine had not been drunk. After a cordial conversation, the physician had left in high good spirits. No one – officially – knew anything otherwise, and certainly, the ushers had warned us, any talk of poison would be met with instant dismissal.

I tightened my jerkin, fumbling at the buttons. I'd decided not to wear my livery on the journey back to London. I wasn't going as a cardinal's man, but as a servant of Sir Thomas More – an unwanted servant, but one who knew something of the crimes. Undoubtedly, the scholar knew that I'd be in his service as a spy for Wolsey, though I hadn't seen the cardinal since I'd left his privy chamber the previous day.

'Goddammit,' I hissed, missing a loop.

'When are you off?'

I jumped, but I got the button through. 'Mark,' I breathed. 'Um? Now. As soon as I can.'

'It's a bad business, this,' he said. He kept his voice low. 'Couldn't sleep right. Gonna be in rage all day, I reckon.' He looked over his shoulder. In the half-light, other men were about their rising. A huddle stood around the ewer, towels over their forearms, their nightshirts all loosened, whilst the barber inspected them to see who had need of a shave. I was glad I'd beaten them all to it, and so hadn't had to wash in the hair-choked soup of their leavings. I was gladder still that I'd been able to hide the little phial in my purse, clutching the leather thing in my hand through the night, until it was hot and damp. I'd barely slept myself, frightened of the dreams that might come, managing only what felt like an extended, deadened blink. 'Can't believe someone here would. . .'

I could, and so I said nothing.

A figure detached itself from the crowd and moved towards us. We both stood a little straighter as Harry Gainsford bore down. 'I say,' he said, his face set grimly. 'It is a job silencing all this . . . this damned seditious talk.' Audley, I thought, had given his young acolyte his orders, then. 'It is said His Majesty fears . . .' He looked around before lowering his voice. '. . . poison. Above all other things.'

'Bully boy here,' said Mark, 'will be right glad to be gone.'

'Mm,' said Harry. 'Quite.' He loosened a little, tilting his head down at us. 'I shall be glad myself to be quit of this house. It is become a. . .'

'Charnel house,' I offered.

'Shit-hole?' suggested Mark.

'Cursed place,' said Harry.

'It's not the palace that's done it,' I said, again darting a look up-chamber. 'It's a man.'

'Ay,' Mark said, 'and the whole pack of us'll be going on to York Place. Can't be in any worse case than here, but.'

I pictured the household moving, some on barges and wherries, some on horses and mules. Amongst the great chain of bodies, someone knew something. And I doubted they'd be satisfied with killing a pair of old men. Whatever they sought – to halt the parliament, to embarrass Wolsey, or even to simply silence the cardinal's enemies – they weren't finished yet. The parliament was still to meet; and Wolsey was not only set on burying the whole matter and regaining the king's favour, but he had enemies aplenty if someone had a taste for ridding him of them.

'When I'm gone,' I said, disliking the words – there was a finality about them, 'when I'm away with Sir Thomas . . . keep an eye on Hal Percy, will you?'

'*Lord* Henry,' said Harry, 'is a nobleman's son.' He went no further, as if that should suffice.

Mark was more forthcoming. 'Here, you don't think Percy's something to do with it all?'

'I don't—'

'Have a care,' said Harry. 'It is unmeet to speak loosely of such a fellow.'

'I'll watch him,' said Mark, rolling his eyes. 'I'll do it. I don't mind. I ain't so nice about it. He won't see me watching, neither – he don't even look at me.' He clucked his tongue. 'But he don't have the brains for burying murders, you ask me. He couldn't think up nothing like that.'

Harry's face screwed up, his head shaking. But he didn't disagree.

I couldn't see the stupid, handsome Percy in the crowd farther up the chamber. Probably he was still asleep, buried under blankets inside the privy chamber.

'I'll let you know if I see anything,' said Mark, following my gaze. 'Officers'll be following you to London today. We'll be behind 'em.'

I said nothing for a few seconds, thinking. 'Yes. I – yes, I'd better get on. Dawn, More said.'

'*Sir Thomas* More,' said Harry. 'Quite. Do not keep him waiting. Though I understand he is not a hard man to those in his service.' He drew himself up. 'Well. Mr Audley has asked me to remind you who your true master is. And to be ever cautious in what you say and how you deal.' I tried, and failed, to give him a smile. So Wolsey, I thought, intended no more privy meetings with me – at least not until I might prove myself more effective. I felt, stupidly, a little pinch of dejection. I'd been set to a task, failed, and was now being shunted off to some other man's service. Perhaps something showed on my face; to my surprise, Harry stepped forward and took me in a rough embrace, before retreating a step. 'God go with you, and my love and true heart, my good friend.'

'Uh, yeah,' said Mark, stifling a laugh, by the look of him. 'Bye, then. I'll see yer trumpet comes with us.' He gave me a punch on the arm. 'You ain't getting no lover's heart from me, boy.'

I smiled, more naturally, and stepped away from them.

There was no point in tarrying further. I left the outer chamber and began, I realised with a grimace, to retrace the last steps Mordaunt had taken before his insides revolted. I didn't look at the closed door the waiting chamber; I'd had death enough.

London would be free of creeping murderers.

Londoners were honest enough to stab you in the guts if they wished you dead.

I hoped.

13

The prow of the barge nudged to the left, swinging around, and sending up a cacophony of angry gulls. The river was looking fair and blue in the noon sun. I looked to the right, barely feeling the turn, as one would in a wherry, and saw the light glinting off the roiling waters. Business was afoot. Boats were careering across the water, carrying people to and from Southwark, to and from Dowgate just ahead.

It was a novel thing to be travelling in high style, not as a trumpeter but as a passenger, of sorts. Sir Thomas More was an easy companion – or master. For the majority of the time – long hours – he had dozed on his high bench at the rear, his hat pulled over his brow, whilst royal servants had plied the waters without any of the curses and tiresome banter the London wherrymen traded in. It was the thickening of the air – with voices and stenches – which seemed to animate him. That, I thought, and the sight of the spires and red tiles and slate and thatch had all banished the sleepiness and brought him to talkative life.

In his moments of conversation, he'd talked about some of the murderous sights he'd seen, in his time. He spoke of the king as if Henry was a young friend – as if he was no different to me, despite the ten years and glittering crown he had on me. He spoke of his time on the continent, at Bruges and Paris – not bragging, like a young man, of basse danses, tourdions, and women's hips, but of the storminess of seas and the strangeness of foreign foods.

And he spoke of murder.

'Tell me,' he'd said, as we'd glided towards the bend near Westminster, 'what causes His Grace to engage such a . . . a young man. Like you. In such a matter.' I repeated my lie about having investigated some brawling. My assumption was that it was a test, to see if I held to that nonsense. It seemed to satisfy him. 'Let me tell you of a murder. A prisoner is found in his cell. A great heretic. Hanging by his own girdle. How did he die?'

'Suicide?' The smudges of smoke, the varicoloured bricks of houses and palaces, disappeared. I was intent upon Sir Thomas More.

'His hair is well-combed. His bonnet rests on his head. His countenance at peace with the world. Drops of blood appear to have issued from his nose. How did he die?'

'Sui – self murder?' I didn't know what he expected of me.

More pinched the bridge of his big nose for a beat, before working his jaw silently. 'Mm. His neck is marked. Yet the girdle is weak. Too weak to support him. The stool he might have used to reach the beam lies clean across the room. His coat is found folded under his bed, soaked with blood.'

'You said only drops—'

'My apologies.' His hand waved me to silence. 'I said the clothes he was wearing were merely spotted. His coat was soaked with it.' He'd switched, I noticed, from the present to the past without comment.

I considered this, my head turning over to the rippling dazzle of the water, but my gaze seeing into this sealed chamber.

Sealed?

'Was the chamber locked?'

More smiled. 'From the outside.'

'Then . . . it's plain. He was murdered. Were there marks on the body?'

'None.'

I gnawed a while on my cheek before looking at him. Evenly, I said, 'If the blood came from the nose, he was beaten about the head. Somewhere that you couldn't see – under his hair. Or – or stabbed up through the nostril.' I tilted my head back for a second, then lowered it. I disliked the size and shape of my nose. 'And his murderer put aside the bloody coat. Hanged him by his girdle, and left, locking the door.'

More said nothing for a moment, looking out over the water himself. At length, he said, 'And how do you know this?'

'From what you said, sir. His murderer neglected to put the stool in place, so he didn't hang himself up. He couldn't have put away his bloody coat and then hanged himself anyway, or he'd have more than spots about his clothes. And they locked the door on their way out.'

'Very good,' he said. 'Very thorough. You would make, my lad, a good inquisitor. Or juryman.' He took a deep breath. 'It is a true enough tale. A body was found as I've said.'

'And he was murdered?' I asked, leaning forward on my own bench, lower than his and running along the port side of the barge. 'It was discovered?'

'It was self-murder,' he said flatly. 'The man was a Lollard. A heretic. He killed himself in despair at his wretched state.'

'But – but, sir, you said – the stool, the coat—'

'I said it was a suicide. So said the Church. So said the king.

Self-murder. Those who reported the said . . . things . . . were misled. Or lying, I fancy. To make trouble for the Church. The state. And what the great bodies of the commonwealth say stands as true.' Something hard had crept over the man's features. His grey gaze fixed on me. 'Do you understand?' I gave a nod. 'We might speak a little more of heresies – Lollardy, and the like – in more private state. I might have questions for you.'

I broke his stare, looking down. I wanted nothing less than to discuss heresies.

When More spoke again, his voice had returned to its usual, gentle rumble. 'Enough of that, though. Let us turn to lighter fare for the rest of the journey. A woman who caused her husband to be strangled with a linen scarf and his remains roasted clean away in her oven.' My head jerked up, to find that slight upturn at the side of his mouth. A laughing man, I realised, who made jests without clowning. He proceeded to unfold his tale, which was, mercifully, without taint of talk of heretics.

At Vintry, the Thames met the outflow of the Walbrook, a small river that ran from the city, cutting partly through it, partly under it. It was there that our barge turned northwards, so that we began to stab at the heart of London. We could proceed only fifty yards or so between the red-roofed houses; still, I could see the sloping top of the skinners' Copped Hall – an austere grey slate jabbing at the clear sky.

'It's a fine thing to travel so,' I said, standing, stretching, putting my hands to the small of my back. The flat-bottomed barge had come to a smooth halt amongst some reeds, hard by a shallow flight of stone steps.

'Is it?' asked More, giving no indication that he wished

to move. He gave a wondering look around. 'I suppose it is.' He seemed unimpressed by the smooth wood, the white and green paint. It was a far cry from the king's personal barge, and further still from Wolsey's floating palace, but it was still a luxury. 'We arrive no quicker,' he observed. 'Slower, in fact, than if we'd ridden. But no matter. I regret I am become a public man. The young king likes his public men to be. . .'

'Public?'

More smiled. I had, I thought, won him to my trust on the journey. He thought me young. That was good. 'Well, to home.' He shoved himself off his bench without much grace, moving down the barge and stepping past me. He didn't disembark immediately; he went along each of the boatmen, thanking them for their troubles. When he was beside the stairs, he frowned back at me, past me, squinting. 'Hat!' He began patting down the front of his gown – the same one, I thought, as the day before, and which hadn't seen a wash barrel.

'Sir,' I smiled, tapping the side of my head with a finger.

'Mm?' His big paws reached up and felt about his own head. 'Oh. Oh. So it is. Thank you. Come, now. This way.' He stepped down heavily onto the steps, leaving me to scurry in his wake.

The road above the out-flow of the Walbrook ran north. More looked at it as though seeing it for the first time. And then he set off, moving like a bull, chattering to me over his shoulder. 'This way, lad. Beyond Cousin Lane.' I followed, skirting a pair of gulls fighting over a scrap larger than their beaks, both pairs of wings spread in furious display. Amused, I watched as, as they were busy fighting amongst themselves, a littler blackbird swooped in and carried off the prize.

More's head twisted around, upwards, back to me as he walked. He seemed to look at everything except what was in front of him. His commentary went on. 'You see, over there? The skinners have had the run of the place. You see, across the way? The herber, yonder.' He pointed across from the Copped Hall, to where a stone archway led into the courtyard of a house, the tower and walls of it crenelated. 'Old home of the Nevilles, Warwicks, and Clarences. Living shoulder to shoulder with the innholders, their hall. A noisy manner of living, I think.'

This went on.

Occasionally, a wandering friar or well-hatted man would cry out: 'God give you a good day, Sir Thomas,' drawing a vague salute of the great man's left hand. More than once, I had to beg pardon of some man or woman whom his barrelling gait sent dodging into the gutter. A hospitaller in a black gown, with its stitched white cross, stopped and began a greeting, which More cut short with a clap on the fellow's back. Yet I sensed he was enjoying himself immensely, enjoying showing off the city he didn't seem to think I might know well enough already.

The air grew sourer as we passed the hulk of St John the Baptist ('a freshening needed of its masonry, I think – but they will *resist*') and continued up Walbrook. The houses on either side of the street were fine, large, but somewhat run down. From what I'd heard, they had once been homes for courtiers, before the fashion had begun for riverside manors and palaces. Now they sat about, looking gloomy, dreaming of better days – waiting, probably, for merchants to decide to give them fresh paint and new tiles and a touch of their old glory.

'Empson's house,' announced More, pointing across the sewer channel to a dejected-looking stone building that dwarfed a small inn – Torlington's, I thought it was called. 'A foul creature – a tax collector. Justly executed for his treasonous crimes when the young king came to the throne. Yet the house is fine enough, I think.'

I shuddered.

King Henry had few people executed. I could really remember only the duke of Buckingham, a couple of years before, when I'd been living at my stepmother's house. She'd been full of it, condemning the condemned, as it were, as a fat fool who meant to unseat Queen Catherine (and, I'd pointed out, the king with her). We'd heard the cannon boom out from the Tower to announce it, as though the head being severed was a cause for celebration. Afterwards, it had felt even more like it. Folk round about had got drunk in the taverns, lit bonfires, cheering the king for surviving the treacherous duke's. . . Well, the story varied as to what he'd actually done, from plotting to kill the royal family to raising a rebellion to trying to burn down palaces.

'St Stephen Walbrook,' called More over his shoulder, pointing this time at a grey-stone church, whose tower clawed the sky. 'A fine building, I think. Ancient. In a manner seldom seen in our times.'

'Sir!' I gasped. He'd nearly collided with an apple-wife, whose lipped wooden tray was on strings around her neck. One of the things went rolling onto the street. She began muttering as I picked it up before it could hit the sewer. 'It's dirty,' I said, shaking my head in apology.

'Shut up. Put it back,' she hissed. I did, perching it amongst its fellows on the tray. 'Now bugger off.' She continued on down Walbrook. 'Pippins! Fresh! Fine! Who'll taste me pippins?'

I gawped after her.

'This way!'

Turning, I hurried through the shade of the overhanging galleries, trying to stamp the woman's face on my memory, so that I might never buy anything from her.

More had turned and was heading left, where a street opened up just across and along from the church he'd pointed out. The smell, still strong, deepened further. 'The conduit,' he said, finally slowing as he turned into Bucklersbury Street. 'I would speak to the city authorities about its abuse but . . . I feel I cannot rightly complain about the stink of other men's piss until mine flows out like rosewater.'

I was surprised. The man seemed to have opinions on everything and was not shy about sharing them. He swung left, passing under the gateway of a cheerful-looking place of whitewashed stone, the wooden shutters of which were hung with garlands of primroses and peonies. I followed, nearly colliding with his back. He had paused in the shadow of the gate. A rush of cool, tangy herbs washed over us, as though on its way to do battle with the pissy reek of the street.

'My home, when I am in the city. The Barge. A humble place, not much. Convenient. Rich in memories. An old relic, you might say. But fit for an old cur, I think.'

He moved on, so that I had the impression only of his broad back. As he turned right, the garden beyond spread before me. I smiled. It was hard to believe the place was in London, a step away from gutters and piss and dirty apples sold as fresh. Gravelled pathways crossed neatly between turf seats and small trees. Arbours, their greenery still pale, arched over some of them.

I stood for a beat, drinking deeply of the air, when More's voice boomed out.

'I return, wife. Wife?'

With care, afraid of disturbing the gravel, I set off after him. He turned left, going off into the garden first and passing under an arbour. Against the box hedge that formed an outer wall stood, stacked on top of one another, small wooden cages with barred iron fronts. A rainbow of colours seemed to melt and shift inside some of them. A pair of mean-looking eyes set in a confusion of dark fur gleamed in another, this last issuing its own musk.

'Birds of Spain,' he said. 'And the Africs. I make a study of them.' He bent down and found a small, covered wooden bowl on the gravel before the cages. Lifting the lid, he produced some grains, rose, and passed them through the bars. A wittering trill began. 'Fine creatures,' he said to me without turning. 'Perhaps from the same shores as your forefathers.' I said nothing to this. Softly, he added, 'It must be a fine thing – a great and special thing – to be descended of a people in lands of such wonders and marvels.' He must have sensed my discomfort. He stepped back, wiped his hand on the front of his gown without care, and said, 'A wise friend of mine once said that birds deserve our especial regard, for they have their kindnesses and feuds, as well as we.' He smiled, and then nearly barged into me as he made his way back towards the house. 'Wife!' he cried, more insistently.

The main entrance into the house lay to the right of where we'd entered: a doorway with steps up to it, probably left over from the ancient days when the Walbrook lapped close by and heavy rains encouraged it to invade the streets. It opened as More reached it, a small figure blocking its way.

'Husband,' boomed over his head, though I couldn't tell whether it was seasoned with delight or surprise.

More stopped in his tracks. 'Wife,' he said.

Happily?

Lady More stepped down onto the gravel. She was a stout woman, short, her eyes heavy-lidded and the tip of her nose jutting and thick. A heavy gable hood covered her coif and hair. Yes, I thought – there was pleasure on her face.

She raised out arms to her husband and then, spotting me, let them fall. 'A . . . who . . . a servant?' Her voice was strong, sounding like it came of respectable folk. But I recognised the look on her face. I could read her thoughts.

What on earth have you brought? What is it – a captured slave of Spain? An Italian?

More half-turned. 'A new man. His Grace has him at my . . . service.'

'Old Wols. . .' she began. And then she looked at her husband. He turned to her and I imagined a brief eye conference was happening. She cleared her throat and then stepped around him, coming towards me, her hands on her hips.

'Why, lad, you're all hither-and-thither. Draggle-tailed.' She reached out to my trailing cuff. On instinct, I hopped back, excuses forming.

Mind your business, old woman!

'Leave the boy in peace, madam,' said More. 'You may kiss me.'

Lady More tutted. 'Husband, this new man is as bad as you. A good match, ay, all at sixes and sevens.' She shook her head, looking at my upturned collar and then down at her own dress: a sombre bodice holding her in, grey gown and white kirtle. And then More took her around the waist, smiling, no shame.

'You'd have me nothing otherwise than I am, I think,' he said.

'Oh, for shame, sir. Off, off!' But she let him embrace her and turned, kissing both of his cheeks and then his lips.

They love each other, this pair, I thought. A lucky thing, for married people. I tried to imagine the king doing something similar with Queen Catherine and couldn't. I'd only seen them in public places, of course, but they sat apart, like statues, carved things. Imagining anything else seemed obscene, almost blasphemous, like imagining saints naked.

Finally, Lady More broke free of her husband's embrace, but she kept hold of his hands. 'How does the king?'

'Well. I have matters to discuss with my new charge.'

Charge?

'You'll be wanting to see the children?'

'Very much. Very much. But a little later.' He looked up at the sky. 'After their learning. They're at their learning?'

'Of course. I'll – the servants – I'll have them bring you in something. You're hungry? Ah, but you're dusty. . .' She continued making comments on his dress, on his state, on the muck he was tracking in from the road. And he let her, taking the gentle scolding as though it was something familiar, even welcome. At length, the two passed into the house. I stood for a beat, unsure.

'Well, come, lad, if you're coming. You're welcome to our home.' Lady More's voice would brook no opposition, and I followed.

Inside was a fair reception hall, with painted cloths depicting scenes from saints' lives. One I recognised, because my mother had something similar: a large wheel in the foreground, and behind it, in it, St Catherine, in profile, her hands clasped before her, turned up in prayer. 'CATERINA' was painted in mock-gold, just above those unnatural-looking hands. Along either side of the room, cabinets were covered in bowls of flowers similar to those hanging outside the shutters. They filled the air with their scent – faintly sweet, faintly damp, with good sprigs of rosemary, to sharpen the memory, threaded amongst them. Doors led off either side of the hall, and a staircase at the back led up; to its side, carved screens hid what I assumed to be the servants' areas. Lady More marched towards these, already shouting, 'The master is home. Be up and about, lads – the master is home.'

More stood still, watching her disappear behind the screen, before dragging himself towards the stairs. 'This way,' he said. 'I apologise if my private chambers are something . . . less. Fit enough for a poor old scholar, though, I think. Not, perhaps, what a cardinal's man is accustomed to.'

Nothing coloured his comment. Yet I could detect criticism, like a faint, sour smell.

He led me up and along a small upper gallery, passing those open shutters that looked down on the street below. Faint sounds rose up – shouts and cries from Bucklersbury: the dim sounds of life and laughter. From somewhere in the house came another sound – a strange sound.

Latin?

I didn't speak the language, but I could recognise it well enough. What was strange was the melody of it, the quality. It was, I realised with a start, a woman's voice, a young woman, singing the language from some other chamber with more grace than even Wolsey spoke it.

Odd.

Pretty.

More had moved on, leaving me caught between the guttural barks of the street and the strange music. Pushing open a door at the far end, he jerked his head and put his hands up, already removing his hat.

The chamber was large – but, in its dress, it was much like the little room he'd kept at Richmond. Papers more than books dominated. Those tomes that were present appeared a little well-used. Typically, I knew, books were items for display, sometimes with jewelled covers to proclaim their worth, laid out on their sides in cabinets or on tables to show off the gilt edging. Here, they were useful things, selected, apparently, for that reason alone. The air of the room carried the same vinegary sting of ink as his Richmond chamber, though it mingled with the scent of more bowls of flowers, which I assumed Lady More had put there in in his absence. A desk dominated, but every inch of it was covered in the stuff of writing.

When I was inside, More closed the door with a gentle thud. He ran a hand through his hair, further messing it, and screwed his mouth up on one side. 'Flowers,' he said, squinting and finding a bowl on a sideboard. 'They die as soon as they're plucked up.'

I said nothing as he moved over to his desk. He picked up some papers absently, looking at them, replacing them, and then moved to the side of the room where a cushioned bench sat. Heavily, he slumped onto it. 'Sit, will you?'

'But I—'

He tutted, thudding one paw on the cushion beside him. 'You would have an old fellow break his neck looking up at you? Sit, will you. . .'

I did, gingerly, removing my own cap first. I perched there whilst he sank deep into the cushions, tilting his head back to look up at the dull blacks, whites, and yellows of the painted ceiling. His hat dropped to the floor and he booted it away in annoyance.

'Now,' he said, folding his hands over his stomach. He inhaled deeply. 'I enjoined you to honesty. That we might be both of us perfect friends and true.' I bowed my head. 'Have you had any thoughts on the terrible . . . these murders? Since we spoke yesterday?'

I swallowed. I had, of sorts. 'Sir, it's . . . since yesterday, it's occurred to me. . .' He made a little sound in his throat. 'Cosyn,' I said, grasping at the name. 'Mr Cosyn, murdered first. It's occurred to me that, uh, perhaps he sold his goods to some low, scheming creature. That creature then killed him to retrieve the money.' Even as I said it, I thought it unlikely. The next murder, of Mordaunt, who as far as I knew had sold nothing, spoke against it. Nor could I truly see some hard London rogue passing in and out of Richmond unseen – especially not twice.

More grunted. I could hear the demurral in it. And then he swivelled, so that he was facing me. I straightened my back. 'Tell me,' he said, 'more of this meeting the late Mr Cosyn had.'

I repeated all I knew, what little I'd learnt of the innkeeper. He nodded as I spoke, slowly, to himself.

'I shall come to the point,' he said. 'Mr Cosyn and Dr Mordaunt were friends. Oh, a circle of us. All friends. All champions of good Greek learning. Myself. Mm. And Mr Rowlet. Others, too – friars, divines – a fair bunch.' He paused. 'Once, your master my lord cardinal we counted a friend.' I stared over towards the desk, tracing its edges, the curve of quills, the straight lines of papers. 'Lately – in these times, His Grace was . . . less favoured. Mr Cosyn, in particular . . . he has long been a critic of the cardinal. Of his Grace's . . . manner of living.'

I turned to More. 'I know that, sir.'

It doesn't mean Wolsey had him killed!

Does it?

'Mm. Dr Mordaunt too. He advanced in these past months . . . from arguing for better learning amongst priests and students, to . . . larger . . . more advanced disputations against the state of the Church. And its princes. And so they thought that your master – both thought your master a very Ahitophel. More – rather an immovable Niobe in his vainglory; their words, I assure you. Do you take my meaning?'

'Yes,' I said – and it was only partly a lie.

So they both hated Wolsey; so they both died in his house; so what?

'And you tell me,' More went on, his voice turning gentler, like soft butter, 'that Mr Cosyn met a man or men.' The hairs on my unburnt arm began to tingle under my shirt. 'And so I wonder. . .' The rest of his sentence died softly. He scratched at an ear. 'Tell me, have you heard of Lollardy, young man?'

I felt my stomach drop.

I had.

The Lollards were men who went crazed with false

religion, who denied the Pope and I didn't know what else. 'Yes,' I whispered.

'Good. It gives me no pleasure to speak of them. Yet . . . in these times – the times grow wicked, I think – in these times, such men as the Lollards are overgrown in boldness. They pick up heresies from abroad, from crazed creatures like the monk Luther. And they would infect our realm.' Something in More's voice changed. A hardness came into. I'd heard it before, when he'd spoken on the barge of the suicide-that-wasn't-a-suicide-but-was. 'They would pluck down not just your master but the Church, the whole Church, and with it the law, and the commonwealth. All are too much connected for it to be otherwise. An evil – a mad, canting sort of evil we cannot perceive without drinking of madness ourselves.'

I didn't want to. 'Like Cosyn? You think . . . was Mr Cosyn . . . Dr Mordaunt – were they Lollards?'

More hunched forward, putting his elbows on his knees and his head in his hands. 'No.' Then more firmly, 'No.'

Oh.

Then what?

He supplied the answer, croaking into the sweet and sharp air before him. 'Yet I give you this possibility. Mr Cosyn – and, I think, Dr Mordaunt – have – *had* – grown stronger recently. In their disputations, as I said. More violent, I should say.' I recalled seeing More with the physician at Richmond, on the day of the Maundy. 'They tried to draw me in. I spoke with the doctor. He protested he was no evangelical – no wicked heretic, not . . . not infected. Mr Rowlet and I both grew. . .' He made a swallowing sound. 'Troubled. In our minds. At his more turbulent courses. Yet he said – he protested, as I said, that he meant only to correct our Church, not to strike at its foundations.'

I followed – or thought I did. But arguments for or against the Church were nothing to me. I wished things to continue as they were. My father had always warned me – had warned me when I went into service the first time – to meddle with nothing, to say nothing, to think nothing that tended towards criticism of anything.

Let da learned divines do their talk, and you smile and work and serve your master and no more.

Good advice.

'This talk frightens you,' said More, twisting his head, still resting it on his chin.

You're goddamned right it does.

'No, sir.'

He gave a little snort of laughter. 'I mean no harm in it. No. What I tend to is this. It might be that Mr Cosyn, in his extremity, met with someone who was likewise . . . ah . . . a speaker-out against my lord cardinal. This fellow, perhaps, was no simple Greek or gentle reformer, like dear old Cosyn, or Mordaunt, or, God-help-me, my own self. No, this man tried to . . . persuade . . . the old man into wickeder courses. Into this new form of Lollardy the demon Luther has devised. And then, finding Cosyn to be only a gentler person – moderate in his desires – he killed him. Perhaps this fellow did the same to Mordaunt. Tried and failed to make a true heretic of him, and so killed him in his fury. These . . . these *Lutherans* . . . it would be in keeping. Think they are the first men ever to read the Scriptures. They are the deepest depth of filth. They breed in the sewers. They feed on the spew and poison of the foulest gutters and spit it back into the world. They—' Spittle had flown from his own mouth, landing in droplets on the rush-strewn floor. 'Forgive me.' He gave himself a little shake. 'But this is possible, I think. Our Lutheran scum might thus achieve much. He might strike at the cardinal and kill two fellows he had failed to seduce with his lies into his devilry. His heresies and devilry. Such low creatures would delight in enterprising at murder.'

Jesus.

I drew my knees together.

So that was More's deduction. Cosyn and Mordaunt, enemies of Wolsey, had attracted some more extreme enemy of the whole Church. The old fellows had disappointed him, and they'd been slain for it.

I nearly laughed.

For Wolsey, the murderer was some French agent, out to make a ruffle in English policy, to cause trouble and ruin the king's and his own plans for raising money from the parliament.

For More, the murderer was some heretical Church-hater, out to kill – *slightly less heretical?* – cardinal-haters, whom he'd failed to draw into his own extremity.

And me? I still suspected everyone for every reason and would until someone and something showed themselves plain.

I was saved from offering anything by the door opening. Lady More herself entered, carrying a wooden tray of sliced bread, cheese, and what looked like broken pork, the cold, greenish sauce already congealing on it. A pair of cups, already filled, sat alongside it all. I sprang up, my hand out, to help her.

'Peace, lad. I made it this far.'

I stood back, a little awkwardly, as she set the tray down on a sideboard. The light spilling in from a high, open shutter had dimmed. It was growing late. The days were still short.

'That was well done of you, wife,' More said.

Lady More gave a little bobbing curtsey, sarcastic-looking, I thought. 'You've not tasted it yet,' she said.

More, who had stood too, smiled. 'This is true.'

She left us again. I watched her depart with dismay. She was welcome – anyone was welcome. I didn't wish to be alone, discussing heretics. I would almost prefer the murderer to be some ruffian in my own household, acting on Wolsey's orders or otherwise in shutting up the damned dangerous old men. Even my milksop idea of some rogue killing for money had the benefit of not involving yet more dangerous courses.

'Eat,' said More. 'You're young yet, and thin. Eat.'

I did, without much enthusiasm. More joined me, and we chewed and swallowed in silence. The food was rich. My stomach welcomed it, even if my tastebuds shrank from the slippery, greasy taste. The wine was better – strong hippocras, so sweet it curled my tongue.

'I have taken you,' said More, at length, 'into my confidence because my lord cardinal wills it. I trust, if we are to think on this matter further, we will be open and honest in our dealings.'

'Yes, sir.' I put down a crust of bread. 'But what – what do I – you – what do we do?'

More considered this awhile, chewing. A trickle of grease had wound its way down his stubbled chin, and he fingered it away absently. 'Do? What, indeed? On the morrow, we might engage in uncovering some of these . . . scum. These evangelical creatures, as they call themselves. Followers of the Lutheran heresies. We might lift rocks down by this inn – the Bottle? – and see what scurries from the light. If there are heretics . . . seducing . . . men with their wickedness . . . I have friends in the city who will know where they've been. Their names and where they lodge. Better that we flush them from their dark places now. Before the king's parliament. His Majesty will wish the realm at harmony with so many fellows from without coming newly to town.'

'Yes, sir.' I said, my mouth a desert. 'And I?'

Please say I can return home – any home.

I was no informer against heretics, nor ever had been. I'd spied for Wolsey on household matters, nothing more. And I *wished* nothing more than to be released: to lie down by my stepmother's oven and drink small beer and pass out for a good few days. Until the parliament was safely open, perhaps – until it was all over. For something to do, I clutched at my cup and downed more drink, feeling my head swim with it.

Let good Sir Thomas More catch heretics himself.

'Where do you lodge in town?'

I told him.

He considered it a moment, wiping his mouth with the back of his hand. 'Should I require you, lad, I'll send someone for you.'

Thank you, God!

'Yes, sir,' I said, probably too eagerly. The wine had made me slur. 'I should probably get back there now, sir. Let you – your family. Let you see them. Thank you, for your hospitality.'

And your dangerous confidences.

'Mm. Yes. The time, the night.' He frowned towards the

shutter. Without another word, he went to the door and opened it. 'Alice!' he cried. 'Wife?'

Her voice echoed in response, but I couldn't hear what she said. Her steps, however, clattered closer. More remained in the doorway, speaking softly to her. I stood, still feeling trapped, dancing my fingers along the edge of the sideboard.

Further clattering sounded from outside, followed by more of Lady More's voice calling, laughing, muttering. Eventually, her husband turned to me, a glowing wooden box in his hands. It took me a few beats to place it. A dark lantern: it held a candle, enclosed on three sides, with a shutter that could be lowered to hide its single beam.

My heart fluttered.

Foreigners were made to carry candles about the streets when night fell. Otherwise, the king had decreed, they could be taken up as foreign enemies, agents of France or Spain.

Or Turks?

Am I being suspicious?

The problem was, I could seldom see when insults were meant, or not meant, or not insults at all.

'To light your passage home,' said More, evenly. 'The streets are turned wicked, I think, in these days.'

'Thank you,' I said, perhaps a little shortly.

He stared at me for a beat, his gaze difficult to read. 'Oh,' he said. He passed me the lantern. Its flame wobbled. The smell of beeswax – not cheap tallow – nipped at me. As I stood, he began muttering to himself, fussing around another cabinet against the wall.

'Ah! *Hic est!*' He turned to me in triumph, a small, bound book in his hand. 'A gift,' he said. 'My own poor work, I'm afraid. But I've nothing better to give you. No, boy, don't argue. I believe new men should be bound over with deeds of friendship.' My mouth fell open.

A book!

I could write well enough, but only to the extent that I still felt, childlike, a flutter of satisfaction at the end of each careful line. To write a book – to have read enough of the right books to write a book: that was a thing above me. This was a gift above me.

There followed an awkward little dance as he tried to pass over his book, and I fluttered around with the iron ring on the roof of the lantern. Eventually, I managed to take it, in my bad hand.

He looked down. My cuff had ridden up. He seemed on the point of saying something. Before he could, I said, 'Thank you, sir. Though there's no need.' The thing, I could guess, would be in Latin. I couldn't read it, but I could give it to Harry, who'd no doubt enjoy it. 'This is a kind gift.'

More's half-smile twitched. 'You haven't read it yet.'

I had the wit to say, 'This is true.'

He laughed, naturally, and led me to the door. I managed to wrestle the book into my belt as I walked, my fingers wine-clumsy.

Together, we retraced our steps back along the gallery, downstairs, through the garden, and to the gate. Shadows now hung deeply under arbours, under trees, under the gate's low roof.

'God give you good evening, Anthony Blanke,' he said, 'and grant you safe passage home. Think on what I have said to you this day. Mark me: there is some devilry abroad in the city. I regret it has taken two old friends. Let us pray it takes no more.' I couldn't see his face clearly, but I thought he smiled. 'Mr Cosyn. Dr Mordaunt. It shall be me next, if the heretics can have at me.'

'I pray not, sir,' I said, and meant it. I liked the fellow. I liked his rambling house, and his bold wife.

And his wine.

I didn't so much like his suspicions. 'Good night.'

I managed a bow, despite the lantern. Its beam found only More's middle, and then his side, and then his back, as he began whistling his way back into his house. I turned too. Night didn't just come on fast in London in April; it fell, as though the heavens carelessly tossed a cloak over the place. My vision, thanks to the hippocras, was dulled enough.

Long walk.

It was too late to visit an apothecary with my phial. That could wait until the morrow. The thought seemed almost funny. I'd spent the day and evening in the company of a great lawyer and man of justice, with an empty poison bottle in my purse. There was a boldness in that – a mad kind of boldness.

The streets up towards Poultry were already quiet. My little flame, uncovered, in fact seemed to make the world darker; it gave a faint glow ahead of me and, as though annoyed, the shadows hanging underneath the roofs fought back, thickening, lengthening, making pure blackness of everything the lantern couldn't reach. Where Poultry branched, I opted for Threadneedle Street, hurrying past the tower of St Christopher and the even more forbidding cliff-face of St Bartholomew. The good old buildings, so cheerful in daylight, were sensibly shuttered against the night. They'd become sentinels, brooding over the streets, judging those who stirred abroad when soon enough it would rightly be time for the watchmen.

I shivered. It was turning cold, and I'd a fear of being out alone in the streets at night. It wasn't the thought of people that bothered me, so much as what might be lurking amidst the lack of people. Often, it was said, robbers and cutpurses drifted about, making the world their own; but they'd have slim pickings.

One wine-sodden trumpeter with a book and a lantern!

St Anthony's loomed up on my left, giving a little cheer. It was no less dim than the other great buildings, but I knew it – it had a pleasant solidity. In the past, I'd been walked by it by both my father and stepmother; according to him, it was where my name had come from. The thought blossomed, bringing on a sweet, spicy burp.

The tunnel of a street stretched before me, terminating in a wall of nothingness: unlit buildings screening the priory I knew was hidden somewhere beyond.

Up Bishopsgate?

Down and along Leadenhall?

I'd go up, I decided – follow the wall after the Bishopsgate. The houses were finer along there. There would surely be some servants of the big places about. Candles would shine down from the windows. There would be the sound of prayers being sung out.

Before I hit Bishopsgate Street, one last church tower climbed to my right: St Martin Outwich.

I'd wager More could tell me something about that place.

Gripping the lantern, I turned it left and right.

'God-i-goden,' hissed at me. The voice was close, coming from somewhere in the shadows of the church.

I stumbled, nearly falling backwards.

The beam of my lantern went upwards, to the side, upwards again.

Out.

'What?' I gasped. Then louder, 'Who's there?'

Something stepped into my path. A shifting, darker blackness, in the vague shape of a man. Fingers tightened round my wrist. The lantern fell, hitting the muck with a flat tap. My voice came out strangulated. 'Get off me!'

Who? Who are you?

I could barely see; no light spilled from the church.

'Been sent to meet you,' the figure said. And then, low, 'Fucking Turk!'

That voice!

'You,' I gasped.

My spine stiffened. I lunged forward, ignoring the hands around my wrist, digging, seeking to scratch. My fingertips brushed the front of a cheap, canvas jerkin, but they found no purchase. I hissed, making to lunge again. The shape of the fellow remained before me. It laughed; it fairly cackled with laughter.

'Ow!' I cried out before I felt anything. And then the pain came, slow and spreading, at the base of my neck.

There's more than one of them, I thought, stupidly. I'd walked into a trap.

And then, more roundly, another blow struck, and I thought no more.

14

Darkness.

A low throb, like a heart beating dully in the base of my skull – out of place, causing low tides of pain.

Things darted on the edge of my vision: lights, shapes. I tried to focus on them, and they fled.

Voices fluttered over me, indistinct and muffled, as though I was hearing them underwater.

Alive.

I was alive.

'Urgh,' I said. It wasn't what I'd intended; but I needed to be making noise. I needed to speak. 'Urgh.'

The voices deepened. Something nudged me in the ribs, making me squirm. I forced my eyes open in protest. Lights hovered, dancing around me, above me. I squirmed again, and wiggled movement into my hands. My fingers slid in coldness, wetness, the slime and mud of . . . *the street.*

But I was alive.

I tried to arrange my thoughts, to sort them into order.

Sir Thomas More's house came forward, in a blur of St Catherine and her wheel, flowers, arbours, caged birds, books, and papers. And the scholar himself, rumpled and ranting. I tried to form his name and found I couldn't. The pain flared again. My eyelids screwed shut against it. 'Urgh.'

And then I felt something; my restless hands, still flailing in the muck, came upon it. It was hard, smooth.

Stick?

My fingers danced around its edges.

But why was I alive? How?

What had happened?

Bucklersbury and More refused to make way; they stood in my mind, refusing to let in anything that might have happened afterwards. My mouth was dry, my breath stinking in it.

'Stand.' The voice blasted at me.

Again, I opened my eyes and saw the lights, close now. It was still dark; we were deep down in the gutter of the night. And still I couldn't seem to form clear thoughts. 'Stand, you dog!'

Dog?

A little mongrel danced through my mind, its tail wagging in the air.

I laughed.

'Get the creature on its feet.'

And then I was being handled. My head lolled forward, my chin dipping to my doublet. Pressure forced its way under my armpits, and I was lifted, I was flying up, up. My head jerked.

I'd been attacked, I realised – I couldn't remember it, but surely I'd been attacked by cutpurses, night-rogues. I swallowed, bringing on a fresh wave of pain, and raised my head. Suddenly, I was released; I remained on my feet, swaying but not falling, as my saviours moved back from me. There were two lights, I saw: two men.

Didn't I have a lantern?

'Attack. . .' I managed. I blinked, and then repeated it over and over, until the fellows and their torches ceased their wild swaying. I'd been attacked, to be sure, and these were my saviours. 'Thank you. God . . . thank you. Attacked.' My words, in my own ears, were diffuse. I'd been drinking, I remembered – wine – hippocras.

A giggle burbled up in my throat.

A hiccup killed it.

'Thank you,' I said. 'I'm . . . attacked.'

Two faces resolved themselves: two bearded, hardened faces, floating indistinctly above their lights. They looked at each other, not me. 'Drunk,' said one to the other.

I am that, sirrah, and thanks for noticing!

'Attacked,' I croaked stubbornly. I took a half step forward and the two men – watchmen, I realised, in city liveries, the crosses and swords on their badges faded – hopped back in twin waves of light.

'Halt,' one cried. 'Come no farther, villain.'

Villain?

I opened my mouth to ask just that, but they began talking loudly. 'Compter?'

'For this deed?'

'I ain't carrying no murderer all the way to Newgate in the dark. Compter for the night.'

'Ay, for the night.'

I tilted my head forward, blinking again. 'What?'

'Don't reckon 'e'll give no trouble. Damned drunk.'

The other fellow held up his torch; it blazed in my face and I nearly fell back from it. 'What is it? A Moor or a Turk or a Spaniard or what is it at all?'

'Look at the neck. That's burnt. From a boat cannon. I'd

a brother gone for a soldier and the same thing 'appened. Reckon this one got it in the Grand Turk's army, like? See 'ow 'e tries to 'ide the marks from us. Marks of 'eathen wars, them. The Turks is even more bloodier than the Moors – even darker – how'd ya say? – more inwardly even than outwardly.'

They were speaking too quickly. I grasped only at 'murderer' and 'marks', and I raised my hand to screen my neck. This brought on a wave of protest from the pair of them.

''Old! Mark 'im – 'e makes trouble!'

'Christ, let's lock him in the Compter. Chain him. They can do what they will in the light. Gives me the spooks, in the dark.'

A face came closer. 'Look 'ere, young . . . feller . . . you won't give us no trouble, will you?'

'T-trouble?' I asked.

Why would I? You saved me from a murderer.

'Just you walk with us quietly and we'll bed you down,' said the other. 'And you can explain this wicked deed in the morn.'

Two things happened at once. Both watchmen circled around again to my side, and again they aimed their torches towards the ground.

'Oh! Oh no!' I cried. And then my arms were pinned against my sides. I made no move; I was rooted to the spot, staring down.

Their lights had brought to life what had been an inky nothingness on the ground – a sea of blankness. And there, in the midst of it, was sprawled a body. In the flickering light, I could see the sandy hair, the pale face staring upwards, the dark splatters trailing from bloodless lips. The flesh looked a clammy bluish white, robbed of life of warmth. Familiar, somehow – familiar.

And I knew him.

And I remembered.

'Him!' I shouted. 'It's him – it's him!'

'Quiet. You'll wake the town. You can explain 'im in the morning.'

'And that,' said the other, though not to me. 'Reckon we should take it?' Without waiting for an answer, he released me and dipped to the ground. He rose with the thing I'd taken to be a stick and held it up. It was a small eating knife, well-sharpened and still stained.

Nothing made sense.

The corpse on the ground was the young rogue, the apprentice or whatever he was, with whom I'd nearly fought outside the Bottle tavern. How he'd come to be here, dead, at my feet, I had no idea.

I didn't do it.

'I didn't kill him!' I said. 'I wasn't – this wasn't – I didn't—'

A hand struck me on the back, forcing me forward, forcing me to look closer. 'Shut up. And come with us, lad.'

Clamped between them, I wobbled forwards, was turned away from the body, and was half-carried along the dim tunnel of the street. There, I thought: a dark lantern lay forgotten. 'That's mine,' I breathed, and was ignored. They moved me on.

Threadneedle Street.

The huge tower and cross of St Anthony's.

St Benet Fink on the left; St Bartholomew's on the right.

All dark, shuttered and. . . *familiar*.

Memories began to form.

Yes! I'd walked this way – not long before. I'd walked this way and been attacked. It had been him, the rogue – his name was . . . *Robin? Rafe?*

Rob.

A flare of pain at the back of my neck reassured me I was right. Someone had struck me, knocked me out and then . . . and then they must have slain the young brute. Slain him and cried out for the watch, leaving me lying in the gutter beside him, stinking, the bloody blade at my side.

'I didn't do it!' I cried. 'It wasn't me. It was some other. Made to look like I did it.'

My captors said nothing. They simply kept jouncing me along the rough road as it curved by St Christopher's on its way to meet Poultry.

Poultry.

The Poultry Compter.

I was being locked up, gaoled, like a criminal, like a renegade

Turk.

All thoughts of what might have happened were drowned by what was about to. 'No,' I said, trying to shake them. 'No, you can't. I didn't do anything. Get off me – let me go!'

I was only gripped tighter.

Absurdly, I wanted to laugh again.

We all three turned towards a plain, grey-stone building with a porch and gatehouse which looked very much like one of the old manses which littered the city. The only difference was that the entrance into the courtyard was no open space nor even an iron grate, but a thick oak slab set in a whitewashed portico.

My spine stiffened. I dug my heels into the soft gravelly mud of the street before it.

And one arm was released, left numb.

The watchman at my right peeled off, stepping over to the door and beating on it with a forearm. 'Rise,' he shouted. 'Be up, sirs, and rise – we've goods for you.'

At length, a little window in the door opened. I couldn't see the face, but I heard a voice, pouring out aggrieved questions. My captor gestured in my direction, half-turning, before resuming his answers. The broad door screeched open, and I could see partly into a yard lit with braziers.

'Well, 'op to,' said the man still holding me. He jerked me towards the door and then let go. I stood there, on the threshold of freedom and the lowest kind of captivity, whilst the night gaoler looked me up and down.

He let out a whistle before speaking. 'Dark murder done in t'night by a dark murderer, then, is it?' His accent wasn't London. It sounded northern to me. I said nothing but managed to shake my head.

The watchmen had stepped back, as though they didn't want to get too close to the place. 'Reckons himself an innocent,' said the better-spoken one.

The gaoler snorted laughter. 'Don't they all, lads? Well, get ye in.' He looked over my shoulder. 'But just for t'night, mind. Don't want murderers infecting t'place. Gives us a bad name. Give you lads a bad name bringin' him no further than t'end o' your noses.'

This isn't happening.

This isn't real.

'Well, come, now. No sense in struggling. Better in than without, heh?'

Still, I resisted. Something snapped within me. If they wanted a Turk murderer, I thought, my head swimming with the vapours of wine and the madness of everything, they'll have one.

''Ere!' cried the fellow to my left. He let go as I threw myself to the side.

'Get away from me!' I cried. 'Go!' With a start, the man on my left fell back, squatting and assuming a grappling position.

Like hell you do!

'Come, then!' I shouted. 'You'll be the worse! I'm Wolsey's man – you'll swing for touching me. Come, then!'

The gaoler stepped into the broad doorway, putting his hands to his hips but saying nothing. Both watchmen now stood back, wary, their eyes on me.

I swivelled, turning resolutely away from the doorway, allowing them each to take tentative steps towards me.

'Don't think it,' I said, my voice low and cracked. 'I'm the cardinal's man. Touch me, and you'll die for it.' This, I knew, was nonsense. Wolsey would never get involved in anything so grubby. But his name was enough to stop any man in his tracks.

I stepped away from the gaol – just one stumbling step, my back straight and my chin up. Out of the corner of my eye, I saw a brief eye conference take place between the two watchmen, but neither moved.

Confident now, as strong drink can make you, I took another shambling step.

'And don't dare try to follow—'

A tremendous force hit me from behind, smashing into the small of my back and sending me to my knees. I could say nothing.

My head wobbled from side to side. The watchmen were relaxing their stances.

Gaoler?

'That's done him. Talks too much, this one.' The fellow's voice rumbled over me. My middle was looped in a strong arm, and I was lifted off my feet, still fighting for breath.

'I'll see him fastened, right well.'

'Get off me!' I gasped, as he began hauling me back towards his door. 'You . . . big bastard!' I'd never learnt the art of cursing to witty effect.

'Hush, now, lad. Eeh, 'ow did you think this would go?'

I wriggled and jerked, but the enormous bear of a creature had me locked tight in his embrace. Instead I began spluttering a list of names: Wolsey, the king, More – even Mr Richard Audley, private secretary, must have had red ears, for I boldly shouted that his intervention would have the gaoler's balls strung up on the Cheapside pillory.

And then one of the watchmen stepped forward. 'Just see 'e don't go nowhere till the morning. Till we know what 'e is and who yonder poor English boy is what 'e's slain. We'll be about gettin' 'im to 'is rest somewhere.'

'Don't you go anywhere, you little shit,' I cried. 'I want your names. Both. Ow!' The gaoler's arm tightened and I thought of biting down on it.

Still, I wriggled, just in time to see the watchmen and their torches fading away back in the direction of Threadneedle Street. And then the gloom of Poultry was being scraped away as my new captor dragged me a few steps farther, releasing me as soon as we were through the maw of the doorway. I cradled my middle as he started whistling and fumbling with a jangle of keys.

Something came upon me. It was an urge to run, to throw myself at the door. Rising to fight it was a desire to throw myself to the ground and tear at my clothes.

What would my stepmother say?

What would the cardinal say?

What would His Grace's household – my friends, those around me – say?

All of this seemed more important than what I might do. All were questions to focus on.

'Right,' said the gaoler, giving a satisfied little cluck at the locked door. ''Appen you've becalmed yourself.'

'Calm! Unlock that door. I have friends – high friends.'

He gave me a blank look, as though he'd heard it all before. Which, I guessed, he had. Accordingly, I affected the highest court accent I could manage. 'You, gentle, will be well rewarded for seeing to it that I am freed.'

He yawned – yawned!

'Murder, then. Naughty, indeed. We don't take no murderers, in t'common run o' things. Come on.'

He nodded his shaggy head into the large yard. It was gravelled, without any hint of tree or bush or flower. High stone walls and squat buildings stood about, lit in fiery fingers by the dancing glow from the braziers. He set off ahead of me, swinging the ring of keys around a finger, heading in the direction of a stone block of a building.

I remained where I was.

'Make me,' I said. It came out not with the boldness I

imagined, but with the petulance of a child. The gaoler only turned, one hand on his hip and the other flexing. Embarrassed by my childishness, I stepped after him.

'I'm not lying,' I said, my shoes skating over the gravel. 'I am what . . . I say. I am Cardinal Wolsey's man. If I'm ill-treated, I swear before God, His Grace will see that you're stripped of office.' No reaction. I dropped the accent. 'And that your privates are mashed into quince jelly and fed to the queen's pet monkeys.'

'Nasty tongue,' the gaoler smiled. 'For a man of a man of God.'

'You'll know nasty soon enou—'

'In here,' he said, 'ye'll rest easy enough, lad. What are you, Moorish? Off the boat from abroad?'

'I'm English.' I managed not to stomp my foot.

This caused him to turn. 'And are you, at that? Ye sound it, right enough. Sound London. Yet. . .'

I stared. I saw myself as he must see me: dressed in my own middling clothes, caked in mud, scarred at the neck and hand. This was how the watchmen had seen me – how they'd found me, sprawled next to a corpse, and thought, 'A-ha – here's a stranger, near at hand to the doing of his evil.' The drink-fuelled fire damped within me. I saw clearly enough how it all looked.

How it was made *to look.*

'What happens?' I asked. I didn't know – didn't want to and shouldn't have to – what the course of arrest was. I licked my lips, leaping on whilst he opened the door. 'I've come from Sir Thomas More's house. Honest to God. Not far. Sir Thomas More. I assure you I work for the cardinal. I'm of his house. If I'm lying, may God strike me down.'

This paused him, but he only turned to me with amusement. 'Old Wolsey, Wolsey, Wolsey, eh? That's new. Usually it's the king folk cry on.' He mimicked, 'I'm King Henry's hawk-man's lad! I'm brother to t'king's own under-cook! I make cards for t'king – let me go!' He pushed the door into a room in full darkness.

'No, you don't – I was – I do.' Indignation rose. 'I am the cardinal's man. I am!' Something slid into place in my mind. 'I've been followed. I was followed – someone watched me – dispute – with that lad. Days ago. And now they've killed him and made it look like I did it.'

I could see how crazed my words looked – I could see it reflected on his face. He wore a kind of amused detachment. But it was being pushed. 'Come on, lad. It's late. You can make your case when we put you to t'Newgate in the morning.'

The Newgate.

No.

'But – but . . .'

He tapped on the door with impatient fingers.

Inspiration struck.

I grasped about my belt, making the gaoler straighten and raise a fist. 'No – look. Look!' Thank God, I thought, that it was still on me. I pulled More's book free from my belt. 'You see?' I held it out to him. He eyed it warily, his head tilted back.

Not so clever now, you great hulk.

'From Sir Thomas More,' I said. 'I've been serving him. Tonight. You see?' He took the thing in his fingertips but only briefly looked at it.

'In, lad. In.'

I stood my ground for a second and then nodded. 'If you

promise me you'll summon Sir Thomas in the morning.' I waited until I saw a flicker in his eyes, and then I tried, and failed, to muster a smile. 'One night,' I said. 'You can – you *will* send someone to Sir Thomas's house in Bucklersbury in the morning. It's not far. It's—'

'I know where Sir Thomas lives,' he said. He jerked his head into the darkness again.

'Good. First thing.' Bowing to the inevitable, I stepped through the doorway, cradling my elbows.

Once I was inside, he followed, produced a tinder box and rushlight tapers from inside his jerkin, and lit a torch set in a bracket on the grimy stone wall. It cast a shallow pool of light, making the room if anything more cheerless. The floor was hard-packed earth, gritty, and the ceiling still lost in blackness.

When he'd finished, he blew out his taper and threw it down, before stepping towards me. I shrank back. 'Peace,' he said. 'Mean no harm. But ye must be searched. No trouble, now.'

No.

'No. You've no warrant.'

My back bumped a wall.

There was no point in struggling, though. He had me.

I stood, whilst he stripped me out of my doublet. It fell away, as though I was being disarmed as well as disrobed. My shirt was torn off in shrieks, exposing the scars from my neck down my chest and arm. He whistled at the sight. 'These are beauties,' he said. 'You at the wars?'

'Fire,' I breathed.

'Ffft. Nasty, that. Knew a lass, once, left her babe sleeping too close to t' hearth. Got nearly as bad, poor baba.'

Closing my eyes, I said, 'The man who did it is dead now. For his sins against the cardinal and king.'

'And what's this?' He was feeling around my belt.

My eyes popped open.

Shit.

'It's nothing!'

He had reached my purse and already his fingers were digging about in it. He produced the phial, holding it up, sniffing at it, squinting. 'Strange thing. Some kind of medicine?'

'Yes,' I said. 'Mine. For – for the. . .' I hesitated over the word, my gaze falling into the gloom beyond the torchlight. 'Scars.'

'Oh, ay. Hm.' He frowned. 'Well. We'll send this down to Sir Thomas with the book. And that doublet. See what he has to say in the morning.'

Double shit baked in a crust.

'Oh,' was all I managed.

'Now, just you sit down . . . ah. Here.' He'd moved a little along the wall beside me and tapped on it.

'The upper part of the chamber, I hope.' It wasn't very funny.

'Heh. Just sit down and ye might have a sleep.'

'Sleep,' I echoed, moving towards the wall. 'I barely sleep in York Place's dormitory chambers. What chance in a dungeon?' Yet, as I lay my back against the wall, I suddenly ached not to be on my feet.

One night.

This will be sorted in the morning.

The torn shirt rode up my back, my skin scraping the wall as I slid to the ground. I didn't care. 'There's a good lad. Now raise your hands so.'

I started to do it, too. And they froze in mid-air.

'What? Why?'

His hands clamped around my wrists. 'No!' Realisation dawned. I lifted my knees as he straddled me. 'Get the fuck off me!'

'There's that nasty streak again, lad. Watch it.' He lifted my arms. I shook, uselessly fighting against the strength of him, trying to push back. 'It's a horse's bridle you need, my boy.'

'No!'

'Peace, now,' he said. 'Can't have you making no trouble in t'night.'

'I swear to God, when I'm out of here, I'll have this place razed to the ground with you in it!'

My protests availed me nothing. With practised hands, he got my wrists into iron manacles jutting from the walls. These he clasped shut, finding yet more keys on his seemingly infinite ring.

I sat there, my legs out, my arms raised above my head and fixed to the walls, staring up at him. Again, laughter threatened. I fought it back. He stepped away from me, surveying his handiwork. 'But I didn't do anything,' I said. The fight, again, had burnt out of me.

'And you'll be heard in t'morning. The least of the king's subjects has justice, lad.' He was bored with me now. I was contained, restrained, and couldn't dig or claw my way out from his gaol. Nor could I murder anyone else, in my dangerous strangeness, locked away alone in the worst place he had.

He didn't bother with a farewell, but went off whistling,

closing the door behind him. The infuriating jangling sounded again, muffled this time, and followed by a more definite click. That voice in my head sounded again, in what was becoming a refrain.

This isn't happening. This isn't real.

I sat there – what else could I do?

The least of the king's subjects has justice.

This time I did laugh – just a series of short yips, mingling with tears.

King Henry's justice.

Why did we believe such things?

I supposed it was for the same reason we believed it when the chroniclers told us of the virtues and misdeeds of long-dead heroes and villains. We forgot – we chose to forget – that the writers had never actually *seen* their subjects.

This gaoler had surely never seen the king, and he wasn't seeing justice now.

Perhaps Sir Thomas More would bring some if he came for me.

Or perhaps he'd see a lying murderer, with a knife found by him and a poison phial found on him, who'd been at all the sites of bloody murder – and he'd say, 'It's plain – this Moorish serpent our commonwealth has nourished is a murderer.'

And what the great bodies of the commonwealth say stands as true.

I remained awake, my back stiff and my backside numb, my mind fighting to work, fighting not to envision even worse places.

Newgate.

The Tower.

Thank God there was no torture in England.

Or is that another one of those things we believe because we wish it to be true?

There was no way of telling how time passed, save that I felt it inching by slowly, eating as it went at the torch on the wall. The thing flared, widened, was darted at by the cloud of insects which had appeared around it, and died.

15

Why, I wondered, were prisons always dank places? Why was darkness so terrifying and evil a thing that it was judged a fit punishment for the condemned? Light and white were to bathe honest men; dark and black were for the dishonest, the criminal, those who ravished women and broke the law.

My mind ran this way and that, like a Bedlamite, refusing to be tied down to anything, refusing to make sense. I tried to listen out for things, to let noises anchor me in the world beyond, but there was nothing. That was the worst thing, worse even than the pain and strain. In the dark night were no distant church bells carried from the city. There was no hum of constant conversation from fellows who ought to be sleeping but weren't. No whisper of brushes as lower servants set about their work. Not even the wind made a hue or cry. In the silent darkness was negativity: a threatening, overbearing accumulation of nothing that dulled all the senses. I gave up even trying to judge how time was passing. Stretched nerves are poor timekeepers. A minute might have been an hour and an hour two minutes.

Strangely, I couldn't think back over what had happened. I shrank from reason, from memory, imagining instead escape – running home to Shoemaker Row, feeling vaguely that everything was a bad dream; that I wasn't chained up in a gaol at all.

Eventually, after however long, the retreating night introduced me to my cell's windows: high, barred things, half-hidden under the eaves of the slate roof. As the dawn broke, I traced its faint light as it inched up the blank walls.

I hadn't slept, of course. My head might have slumped forward at some point; I might have lost consciousness, but that was all. And worse – my mind couldn't focus on any one thing. Instead, it raced through images; it was as though I was whirling through a hallway of painted cloths and tapestries, seeing nothing long enough for it to make sense.

Watching the light had at least been something to do, as had tracing the uneven lines of the brickwork once they became visible. This, I realised, was the worst place. The Compter was typically a gaol for debtors or other minor malefactors – folk who broke the civil law. This little-used chamber must have been reserved for those who became frantic or wild, who had to be restrained.

I'm the first murderer here, perhaps.

Only I wasn't a murderer.

I ought, in the Christian way of things, to have had some sympathy for the dead lad. I didn't, though. I thought only that I'd been falsely accused – beaten and left there to take the blame.

As if in response, the ache which had dulled during the night throbbed again.

Throb, Rob, dead, didn't do it.

My heart lifted, just a little.

If only someone would listen to me, I thought. If only I could make an unlikely tale sound a little likelier. If I couldn't

– if I couldn't even have hopes of it – despair would set in and then I'd be lost.

Voices drifted in from the yard outside – a dozen or so by the sound of things. There was laughter amongst them; they had the cadence of banter, good-natured. My fellow prisoners, I guessed, being let out into the yard for the day. I'd heard that the gatehouses of some of the lesser prisons were sometimes left open – open, but not unattended – so that family members and pedlars could wander in, bringing or selling things to the unfortunates.

I could escape, I realised, if I had to.

And go where?

The by-now hideous tinkling sound announced my door being unlocked. Light spilled in, making me turn away after the briefest impression of my gaoler. 'Good morrow,' he said cheerfully. 'I won't ask as how you slept, all things being equal. But we can get you out of them manacles for a spell.'

Aren't you the gentleman!

'A drink,' I said. The words were half-formed. They scratched their way up my throat and had barely the strength to reach beyond it.

'How's that? Ah, but you must have a thirst.'

I had more than that. I had a dozen questions, growing from angry to pathetically pleading.

Have you sent someone to Sir Thomas More?

Has the body been examined?

Will I be heard?

By whom?

Will my stepmother hear about this?

Can she not?

Will you please write the cardinal?

Can I go home?

'Drink,' I said.

He whistled as he loosened my chains and my arms flopped. There was some pain around the wrists where my skin had rubbed and chafed, but otherwise, both limbs felt full of wet sand. I let him lift me to my feet. It was no use, though; he had to circle my waist with one big arm and almost carry me towards the door.

The bright, white light of morning rejected me, or I rejected it. Moans emerged from somewhere in my throat. 'Come, now, lad. One night in chains. You'll be thanking God, or whoever you pray to, for it when you're in t'Newgate, amongst all them other damned souls. Waiting on judgement.'

I felt myself become a dead weight. He grunted as he hauled me back up. 'Not Newgate,' I said. I would climb the walls of the Compter hand over hand and run wild into the streets, crying Wolsey's name, before I let any man carry me to a worse place.

Once again, I was being led, pulled and hauled, like an old sack – this time, there was no respite. The light was remorseless. I steeled myself to it, looking up and around. Men – well-dressed, mainly, well-groomed – stood around in groups of two or three. Their heads turned to me. Silence fell.

'You can stand well enough.' The gaoler released me and, I found, he was right. I couldn't stand straight, but neither did I collapse. Blood had begun to pulse through my legs again; it was as if the light had caressed them back to life. 'You slept well enough, then?'

I tilted my head towards him, my eyes narrow. 'In Hell's

waiting chamber?' I croaked. 'Christ, but,' I dry-swallowed, 'a witty clown for a gaoler.'

'Heh. Water butt's over there, if you've nowt to pay for ale. Pissing corner there.' He didn't need to move the finger he'd pointed: both water and jakes were feet apart – a barrel by the far wall of the gaol and a gutter running alongside it.

I managed a halting walk, ignoring the men. Whispers rose around me. If they'd been laughing together when I'd heard them through the windows – well, now they were bending their heads together like old gossip-aunts. I ignored them, made my way to the wall and, cupping my hands, slurped down the fetid rainwater before relieving myself without shame.

I turned, when I was ready, my hose half-up, my shirt ripped and loose, and found the gaoler watching. 'I wish to speak to someone of Sir Thomas More's household,' I said, surprised at the strength in my voice. The water had, oddly enough, restored some fire to my belly. To my chagrin, some of the men about the yard heard. Now they laughed. My fist balled. 'I assure you. I am of Cardinal Wolsey's household and engaged at present by Sir Thomas. I make no idle threat.' My voice managed a little of the court again – enough, at least, to make the gaoler hold up his palms.

'We don't want you to catch fleas amongst this lot, then, sir,' he said, essaying a little bow. 'Come, back to your fine chamber.'

I swallowed. The foul water threatened to make a return. 'I wish you to send some man to Bucklersbury.' I blinked. 'Now. Or I will. . .' I stepped forward with what I hoped was a look of menace. 'You will have trouble in your house here.'

He gave a little amused grunt. 'Peace,' he said, shaking his head. 'I've sent our horse boy down there. With your book and your little glass bottle.'

Dammit.

'And? Will he come?'

'How should I know, lad? Sir Thomas More don't write me no pretty little love notes and I couldn't read 'em well enough if he did.'

'But – the boy – is he returned? With word?'

'Not yet.'

'And the cardinal – I would have word sent to the cardinal. He was at Richmond. Might be at York Place by now.'

'You talk too much, lad,' he said. 'Sir Thomas will come, if he's coming. Told the boy to tell him your fond fancies and tales. And,' he added, without expression, 'to tell him how you were found. What next to. The men who brought you – they told me what you'd done. The blade near enough bloody in your hand.'

I wheeled, making the world spin. Facing the featureless grey wall, I reached behind and tore further at my shirt, exposing my back. 'Look!' I cried. 'Look – feel there. I've been struck – struck down. Could a man struck down have killed another? I was. . .' I choked for the word. 'Insensible! Struck! You have eyes to see, don't you, as well as arms like ham hocks?'

He didn't come any nearer, and I turned again, slowly. Still, his expression betrayed nothing but a kind of distant amusement. The prisoners were watching us with undisguised interest. I must have been a rare sight to them: a half-Moor – or, if they were less attentive, a something different, at least, crying out affinity with great men of the state and exposing his skin like a madman.

And to hell with them.

The lump I'd felt on the back of my neck was my trump card. I might have trouble explaining the phial, but even Sir Thomas More couldn't deny I'd been knocked down and lain out by whoever killed the damned apprentice.

And whoever that someone was, he'd certainly killed Cosyn and Mordaunt.

'Come,' he said. 'Back to your chamber.'

'My cell!'

'As you like it, lad. Come.' He stood back to make way.

'I won't go into those irons. Don't you even try it.' I meant it. I was aware of his trickery now. I could probably manage to hit him in the nose with my forehead if he tried. I didn't relish the kicking I would take, but it might be worth it.

'No irons,' he said.

I let a pause draw out between us. 'Good. In England . . . in England, I think you know I am an innocent man.'

Until. . .

He said nothing. I moved past him, back in the direction of the cell. Better in there than out in the yard amongst the strangers, the criminals. I knew none of the men, knew none of their faces – not even the gaoler. That lack of recognition only lent more unreality to everything as I scudded across the gritty yard.

Once inside, I sat down on the floor – the glorified ground, as it was. My captor didn't come in; he simply closed and locked the door from the outside.

The morning wore on. Outside, the singing of Mass. A chaplain had evidently come in; one of the pathetic little shacks must have been a chapel. Strange that I wasn't invited, I thought – not that I'd have wished to go.

Someone would come – of that I was certain.

I dismissed the idea of the gallows outright. It couldn't happen. I was innocent. I'd seen hangings, of course: for theft (a little much, perhaps – but then, I'd never been robbed and might change my tune if I was); for murder (much deserved). There was a process that had to be gone through. The whole system of justice I imagined to be like a great household, full of officials, giving a good appearance of smooth and stately order.

Every appearance.

In every household, if you looked closely, you'd find corners cut. Men would be taking bribes somewhere. Some would go unpunished for offences because they had high friends. Others would be punished unfairly. The important thing was always that *appearance* of order.

My execution, swiftly carried out, would provide that.

At some point, I ceased to listen to the weak sounds coming from outside. I lay down flat, scratching occasionally at my tattered clothes, and tried not to think about how my case might look. The light in the room shifted, dull to brighter, brighter to dull, until it became impossible to judge the time even by the length of the shadows. My stomach turned in on itself.

Could they hang me?

Was there some worse punishment for a man who had stabbed and poisoned?

I prayed. I got to my knees and pleaded with every saint I could think of, aloud and silently.

As if in answer came the familiar sound of the key in the lock.

I scrambled to one knee, blinking as light spilled in.

'Gaoler?' Even as the word tumbled out, I could see from the outline it wasn't him. This was a familiar shape: bulky, all uneven surfaces and a squashed hat sitting askew.

'Thank God,' I almost shouted. 'Thank you, Sir Thomas!'

The figure remained in the doorway for a moment, so that I couldn't see his expression. And then he heaved a long sigh and slouched into the room.

'Shall I leave you with him, sir?' The gaoler's disembodied voice was rich in deference. 'He's all unchained. He might. . .'

'Mm? Oh. Mm. He shall give me no trouble, I think.'

I licked at my dry lips, making fumbling, desultory attempts to straighten myself up. Yet I remained on one knee, gently swaying. What was that in his voice? Fatigue?

No.

Sadness.

'Sir Thomas,' I said, 'I thank you. I thank God for bringing you. I've been locked in here – chained, like a beast.'

The door closed behind him, leaving us in the dimness of the cell. He remained, however, standing by it. 'It was not God, Anthony Blanke. I received word from the gaol that you had been taken up. In the night.'

'I didn't do it – it wasn't me; it was him. I—'

'Peace. You look ill-humoured.'

Well, perhaps if you hadn't poured a bottle of hippocras into me and launched me into the night when a cunning murderer was abroad . . .

I bit this back. I needed this man more than I'd ever needed anyone.

He reached under a fold of his gown, muttering as he did so, and produced something. I knew what it would be before it glinted. 'This,' he said, holding up the phial, 'was found in your purse, I am told.'

I said nothing for a beat. And then, my voice small: 'I found it. Lying on the floor. In the cardinal's lodgings.' I was aware of how lame that was; I'd tried, and failed, to think of a more plausible lie. Only then it struck me: I might have said the murderer put it in my purse when he'd struck me down. But no. Building up lies was only an invitation to someone to knock them down.

'Is that so?' asked More. His voice betrayed nothing. 'It was brought to me this morning. That and my book. I took the liberty of visiting an apothecary on Cheapside.' The bottle disappeared back into his gown, and he tapped his chin with a finger. 'Do you know what he told me?'

'Poison,' I breathed. I hurried on: 'That's what I was going to do, sir. Go to an apothecary. See what he might tell me.'

'And yet you mentioned none of this. You found this phial, suspected it, and said nothing to me. Is that what you confess?'

Confess?

'Yes,' I said. My heart began to thud. I'd been hoping he would march in and order me freed. He had the power – not as much as Wolsey, perhaps, but power enough to do it. Even if he'd meant to interrogate me, I'd been fool enough to hope it would be away from here. 'It's the truth, sir. I . . . I'm sorry. I didn't . . . I thought I might. . .' I shifted my gaze into the room's darkest corners.

'Mm. This little phial . . . I took to the apothecary. The gentleman held it to his nose.' He paused. 'Nothing.'

I collapsed onto both knees and folded onto my backside.

'Wha – it – it wasn't poison?' I nearly laughed. I'd thought myself so cunning.

'I did not say that.' More patted at his breast, cleared his throat, and gave every appearance of enjoying my suspense. 'There are certain. . .' he cut the air with a hand, 'certain arts scientific which wise apothecaries can perform. On suspected things, you understand. This the fellow did. The phial was without scent or colour. He tipped a little of its effluence – very little – onto a spoon and put it to a flame.'

I shook my head. I'd seen such experiments. Still, I didn't understand.

'There arose,' said More, 'a most puissant smell. Not unlike fresh-cut garlic.'

'I don't know what that mea—'

'Poison indeed,' he said. 'I am assured and contented that it is a most potent poison. In strong doses it can kill in hours. Before death, it . . . it misbalances the vital parts of a man. A cruel death. Dr Mordaunt's death.'

'But then . . . it's as I said. The murderer poisoned him in the cardinal's lodgings and threw it away. Or dropped it.'

More said nothing for a few seconds. Instead, he seemed to watch me, his face flinty, as though he were measuring up a cut of beef. 'Yet this foul poison – or the phial which carried its substance – was found on your person. And you were seen, it has been reported, about the kitchens before he was murdered.'

I remembered the Frenchman in the wine cellar.

Blabbering to More's creeping little spy Rowlet!

'The boat – I was just off the wherry. I've already—'

'Item the second. You were present when the late Mr Cosyn was foully slain.' I said nothing, my eyes widening.

I knew this. I knew how it looked. 'Item the third. You were found, as the Scots say, red-hand. A dead lad before you. The knife that took his life near enough clutched in your hand. The boy was killed with expert cunning. Not animal savagery. A neat blow through the heart.' Something shifted in my mind at that. But More went on before I could gain hold of it. 'You understand how the matter looks. Tell me, Anthony Blanke, how you might explain this . . . strange appearance. All these strange appearances.'

I took a breath. I'd known, more or less, that I'd have to give some account of myself. And so I launched into it, telling him all I could recall and seasoning the telling with my suspicions. To my surprise, he produced a paper, a small, stoppered silver inkwell and quill, and began writing, leaning on the wall. He cursed occasionally, as ink dripped or blotted, but didn't interrupt until I reached what I fancied was my climax: the proof of my suspicions.

All shame of my body, of my damaged skin, had long since fled. It was now my salvation. I stood, eased my shirt down my back and turned. 'You see? I was struck about the neck. From behind. So it's plain, isn't it? Someone knew where I'd been – probably where I was going. And they brought that boy up. Paid him, maybe. Struck me down and killed him. Made it look so I'd done it. I couldn't have – if I'd been knocked down? See? I can feel the raised part.' I felt around for the bump, almost enjoying the pain brought on by pressing around it.

Behind me, a rustle signalled More putting down his writing stuff. I felt him creep towards me. His breath warmed my neck for a moment and was gone.

I turned back to him, feeling the manic grin yanking at my cheeks. It caught there, freezing.

'I admit,' he said carefully, 'that this . . . makes me unquiet. In my mind.' He was staring at me again, as though willing some proof to leap from my eyes. And then he broke his gaze, chewing on his cheek and looking up. 'It is not for me to say anything. No, neither yea or nay. Nor guilty or innocent. Not for me.' He cleared his throat. 'The city coroner, I think, will inspect the dead lad. I doubt the need for an inquiry, given we have a . . .' Something business-like took a grip of his wavering tone. 'The matter will proceed to trial, if you stand upon your innocence. At Westminster, I should think. His Majesty will have an interest. Not, perhaps, in the boy's murder – but in the others.'

His words left the room even colder.

More gently, he said, 'You might make your case fully and in open court.'

'"The least of the king's subjects has justice,"' I said. My voice was distant; I scarcely heard the words and dropped again, the ground sending needles of pain up my knees.

'Quite. Quite.'

Proceed to trial . . . at Westminster.

'You see the case.' He stooped with an old man's grunt to retrieve his paper. 'You ask . . . you ask that I should believe that a murderer of two men has made some – some study – of your movements.'

'He followed me,' I said. Still, I was speaking and barely hearing.

'And devised that you might be accused of his crimes. By placing you next to a third victim. A poor no-one. Some street nothing.'

'He was watching me.' Something lit within me, finally – though it wasn't bright enough to show the face of that unknown he. He remained formless, watching, lurking. But he knew *me* well enough and knew how well I'd fit his murderous shape and wicked deeds. Because I was. . .

Darker . . . more inwardly even than outwardly.

'He saw me. He's been watching from the start. I nearly brawled with that. . .'

Bastard.

'. . .poor dead lad.'

I remembered the feeling I'd had outside the Bottle: that sense that someone in the street had been watching me.

And I remembered something else.

'I need to get out,' I said. 'I need to go and see the old woman – I—'

'If this is the truth,' said More, 'then you might make these claims in court. You might find you a lawyer. I shall send someone, if you wish – a trusted man. The matter of your guilt in the lad's death – that shall be the ground of the case, I think. The rest . . . that shall be for. . . Mm.' He fumbled again at his gown, as if remembering something. Out came the book. 'I see no reason why you should not keep this. You might read to pass the time. The hours, I think, might be long ones in the weeks coming.'

He held out his present to me. It hovered a moment in the empty space between us. My hand – my bad hand – reached up and folded around its firm, cool cover. 'I don't read Latin,' I said.

'Ah. Then it is a poorer gift than I first thought. I apologise.' Still, he left the thing in my hand and stepped back. A frown passed his face. 'It is a strange matter. As I said – it leaves me

. . . unquiet. But you shall have justice. The law will proceed. All will be well enough. If you are innocent. If not, I pray you make your peace with God that he might pardon your soul. Have hope. The law has not yet judged you guilty. Nor is it satisfied of any innocence. You are . . . between states, as it were. If your guilt is proven, you might think with care on who set you to this great evil.'

I could think of nothing to say.

'Don't go. Don't leave me here, sir,' made its mewling way out.

'You shall be taken to some other place, I think.'

'Newgate?'

'No.'

The Lollards' Tower!

More turned. I'd made him uncomfortable, I realised; I'd unquieted his mind. And I didn't care. 'This isn't justice!' I cried. 'You can't leave me locked in here!'

'Have faith. The king is the fount of all justice,' he said, his back lumbering towards the door.

Cardinal Wolsey *is the fucking king!*

I had the wit not to actually say it, or anything like it, but Wolsey, I'd realised, was now my last hope.

More rapped on the door. The gaoler, however, didn't answer. He tried again, before calling out, 'Gaoler!' When there was still no response, he turned to me, a kind of awkward apology on his hard features, and opened his mouth to speak.

Before he could, the familiar metallic tinkle came, and the key turned in the lock. More fell back a step as late-afternoon light washed over him.

'Begging your pardon, sir,' said the gaoler. His breath was

short. 'Young man come. For our friend here.'

I jerked forward, palming the ground and hoisting myself up.

'What is this?' asked More. His voice had turned inflexible. He reached out and plucked something from the gaoler's hands – a paper. He muttered aloud as he read, but I couldn't make out the words.

'All sealed, sir, correct. And the feller who brung it in His Grace's livery.'

More tutted. And then he turned to me, half of him bathed in light. He chewed again on his jaw. Disapproval coloured his words when he spoke. 'It seems,' he said, 'that your master is not only aware of affairs but . . . has taken an especial interest. I took the liberty of sending word to York Place before I visited the apothecary. Of your case, I mean. My lord cardinal has ordered your release and return to his household.'

Cardinal Wolsey! Cardinal Wolsey, you marvellous old bastard!

I could have bent to the ground and kissed it. I settled for folding his book into my belt, where it hung down under the rags of shirt. 'No trial,' I breathed. 'No nothing – no trial!'

'It is not,' said More, 'the proper course. That the lord chancellor might exercise his— But I say nothing against it.' He drew himself up, inhaling deeply. 'His Grace has the authority. The law judges you unmeet to be brought to open trial, it seems, by my lord's will. And so it is right that you do as you are bid.' He seemed to be arguing with himself, forcing his mind to conform itself to this lapse in how things should be done. With a show of acceptance, he folded the paper and handed it back out into the light. 'It is just. He must go as His Grace commands. The law has spoken.'

And my sweet, blessed Cardinal Wolsey is the law.

'Law. . .' I forgot myself. 'I don't give a red plum! Can I go now? Can I leave?'

'You're damn right you can,' piped a new voice from outside.

Mark!

'Oh. Sorry, sir. Didn't mean no harm. I come up to fetch him. Anthony Blanke, I mean. For the master.'

More raised his chin and stepped out of the cell without a word. Mark pushed past the gaoler and slipped easily into the space the scholar had vacated. He let out a low whistle. 'Christ alive. What a shit-hole. And what a turd you look to tenant it, my friend. Get up. You're coming home.'

I threw myself towards him, wrapping my arms around his shoulders.

'Steady. I've heard what prisons turn men to. You've only been here a night!'

I pulled back, feeling tears begin to cut tracks down the grime on my face. 'Thank God,' I said.

'Thank old Wolsey. Though he has God's ear, I s'pose.' Mark lowered his voice. 'Here, old Sir Thomas More didn't seem too pleased. About Wolsey ordering you out, like.'

I didn't care. A great trembling had taken hold of me. I had to lean on Mark's shoulder as he led me out into the light. My eyes stung as it enveloped me. In the yard, the other prisoners began whooping, as though it pleased them to see one of their own – or near enough – find an escape. 'It's over,' I gasped. I clung to Mark, for fear I'd punch at the air and return the salutes of the damned criminals. Giddiness threatened to overcome me – I felt almost boyish.

He said nothing as we lurched across the gravel.

Only when we reached the entrance to the place, to which the gaoler had already padded, did he answer me.

'Um. So, maybe not quite.'

The great oak door loomed up, suddenly less pleasant. I turned to Mark. His round face was blotched, but he met my gaze evenly. 'What?'

He wet his lips and gently lifted my arm from around his waist. Then he turned to watch as the whistling gaoler unlocked the door. 'It's . . . the cardinal . . . he wants you out. No shame to his house, like. But . . . so's not to make too great a ruffle, I s'pose. . .'

Get to the point, Mark!

He turned to me again, as the door slid open on the hurrying people and pervasive stench of London. 'You're freed, yeah. But only for you to prove yer . . . well, yer innocence. You're out until you can find who murdered this lad they're sayin' you done in. If you can't . . . you've to be turned back over to the law.'

16

I sucked deeply at the afternoon air, foul as it was. There was still a sweetness to it – there always was, in the city streets, whether it was that undertone of bread from a bakehouse or burning herbs drifting out from a kitchen building or tavern. The door to the Poultry Compter slammed shut at our backs.

Turned back over to the law.

I'd die first. I thought it and I meant it. If it came to it, I'd throw myself into the Thames before I let a gaol and a gallows have me. If that was evil-minded thinking – well, people did it all the time, and God let them.

Ahead of us, life was going on. Men and women walked the streets with their heads turned pointedly away from the prison. It was as though it was a shameful part of their street – of their city: a part which they'd prefer to hurry by and pretend didn't exist.

'Here,' said Mark, patting his swollen gut. I frowned, only just noticing his usually stocky but slim frame had blossomed. He twisted an arm, hooking it up under his doublet and yanking out a red bundle. 'Brought yer livery. And a good thing, too. They strip you?'

Awareness hit. Strangely, I felt no embarrassment. I'd had strange dreams often enough, in which I'd found myself out in public either shirtless, my skin exposed, or, less explicably, shoeless. Yet, finding myself out in the streets undressed,

I felt nothing. I didn't care. I'd been fumbled at, stripped, called a murderer. . . I didn't care. Let them look. After all, men enough had judged me a killer even when I'd tried to hide the marks.

To hell with them.

'I don't want to be wandering about with no undressed moon-man,' said Mark. 'Get it on.'

I snatched the bundle away, rolling my eyes, and pulled on the doublet, not bothering to button it up. Though, in defiance, I carefully folded back both cuffs. Let them look. I would welcome a sneer or a disparaging comment. I'd tell them how I'd just been released from a gaol for murder and enjoy the look of terror on their faces.

Mark cast a glance back up at the Compter and stuck out his lower lip. In a small voice, he said, 'Was you locked up in that place – that cell – alone? All night?'

I followed his gaze, but only for a beat. 'Not quite alone. At some point, a family of lice joined me.'

His eyes widened and he hopped back. His laughter, bright and clear, rang out. 'Christ, man. Glad you're . . . yourself. You've got that – ah – that bite back.' He shook his head. 'Question. You're the same as me. Always say you like the city. Why? It don't seem to like you. Reckon every time you fart about London, it's me has to come and save you from . . . all kinds.'

I gave him a weak smile. 'Thank you. For coming, I mean.'

His chin rose and he showed his good teeth. 'Truth was, it was me asked to come. Special, like. When the news got about this morning. Friend Harry – he wished to come up. Can yer imagine that? Handsome Harry Gainsford setting his pretty big feet in a shit-hole the likes of that? Walkin' amongst all them scum?' He grinned. 'But his Mr Audley's got some kinsman up from Essex, for the parliament – so our friend's runnin' about wipin' his arse and feedin' him sweets. So I said I'd come. I'd get you free.'

'Thank you.' I blinked. 'Do folk know – in the household, do people know I was . . . in there?'

'Some might,' he hedged. 'They'll reckon you must be harder than what they thought, if they do.'

I gnawed on the inside of my cheek. An ill name, once got, was never put lightly away.

Too bad.

I swallowed the shame, the embarrassment. 'Is Wolsey. . . Is the king not at squares with him anymore?'

Mark shrugged. 'Pfft. King needs him. Can't be at squares. All else goes by the board with the parliament coming and His Grace master of all.'

I accepted this in silence and looked out across the street. It was late and, I realised, a Sunday to boot. I could tell it by sight: boys hurrying home with stuffed bladders under their arms; swains and maidens returning from illicit walks in the woods and fields; folk being turned out of their neighbours' houses. Somewhere, bells began to ring, and then the sound grew as it was taken up by the neighbouring churches. Dimly, I wondered if they had some system – if the churchwardens of a parish perhaps arranged who should signal the beginning when it came to ringing out the hour.

Time.

'How long?' I asked. 'How long have I got to find who did this?'

Mark bit his lower lip. 'I. . . Cardinal wouldn't be telling a nothin' like me that. Only know what I told you. You're out until you find this . . . murderer. The one what done it. You can see why. I mean – otherwise, the family 'n' that'll cry fie upon our old Wolsey. The dead lad's master too, if he had one. Don't look good, His Grace freeing a guilty man. Not that you are one. I mean, just how it looks.'

I waved this away. 'Not long, then. You saw More?' Mark nodded. 'He didn't like it, I don't think. That the cardinal got me out.'

'Not for him to like or not. His Grace runs the world.'

I smiled a little at this. Mark wasn't far off. Still, there were limits even to what Wolsey could do for his people. If matters got any more unpleasant, I'd be cut off, whether he wished it or not. I was his man, to be sure, but I was still amongst the lesser of them.

'We should get back, now you're out and . . . er . . . clothed.'

Back.

'You're all at York Place?'

'Yeah. Yeah. All shifted.'

I considered this. 'Hal Percy,' I said, remembering the shiftless nobleman. 'You've kept a watch? What's he been doing?'

Mark nodded. 'Sleeping, mostly. Drawing with his chalks – pretty pairs of eyes, I've heard. And hiding from work. You don't really think. . .'

'I don't know what I think,' I said. 'It's this creature – they're clever. It's got to be someone who can come and go from the court – or can pay someone to.'

'That's everyone. With the move, and the parliament, and messengers coming and going. That's everyone. All froing and toing as me old ma used to say.'

I considered this. It was a fair enough point. But some

people were noticed in their comings and goings more than others. 'Someone who knows what I've been doing. . . For Wolsey, I mean: seeking out the truth. He has to know enough to follow me and – to try and have me put away for his crimes. Even doing one especially for that.'

Mark tutted. 'Bastard. Utter bastard. An arse with ears.'

'And a mind between them,' I said.

'Someone of the household, then.'

'Maybe. Possibly. I don't know.' I swallowed. 'We can't go back. Not yet.'

Mark didn't demur. Instead, he smiled and looked out into the street. 'What's in the wind, then – what are we doin'?'

I smiled, in spite of myself, at the 'we', as I always did. 'Would you know how to capture and question some wandering rogues? Roaring apprentices – that kind of low rascal?'

His chest rose, displaying his badge. 'Oh,' he said. He drew his cheeks in. 'I see. You reckon because I'm outta the gutter, I know every low varlet what roars about the town?'

'What? I – no, I'm sorry – I didn't mean. . .' I shook my head.

'Oh, so you reckon I *don't* know no one?' I frowned at him this time. 'Reckon I can't hunt no bootless rogues? That I've gone soft lying on pallets and eating with spoons at court?' He reached up and stroked his collar with both hands. 'I know folk.'

'But you just said. . .' I saw the grin spread across his face.

'Just tryin' to lighten you a bit, son,' he said. 'Turn yer mind off all this . . . rottenness.'

I cuffed his shoulder. 'So you do know how to scare some answers out of the rough sorts?'

Mark shrugged. 'Dunno. I must. I'm from Deptford.'

'Well,' I said, giving a short laugh, 'we don't have to go that far. Last time I saw them, they were at the sign of the Bottle, down by the river.'

'Now?'

'If I'm on borrowed time, then I'd rather not wait.'

I took off, leaving him in my wake.

* * *

We didn't have to go into the Bottle. Nor did we even have to climb up the scaffold-like steps of its outdoor gallery. The lads who had been friendly with the late, lamented Rob were grouped on the shallow steps up to the cross at St Andrew Hubbard on Botolph Lane. I recognised them only by the spindly, young one; but you couldn't mistake a threat of prentices. You learned, in London, to spot them lounging about the streets, the better to avoid them.

'This the rights ones, is it?' breathed Mark, not far from my ear. We'd already passed small gaggles of similar creatures on Leadenhall and at the corner of Gracechurch and Little Eastcheap. The evening belonged to lads, their days of work done and nothing else to do save avoid their masters.

'I think so. Yes.'

'Let's go, then.' Without another word, Mark broke from me and began stomping over the paved ground in the direction of the cross. 'Holla, lads,' he shouted, as though commanding horses.

Heads snapped up, each glaring. I sloped after Mark, watching as the lads turned their attention to each other, their whispers hissing into the evening.

'What's the news?' asked the tall boy. If I'd heard his name before, I couldn't remember it.

'Just passing the time of night,' said Mark. He drew close to the steps, me at his heels.

''Ere,' said the tall boy. I judged he'd been elected leader already – or put himself forward for the role. 'It's the whatever-he-is. The Turk.'

'Watch your mouth,' said Mark.

The lad pushed himself off the steps and glowered down. It was an odd thing, seeing so youthful a face on a rangy body. 'I can speak for myself,' I said. My voice came out clearly enough, but no one paid it any attention.

'My friend here's an Englishman born,' said Mark. 'We heard about your friend.' Sincerity flooded his voice, and he removed his cap, freeing his brown curls. Grudgingly, I did the same. 'We're right sorry.'

Muttering rose and fell throughout the group. The name 'Rob' sounded here and there: 'poor Rob;'§ 'our Rob.'

'We was wondering,' said Mark, 'if you knew anything.'

The leader gave him a long look, which lingered on the livery. 'We don't say nothing to no one.'

I stepped around Mark. 'Your friend was murdered. Slain. Don't you seek justice?'

Another ripple ran through the group. The tall lad held up a hand. He looked, I thought, nervous, unsure of himself and his new station amongst the little crew of prentices. 'Justice been done,' he said. 'We heard, didn't we, lads?' And then his eyes widened and turned to me. 'Heard it was some stranger. And Rob. . .' he crossed himself. 'Rob said he was going for to meet some rich stranger.'

My heart leapt.

'What?'

'Seems to me you look strange enough,' piped the lad. He turned to his friends and received some murmurs of approbation. 'And you remember, boys? This one was fighting with our Rob. Rob would've killed him.'

Mark cut the air with his hand. 'Have a bit of sense, lads,' he said. 'You heard someone's been taken up. Would my friend here be standing before you if he was the murderer?'

This seemed to defeat the lad.

I jumped in. 'If the murderer was taken up, he'd still be in gaol, wouldn't he? They'd hardly let him go. And if it were me, I'd be rotting in there as we speak, wouldn't I?'

He now looked thoroughly lost. Colour flooded his face, making it looking purplish in the poor light.

Good.

These riffraff wouldn't have heard about my release – not yet, anyway.

'Get out of it,' was the best the lad could think of to hide his embarrassment before his friends. 'We don't say nothing to no one.' He turned his back on us.

I sighed.

Out of the side of his mouth, Mark said, 'Give him somethin'. Make him look big in front of them lot.'

Give *him something?*

I replaced my cap and felt about my belt. 'Here!' I said. 'We're trying to seek justice for Rob. If you help us, you can have this.' I freed More's book and held it out. The boy wheeled. Instantly, his eagerness melted.

'The fuck is – a book? Don't want no book.'

'It's worth money,' I said. 'A lot of money.'

Mark whistled. 'Ay, and it is at that. You'd fetch a good

price for the likes of that up Cheapside. Or down by St Paul's. Enough to keep you in ale for a good few weeks. Wine, even, if you've the guts for it.'

Whether it was the word 'guts' or 'ale' that prompted it, I couldn't say; but the boys began cheering on their leader.

'Take it, Peter.'

'Take it!'

'We'll have a drink to Rob with the money.'

The tall boy – Peter – gave a big, childish grin. As I watched, he mastered it, affecting an air of indifference. 'Give it me.'

I jerked the book back. 'When you help us find Rob's murderer.'

He considered this. 'I . . . don't know nothing.' I didn't think it was truculence; he looked little-boy-lost, his eyes darting to the ground. 'The murderer's in gaol.'

I had a short eye conference with Mark, before saying, 'We need some proof against him. You won't have to speak to anyone, none of you. Just us. And then you can have the book.' He didn't answer, but he did look longingly at my hand, curved around the little volume. It was worth money to him now. And he'd made a show of wanting it before his friends. He'd either have to talk or beat both me and Mark and take it. 'It's not much,' I said, keeping my voice gentle. 'Not much we seek. Just . . . we think your friend Rob was . . . uh . . . brought away from here. Up through the streets. By a false man – a man who maybe made him fair promises. But he killed him.'

This brought a collective cursing and spitting from the boys; a hailstorm of gobs of spittle flew threw the air and began peppering the steps and ground below.

'It was a feller,' said Peter.

'What?'

'Rob said – last night – he said some rich stranger had asked him to meet him outside the Crown.' He jerked his head to the right. 'Up Philpott Lane.'

I knew the place: an old tenement building. 'A rich stranger?' I said. Stranger could mean anything – a foreigner, an outlander, an unfamiliar face.

I thought Rob no great loss to the world of intelligence.

'Ay,' said Peter.

'Did you see the man?'

'No. Rob just told me. Said the feller had a job of work for him. For money. Said it was a job would please him – settling a reckoning by revenging himself on some trash. Went off last night for to do it. Then we heard this morning he'd been slain up somewhere. And some stranger taken up for it. We was going to go up to the Newgate and spit through the bars.'

It was what Rob would have wanted, I thought.

'Did he say anything else – Rob, I mean?'

Peter appeared to consider this, frowning down at the steps. Some spittle still glowed a fizzing white. 'Only . . . said the man was rich. Ah, I said that. Rich-spoken. And said as how he'd told him that he'd – I mean Rob – he'd enjoy the sporting and get some revenge.' He looked up and shrugged. 'That's all. Never saw him again. Rob, I mean.'

The book was warm in my hand. I held it out. 'It's yours. Take it to St Paul's – you'll get a better price there.'

Peter snatched the book without thanks. His chin rose and his eyes slid to his friends. 'Now get out of it,' he said, deepening his voice. 'This is our place. Get out of it.'

'Gladly.'

I stepped back. Mark turned, giving me the side of his face. 'We're done?'

Done, I thought.

Like Rob.

Together, we backed away into the shadows, part-way down Botolph Lane, and paused under the heavy shadow of Lombard's Place. I stared at the ground, thinking. Some children, I supposed, had drawn things in the ash-pile there – geese, they looked like: fighting geese that would only see flight when a strong wind blew down the lane.

I'd been right.

This rich stranger – he was still a shadow, but now a little less indistinct – had followed me to London when I'd come in the wake of Cosyn's death. He'd seen me fight with Rob and, at some point, decided he could be rid of my meddling by having me taken up for the lad's murder. A neat job it would have been, too, if Wolsey – God bless him – hadn't determined to thwart it.

And then I remembered the other thing that had troubled me that night.

'Come on,' I said.

Mark had had the grace to be silent as we stood in the darkness. 'What? Home?'

'No. Quick.' I tugged at his sleeve, my fingers sinking into soft wool. 'Not far.' I crunched onto the broken, mud-spattered paving stones.

'Here,' said Mark, at my back. 'You wasn't meant to give them nothing. Just snatch the book back and run away!'

I ignored him, heading riverward, crossing the eerily quiet expanse of Thames Street. As the air became wetter and thicker with its fishy stink, I swung right, into the gateway which led to the courtyard of Cosyn's house.

'Yip! Yip-yip-yip!'

Yes!

I recalled how, on the night I'd left the place, I'd heard my little mongrel friend barking. Someone else had surely gone in after I'd left.

A rich stranger, perhaps, who'd been trailing me.

'Dog,' said Mark, once we'd passed into the gloomy yard with its quadrangle of buildings, Cosyn's own hanging down like an embarrassing afterthought. 'Here, it's a little pupper.' He bent to the dog and began stroking between its ears. 'Scabby-looking thing, ain't it? You got a name, boy? You got a name?'

'Leave it,' I said. 'It just wants food.'

Mark immediately began digging about under his doublet and, as I'd done, he produced a bundle and began feeding the beast on scraps.

'Come on,' I said. 'He was here – the murderer was here!'

A sharp crack rang out over our heads. I looked up, looked everywhere, for the source.

The shutter that opened onto Cosyn's little balcony fell open. A flame appeared, wavered, and then dropped, extinguishing as it flew downwards. 'What's it—' Mark cried.

A shriek cut him off.

It fell silent.

It came again, insistent, full of terror.

The three of us – myself, Mark, and the dog – seemed to hold our breaths.

'Mistress Cotes?' I shouted, her scream still ringing in my ears. 'Mistress?'

Her voice, when it came tearing down from the balcony, was louder even than her scream.

'Save me! Save me! Mercy! The cardinal's man is come! I am murdered! Save me!'

'What the fuck?' cried Mark.

I wrenched him by his elbow, up off his knees, and he stumbled into me. 'My God,' I said. 'Come on!'

I threw myself across the yard, Mark at my side, excited yips behind us and screams pouring out over our heads.

17

The door was locked. 'Stand back,' Mark shouted. 'Gotta hit where the lock is!' He aimed a kick squarely at the centre of the door. It moved but didn't open.

'Hurry!' I shouted.

He was good enough to ignore me. He kicked out again, and again, and again. The door fell inwards, only just clinging to its hinges. Mark hopped back, as though hesitant to go first. I charged in, saying nothing.

The stairs marched upwards; I took them two at a time, one hand braced against the plaster wall. At the top, the chamber was lost in darkness. It took my eyes a few moments to adjust.

Where is she?

'Mistress Cotes?'

Her cries, her screams, had stopped.

When?

As Mark was kicking at the door. I hadn't realised; they'd just stopped.

The makeshift table resolved itself. I stepped towards it, squinting, her name forming again on my lips.

Something stubbed my toe, nearly tripping me.

No.

There, on the floor, was sprawled a dark form.

I bent and felt soft cloth.

Some gurgles drifted up, sounding horribly slick, wet, as though someone were slurping at a mug of ale. I jerked back.

'Jesus Christ,' said Mark. I turned, looking up at him. His face was clear enough. It was pure white in the darkness, like a Eucharist held aloft. 'It's – she's – is she dead?'

'I – I. . .'

'Where'd he go?' he asked. His face twisted from side to side. 'He still here?'

'She's still alive,' I said. 'I think.' I looked down again. I could see her more clearly now. The old woman was lying on her back, her hands up around her dark throat.

Dark!

'Her throat's been cut,' I breathed. I repeated it, more wildly. 'Mark! We need to fetch help.'

'But the man who did this—'

'To the devil with him! She's dying!'

Our voices had risen, not to argument or anger but to the borders of hysteria. 'Help!' Mark spluttered. 'Ay, help!'

I stood, and immediately slid, falling against him.

Blood.

The floor was soaked with it.

'Come,' he said. 'Help.' He kept repeating the word, as though it would summon someone.

I gripped his arm and began moving back towards the doorway. I needed air, fresh, clean, bloodless air. We could cry out, I thought, cry out into the night, raise a great tumult, a great hue and cry. All London could be roused, if need be.

With Mark at my back I took the first few steps.

'Help. We'll fetch help,' sounded at my back.

He's never seen a murder unfold, I thought, never like

this. He's enjoyed my stories of it, but they've always been just that – stories.

Lucky him.

I was still thinking it when I reached the bottom of the stairs.

I was still thinking it when I realised the door had closed.

No, not the door.

I frowned.

Mark let out a little croak behind me.

Someone had come into the doorway, someone bulky and solid. They were standing there, blocking it.

I drew up short, Mark hitting me and sending me forward again.

Two great paws clamped around my shoulders.

'Get off of me!' I cried. I squirmed, jolting from side to side. 'Off!'

'Peace,' hissed a familiar voice. I stopped resisting at once. I looked into the eyes, stained dark in the gloom. I traced the jutting nose. I looked up to the battered hat, sitting askew. 'What the devil has gone on up there?' asked Sir Thomas More.

I fought for words. There were too many of them; I could find nothing that would make sense.

'Woman's been murdered,' said Mark, his own voice still edged with wildness. 'Just now – she cried out – we run up – she's alive – she's murdered.'

More released me. Feeling rushed back into my shoulders. 'Out of the way,' he said. His voice was very much under control. 'Make way.'

Gratefully, I flattened myself against the plaster. Mark did likewise, on the same side. The fellow stepped in, and only then did I realise he had brought support: a smaller figure I recognised as his friend Rowlet. More's heavy footsteps thunked their way up, followed by the physician's assistant's lighter ones. We watched them go. Mark whipped off his hat. 'That's Thomas More,' he said.

I said nothing for a beat, chancing a glance out into the yard. 'And his spy,' I said, under my breath.

'Yip – yip – yip!'

Looking back up the stairway, I swallowed. And then I followed in the pair's path.

Light sparked on and off, finally catching. More had managed to find the tallow candle on the table and bring it to life. It sent wandering waves of light over the scene, casting him in shades of grey as Rowlet bent to the stricken woman.

'She is gone,' he said. His voice was choked. 'By the Mass, *gone.*' His hand twitched in a sign of the cross. More said nothing, turning his hawk nose to us.

I tore off my cap.

Mark, doing the same, said, 'It wasn't us, sir. We just got here. Heard her cry out. We was tryin' to help.'

I forced myself to look down. The old woman lay in a pool of blood. Streaks of it were everywhere, sprayed, it seemed, on walls as well as the floor. It looked as though she had danced around the room, bleeding as she did so, revelling in it. Her eyes were closed, her pale hands still up at her ravaged neck, mercifully hiding the wound. A few strands of white had escaped her cap and stuck about her face and throat.

Death, I'd always been assured, should be a release from this sinful, fallen world.

Release.

It sounded soft, welcome, like freedom. Too often,

though, the end was ugly – as though God expected us to pass through thorns to reach paradise. It was a remorseless, painful negation.

More helped Rowlet up off his knees; the fellow rose silently. 'I know,' said the scholar. A little sob choked in his throat. Rowlet, for his part, moved over towards a wall and leant his forearms against it. 'Forgive me. I knew the lady a little. Mistress Cotes. We both did. She was . . . vehement of spirit. We all knew her, we . . . we friends of Mr Cosyn. This creature – this monster in nature – seeks to be rid of all of us who ever spoke out in the slightest . . . against the Church as it is. The state of the world.' He appeared to remember our presence. 'Forgive me again. Yes – I know your late movements as well as my own.'

Rowlet spun. 'We witnessed them,' he spat, half-shaking his head. 'Coming upon her.'

'What? Sir?' I asked, dumbly, looking between the older men.

More gave me a hard look. 'We know. Mr Rowlet here watched you leave the Poultry and reported that you went south. I thought it might be . . . instructive . . . to see where it was you went. I joined him and saw you trafficking with yonder poor boys and then coming down here.'

You pair of old foxes.

'And we heard,' Rowlet said, 'the lady cry out. "The cardinal's man. I am murdered." A strange and unearthly thing.' He wore the same look of shock when he had first looked at old Cosyn's wounds, I thought. And the same steel edged his words.

Mark and I looked at each other. His eyes were two blank discs. I'd forgotten what she'd been raving.

This murderer is still trying to cast the blame at my door, I thought. How can he know my movements before I do?

'But he'd gone,' said Mark. 'Time we'd got up here.'

More's cheeks drew in, giving him a gaunt look. Before Rowlet could speak, he said, 'It seems to me a most simple scene. The lady cries out against the cardinal's man. Two cardinal's men attend on her. She lies thus, devoid of life.'

Rowlet crossed his arms over his chest, glaring at us, his tiny features hardening.

'You don't mean you think we. . .' I began, sensing Mark stiffen.

More tutted, looking back down at the body. 'No. No.' He turned back to us. 'If you had done this . . . so quickly . . . you would both be soaked in the poor lady's blood, I think. Is that not so, Mr Rowlet?'

The fellow's face slackened. 'I. . .' He glanced down at the body, winced, and returned his gaze to More.

'Well? You are expert on the inner workings of the body natural. Is it not so? These men could not have done this foul deed? They are neither bloodied nor befouled. They disturbed the murderer, rather. And he fled as they entered.'

'I. . . Yes, Sir Thomas.' Rowlet lowered his gaze for a moment. Looking up, he added, 'Unless there is some greater conspiracy in that household. And these men came here to alert the brute to run. Else some black sorcery is at play.'

More looked around the bare room. 'Run?' he murmured.

'Here,' said Mark. 'No, we didn't – we didn't chase no one. Look – there's a door.' He pointed at the far wall, opposite the stairway. I began moving towards it, eager to be away from the body, my eyes on the floorboards to avoid the pools of blood.

'Remain,' snapped More. 'Stay.' He moved to the door himself, Rowlet following. A rusty ring hung at its centre and the scholar grasped it, shook it, and pushed. The door fell inwards.

As the pair entered the next room, I looked instead at the cracked and broken square board balanced on the barrel, with its stinking source of light.

There, exactly as before, were laid. . .

Just a spoon . . .

Before, I thought, there had been both spoon and eating knife.

Eating knife.

'Sir Thomas,' I cried. 'Sir Thomas!'

He reappeared, frowning in the doorway, questions written in the wrinkles of his brow.

'There was a knife here. On the table. When I was last here. It's gone now.' I tried to think, tried to recall the look of the knife I'd nearly touched – the one which had slain Rob. I couldn't. Both were knives, like any other. I decided to press my case anyway. 'The same knife, I think, which killed that lad. The one they found lying by me.'

'What?' More frowned harder. 'Yet that knife didn't cut the lady's throat. It is locked most securely in the Compter. I have examined it myself.'

I said nothing. I didn't want to risk saying too much.

'So what killed her?' asked Mark. 'Sir.'

More didn't answer directly. He reached up and scratched his stubbled chin, before shrugging, turning, and stepping into the other room. We stepped carefully across the floor, and stood in the doorway, looking in.

Jesus Christ.

'Christ's bloody wounds,' said Mark. 'Ah, sorry, sir. But – is this how this old dame's been living?'

Only a few tongues of light lapped into the room, but they were enough. Like the outer chamber, the inner one was bare of almost everything. Only a small sackcloth marked out where the woman must have slept. An unpleasant odour lingered in the air: faintly herby, with an undercurrent of urine. There was nothing else. On the far side, a window admitted a little ambient city light, mingled with the weak glow of the moon. Rowlet stood by it, almost lost in shadow.

'The shutter,' said More, 'is open. Come. Look.'

Mark nodded at me to go first and I creaked across the boards to where the older men stood. Looking out, I could see only a straight drop to a small alleyway, which ran between the back of Cosyn's house and the wattle-and-daub wall of another building. 'The means of escape,' More rumbled.

I looked down, a little doubtfully.

Only if he has wings.

'Maybe,' I said. It was possible. I leant out the window and tried to see the outer wall of Cosyn's house. 'No blood,' I said.

'Mm?' asked More. I cleared my throat, sliding back over the rough wooden lintel. 'You said, sir, that if we'd – that whoever killed the lady – would be as soaked in blood as she is. Mr Rowlet agreed.' I looked at him, but he said nothing. 'If this creature jumped out the window or climbed down . . . but there's no blood there.'

More's eyebrow arced. 'No. No, there is not. Curious. A most curious thing. It should be bloodied, should it not?'

Rowlet's voice was barely audible. He was, I thought, on the verge of tears. 'Yes.'

'But I think, sir . . . the knife.' I was unwilling to let the thing go. 'I think there is some connection between the murderer and the dead woman. He followed me here. He visited with her when I'd gone. I don't know why. And he's been back since. He took that knife and used it on Rob – on the dead boy. And now...' An idea fit neatly into place. 'And now he's silenced her.'

'You are forgetting something,' said More. He stepped away from the window and, taking Rowlet's arm, moved back towards the light falling in from the outer room. As he did, he gave Mark a searching look. 'I heard, with my own ears, the lady cry against a cardinal's man. Why should she have done so?'

'Because a cardinal's man killed her,' offered Mark, before immediately staring at the floor and biting on his lip.

'So I would guess. And yet why should this lady have traffic with such a man?'

I considered this. 'She worked for Cosyn. Perhaps ... uh ... perhaps she loved him.'

'Mr Cosyn was a good man,' snapped Rowlet, shaking himself free of More.

'Peace,' my friend, said the scholar. 'We are all disturbed by this tragedy. Go on.'

'Perhaps this cardinal's man...' Loyalty forced me to qualify. 'Or someone claiming himself a cardinal's man ... offered to help her. My master – he told me to tell her he'd see to everything. The burial, the removal of Mr Cosyn's body to the parish. Everything.'

'And who knew His Grace had made this offer?'

I swallowed. 'I did.'

Mark stepped forward. 'So did I. We all did, in the household. It was – uh – common knowledge, you'd say.'

Bless you, Mark!

More sighed, pinching the bridge of his nose and then giving his head a hard shake. 'I am unquiet in my mind,' he said.

Is it ever quiet in there?

'I must see that this terrible thing is . . . well handled.'

'May I cover her, sir?' asked Rowlet. 'I cannot . . . she had no . . . I cannot. . .'

More murmured assent, and the other man deftly began unclasping his own woollen cloak. 'I must write to the king.' He looked up. 'And your master. And see that trusted men of the city can attend to . . . all. Discreetly, without causing fear or tumult. First, I shall examine the room yonder, I think – and Mr Rowlet shall secure any other means of passage from this house. And call up chaplains. The lady died so suddenly, I fear her soul—'

'Her soul is flying heavenward. Her. . . She was pure in spirit,' said Rowlet.

I gulped down a breath. 'Sir, you said that this creature is intent on murdering those who spoke against the cardinal.'

'Against the Church,' he said. 'Certain perceived abuses. Not your master in especial.'

I conceded with a nod. 'But that Rob didn't.' He gave me only a wan, blank look. 'It's . . . I see some pattern here, sir. Some bloody design. Two men go to the cardinal to be . . . over-bold . . . against him. And they're murdered, right there in his house. Boldly. This street lad – and this old woman – they aren't of the design. Nowhere near the cardinal. Or they've been killed quickly, suddenly decided on – to aid it, perhaps. Or to provide someone to blame it on – someone,' I swallowed, 'in the cardinal's household. Whatever it is

– 267 –

. . . this . . . design,' I finished lamely, already regretting speaking.

More had drifted off during my little ramble, staring into darkness. Rowlet, however, was watching me intently, and with something, I thought, like respect. He was, I guessed, engaged on the same matter – and perhaps he was working towards the same conclusion. The scholar looked at us, as though suddenly remembering our presence. 'Order,' he croaked. 'You have been ordered to return to the cardinal, have you not?'

'We have, sir,' said Mark.

'Then get you gone. Go. Go now.'

Rowlet coughed. 'Better, perhaps, Sir Thomas, that I accompany the lads. Openly, this time.' His little features had tightened, his lips pursed. He stood with his back to the wall, shivering a little without his cloak.

To see what black sorcery we're about?

Ass.

More appeared to consider. 'Why . . . yes, I think . . . His Grace's household might be enriched by extra service.' He gave me a crafty look. 'As His Grace was kind enough to put you at *my* service. You will be well watched and cared for once you are home.' Silence fell, punctuated only by the distant snuffling of the dog. 'Wait in the yard a space. I should like.

. . Wait downstairs.' In the candlelight, the old man looked very grey, very much older than he had when I'd seen him even that afternoon.

Mark needed no further invitation. He flew downstairs ahead of me.

Slowly, I followed, my mind churning with possibilities.

None of them was particularly attractive, still less likely.

I moved slowly, pausing a couple of steps down and listening to the whispered conference that immediately erupted in the dead woman's room.

'There is something rotten drifting from that household,' hissed Rowlet. 'This rottenness in the Church which Cosyn spoke of – it takes evil and unnatural shape.'

Whatever More responded was lost, and I slid downstairs.

Familiar yips met our arrival in the yard. I sipped at the cool evening air; it washed away the memories of wild screams and the reek of tallow mingled with the tang of blood.

'Here, boy,' said Mark. 'Here, lad.' Already, he was moving towards the source of the barks. He turned to me. I saw that he was shaking all over; his eyes were still huge and bright. I knew the look. I'd worn it myself in the past, when foul murders had still been strange and unusual things. 'Here he is! What's that you've got, boy? You don't want no rubbish. It's an 'ome you want.'

I padded over. Mark had wrenched away a little jagged piece of dirty wood from the mongrel, drawing annoyed growls. He hurled the thing into the yard and grasped the dog at the scruff to stop it playing fetch. 'It's food you want, and an 'ome.'

'Leave the damned thing,' I said.

'But it's. . . It ain't got an 'ome. If yonder old bird was feeding him, God rest her, it'll – it'll starve.'

'Dogs don't starve in London,' I said. 'They eat better than most folks.'

'Still,' he said, releasing the thing. It didn't run off, or bark, but began wagging its tail. 'I s'pose. I s'pose I could take it, couldn't I?'

'What?'

'Give it a home, like. Take it.'

'But you can't – it's—' I looked at the foolish thing. And then at the dog. I smiled. I'd only just realised how much I needed to smile. And then I thought of the old woman, feeding the mongrel scraps, probably – using it as her guard dog. She'd been an unpleasant, cracked old wench, making dangerous accusations, and living in her own filth. But she didn't deserve a bloody death in the crumbling remains of her master's house. No one did. I sighed. 'Well, I lost the present I meant for Harry. This can be yours.'

Mark grinned down at his new friend. 'Come then, Bo.'

'Bo?' I asked.

'I'd an uncle,' he said, 'kept a dog called Bo. Always said I'd name me own dog that one day.'

I smiled again, more deeply. 'Reckon we can get a wherry to carry us both and a dog along to York Place?'

Mark lifted the unprotesting Bo, who immediately began lapping at his face. ''Course.' He turned to show me the 'T. C.' on his back. 'Wolsey runs the river, don't he? Better wait on that other lad, though.'

I cast one last look up at Cosyn's house. Light still wobbled from the shutter at the balcony. Distantly, I could hear Sir Thomas More's voice, droning slowly on in Latin as he prayed over the dead woman.

18

In the evening gloom, York Place presented a vast wall of lights. There wasn't a single wooden shutter in the palace, as far as I knew. Every window was glazed with French or Flemish glass. Those lights danced in reflection on the Thames as we pulled up to the marble landing stage and water gallery, which jutted out from the riverbank and was covered over by an arched roof. Our wherryman drew us in close by the grey steps, just a little way down from Wolsey's own enormous barge, which might almost have been an extension of the palace.

There had always been an archbishop's house there, I knew; but wherever and whatever the old building had been, exactly, I couldn't tell you. Wolsey had repaired it out of existence. The cardinal built, I thought, as though privately worried about his own impermanence. To combat it, he sought to will himself into the world in brick, mortar, and gilt. The vast archiepiscopal palace, unlike white-and-red-brick Richmond, presented a warm face to the world, its brickwork washed in the faint yellow called king's gold. The slate roofs, stained grey by the night, offered a votive violet under the sun.

Throughout the journey, Mark had entertained the dog whilst Rowlet had sat demurely, trembling with cold. At one point, he had begun asking me questions about life in Wolsey's household – was there suspicion? Good cheer? – but my single-word answers seemed to have forced his mind back on the dead woman, and he'd fallen silent.

We alighted, Rowlet paying, and began moving along the path of the covered water gallery towards the palace proper. The golden cross at the prow of the barge gave only a dull sheen.

'Here,' said Mark. 'This way!' The dog grizzled a little, as though the barge was a great water beast; it moved only with a yank.

We tapped our way along the marble, past the smooth expanse of canvas cover over the rowers' section. This ran all the way up to the enclosed glassed part at the rear, where Wolsey's great seat was, and then we were past the glazed enclosure, past the musicians' section, past the painted wooden cardinal's hat, and the barge was behind us. 'A fine vessel for a poor priest,' muttered Rowlet, getting no answer.

The path led directly through a gatehouse, where a porter nodded us through, crying out only at the sight of Rowlet. 'Sorry, my friend. New means of, uh, looking to our locks, as it were. Don't wish hazardous men sneaking in amidst the poor trash who beg alms, eh?'

'And are given crumbs and soured sauces, doubtless,' sniffed Rowlet. 'I can see the way of it. Great men grind down littler ones, then offer to pick them up. And demand love and fealty for the doing of it.'

We ignored him and, after a moment's silence, the porter went on. 'Uh. Well. You wait here until I send word up to one of the officers. Have you checked, as it were. For safety's sake.'

Rowlet looked on the point of making a fuss. 'It is late, sir, and cold.'

'Shan't be a minute,' chirped the porter.

'We'll let an usher know you're here,' said Mark. 'Straightaway.'

'I . . . I must get word out. To Sir Thomas, to let him know of my safe arrival. You, porter – have you means of writing? Of despatch – swift despatch? This is a fine house. I'm sure it would look well on you if you would see your way to letting me write to Sir Thomas More, the king's own counsellor and friend.'

To let him know we haven't tossed you into the Thames!

'We've old papers and inkhorns here,' said the porter, looking suitably convinced by the summoning up of the king's presence. 'You can send word out by the wherrymen. And it won't be no more than a minute until I can let you pass, I'm sure.'

Defeated, Rowlet said nothing, but huffily moved towards the door of the gatehouse. Well, I thought: security was tight enough, at least.

As Mark and I passed on into the courtyard, he mouthed to me, 'Fuck him. Leave him there all night, all I care.' I smiled, and together we stepped into the great open space, watched over on the north side by Wolsey's privy chamber, and the secret lodgings – the withdrawing chamber, bedchamber, and privy gallery – one floor up. I craned my neck as we entered into the cobbled courtyard. The lights were lit up there too, of course. From somewhere, music drifted. It was getting on; this was the time when the men of the household would spend their recreation in – *silent prayer and contemplation* – gambling and gossiping.

As at Richmond, open wagons stood about. We wound our way through them, intent on the grand doorway into the White Hall: the whitewashed stone foundation that housed a grand chamber directly below Wolsey's lodgings.

'Yip!'

I turned. I'd grown used to the sound on the way – the dog was simply a nervous, city-bred thing. On our moonlit journey westwards, Bo had become Jackfoot ('me other uncle had a Jackfoot'); Jowler ('he looks like a Jowler'); Nosewise ('see how he sniffs at me – boy's got a nose'); and finally, for reasons Mark kept to himself, he'd been christened Marchpane. The wherryman had provided a length of rope, which had been fashioned into a collar and lead.

'Here, he's seen something. What is it, Marchpane? What is it, March?'

The dog had lifted its tail and was staring at one of the wagons. It crouched low to the ground and began growling in its throat. Looking, I fixed my own gaze on the thing, looked above its wheels, saw. . .

'Jesus!' I cried.

The wagon was stacked high with straw.

From it stuck a human arm and leg.

'What's it?' Mark caught up with me. 'Wounds!'

I looked around, up at the blazing windows, around the maze of wagons and barrels and coffers which still littered the courtyard. And then I stepped towards the body, reaching out. My fingers shaking, I touched the hand.

'Bugger off!'

I jerked back. The dog began yapping excitedly. The straw shifted, and the hand curled. A little way along, a face emerged, sticks of straw littering a beard. 'Bugger off,' it said again. 'Find yer own place.'

I murmured apologies, feeling my cheeks heat.

Mark laughed, swearing with abandon. 'Christ,' he said, when his attack subsided. 'By the hole in Christ's sweet side. The whole place is filled up. All them great men in for the parliament what can't get a place in the king's house and won't sleep in the town. Them and all their folks – the cardinal's lodgin' them as he wishes to favour. Christ,' he said again. 'We're jumpy as March here.'

With good reason!

My heart was beating erratically.

At length, I said, 'You'd better find somewhere for the dog.' I lowered my voice. 'You know what Wolsey's like about them.'

Mark's knuckles whitened on the rope. He knew as well as I did that the cardinal detested animals being brought indoors. The mastiffs and hounds that courtiers filled palaces with – he'd happily see them all thrown in the Thames.

An idea struck. 'Put him with these parliament men's dogs. They must have been put somewhere.'

Mark clucked his tongue. 'Ay, a fine thought. Come, March. Come, boy. You're going to make some friends and show 'em how a London doglet does.' He looked up at me. 'I'll see you soon, man.'

I nodded, as he traipsed off whistling and cooing to his new friend.

Let's hope the thing isn't rife with fleas.

When they'd disappeared amongst the courtyard stuff, I made my way to the entrance to the White Hall, knocked, and was admitted by one of the lesser ushers. Inside, the place was crowded with men I didn't know, and who paid me no attention. These, I supposed, were the parliament men: the squires and burgesses Wolsey would have to pretend to love over the coming weeks, or however long these great conferences lasted. They looked the part, too: their suits – their doublets and coats and hose – were of decent quality and varicoloured, probably the best they had, but ill-fitting. I had a vague notion that probably these were the only fine clothes they owned, bought perhaps for their weddings or some other celebrations and barely altered as the fellows fattened and sagged.

The room itself was large, lined with tapestries, with deep-set fireplaces and Turkey carpets covering almost every inch of the oak floor. Probably, the fellows assembled had never been in such a place. Some of them stood by the grates, talking as their cups were refilled by pages. Others sat on stools at low tables covered in cards. The more countrified stood by themselves, appearing ill-at-ease, gazing up – at the woven images of David playing the harp and the Prodigal Son returning home – with undisguised fascination.

The harp...

I realised what was missing.

Keeping my head up, I passed through the room, making for the doorway hidden in the far-right corner. Sure enough, some men I knew were busily polishing and gathering up rebecs and lutes. That, at least, explained the silence, which pressed down on the chatter of the gathered men in the room.

Standing before them, his arms folded, was Mr Deacon, the usher, attempting to hurry them on with fluttering hand gestures. I cast one last look at the men enjoying Wolsey's hospitality, and then I raised a hand in salute as I approached the musicians.

Deacon sensed me coming and turned. His eyes widened. 'You,' he said. 'Blanke! You've returned.' He swallowed.

I didn't know how much he knew, so I simply said, 'Yes.'

'Good.' He peered over my shoulder and lowered his voice. 'His Grace is assembling his whole household in the hall. He has a most important. . . He will speak to us all.' He surveyed my livery. 'You need brushed. But you have ceased to look so bedraggled.' I looked down at myself. The upturned collar and the floating cuff seemed foolish now – an affectation. Probably they'd done more to draw attention to what I'd wished to hide than actually hidden it.

'What's it about, this . . . assembly?'

Deacon cooled. 'Do not be impertinent. You will discover it with the rest.' He clapped his hands together. Authority sat ill on his beardless face, and he turned it from me, his eyes darting about. 'Musicians, please. Would you keep His Grace waiting?' If anything, the musicians began moving more slowly. I met eyes with one and gave a little smile. 'Wipe that foolish look from your face, trumpet,' said Deacon. 'You ought to have returned sooner. It is disorderly to be . . . about the world. You are sought.'

'By His Grace?'

'Certainly not. Our most excellent master is labouring hard for the good of England. Mr Secretary Audley has expected you these past hours. Go to, now.' He dismissed me with a wave of his hand. 'Musicians, will you hurry, please.'

My heart sank.

'Wait,' I said. Deacon turned, question and irritation on his face. 'Sir Thomas More has sent up a fellow. To be lodged.

At His Grace's service. One Mr Rowlet, assistant to the late physician.'

'At His Grace's serv— At His Grace's *expense*.' Deacon looked torn. 'Where is he?' I told him. 'Blast and damn . . . as if we hadn't enough . . . I shall deal with it. Lodgings, lodgings. . .' He bustled away, barking at a young page who darted in the direction I was going, leaving the door open behind him.

I watched until Deacon had moved off towards the door to the courtyard, and then followed the page into a small hall, passing in and out of the torchlight from the bracketed sconces. Only painted statues gave me company until I reached the end, where some liveried fellows stood outside the door that gave into the presence chamber. I emerged at the top, just at the edge of the dais. Standing up there, just ahead, his arms folded as he surveyed the crowd – dozens of men of the household were already buzzing with chatter – was Audley.

I took a half-step towards the dais and he saw me. No surprise crossed his face, but his lips drew into a single, flat line. He reached up and tugged at his forked beard, looked again across the assembled household folk, and returned his attention to me. I remained where I was; I wasn't allowed on the raised dais. He appeared to realise this as I did and began marching over, finding the wooden steps and coming down to my level.

'Anthony Blanke,' he said.

As God made me.

'Anthony!' We both turned as Harry Gainsford strode up the hall. I finally remembered to remove my cap.

Audley gave his servant a hard look. I knew he disapproved

of my friendship with Harry – always had. It seemed to trouble him that a gentleman might be friendly with a trumpet. 'All is well, Mr Audley,' he offered, his voice becoming business-like. 'Save for the musicians not yet come.'

'Yes,' I said. 'Mr Deacon is fetching them.'

Audley sucked in his cheeks and then released a breath. 'You, Blanke, have been expected some time since. Byfield brought you, yes?'

'Yes, sir. Mark did.' And then, looking down at the rush matting, I said, 'I thank His Grace with all my heart. For . . . what he did for me.'

Something approaching amusement passed the secretary's face. 'His Grace,' he said, 'would not have it noised abroad that his own creature committed any such evil act. The world might see this lad you were accused of . . . and look back upon the two better men killed and . . . believe the cardinal had hired your murderous services in ridding him of his enemies.'

I saw Harry whiten. He shuffled, just a little on his soft shoes, to stand closer to me than to Audley: 'We know,' he said mildly, 'of your innocence.'

'We know nothing,' said Audley. 'Recall my teaching, young Mr Gainsford: we know nothing until we know everything.' Harry focused on the ground, looking abashed. Audley appeared to enjoy the power he had over him. With a show of magnanimity, he added, 'You learn well, Mr Gainsford. Your coming on pleases us.'

Harry looked up instantly, his neat features blossoming in a smile. He made an effort to control it. 'Thank you, sir. I thank you.' One hand clasped over his breast.

'I can explain to His Grace,' I began.

'His Grace is in no humour to see you.' Audley looked again into the hall, narrowing his eyes. 'You have brought nothing but troubles.'

'I didn't do—'

He silenced me with a frosty glare. 'The cardinal's friend, Sir Thomas, I understand, has been troubled with you.'

More than you know.

'We have just this minute had to find room,' said Harry, his voice booming with authority. 'Sir Thomas is having his friend Mr Rowlet installed in our house tonight.'

Anger passed Audley's features. 'What?' Harry moved forward and whispered in his ear: something about the page bearing the news. 'Hmph,' said the secretary. 'A fair exchange. We must do with his spy as Sir Thomas has had to do with you. And we might hope he brings less trouble.'

And so, I thought, More's pet spy would indeed continue breathing over my shoulder as I sought to find the murderer, at least until—

Audley finished my thought. 'His Grace has had you released until the opening of parliament. On Wednesday coming. If the doer and begetter of these vile deeds is not discovered before then, you shall return to await trial. For the killing of this creature in the city. No other. Do you understand? No other word shall be noised of any other . . . accident.'

I was barely listening.

What day is it, again?

'We shall find him,' said Harry. I looked up and saw a kind of pained hope on his face. 'It shall not be otherwise. As you are innocent, so shall the guilty be revealed.'

Before I could answer this, the door opened behind me

and the musicians passed in, followed by Deacon and the others in livery who'd been waiting outside.

'Go to,' said Audley. 'To your places. Mr Gainsford, you might stand by me. With the gentlemen.'

Harry reached out and clapped my shoulder, before moving off in Audley's wake.

Old bastard.

I stepped into the hall myself, passing the gentlemen, on down to the middle of the hall. Mark, to my surprise, was already there, and dogless. He must, I realised, have come in through the lesser door. 'What's it about?' he asked, hooking an arm through mine as I reached him.

'Don't know,' I said. 'Haven't you heard anything?'

'Only that Wolsey is in a temper.'

That temper squealed into the room. Evidently having given me and Mark up for the night, another pair of trumpeters had been sent up to the dais. Their treble-blasts silenced us all. I stood a little straighter. Mark released me to remove his cap, as I slid off my own. Up and down the hall, heads were bared. I looked over the bumpy landscape of thatch, curls, and smooth domes, up towards the top of the room.

From his private entrance behind the dais, Wolsey appeared in a blazon of scarlet, supported by his chamberlain. He made his way smoothly up the steps and onto his carved throne, and settled down on it, staring out at us. His ushers and the officers of his household, all in liveries, arranged themselves until the dais took on the look of a . . . *clotting pool of blood* . . . flowering rose bush.

Wolsey nodded, and his chamberlain stepped forward. The tall, nervous-looking man cried, 'Come forth, the Lord

Henry Percy.' A chorus of whispers fizzed through the room. I gaped at Mark, mouthing 'Hal Percy' silently. The chamberlain stamped his foot, making a hollow, tumbling sound which reverberated up to the carved ceiling. It brought a reluctant silence. 'Step forth, Lord Henry Percy.'

I watched – we all watched – as the tall, good-looking figure stepped from the upper part of the hall, where he'd been buried amongst the gentlemen. Those men – his friends and colleagues – shrank back from him, making a path up towards the dais. He took it. From behind, his head and cap appeared steady, his legs less so. When he got with spitting distance of the dais, he sank to his knees on the rushes and released his dirty blonde hair.

Silence ticked over.

We all waited, watched, transfixed.

So silent was it that we could hear Wolsey's long, plaintive release of breath. His lazy eye twitched and fell, before rising again.

'I marvel,' he began, 'not a little. At your peevish folly, young son of Northumberland.'

My heart leapt. Wolsey knew. He'd discovered the young nobleman's love affair with Mistress Anne Boleyn.

More of Percy's hair appeared; he was looking up at his master.

'That you, boy, should so entangle – yes, and ensure yourself – with a foolish girl yonder in the king's court. I mean,' he added, giving a brief glance into the chamber, 'Mistress Anne Boleyn.' He returned his gaze to his victim. 'Do you not consider the estate that God has called you unto in this world? After the death of your noble father, you alone are like to inherit and possess one of the wealthiest earldoms of this realm.

'Therefore, it would have been meet – yes, and convenient – to sue for the consent of your said father in that behalf. And the king's, also. You have sought by degrees to hide your actions from His Majesty.' Wolsey thumped one hand on the armrest of his throne.

He's enjoying this, I thought; that's why he's making a public display of it. There was a thing I'd heard whispered about the cardinal: that he was born of base stock and, having climbed so high, he enjoyed nothing more than mortifying those who'd been born of high degree. It was why the old blood of England hated him. He'd never attack them outright; he'd use what subtle means he had to humiliate and degrade. And he might veil his attacks in the velvet glove of King Henry, who had raised him high.

'You have scorned, we think, His Majesty's princely favour by submitting nothing to His Highness. That good prince who would not only accept thankfully your submission, but would, I assure you, provide so for your purposes that he would advance you nobly and have matched you according to your estate and honour.' Wolsey paused for breath, tutted, sighed, and went on. 'Whereby, you might have grown by such wise and honourable behaviour into His Majesty's high estimation.' He shook his head, affecting sadness.

'But no. Now behold!' He looked again into the room, though he continued addressing the unfortunate Percy, whose back had straightened. 'Behold what you have done through your wilfulness, lad. You have not only offended this household, into which we have nourished you, but offended your natural father and your most gracious sovereign lord.

You have matched yourself with one such as neither the king nor your father will be agreeable. And thereof, I put you in no doubt that I will send for your father, and at his coming he shall either break this unadvised contract or disinherit you forever. The king's own Majesty will complain to your father of you and require no less than I have said: that you will be unmatched with the Mistress Anne and put to some fitter match. What say you, boy?'

Silence again blanketed the room.

I craned my neck, trying to see, trying to hear.

Whatever Percy mumbled up there, however, was lost. Even Wolsey had to lean forward, his face puckered. And then the younger man's voice came again, clearer, fired with defiance.

'She is fit. She is my equal.'

A collective intake of breath hissed through the room.

Good, I thought – good for Percy.

I didn't know he had it in him.

My gaze shifted up to the throne. The cardinal, with something like grudging respect on his face, sank back, pulled out his silken handkerchief, and mopped his brow.

Percy went on, his voice losing its confidence. 'I – I – humbly, I – require your Grace . . . require . . . your especial favour. To entreat the king – the king's most royal Majesty, lowly – on my lowly behalf. For his princely benevolence in this . . . in the matter . . .' He was tottering. And then, suddenly, strength re-emerged, gilding his words. 'I cannot forsake or deny the lady. I shall not.'

As though we were watching the king at tennis, all our heads turned again to Wolsey. The cardinal, looking weary, shook his head a little before leaning to one side and saying something, too low to be heard, to those who stood about him. He cleared his throat, the sound splitting the hall, and croaked, 'His Majesty and I understand the matter very well. We will speak of it. In the mean season . . . in the king's name, I command that you presume not once to resort to the said Mistress Anne Boleyn's company. And this is our final will and express command.' His chin rose and with it his hand, flicking in dismissal.

Percy rose unsteadily, bowed, replaced his hat, and turned. He looked at no one, his eyes fixed on the floor as he began walking down the hall. He didn't return to his place; instead, he kept coming. As he passed me and Mark, I saw how wet his eyes and cheeks were. And then he was gone, passing the lower servants. The smooth sound of a door being opened and slammed signalled his departure.

We turned as one back to Wolsey; he'd already risen, and was back on his chamberlain's arm, being escorted to his privy lodgings. As soon as the red back had disappeared, the room exploded in noise.

Well, I thought – if there had been any gossip about my imprisonment and sudden return, it would be buried deep already.

'Christ's wounds,' said Mark, his eyes popping. 'I wasn't expecting that.'

Nor was I.

I regarded my hands for a beat, tracing the neat stitching on my cap. And then I looked up. 'He's going to call down his father,' I said. 'Wolsey is, I mean.'

'Sounds like it. High and mighty Hal gettin' his balls booted by old Northumberland. Shame we won't get to see that.'

I shook my head. 'No, but – won't the earl be here? For the parliament?' Mark only shrugged. And then it hit me. Another piece of mischief on the cardinal's part: to say nothing when old Northumberland was in town, only to let him return home and then cause him twice the inconvenience by recalling him to London.

I almost felt sorry for Hal.

And Mistress Anne Boleyn.

A foolish girl.

Although I didn't know her well, the one thing I didn't believe Mistress Anne to be was a fool.

'Wonder what he'll do?' said Mark. 'Percy. Didn't look too happy.'

I shrugged. 'What can he do?'

'And I wonder who told him?'

'Mr Deacon.'

We both whipped round. Harry had joined us and we scrambled for our caps, forgetting they were still in our hands. 'What?' I asked.

'It was Mr Deacon. It's no secret. He told the cardinal what shameful bruits he'd heard about Lord Henry and the Boleyn girl. Mr Deacon watched and came upon them saying goodbye at Richmond. With kisses,' he said, tutting and shaking his head, giving every impression of a scandalised old maid. 'It was right that His Grace reminded Lord Henry of his father. And of the king, too. To carry on so in this household. It is . . . without respect or honour.'

Jesus, Harry.

Sometimes I wondered which were his own thoughts and which had been poured into him by the old goat Audley.

'Perhaps they're in love,' I offered.

Harry made a tsking sound. '*Ubi amor, ibi dolor*, I say.' And then his face changed, softened. Redness suddenly blossomed on his cheeks. 'It . . . it is not how matters should be done.' He swallowed, looking briefly at Mark, and then at me, and then at the floor. 'I . . . have been meaning to tell you. I, too, have a sweetheart amongst the queen's ladies.' Before I could speak, he went on. 'Yet I put my suit before Mr Audley, and he put it before the cardinal, and His Grace will put it before the king, and then it might be taken to the lady's father. That is how such things might rightly proceed.'

The stuff of poetry.

My mind boiled and I felt a grin jerk at my lips. I was amused, in spite of myself – and curious about which of the sheeplike queen's ladies might have tickled Harry's fancy.

'*You* have a woman? *Sir?*' asked Mark. His tone was hard – less disbelieving than, I thought, annoyed.

Here we go.

Harry ignored him entirely. 'At any rate,' he squeaked, lifting his chin, and clearing his throat, 'the matter between Lord Henry and Mistress Anne is done now. His Grace is most troubled in his mind and has retired.'

'Away to have a drink and laugh himself to sleep,' said Mark, drawing a look I was sure was all Audley.

Harry turned his head up-hall for a moment and then looked evenly at Mark. 'Perhaps just a little French wine. To keep out the cold.' To my surprise – and more, I felt, to Mark's – he winked. 'Now. To bed. The cardinal must rise early tomorrow. Before dinner, he shall take his barge to Blackfriars and inspect the ready-making for the parliament house. Mr Audley wills that you play him out and in.' He gave a firm little nod.

'Does Mr Audley wish me to have any time to discover the murderer? Or does he wish to see me dance at the end of a rope?'

Harry gave an anguished look. '*Libertas perfundet omnia luce*, my friend.'

'I don't know what that means,' I said.

He said nothing more but gave me another clap on the shoulder before turning and moving back towards the gentlemen.

'He's an arse with ears,' said Mark. 'Audley, I mean – not him. But I don't see as why some high-born gent should get to have himself the right to court no woman when the rest of us can't. You tell me how comes that, then. It ain't – it ain't fair.'

'Yes,' I said, noncommittally. A yawn overcame me.

'Bed?'

'Bed,' I said.

Though my body demanded it, I wasn't thinking of sleep. I was thinking of where Hal Percy had gone, and where the spy Rowlet had been put, and what else Mr Deacon had been doing, and how long it was until the parliament, and pools of blood and stolen knives and expert and inexpert wounds.

19

It was a mark of York Place's greatness that even its servants – if they weren't the folk of visitors – had their own quarters. There was no bedding down in the great hall on straw or bundles of sackcloth. Instead, off the huge chamber was a whole network of small connecting dormitories.

I'd shared one with Mark and enjoyed a long void of sleep: a needed, welcomed sense of deadness, untouched by dreams good or bad.

Unfortunately, waking life soon found unpleasantness enough to compensate.

Mark's voice intruded on the pleasant nothingness.

'Get up,' he said, clearly enough this time to brook no argument.

'Mmph.'

I opened my eyes and fought the urge to pull the kersey blanket over my head and shut the world out. It was a rare thing for me to be so sluggish; I could be up at a trumpet's blast. I focused my mind on that knowledge and sat. 'I'm up.'

Mark was leaning over me, his face rosy. 'Quick. Come quick.'

My heart sank. I tried to swallow and found my mouth dry. 'Oh God. It's not – it's not another.'

'No. Not that. Come an' see. Everyone's seen it – you'll

be last. It'll be gone if you ain't quick. Don't bother about a wash. Move yer tail!' He began tugging at my blanket. 'Just throw your doublet on over your nightshirt.'

'Leave off,' I said. But I put my palms to the floor, hissing as a stray piece of rush matting jabbed at me, and fumbled around for my livery, sliding it over my head in a haze of red. I tutted as my little woollen nightcap slid off and lost itself down my back, hiding there until I could tug it out and toss it down. Mark had been as good as his word at Richmond; all my things, such as they were, had been brought over with his and unpacked. I'd barely rolled up my hose and wrestled on my shoes – still mucky – when he was at me again, grabbing and pulling.

'Come *on*, man. And watch yer face don't trip you. Moody.' *What's the hurry?*

He dragged me out of the side room and into the great hall, where already people were up and about. Men stood everywhere, grouped together, their heads bent. Rather than the usual morning song and chatter, everything was whispered. The occasional laugh was quickly stifled.

The ancient great hall of York Place lay at a right angle to the presence chamber in which Percy had been dressed down, and its main doorway led to another small, interior courtyard. It was to this that Mark pulled me. Snatches of conversation met me as we strode through a chamber barely punctured by light, blocked as it was by the high, leaded windows.

'I saw it.'

'Chalk.'

'Did any of those come into the house see it?'

'What did the cardinal *say*, though?'

It?

I shook my head to clear away the wool as we approached the great double doors. Knots of lower servants were grouped by them. Occasionally, a fellow would break off and scamper up-hall, presumably to pass on anything he'd heard being said outside.

Mark reached them before me and beat on one. It opened a crack and he whispered something out of it, before turning and gesturing to me. The door opened farther, and silence fell behind me, making me turn. Faces – lowers, middles, and gentlemen – made great clusters of white buds, each one turned towards the shaft of sunlight spilling in.

'Come on,' said Mark.

I did as he bid, stepping out onto the paving stones of the little courtyard and immediately lifting a hand to shade myself against the onslaught of morning light. I blinked stupidly, looking around at the assembled officials: Deacon and Cavendish stood with some other ushers, the whole lot with their heads bowed. Beyond them, against the wall of the chapel on the far side, men stood with buckets and washcloths at their feet.

A thud announced the door closing behind me.

'Look round,' whispered Mark, close by my ear.

I did.

And first confusion, and then a wave of laughter overcame me.

On the huge doors to the great hall had been scrawled what looked like a poorly rendered drawing, in white chalk, of a phallus, standing tall, with a cardinal's hat hovering over its tip. Sprouting hairs had even been added to the cods at its base. My laughter – stupid, unbidden, and dangerous – died in my throat. Underneath the drawing was something else

PRYDE HAS MAYDE HIM

YE DEVIL TAYKE HIM

I swallowed, managing it this time, as I stared.

'You find matter fit to amuse you?' snapped Deacon, making me jump.

I wheeled. 'No, sir. No.'

'It is frightful. Frightful. Disorderly. This whole house is fallen ill with slack disorder.' He seemed more nervous than outraged. 'Word has been sent up to His most princely and benevolent Grace. But so many have seen it.' He wrung his hands. 'And with these late . . . all these affronts. It must be that. . . You are engaged in the matter. You have been . . . prying into it all.' He looked at me with vaguely accusing eyes. Deacon, I knew well enough, had been there when both Cosyn and Mordaunt had been found. He turned his gaze on Mark.

Stepping between them, I said, 'Mark knows all too.'

Deacon looked doubtful, gnawing on his lip and throwing glances up at the doors. 'We've had the servants draw water . . . we didn't know . . . if this was some kind of message.'

Well, it is clearly that.

Another tattoo was beat on the door. Deacon pushed past us, opening it again. This time Harry emerged, pulling it closed behind him. He gave me and Mark a curt nod before turning. His face coloured instantly. 'Mr Audley – His Grace – says wash this filth clean away. Immediately.'

'Yes.' Deacon turned and began shouting across the yard. 'Be about your labours, men. Every filthy word – every filthy – all of it – must be gone. Forthwith.'

Mark, Harry and I all stood off to the side as the grunting, smirking servants began hauling their slopping buckets across the paving stones. We watched in silence as they worked, the ushers urging them on with, 'Up there;' 'Reach the . . . tip;' 'You there – you've left a hair.'

'Disgusting,' was Harry's assessment.

'I dunno,' said Mark. 'Looks well done.' He received only a look of rebuke. 'What do you say, Anthony?' he asked mildly. 'Has our friend turned painter?'

I considered this. 'No. Probably not. A murderer doesn't stoop to writing messages in chalk. To insulting . . . to this.'

Harry raised an eyebrow at me. 'That is what Mr Audley said when the news was brought.'

That didn't surprise me. Audley was an unpleasant creature, but he wasn't a fool. 'The ushers – Deacon – seem to think I should care.' Because, I added silently, they were certainly fools.

'His Grace wishes the vile slanderer found,' said Harry. His brow wrinkled. 'Though – when I came from Mr Audley and the cardinal – His Grace seemed more . . . I almost thought . . . more amused than angry. Until he heard the words written. They troubled him.'

'Left him unquiet in his mind?' I asked.

'I beg your pardon?'

'Nothing. Harry – is Hal Percy returned? Did he sleep in the upper chambers last night?'

'Lord Henry? Why – yes. Yes, I saw him this morning. Early.'

I nodded. 'Would you do me a favour? Have him attend upon the cardinal.'

'But he is. I saw him go up to the secret lodgings. He aids the cupbearer.'

'Good. Come.'

The three of us hopped over the pooling slosh of water whilst one of the servants opened the sodden doors, just wide enough for us to pass through. Again, heads turned. Some questions flew our way; Mark brushed them off with banter and winks.

Thanks to Harry's friends amongst the gentlemen, we found Hal Percy's dormitory room easily enough. It was a duplicate of mine and Mark's: a small cell-like closet without a door, clutched against the side of the great hall. The only difference was that Percy had his to himself.

I stepped inside.

'You cannot,' said Harry. 'It is dishonourable to intrude upon a man's private space. We must wait until he returns. I shall send for him.'

'Have a care,' said Mark, crossing his arms. 'Ain't no point in searchin' if we tell him we're searchin', is there? He won't hardly like that, if he's somethin' to hide.'

Harry gibed, crossing his own arms, working his lips, but he said no more.

Nor did I.

I stepped lightly into the closet and looked down. Rather than a kersey blanket, Percy had been provided with a good woollen, laid out over a featherbed. His possessions were piled neatly beside it: a suit of blue velvet in which I'd never seen him, a feathered hat, leather outdoor boots for riding. I bent over and began lifting them and placing them on the empty floorboards. Underneath the clothes was a stack of papers. These I lifted. There was no writing, but several drawings – not bad, but not great – in the old style, mostly women in profile or three-quarter faces. They'd been done in charcoal. I touched one and some blackness came away on my finger. With a start, I realised that the same woman had been drawn, over and over: a woman made and remade, more of straight lines and angles than flourishing sweeps and curves. As I turned the pages, I saw that some were simply tilted eyes, floating on the yellowish paper.

'Told you,' said Mark. 'Heard he sits of an evening drawing eyes. Weird.'

These eyes, however, I vaguely recognised. He'd overdone it a little, but the upwards tilt, the deep black of the pupils and irises, the little flicks of charcoal to mark out lashes.

The Boleyn girl.

Mistress Anne Boleyn.

I felt dirty, looking in on his drawings.

Did Wolsey feel even a little of this, in ordering him to break with her?

I set the drawings down where I'd found them, wiping my blackened finger on my doublet. I wanted to stain the badge a little, to cast a little dirt back on the cardinal.

'Here,' said Mark. 'Look at these boots. Real leather. Like what you'd—'

I heard the hollow thud and turned, frowning.

'What's this?' asked Mark. He stooped, stumbling after

something as it rolled away on the floor. Whatever it was, it hit the featherbed. Mark rose, holding it up between his fingers as he twisted to us.

'By St George,' breathed Harry.

I looked at it without surprise. A small end of chalk. It was the kind artisans used in marking out their designs. The stuff was everywhere in Wolsey's houses, so wild was he about building and altering and improving.

'Looks well used,' I said, looking out into the hall. No one was looking in at us. Everyone, it seemed, was still interested in the door to the courtyard.

'I shall tell Mr Audley. He shall inform His Grace at once. And Lord Henry – a son of the ancient blood of this realm. To stoop – to – I cannot. . .'

'Then don't,' I said. 'Say nothing.' I reached out and took the chalk from Mark, who seemed eager to be rid of it. 'I'll throw it in the river.'

'But—'

'Leave it, Harry. I knew – I thought – we'd find it.'

Mark, glancing out into the hall himself, said, 'Then why seek it out?'

I closed my palm over the thing. It began to warm; it was like clutching a cool pebble. 'Because. . .' I took a breath, shuffling my thoughts. 'I might tell the cardinal myself. Find a means of telling him. Softly. If he's truly not . . . in a temper.' It was easy enough to read Wolsey, I thought, if you knew what to look for. The crude drawing, I guessed, was Percy's own; the words, I suspected, had long since been put in his mind by his young lady.

'But why?' Mark persisted. 'You don't think Percy – the other stuff?' He blanched. I could almost see him recalling the dead woman, lying in her own blood on the bare floor of her master's house.

'No. Or . . . no, I thought it possible. I did. But this,' I said, holding up my fist with its hidden chalk, 'this I think proves otherwise.' I wasn't making myself clear; I could see that on Mark's baffled face and Harry's indignant one. 'A child might have done this.'

'A wicked and ill-trained child,' sniffed Harry. 'It is a short step from foul slander to fouler murder.'

'In this matter, that would be a step backwards. This – it was the act of a child – a wounded one. Mindless, rage fuelled. This is not of the same – the same character – as the deeds that've passed.' I hesitated for a beat and then said, 'The murders. No sudden act of anger or defiance moved that hand. They were – there was a design to them. A plan.'

'You keep speakin' of design,' said Mark, a little huffily. 'Murder's murder.'

'And misbehaviour is misbehaviour. Without honour or grace,' put in Harry. His chin was in the air. 'I feel strongly that I ought to inform Mr Audley.'

'Please, Harry,' I said, with a confidence I didn't feel. 'I'll be on the barge with the cardinal. Soon. So will Mark. I'll . . . if I can, I'll speak with him.'

'On your honour?'

I put one hand on my heart. 'Satisfied?'

'Yes,' he said, not looking it. And then, more convincingly, 'Yes. If I have your word.' He had the wit not to add 'as a gentleman'. 'But I shall say no civil word to Lord Henry until he has made his apology – his peace – with His Grace. In full submission. And that is my final word on the matter.'

'Let's get out of here,' said Mark, eyeing the entrance to

the hall again. 'Before folk notice. Reckon he'll notice 'is chalk's been lifted, though, daft bugger. Fancy thinking he'd get away with that.'

Mark stepped out first, with me behind him. 'Men like him,' I said, low enough for Harry not to hear, 'get away with everything.' More loudly, I said, 'Come – we have to be ready for – where was it?'

'Blackfriars,' said Harry.

The name, for various reasons, struck me with foreboding.

* * *

We led the small procession, Mark and I, along the covered water gallery. I had no wish to be part of it. I wished instead to be somewhere closeted, thinking, or out somewhere, searching. In truth, I had no idea what to think about anything – yet I knew that there was a solution to all that had been happening, and it cried out for time and thought.

I've done this before and successfully.

That thought repeated in my head, with mocking insistence.

Yes, I'd discovered unpleasant truths before. I'd even just done it, easily enough, with the obvious truth of Percy.

But I couldn't recall – I couldn't rightly understand *how* I'd done it, beyond having enough information to fill in gaps.

Sight.

It was from seeing things – that's what had led me to the truth in the past, I felt sure. Seeing things and recognising them from having seen them before, or things like them.

Knives glinted in my mind.

Blood flowed from wounds.

Things were broken and unbroken.

Shadows flitted in and out of palaces, sometimes visible, sometimes not.

None of them fit together; nothing seemed to make up a whole, clear image. Not this time. Not yet.

A person was at work here, a – *rich stranger* – man.

He was working according to some design, or had been, and proceeded along other lines when thwarted. But a man he still was, and men made errors – they said things they shouldn't or left things they shouldn't or took things they shouldn't.

The Thames sparkled ahead of us, greeting us with its warm breath. The smell was quite pleasant this far upriver – it was reedy, awash with freshness. Mark and I paused, just before the barge, under the high, angled roof with its hanging banners. There was no need for us to blow our trumpets; that could wait until we were afloat, passing each great house or dwelling.

We set them down on the marble and put our backs to the columns that lined the water gallery, making way for the crew of liveried rowers. In solemn silence, they began unlacing the edges of the canvas cover that protected their part of the barge.

'This one's loose,' cried one of them. 'Lazy. . .'

I looked at Mark, directly across from me.

Though Marchpane wasn't with us, I remembered him grizzling at the big boat.

'Here,' shouted a rower. 'Something!'

He fell backwards into the gallery.

The others began muttering. They left off their own sections and made their way.

I felt no shock – no sense of surprise even – when the cry went up.

'It's a man! He's – saints preserve us – I think he's dead!'

20

We weren't a large procession; this wasn't the journey to the formal opening of the parliament. I pushed past the rowers, my heartbeat barely even speeding. The men seemed keen enough to press back, against the other side of the gallery.

The beige canvas had been thrown back, revealing a portion of the straight, polished rowers' benches.

There, flat on his back on top of a pair of sweeps, lay a figure in white, with a black cope over his shoulders.

Friar, I thought instantly.

A Blackfriar.

Black cope, as I recall. Might have been a clerk, of course, or a secretary. Was he here that last night?

The fellows were well known about the city – a well-loved and respected clutch of men. This one was old, his face a map of deep wrinkles, giving him the look of a blanched nut. Only a few strands of silvery white clung about his head. He had been staring up at the canvas with milky blue eyes. They now stared sightlessly at the sky.

I could see, too, what had killed him. The crisp linen of his gown had a red flower about the heart.

The boy was killed with expert cunning. Not animal savagery. A neat blow through the heart.

The same hand, it seemed, had been at work again.

But how?

When?

Forcing myself, I reached down and touched the cold skin, finding a hand and lifting it. Still soft enough, the stiffness not quite taking hold yet. I knew even from my father's death that that came a few hours after death; it was why carts of the dead during times of sickness always appeared to be loaded on the bottom with cordwood – the poor souls who had succumbed first and been left for a while whilst more were stacked on top of them.

Murdered in the night.

'I might not say this enough,' said Mark, making me start and drop the dead man's raised arm, 'but boy – you're the angel of death. Jesus, but another old one.'

Before I could answer, a voice cut over us both. It was Deacon. 'Make way! Make way for His Grace, the lord chancellor of England!'

Mark's eyes widened. 'Wolsey!'

I'd no time to think. I threw myself away from the sight on the benches and turned, in time to see the cardinal making his stately way down the water gallery, Deacon before him and Audley, a casket in his hands, at his back.

'Stop, Your Grace,' I said, yanking off my cap.

'Stand aside, trumpet,' barked Deacon, his voice full of affront. 'How dare you.'

I ignored him, looking up at the cardinal. His face was still grey, but he'd been made especially resplendent: over his scarlet and white robes hung his gold chain of office. He put out a hand and placed it on the shorter Deacon's shoulder, gently pushing him aside before stepping towards me in a cloud of strong, sweet-smelling musk.

'Anthony?' He looked at me and then around at the rowers, who all began speaking at once. 'Silence,' he boomed, and got it. 'What is this? Why are we paused?'

I swallowed. 'Your Grace, there's . . .' I lowered my voice. 'Another one. In the barge. In your barge, laid out.'

To his credit, he understood immediately. With barely a twitch of his eyelid, he turned and whispered to Audley. Loudly, he barked, 'Seal the gallery. Rowers, we shall have need of you. Go to – prevent access. Mr Deacon, instruct them.' They did, nodding as one and fleeing back towards the gatehouse ahead of the usher. Wolsey paused, looking again at Audley. 'Some accident, we perceive. Some mischance. Seal the gallery. Yes. Yes, it must be sealed.'

He stepped past me and moved towards the exposed part of the boat, peering down between the columns himself. I watched his profile as his mouth worked silently. When he turned again, his face – lined, old though it was – had the look of a child, lost and surprised.

'A Blackfriar,' he said. 'Our destination. Why should . . .' He looked again at the body and seemed to remain looking a while. Birdsong rose up. It was cut off by angered squawks; big gulls must have frightened off the littler birds. 'Mr Audley,' he gasped.

The secretary flew past me, his casket still clutched demurely before him. Wolsey didn't bother to lower his voice. 'We know him. This old friar. Gervaise . . . something. Yes. This wandering friar.' I wasn't surprised by what he breathed next. 'He has spoken against us, in the past, this old wretch.'

Back, I thought, to the pattern, the design. Murdering the cardinal's enemies.

Wolsey's mild gaze fell upon me. 'You. We have not yet discussed . . . your late efforts. Yes. We must speak. But first – this—'

'Accident,' said Audley, without a pause. 'An unfortunate accident. I perceive, sir, that the fellow came perhaps to welcome you and act as a guide. He must have thought to inspect the barge and fallen . . . struck himself on something. Pure mischance.'

'Yes,' said Wolsey, though I could see the doubt on his face. 'Unlikely, perhaps. It might hold. Yes.' He began shaking his head, looking over the barge. I followed his gaze, over the rippling water. A few wherries were making their way to and fro on the far side, skirting the morning haze around Lambeth Marsh. 'I scarce know what to make of such unlikely things. Save that . . . in these evil days, what seems unlikeliest soonest comes to pass.'

'Your Grace,' I said, giving Mark a glance first, 'the man who did this. It was the same who killed the lad in London. I'm sure of it. As expert a blow.' I willed him to look at me, but he remained staring out across the Thames. 'I thank Your Grace for seeing my innocence.'

'Innocence?' He finally turned. 'Of course you are innocent. Yet you have not proven it, I regret. Our parliament must open in two days. The eyes of the world are upon us. And still, I find these horrors washed up on our doorstep. Upon our threshold. You have brought me no name. No name of any French-paid agent intent on making an evil spectacle.'

I fought for words: a whole flurry of them jostled for attention. No; I haven't; the old woman; a knife; falseness. But I couldn't get past what he'd said.

Two days.

A commotion somewhere behind us turned his gaze from me and over my shoulder. 'What the devil now?'

I turned too, still squeezing my cap.

Wolsey hissed. 'That wretched spy. See to him. Keep him from us. From this sight.'

I didn't know whether he meant me, Audley, or Mark, and he didn't clarify. As a result, we all began pounding our way along the marble, towards the phalanx of crimson backs which had formed a line of defence against any who might try and get a look at what lay in the barge.

'Mr Rowlet,' said Audley, taking charge, speaking over Deacon. I could see the late physician's assistant, More's spy, peeping over the ridge of two rowers' shoulders – up on his tiptoes, I thought. 'We have been kind enough to lodge you. Is there something wrong with your chamber?'

'What has occurred?' he barked. 'I was watching the cardinal's progress from my window. Something is amiss, I perceive plainly.'

'A trifling accident. There is no need to concern yourself. Be about your day.' Audley gave him a short bow and made to turn away.

Rowlet's ginger beard made an appearance, as he shifted until he stood between two shorter rowers. 'Accident,' he said, his small eyes turning to slits. There was no wildness about him, no terror – just a barely-contained excitement. 'An accident? Tell me, Mr Audley – and let us not speak over shoulders, like beasts – tell me: is this another of these foul crimes? As my master was murdered, and Mr Cosyn – this boy in the city – and . . . and . . . a poor serving woman was slain last night. The Moor boy knew of it. She was Mr

Cosyn's servant. Tell me – has the same dark hand moved again this morning?'

Audley simply stared at him, impassive. I knew the gaze. It could probably last for hours.

Rowlet broke it, and for the first time appeared to see me. 'Yes, I think by your countenance there has been another. Straight murder.' His voice teetered on the edge of outright accusation. 'Who is it, sir? Who has met unnatural death in your household now?' Still Audley said nothing. But I saw one dark-clad shoulder twitch. Rowlet went on, quite calmly. 'I have made me a study of all that is passing, you might tell His Grace. It is what my friend Dr Mordaunt would have wished of me. With Sir Thomas's gracious leave, I have made me a study. And I have concluded, sir, that there must be some. . .' His eyes lingered on me. 'Some black devilry at work. Foul practises of sorcery and murder. I would speak with the cardinal's trumpet there, forthwith. If there is some other evil act done. . . The boy is engaged in this matter and has thus far not proven himself helpful to my master. The thing Sir Thomas might find strange. I would speak with him now, if it please you.'

'It does not,' said Audley. He moved to stand more firmly before me and Mark. 'Perhaps tomorrow, but for the nonce, it does not.'

'It does me,' I said.

Audley's back stiffened and he turned, one eye glaring at me, his profile sharp. 'Do you scorn my authority, boy? I said you might speak with him tomorrow – and have a care what you say when you do.'

I ignored this and spoke loudly over his other shoulder. I'd be damned if I'd have the secretary make me look guilty in the face of accusations. 'I'll be a moment, only,' I said to Mark. 'Just a moment.'

And I'll have all kind of cares.

Reaching the row of men blocking Rowlet's passage, I nodded to be let through. Arms were unlocked and I stepped forward, jerking my head towards the gatehouse. As I entered it, he followed. 'A moment,' I said to the porter – a fellow I felt I was coming to know well. He gave us both long looks, but he didn't leave. Instead, he turned his back to us and made a show of looking back out the open window from which he usually held court, his hands clasped behind his back.

The little gatehouse was a cosy place, with a board, a stool, and, in the corner, a battered-looking and well used straw pallet. After a moment's hesitation, I flopped down on the stool, leaving Rowlet to stand appraising me. 'Well?' I asked.

Rowlet took a breath before answering, as though weighing his words, weighing the potential force of accusations. At length, he raised his hands to his neatly brushed doublet and smoothed it down, and said, 'I see that you are a young man of wit. I saw you and your fellow outwit those base, foul ruffians in the city.'

'You followed us,' I said evenly.

'Just so. I do not deny it. Yet you handled those creatures with wit, as I say.'

'Yet not their friend,' I said. 'Someone else got him.'

Rowlet lifted a hand and slid off his cap, his gaze falling to the floor. 'So it would seem.'

'So it was,' I said. 'I have no doubt the – the creature – behind this evil – he lured that lad up to meet me. Probably with a promise of money.' A memory twitched – something about Rob having been offered the chance to settle a reckoning. 'Or a promise that he might have the chance to revenge himself on me for insulting him.'

Rowlet's brow wrinkled. 'You have some proofs of this?'

'. . .No.'

'I see.' He cleared his throat, looking now at the straight back of the porter, who had seemed almost to cease breathing and stood statue-like. 'I am not . . . of the nature of one of your household's flatterers. I speak as I find. Surely, young man, you perceive that this – this. . .' He gestured towards the window beyond the porter. Diffuse sounds of the men blocking the way to the water drifted in. '. . . is wrong? It is corrupted. Your master is a Churchman, a priest. He has no business – no right – to flout the path of justice.'

I shifted, my hose itching me and bunching. 'He is lord chancellor.'

'He has no right to cloak and bury the deaths of my friends. Honest men.' At this, I looked up and saw plain anguish on his face. 'That. . .' His voice cracked. 'That poor old serving woman. Whatever – whoever – you have found lying out there this morning. He has no right.'

There was simple honesty in the fellow's words. I'd no answer to them. In a whisper, I asked, 'What do you want?'

Rowlet took another breath. 'I say only that two straight minds are better than one. We are both seeking the same thing. Truth. Pure truth. We might better compare our suspicions and see if they make a fair – forgive me – if they make a whole picture of these cruel events. You spoke of some wicked design. I've been thinking on that since. As I said, I have made me a study. I have begun writing down matter, you understand, to despatch to Sir Thomas. Join me, please, and let us see what we see. Together. It is the only good way.' His voice had taken on a lulling quality, had grown soft and persuasive. And there was reason in enough in his argument. 'And that alone, I think, shall prove beyond any doubt your innocence in—'

Voices rose outside the gatehouse, breaking the spell. Deacon's was chief amongst them – he must have come looking for me. 'I – I have to go,' I said. 'I. . .'

'Later, then.'

'I . . . perhaps I'll come to you on the morrow. When today's business is done. *Perhaps.*' The creeping spy, I thought, might be useful – he might have discovered things I hadn't. But I doubted very much that Wolsey would wish me to involve an outsider, someone not of the household, in affairs that touched him so closely. That was the problem, really – my work for Wolsey was unofficial – its scope and limits were never defined. His words came back to me.

Discover, yes. Go where you must.

You know how to keep matters close.

I did, but I didn't know when I should and when I shouldn't.

Deacon passed into the doorway, darkening the gatehouse. 'The trumpet,' he announced, 'is commanded to attend His Grace at the Blackfriars. Good day, Mr Rowlet.'

'But I can see—'

'His most illustrious Grace, my very good lord, has spoken, sir.'

Rowlet appeared to know when he was beaten. He gave me one last look – a look of entreaty written into his little features – and then turned one of dislike to the usher. Raising his chin, he stepped back, replaced his hat and set it in place, and then, as though he couldn't resist a parting shot, he said, 'I shall write Sir Thomas.'

You do that, I thought. Already, I could see the movement of his pen, scratching across the page: 'The trumpet resists me, protected by his master. I perceive the cardinal seeks to bury a hidden crime on his barge, on the said trumpet's return.'

Thank God that More had had the sense to have seen that Mark and I were guiltless in the death of Mistress Cotes.

I returned in Deacon's wake, and once again passed through the now depleted ranks of the pale-faced rowers. Mark greeted me with a relieved nod but said nothing. Two of the men, I saw, already had lengths of canvas in their arms. I watched as Audley, his head bent, directed them in low tones back towards the barge. They marched towards it, and set about securing the body in the canvas. The others he dismissed, sending them with Deacon to see to the uncovering and readying of the boat. Everything, it seemed, was to be controlled, to continue as though another old enemy of the cardinal hadn't just been uncovered, dead.

Whilst the grim work was undertaken, I turned and looked eastward, between the columns. The honey-coloured walls of the palace appeared to rise straight from the river, separated from the water only by wooden pilings built on the riverbank. Windows marched off in orderly rows. One little square of glass, I guessed, would have belonged to the lodging given to More's red-bearded spy. My eyes followed the planks. They met us – they met the water gallery. I could have climbed over the low gilt railing between the columns with ease and stepped down, clambering right along the outer wall of York Place.

I didn't, though. I turned and said to Mark, 'Come.'

He didn't protest, casting only a look down the gallery. The two unfortunate rowers tasked with wrapping – concealing – the old friar's body were already at work; I could just about see their bent backs. Wolsey had already climbed aboard – I could see the domed tip of his red hat hovering over the back of his chair.

As though nothing was happening.

Shivering, I led Mark a few steps along the gallery, to where the gatehouse sat. The porter was already leaning out of his window, his face stricken. Thankfully it was the same man who'd been present the previous night. 'Tell me, do you recall us? From last night – when we came in? We brought a dog. A man was with us – we left him writing letters for despatch.'

'What?' He finally looked at me properly. He was a youngish man, making an effort at a moustache, which was still more wish than fulfilled. 'Yes, lad.' He nodded at Mark too. 'Yes.'

'Did anyone pass through this way after us?'

'No.' He straightened, realising the importance of my questions. 'No, lads. You were the last of the evening.'

'You didn't see a friar approach?'

'A friar – it's a friar down there, is it? I heard yonder red-bearded fellow cry murder.'

'Did you see a friar?' I asked again, more firmly.

'No. Nothing like that. Mass of men coming in by water yesterday. When the sun was up. Early. Then no one until you lads and yonder red-beard. And no one out after you came in.' He put out his chest. 'The door was chained. In these late days, Mr Audley has commanded a strong chain laid against the gate at night, so . . .' His voice became a fair approximation of Audley's cold, flat one: 'No man not well known may leave or enter.' He dropped the impersonation. 'Same at all gates. And no man did leave or enter in the night.'

I considered this. And I didn't like it.

Mark asked, 'When was the boat covered?'

'The barge? After it was washed clean, inside and out – yesterday. Daytime. Before you lads came. Servants passed in and out then, ushered, all proper. Like I said.' The porter closed his mouth with a show of finality.

'Thank you,' I said. I took Mark's arm and began turning him back down the gallery. I paused, glancing back. 'And you saw nothing in the night?'

'I sleep here,' said the porter. 'I lock the gate and sleep. Folk can knock if they want in or out. Only officers have keys of their own.' I stared at him a moment, my mind turning, but said nothing. After a nod of thanks, I propelled Mark back along the marble path.

As we reached the back of the barge, he said, 'When the sun was up.' I looked at him, impressed.

'You marked that too?'

He shrugged. 'I ain't no idiot. But it don't make no sense.'

He was right. We had seen Mistress Cotes' murder the night before, even if we hadn't seen who did it. It had been late, darkness falling. There was no way that a member of the household could have killed her and then returned to the palace in the daylight – he would have to have worked some dark magic with time.

I thought again of the dog and its growl at the barge – a common enough thing now looked like it signified.

Was the old man under there, dead, when we passed? His

soft body didn't suggest that. Was he under there hiding, waiting to meet someone – planning, even, to leap out and surprise the cardinal this morning?

It doesn't make sense – it's impossible.

How, then, did his killer know he would be there – at such a time, in such a place; and how did he reach him there to do murder?

About all I could imagine now was that the murderer wasn't one of the household: that he'd been in London when we were, drawn this old friar – whoever he was – to the palace by river, slain him in the darkness, hidden him, and then rowed off, never even attempting to rouse the porter and enter York Place proper.

Or . . .

I shook my head. If the murderer was some unknown person from without, I was lost. London – the world – were big places. I'd no hope of finding the creature.

'Trumpets,' squealed down the gallery. Mark and I both turned at Deacon's intrusion. He was aboard the barge, crying out for us. We removed our hats as the small, covered form of the friar was carried past us by the stony-faced pair of rowers, retrieved our trumpets from the floor, and clambered up and over the sides of the barge.

'You, white trumpet – be seated at the front.' Mark gave me a look before picking his way along the flat bottom, between the double row of benches, most of which were already tenanted. 'You – His Grace would speak with you.'

I said nothing as I made my way towards the glass enclosure. Wolsey seemed almost carved of painted stone, his hands gripping the armrests. Only his eyes moved, following me as I approached him. On a cushioned bench at his side,

Audley had already taken his place; his little casket was open now, and papers were stacked beside him.

I bowed before stepping onto the oak floor rear of the barge. The air warmed instantly from the heat trapped by the glass roof and sides. 'Your Grace,' I said, gripping my trumpet with one hand and removing my cap with the other.

'You will sail with us,' he said.

As though he commanded the tides, the pair of rowers who had carried away the body hopped over the side, making the boat rock gently. They must, I realised, have dumped the corpse with the porter to be stored until . . . I didn't know what.

'Be seated,' said Wolsey. I sat, on a bench opposite Audley, so that we glared at one another almost across the cardinal's knees. As if for protection, I placed my trumpet between my own. 'You will give me a fair report of all that has passed since last we spoke. Omit nothing.'

Amidst the cries and grunts of the oarsmen casting off, I began to unfold my tale, beginning with my visit to More's house, my being set to take the blame for another murder and later discovery of Mistress Cotes, and ending with the discovery of this latest – this stranger. The air warmed still further with it.

Wolsey, as was his custom, didn't interrupt. Instead, he wore that strange, detached air, which I'd never seen before, as though everything that had happened – was happening – was too strange to be true. Audley, however, used his casket as a table and, as More had done, wrote things down, giving the occasional sharp-eyed look up as I spoke.

'We last heard from our good friend Sir Thomas,' said Wolsey when I'd run dry, 'this morning. A letter written by his own hand last night. He vouchsafed that he was . . . satisfied . . .' he frowned, as if recalling, 'that there lies sufficient reason to doubt Anthony Blanke's guilt in the deaths of the said Robert, apprentice, and Elizabeth Cotes, late servant of the late Lancelot Cosyn. Yes. Of the others, he wrote the law had made no study and thus, as far as the laws of England allow, nothing can be said.' He made a snorting sound. 'Lawyer's speech.'

'As I said, Your Grace,' I chanced, 'this creature has attempted to . . . uh . . . make me guilty.'

'Yet it is the others which trouble me. A prentice churl and an old wench – no man cares.' I felt a chill as he spoke. 'Sir Thomas has not yet heard that, on your return – that this fresh outrage has been arranged. I do not doubt that the wretched spy Rowlet shall inform him.'

I have made me a study.

'I shall – perhaps I shall speak with Rowlet on the morrow, as Mr Audley said. See if he has discovered anything – of those in the city or in your household.' I had nothing else. The man might have turned something up and I might well have to try and make use of him. An idea caught fire. 'He's angry,' I said, abruptly.

Wolsey looked down sharply. 'Mr Rowlet? Good Sir Thomas?'

'No – no – the murderer.' The idea seemed clear enough in my head, but words again eluded its expression. 'Cosyn and Mordaunt,' I began.

'Mr Cosyn and Dr Mordaunt,' cut in Audley.

Wolsey silenced him with a hand, and I went on. 'They were murdered and the guilt to be laid at your door, sir. But it didn't happen, not easily. All that happened was Sir Thomas was asked to investigate. The murderer – he was angry. He knew I was charged with seeking him. I don't know how,' I said quickly. 'And so he decided to murder the prentice and have me take the blame. It's like a design – there was a first design, and then alterations to it, as matters went on.' I glanced across at Audley. 'You said yourself, sir – the world would say His Grace had hired' – *a stranger* – 'me to rid him of his enemies. But the cardinal got me out. And so. . .' My theory began to fall apart. He couldn't have known where I'd go. I rushed on anyway. 'He killed Mistress Cotes. And when that didn't work – Sir Thomas, he followed and he knew Mark and I were innocent – when that didn't work, he killed this old man. On my return. To make me appear guilty again, probably.'

'You speak,' said Audley, his tone dry, 'more of a demon than of a man. A creature who knows things he shouldn't. Who can fly from place to place, unseen.'

I said nothing. He was right. The fellow had shown himself only once, to the dead Rob. The other deaths . . . the other deaths seemed different, somehow. Except this latest – this swiftly forgotten old man.

But what did that mean?

'Only the prentice and this friar were killed in the same manner,' I said.

'You think this signifies?' asked Wolsey.

Again, I lapsed into silence. I didn't know. There was too much I didn't know.

'I fear,' said Audley, plainly not fearing it at all, 'that you must face the law for the lad's death if no other. If you cannot make some discovery before Wednesday.'

I looked up at Wolsey. There was no expression on his pale

face. Staring ahead, he said only, 'It will go hard for you and unjustly. But we can see no remedy for it, save discovering the truth of these cruel events.'

I turned to stare out past Audley. We were passing the walls of Salisbury Court. Ahead, the brighter, steep walls of Bridewell Palace rose, like York Place, straight from the water's edge.

'Blackfriars, ho!' drifted into the enclosure. One of the rowers. It was followed by the distant hoot of Mark's trumpet.

I remembered suddenly my promise to Harry. I cleared my throat. 'The outrage this morning – early, I mean – the writing on Your Grace's door. I looked at it – for the culprit.' I tried to find fit words.

'That,' sniffed Wolsey. 'Young Percy, was it?'

I gaped up at him. 'Yes, sir.'

'We thought so. Young pup. He'll find less reason to laugh when I pull his father down from the north again.' His face darkened. 'You know what His Majesty says? Only poor men may marry where their hearts lie. And they have no knowledge – and no interest in – love. "What have *they* read of it?" he asked me once.' I said nothing. He'd known – probably from the first word of the naughty scrawl being brought to him. '*Young* folk. I am eternally beset by the cares and wiles of *young* folk. They think they are their own masters in these times. They think they are the first to discover that their hearts beat to each other's tunes.' He exhaled. 'The Boleyn wench can go home – and think on her lightness – there. Shameful behaviour. Her father's wings might be clipped too; yes, and rightly.' I pictured the lady, her eyes flashing, when she learned of this. Wolsey would have ears redder than his robes. 'A simple case,' he said. 'A small matter compared to what has come. You do not think that Percy could have . . .'

'No,' I said. 'Definitely not.'

'Yes. But we are glad to see that your mind still turns on discoveries.' He took a deep breath. 'Blackfriars,' he echoed. A little jarring of the barge as we passed over the Fleet's outflow lent emphasis. He gave a small cough and repeated the word. Then he looked down at me again. 'It was our intent only to speak with you today and then release you to be about your own travails. We have not forced you still to come, even after this . . . late discovery . . . for vain pomp. The old man – the friar – he was of this order.' He looked at Audley, who nodded. 'You might discover what you can of him – how he came to be in my barge, slain, in the night. And work with haste, lad. I fear me, if you speak true, that these vile acts have been the beginning only, to whatever this design you speak of is. You understand, there is no more time. This is your last chance to make some discovery. Do what you must. When you leave this barge, your time is your own. Believe me . . . I would not stick to see you plain cleared and removed for a space from the country. But . . . I fear . . . I can do no more to protect you once the eyes of the world are upon us.'

I bowed my head, my mind already racing forward and through the friary, whilst Wolsey began to shift easily into discussion with Audley of those parliament men he had bought ('Your good kinsman Thomas Audley is loyal.') and must buy ('The moneylender Cromwell seeks him a place higher than old Dorset's house – Italian-tongued fellow, as we understand – mark him. . .').

I didn't listen. Hearing from Wolsey that there was the possibility of a trial, a return to gaol, hitherto a dark fantasy which could be dismissed, hardened it into reality.

Find him or face it.

21

I was no stranger to priories. They dotted London – religious houses that sent their missionary brothers out into the world to tend to the spiritual needs of the city or kept their fellows cloistered to read, and write, and learn in sacred seclusion. Blackfriars, Wolsey had explained, before he'd gone off with the great flock of friars who'd met him off the barge, was amongst the most loyal to the crown anywhere in England. He'd said it with pride, as though he wore the crown himself.

And doesn't he?

I'd parted from Mark, too – he'd gone off with Wolsey to visit the huge hall, which stood ahead, before the network of ranges and cloisters farther north. The priory's church – a thing of stone, dyed brown with age – dominated buildings that either clung to it or were spread out around it. I could see its roof, almost black, angled and austere. It was set in a vast green, a clipped emerald park, all within the walled compound of the priory.

The whole place, parliament hall, church and all, suddenly made me feel small, weak – and I could afford to be neither. Dwindling time would allow me to be neither.

To my left, the friars' small fields and gardens were laid out, neat fences dividing squares and rectangles of herbs all the way down to the Fleet. Dividing them from the vast sprawl of monastic buildings was the path up from the water stairs. It ran ahead of me – all the way up to the butt end of the huge parliament hall, alongside what looked like fair stone cottages on the Fleet side, before splitting, one branch running eastward into monastic buildings and the other skirting the sharp-roofed hall.

The friars' quarters, I thought, eyeing the neat red tiles of the cottages. Or some kind of guest buildings for visiting dignitaries.

Very few of the black-and-white-clad men were about. Most, it seemed, had been drummed into showing Wolsey hospitality as he paid them the honour of a personal visit. Keeping to the path, I proceeded towards the little houses, breathing in the sweet air. Not for the first time did I realise that these religious sanctuaries, even if they were in London, somehow weren't. It was as though their walls not only protected the inhabitants from the corruption outside but from even the reek of it.

My mind turned as I walked.

Gervaise, Wolsey had said. He'd named the dead friar 'Gervaise something'.

You might discover what you can of him – how he came to be in my barge, slain, in the night.

At the run of cottages, I spotted a fellow, down on his knees, furiously scrubbing at the low stone wall by the path. Nothing, I realised, must be left to offend Wolsey's eye if he decided to expand his tour to the grounds.

'Good morrow,' I called, not quite sure of myself.

The fellow looked up, started, and then got to his feet, trying to bow and turn at the same time. The livery, I realised, had frightened him. Doubtless the prior of the place had instructed every one of them to do everything they could for the cardinal and his minions.

That will do well enough for me.

'Good morrow,' the fellow said. We were both in the shade of a run of cedars that lined the eastern side of the path, rising in stately lines to our right. But only just. The day was wearing on. My new friend only looked to be in his late twenties; the tonsure, however, gave him that curious, indeterminate quality common to all monks and friars, except the wizened ones. 'Can I help you, sir? Do you require anything?'

'Only some news,' I said. 'Of one of your order.'

That threw him. 'Sir?'

'A Brother – perhaps a Brother Gervaise.'

There!

Something like distaste crossed the man's face. Or was it fear? Dislike? It was difficult to tell – it was there and then it was gone. His expression became mask-like, innocuous. 'You know him,' I chanced.

'Of course, sir. I mean, yes.'

Before I could speak, the bells tolled out, lapping a merry tune into the late morning air. There followed the dim echo of a *Te Deum*, drifting southwards from the parliament hall. A display for Wolsey, I guessed; no other bells sounded from beyond the walls. 'You make good cheer for my master,' I said, giving a smile I hoped didn't look too false.

'Yes, sir. We are honoured to have His Grace – and the king to come on Wednesday.'

Stop reminding me of the day!

I smiled again, knowing it was over-bright this time. 'My master,' I said, laying emphasis, 'has instructed me to discover something of this Brother Gervaise – an aged man, I think? He—'

I was expecting neither the younger friar's expression nor the fury of his words. 'What has he done now?'

'I beg your pardon?'

'Gervaise. He is – you must understand, sir – he's aged, as you say. He – we think he's not quite right in his mind.'

Unquiet, I thought. 'He has given trouble.' I tried to frame my words as both question and statement.

'If he has, he speaks for no man save himself. We're all true and faithful men, all of us. Gervaise,' he said, spitting the name and casting a glance over his shoulder and up the path, 'is a man we were glad to be rid of ahead of the visit. Better we'd kept him confined to his chamber. But gone is as well. He's not – he hasn't offended His Grace, has he, sir?' I followed his gaze towards the rump of the hall. Its roof shone a light grey, and the sun picked out reds and greens in the stained-glass window that dominated its southern end.

I opted for something approaching honesty. 'There has been an accident,' I said, sliding off my cap. 'Brother Gervaise attempted to speak with His Grace. He came to York Place.' A look of abject horror fell over the friar; both hands reached up and took a grip of the collar of his cope, making his knuckles whiten. 'Yet,' I said, 'he fell ill. A palsy. It appears his heart was not in it. It ceased to beat, of a sudden, and he fell down dead before he might have an audience with anyone. Anyone of importance, I mean.'

The friar's hands dropped and snatched about his waist. He seemed baffled, utterly unsure what to say. As though measuring his words, he said, 'I . . . am sorry. God give him rest. I am sorry to hear of his illness. His death. Sudden, you say, sir?'

'Very.'

'Sorry.' He seemed to find the word fitting, worth reuse. He nodded the truth of it. 'It's sorry I am that he is gone. But perhaps . . . God's will . . . that he might go to his rest before. . .' I watched as, with effort, he transformed his face into sunshine. 'Thank you and His Grace for telling me. I'll inform them up at the dormitory. The servants can clear his cell. Thank you, sir.' I sensed a desire for dismissal in his words.

'Perhaps you could show me to his cell,' I said.

'I – but I. . .' He looked with longing at the scrubbing brush at his feet. 'I'll inform Brother Alfred. Of your coming.' He gave a bow and made to hurry off – northwards, in the direction of the parliament hall. I followed, matching his pace, as the sound of joyous singing intensified.

He thinks I might discover something, I thought. He wishes to warn this other friar of my coming.

Sir Thomas More's obsession with heretical doctrines came into my head. This renegade friar's cell might be stacked with evil books. 'This way, is it?' I asked, snapping at the flowing hem of his black cope.

He slowed, obviously in a quandary, as he reached the branch in the path. 'Yes, sir.'

Together we turned eastward, passing an elaborate pleasure garden and swinging left, up towards a loose collection of slate-roofed, whitewashed buildings. I recognised them for what they were: the living quarters of the friars – one with a cross marked out a chapel, clinging to what appeared to be an infirmary; low stone buildings were surely the kitchens, judging by the sweet and savoury smells already drifting from them. The dormitory was a fair, dazzlingly white building on two floors. It must, I realised, have formed the base of one of the cloisters leading from the great church. The young friar made for it, halting outside.

'If you'll wait here, sir,' he said, stepping towards the single wooden door.

'I shall come with you,' I said.

Defeat slumped his shoulders. 'As you wish.'

He didn't knock but pushed open the door. A voice drifted over him. 'He been met and gone in yet? Lot of slaves about him, no doubt—' My young friend's hiss silenced it.

I stepped in after him, to a long, open room. It was well decorated, with painted statues lining the walls, painted cloths showing the Virgin in various doe-eyed poses, and a long desk laden with plate and candlesticks. Behind this stood the careless speaker: a middle-aged, trim man with a grey tonsure. His eyes widened as he saw me.

My guide walked smoothly to the table and said something too low for me to hear, before turning and giving his own too-bright smile. 'Brother Alfred serves as master of our dormitory. Keeps all in order. He . . . he knew Gerv – Brother Gervaise. He shall direct you in your searches.'

'It's not a search,' I said. 'His Grace has asked me only to learn what I can.'

'Brother Gervaise,' said the younger monk, conveying his own meaning to Alfred, 'has died. Suddenly. At York Place.'

'And I am commanded,' I supplied, addressing a golden candlestick, 'to make some enquiries into his life. That's all.'

'Brother Alfred will be pleased to direct you,' said the first monk again, bowing and fleeing the dormitory. When he'd gone, I looked at Alfred and found anything but pleasure on his seamed face.

'He's not . . . a representative . . . of us, Gervaise,' he said. He had a rough accent – I couldn't quite place it. 'We give him a little license. Due his age.'

'License?' I asked.

'To come and go. As he will.'

'He goes out often?' This wasn't unusual for friars, I thought; but he sounded as though he meant it in defence.

'At nights, I mean. Out late. All night, at times. I said, one day, I said, he won't come back – he'll have fallen in a gutter somewhere, dead as a doornail.' He appeared to remember himself and gave a lackadaisical sign of the cross. 'God bless him.'

I forced determination into the set of my jaw. Brother Alfred, I judged, was the no-nonsense type. 'Before last night,' I said, 'when did he last remain out?'

Alfred appeared to consider this. Absently, he straightened a piece of gold plate which was already straight, before rubbing at an imaginary spot on it with his thumb. 'A few weeks back. Came back, though.' He looked up at me. 'Smelling of strong drink. I said to myself, that old man has been in some low tavern. Not ministering to anyone.' He added, disgusted, 'Out in his cope and vestments. Wandering so. Dressed like a friar and behaving as a layman.'

Of course.

'The sign of the Bottle,' I said. The tavern-keeper there had seen him meet with the late Mr Cosyn.

'What's that?'

'A tavern. Did Brother Gervaise frequent it?'

'I couldn't say. I don't frequent low taverns myself.'

'But he had friends . . . on the . . . outside.' I couldn't think of a better means of phrasing it. 'Did they visit him?'

'Visit? No. He had letters, though. Letters in, letters out. One Mr Cosyn wrote him often enough. Not lately, of course.'

I stepped forward and gripped the edges of the table, causing Brother Alfred to fall back in alarm. 'You know Cosyn?'

'Know of him. I don't know him. Just know of him.' He took a tentative step forwards. 'Friend of Brother Gervaise of old. Dying, of late.' His hooked nose gestured downwards. 'This is part of it.'

I glanced down at the collection of fine stuff, all laid out as though in some impossibly rich merchant's shop. 'What? Part of what?'

'The bequest,' he said, as though speaking to a child. Perhaps I looked like one, too, for he appeared to take pity on me. 'A few weeks ago – Mr Cosyn bequeathed everything to this house. This plate. All those painted cloths,' he pointed over my shoulder, 'some kitchen stuff, household stuff. A fine man, to do that. Though, of course, it's a sad thing to see his house broken up for our – for the enrichment of this one. God bless him. And this only the least part. We've inventoried most and still this lies waiting.'

I stood back, stunned.

Without seeing it all, I looked at the little treasure trove.

This was too much – too many connections falling all at once.

Cosyn hadn't met sharp dealers in the Bottle – he'd met this Gervaise and possibly others. And he hadn't sold his things – he'd given them all away to the Church, or at least this little stone within it.

'His room,' I said. 'Show me his room. Please.'

'His cell, you mean?'

'His cell, then,' I snapped. 'Sorry.' I wiped my forehead with the back of my hand. I couldn't think clearly. I couldn't see if this sudden drawing of connections amounted to anything. Or, rather, I could see that it must, but not what it amounted to.

'This way,' he said. He slid along his side of the table and over to the right of the room, opening a door. 'Are you coming?'

I answered by following. He went ahead of me, into a dull stairway, which twisted upwards, round and round itself. My mind went with it.

At the top, a door directly above the one below opened into a long, windowless hallway, panelled well in stout oak. Doors ran along the right-hand side. 'He's at the end,' said Alfred, already floating ahead of me. 'Was, I should say. God bless him.'

I hurried down the hallway, past the closed doors, until we both stood outside the last one. 'Is this it?' I breathed. Somehow, I'd got out of breath from just that short walk upstairs.

'Had a room to himself. No one would share.' He glanced at the door. There appeared to be no handle. He raised a black-clad arm to push it and then froze in mid-air. 'I. . . Before we enter into the dead man's cell,' he said, putting emphasis on Gervaise's late state, 'I'd have it known that the poor old fellow was . . . he was wandering in his mind. If he said your master is. . .'

'What did he say?' I asked, keeping my voice as gentle as I could.

The hard-nosed Alfred appeared to crack a little. 'He said – in my hearing once – that the cardinal was a bad man who deceived the king and would meet a bad end.' I might have been imagining it, but I had a feeling the old fox enjoyed the use of the dead man's foul and slanderous mouth. As if he could read my thoughts, he said, in his former, short manner, 'And I had him punished for it. Rightly. Locked away for private meditation and prayer. It is recorded. He ill-spoke and was justly punished.'

'I understand.'

'Lately, he has been more wandering than ever he was. In his mind, I mean. In his better days, he used to instruct the oblates in writing and picture-making. Yet his love of the new learning. . . I thought it best to check his teaching. It is recorded, the ceasing of his teaching. Since then . . . lately . . . he. . .' Alfred let the sentence die, before resurrecting it. 'Yesterday, he begged forgiveness for what he must do – when the wide world watched, he said. I had it from his confessor – worried, he was, at that kind of talk. We feared he meant some mischief against the cardinal today – were glad to see him go out last night to one of his taverns or friends. But . . . he was not always a man of fiery passions.' He gave me a little smile. 'A maker of pictures, he was, so I understand, back in his younger days. Much sought after by the heralds.'

'Might we look in his room?' I asked. Letters, I was thinking: the man must still have letters.

Brother Alfred pushed open the door and, conspicuously, stood aside to let me enter first.

The room – the cell – was small. It contained only a

brazier in the far corner, a straw mattress on a pallet, a couple of books, and some papers.

Papers!

I fell upon them, kicking the pallet out of the way and scooping them up. 'What?' I asked, frowning down. Light from the high, barred window fell in beams. I shook my head. 'What are these?'

I was looking not at writing, but at drawings, just as I had in Hal Percy's room. These were not, however, of women – a woman – or eyes, and nor were they mediocre. There were in fact excellent drawings of birds, coloured and applied to vellum rather than paper. 'What are these?' I asked. I didn't intend it, but I sounded vaguely accusing.

Brother Alfred finally stepped into the room and joined me. 'I told you,' he said, regarding the images wavering in my hand, 'he was a maker of pictures. He never gave it up.'

'Birds?'

He squinted down. 'It's a pelican. May I?' I passed him the sheaf. 'They're all pelicans.'

'What does that mean?'

'It is a large, foreign bird—'

'I know what a pelican is! I mean – what does it signify?'

The friar appeared not offended but befuddled. 'Well, they're – the most selfless of all the birds.' Memory appeared to rise, drawing his lips into a mirthless smile. 'Yes, I recall. The pelican. A bird of great sacrifice. Far above its squabbling, fighting fellows. It pierces its own breast to feeds its young with its own lifeblood.'

'Why would he draw this?'

'I cannot say,' said Alfred. 'Wandering in his mind. Perhaps

- 330 -

he used to draw such creatures for the heralds. Some family arms or the like. I cannot say.'

I stooped down and this time lifted the topmost of the books. Opening it, I was defeated by the frontispiece, which blared Latin laughingly in my face. 'What has he been reading?' I asked. 'I can't read Latin.'

Alfred took this too. 'Hm. Ah, I know this.' He looked down at the remaining pile. 'And the others on the floor. Meditations on the lives of Saints Perpetua and Felicity. The lady Perpetua was a good Christian lady. She had . . .' he looked at me and as quickly away, 'a Moorish slave. Felicity. Both went singing to their deaths for the sake of their faith. Perpetua welcome death by sword. Five, I believe, went to their deaths at that dark time. Another good Christian volunteered to embrace death with them rather than recant.'

'They went willingly,' I echoed.

'I think such martyrs might find much joy in death. She wrote an account of her sufferings in prison. Much studied.'

'Wrote,' I said. 'Letters. Where are his letters?' I bent and lifted the straw mattress, shaking it out. It made only the crisp, crinkling sounds of its stuffing being dislodged. Tutting, I dropped it and went to the brazier. I scraped the thing across the floorboards and into the light and peered down.

Goddammit.

Thrusting my hands in, I brought up only smears of soot and flakes of yellowish white. 'He burnt them. He burnt his letters.'

'A common enough thing.'

'If you think you'll have no more need of them,' I said. And then I blew out a sigh. There was something here, I felt sure – something. But I shied away from whatever it was. 'How many men wrote to him?' I asked.

'I couldn't say. I only remember Mr Cosyn, because he had dealings with us. Leaving us his goods.'

'But more than one?'

'Many,' he said. 'Several.' He looked hesitant. 'He received one only yesterday. After vespers, it came. I don't know by whom. It's what he said, when he read it in the refectory.' I looked at him, expectantly. 'He said, "It is plain the devil hedges his own." And then something about the world having the scales wiped from its eyes – when it's forced to look. Something like that. As I said, we were glad to see him go, for fear he would make some mischief in this place when His Grace came. Or worse, when the king comes on Wednesday.'

I closed my eyes briefly. 'Do you have a house here for guests?'

'Of course – yes. The houses you must have passed along the path past the church. But His Grace has sent no word that he's staying, surely.'

'His Grace isn't. I am. And I'd have someone – that young friar – whatever his name is – I'd have him read these books to me tonight. Give me their meanings.'

'If you wish it, of course. I'll . . . I'll see to it. Are you finished in this cell?'

'For now,' I said. 'But keep those books ready.'

I left him thinking me, I'm sure, quite mad – madder than the wandering Brother Gervaise had ever been. I fled the dormitory building, ignoring Cosyn's remaining treasures, and sucked at the fresh, sweet, spicy air.

I could go back to the sign of the Bottle.

I could go back to York Place.

I could go home, home, home.

I could flee south, west, east – and take a ship going anywhere.

That last, tempting as it was, was bootless. Cardinal Wolsey no doubt had men in every port out of England and I wasn't made for disguise.

Possibilities of escape fought with each other. Possibilities about what had been going on positively wrestled.

At the very least, Cosyn and this Brother Gervaise had met: two old men, with one of them interested in martyrdom. What did that mean? Perhaps that both had elected to make some demonstration against the cardinal and suffer for it, with the gaze of the world on them. Mordaunt might well have been of their mind – he had tried just that. What I could see clearly enough was that there was some plot between these men – some collusion in speaking out against Wolsey and a willingness to suffer for the doing of it.

What none of this explained was who killed them – and the prentice and the old woman too; they deserved justice as much.

I wandered the grounds, returning to the path and looking out over the herb garden, breathing deeply again of its good, healthful aroma. The parliament hall had fallen silent. Perhaps Wolsey had moved on, to be entertained or feasted in the prior's lodgings.

I might go to gaol for something I didn't do.

I banished the thought – or tried to.

Scuffing my way back along the path, I passed the little cottages. Already I was regretting my sudden announcement that I'd stay; I doubted the dead friar's books could tell me anything, unless he'd made some notes in the margins – which is what I hardly dared hope. But I'd said it, bold or not; and already I could see that the horn windows of one building had been thrown open to air it. I'd have to leave the next day – my last day – and return to York Place, of course. Perhaps, I thought, I'd have had some divine intervention by then. About as likely, perhaps I'd have some sudden flash of inspiration if I had a night to myself, in a single room. It was time to think, at any rate.

Think, think, think.

It was no good trying to force it.

Run, run, run.

'You find 'im?'

I jumped.

'Mark!'

He stepped out from behind one of the cedar trees which spread budding limbs on the side of the path opposite the cottages. He was still tucking his shirt back into his hose. I grimaced as he wiped his hands on the front of his doublet. 'I said, did you find 'im? The dead man?'

I told him what I'd found. He interrupted constantly, interjecting with curses and oaths. 'Sounds like a whole lot of madness,' was his assessment. 'Conspiracy. What's it the cardinal calls them things? Complots.'

'Complots,' I said. 'That's it. But . . . I can't understand it. I can't. . .'

'Forget it,' he said. 'Make it simple. Whatever these old buggers were up to – someone's been murdering them. Murdering others too, to – to hide it. To hide it by blaming you.' I nodded. 'To hell with what they was up to. Who's murderin' them all?'

'I don't know,' I said.

He sighed. 'Well, you said he burnt his letters. See who else has some. He must've written to someone. Maybe he got someone angry. Maybe he just has to die 'cos he knew the plot.' He shrugged. 'Maybe they didn't burn theirs.'

I had no answer – I had nothing better.

'I better get back,' he said. 'Cardinal's bored stiff. Having to eat their first fruits all stewed to buggery up in the prior's palace. Whole place stinks of old man. See you on the barge.'

'I'm not coming back,' I said.

'What?' he wheeled. 'Shit. You ain't thinkin' about running off from the law?' He whispered this. 'You can't – he'll find you. It'll look worse. It—'

'I meant tonight. I'm staying here.'

'Why?' Mark looked baffled.

I couldn't think of a way of explaining that I needed time to think. 'Because I've told the friars. They're making a room ready.'

He looked at me, a little doubtfully. I suspected he still thought I intended to run. 'I won't tell no one if you are—'

'I'll be back on the morrow,' I said. I turned northward and looked up at the parliament hall – at the whitewashed stones and the slate roof and the tall, dyed-glass window. 'I promise.' An idea struck, spurred by memory. 'I only have tomorrow. I have to speak with that spy Rowlet – he was assistant to one of the dead men. More, probably – I think Sir Thomas said he was friends with them all too. He might've discovered something.' I was babbling. Mark reached out to me, and I gripped his hand once, giving it a shake. 'But I don't wish to waste tonight. Can you – would you – ask Audley to do a search? Like what we did with Hal Percy. On the morrow, maybe – a great search of the household.'

'For what?'

'I don't know. Books. Writings. Letters, as you said. Any books on martyrdom – tell him that. Or drawings of pelicans.'

'What?'

'Big birds – good drawings of pelicans. That dead friar was mad on them. They mean something.'

'Pelicans,' said Mark. He nodded. 'I'll ask. He'll think you're mad, but. I'll say you said to do a search.'

'Of everyone. Not just lowers. Gentlemen – everyone. Officers – people who can move freely about without anyone saying anything. No warning, though. It might be that these – these conspirators had a man in our household. A man who betrayed them and killed them. And who's trying to put me in the noose for it.'

'Old Audley knows what he's about. Strikes like a viper, that one.'

I nodded. That was true enough. 'Tomorrow, then,' I said.

Again, Mark gave me a hard look. 'Tomorrow.'

He moved off, back up towards the parliament house, one door of which stood open.

Tomorrow, I thought. It's tomorrow or nothing.

22

Harry led me in silence through the southern range of buildings at York Place. He had adopted a sombre air, more even than usual, as though I were already condemned.

And I might as well have been.

I'd spent an uncomfortable night in the Blackfriars lodging house, listening to tales of martyrs and the young monk's eloquent disquisition of them. I'd learnt that these men and women willingly shed their blood for the love of Christ, and so recall for us all the fact that a Christian life ought to be one of sacrifice – willing sacrifice – in imitation of Jesus, especially His own willing sacrifice on the altar of the cross.

Useless.

What a way to spend one of your final nights of freedom.

The prentice boy had gone willingly for money, for the false promise of a job of work, not to death.

The old woman had cried bloody murder in an effort to be saved.

I'd managed to sleep, easily enough, though this time dreams had intruded. Pelicans flew around in my mind. They opened their sharp beaks and chattered at me, in the words I only recalled on waking as having been quoted by Sir Thomas More.

We have our kindnesses and our feuds.

And so, in the morning, I'd been provided with a ewer – full of clean, herb-infused spring water, had a good – *last* – dinner and taken a wherry westward.

★ ★ ★

The hall stretching ahead of Harry and me was a carpeted tunnel, its sides panelled to the waist and whitewashed above, its ceiling carved. Doors stood at intervals down the left-hand side. 'This is where Mr Audley had Mr Deacon put Mr Rowlet,' said Harry.

Laughter bubbled in my throat.

What a lot of Misters.

I choked it back, letting Harry lead the way down the hall, right to the end. He paused at the last door, but he didn't open it. Instead, he turned a serious face on me. I could see him search for fitting words – for words of comfort, probably – as his jaw worked. He raised a hand towards me and let it fall. 'I pray God,' he said, stiffly, 'that Mr Rowlet had made some discovery which will aid you.'

I do too.

My last hope was that the other spy – More's spy – might have uncovered something which would let me see the whole picture: and a clearer picture, hopefully, than fair-drawn black eyes and well-drawn pelicans.

Without another word, Harry knocked lightly on the door.

There followed a moment of silence, both of us exchanging those awful, awkward, *shan't be a minute, I'm sure,* smiles. Only it wasn't a minute. It stretched beyond one.

Harry said, 'I suppose I might . . . knock again; it would not be rude. . .'

I reached up and thumped on the door myself. 'Mr Rowlet,' I cried. 'It's the devil.'

'Anthony!' croaked Harry.

I shook my head. I disliked the man – he'd been suspicious of me.

To hell with him.

Still, there was no response.

'Perhaps,' said Harry, 'he is taking the air. Sending some message to Sir Thomas.'

I didn't answer. Instead, I took hold of the gilded and polished brass ring and began to push.

'You cannot intru—' began Harry, cutting himself off. 'Oh, go on. His room will be searched soon enough anyway.' I smiled at him. He had informed me, when I'd first found him on my return, that his master Audley was planning a surprise search, as I'd had Mark request. Apparently, the ingenious method he'd devised was having the lowest servants conduct it. They would leave nothing – they'd delight in rifling through the things of their betters. I know I always did.

I pushed the door open.

And I managed to make only a crack. A thudding sound prevented me going farther. 'It's stuck,' I said, unnecessarily. 'Blocked.' I tried again, pulling the door closed and pushing it in again, only to meet the same obstacle.

'Unlocked,' frowned Harry. 'Blocked.'

'You try.'

Harry was bigger than me, stronger, built like a man who had spent part of his youth at the hunt and part of it learning to wield big swords and bows. He put his shoulder against the door and careened into it. It gave, though not without resistance. A loud thunk followed.

My heart began to speed, as it hadn't on the discovery of the friar.

The friar.

Harry swallowed. Though he'd opened the door – he didn't look in. To me, he said, 'Something is amiss. We ought to report. . .'

I ignored him, swallowed, and stepped into the room.

The smell hit me first, making me gag. I put my hand over my nose and lips. It was pungent, throat-catching. . .

Familiar.

'By St George,' cried Harry. He'd stepped behind me and saw what I saw, smelled what I smelled. 'But the great search is only just being under. . .'

The room before us was large – a single, well-appointed guest chamber. Or, at least, it had been well-appointed. Now, it was a confusion of broken wood and torn hangings. At our intrusion, a flurry of feathers began a crazy dance through the air. The thing that made the thunking sound was a sideboard, lying now on its side. Whoever had torn the room apart had evidently placed it there to block the door whilst they went to work.

I stepped over the wreckage of a rumpled carpet. My shoes made a dull squelching sound. Halfway towards the window, I froze.

A bare part of the floorboards had been revealed. It was sticky, like the carpet, with a dull, brownish substance. I bent and touched it, rising and wiping it between two fingers. 'Blood,' I breathed.

'Look,' said Harry. His face had turned chalky, and he was pointing at a wall.

Following his gaze, I saw more of the stuff smeared up the whitewashed part. I thought of the old woman and the volume of blood her throat had gushed. This was different – different, too, from old Cosyn's; it had turned from scarlet to a vinous claret.

But such a quantity.

Mr Rowlet, if this was his blood, had been well-filled.

Had been.

'Where is he?' I asked, trying not to breathe too deeply. 'The body.'

Harry only shook his head. 'The smell, Anthony. The *smell.*'

I ignored this and padded carefully to the window. It was a rectangular thing, like the rest fronting the river. And it was open a crack, its latch released. I pushed it all the way, letting a cool breeze wash in. It did little to combat the reek. Looking out, I could see the gentle swell of the tide. I stuck my head out farther and looked right. Sure enough, as Rowlet had said, I could see the columned water gallery, not far away, stretching out into the Thames.

I turned back to Harry. 'Something's wrong here,' I said. It sounded stupid, even to me. I moved back into the room. 'That smell.' I began picking things up and putting them down – a torn chunk of mattress, a wooden dish, a spoon half hidden by the maroon fronds of the carpet. When I reached the overturned sideboard, I spotted something else – something familiar.

Picking up the glass phial, I brought it to my nose and jerked back.

This one wasn't scentless. It had carried no poison, at least not of the same type as Mordaunt's. Nor did it smell like garlic, as More had told me the stuff used to kill the old doctor had reeked of when heated. I felt around, finding another – and another. Altogether, there were five of the little phials, and each one of them gave off that foul, strangely familiar stink.

My mind turned to it.

'Hark!' Harry bent and stood, a small casket in his hand. Its lid fell open easily and he spun. Lifting something out of it, he said, 'Wounds!'

'What is it?' I asked, stepping closer.

'Blades.' Harry held the casket in one hand and removed a sliver of silver with the other. 'Cutting tools. For spring bleedings. They are clean.'

I stared, dumbly. 'I doubt the creature came here without his own weapon,' I said, unsure. 'Nor used Rowlet's blades on him and cleaned them.' In truth, I didn't know.

'The poker used on poor Mr Cosyn – the monster did not bring that to do his deed. He found and made use of it.'

I nodded. Harry was right.

'We must report this at once,' he said, frowning as he replaced the blade and set the casket down on the floor. 'Wicked practices. *Something* has been done to Mr Rowlet. By a man using *something*.'

'He was set to work – to discover the matter,' I said. 'As I was.'

'Then,' said Harry, 'it is plain he discovered something. And was foully murdered to ensure his silence.'

I dropped the phial I'd been holding. It hit the carpet with a soft ting. 'Where is he, then? His body?' I asked.

Harry looked at the window. It was certainly large

enough for a man to be thrown from. 'The river,' he said. He remained staring at it, his face impassive. 'I have heard . . . I have heard that bodies thrown into the river . . . commonly they wash up at a certain place in Southwark. It is most notorious for it.'

I considered this. The murderer might have slain Rowlet, tossed his room in a search for something – his writings on the crimes, likely – and then thrown his body from the window, to be washed away by the river. Then he might easily have escaped by the same means, climbing down and skirting the pilings above the water's edge.

But why?

Why not leave him to be made a grim discovery, like all the others?

'Go and report it,' I said. 'Report that it appears Mr Rowlet has been slain and dumped in the river. Much blood, tell them – tell Audley. Much blood, looking old, as though it's lain awhile. Done,' I added, with emphasis, 'when I was at the Blackfriars. He can check himself if he wishes. He'll judge this blood was spent . . . it looks like yesterday, I'd say. Not long after we left to visit the priory.'

'Are you not coming?' asked Harry.

'No. I'll – no.' More to myself, I said, 'I wonder . . . when pelicans pierce their breasts, if they do it expertly or inexpertly.'

'What? I cannot – I beg your pardon?'

'Nothing,' I said, unsure if it was. I shook my head. 'Go. I'll . . . I wish to look a little further.'

He paused, nodded, and turned, fleeing the murder room.

When I was alone, I continued moving about, trying not to miss anything. A mistake had been made here, of that I felt sure. I looked up at the painted cloth hangings. They hung in strips, as though someone had taken a knife to them. Parts were missing. Bending again to the mattress, I looked under it, around it, everywhere for a linen sheet.

There wasn't one.

Yes, a mistake had been made.

I went again to the window and breathed the clean air. That foul smell had lodged itself in my throat, making a home, making itself familiar. Putting my hands to the wooden lintel, I pulled myself up, raised a leg, and gracelessly hauled myself onto it. I hung a second, getting my other leg up, before swinging them both out and sitting there, between the foul room and the bright morning. My dangling feet were just a few yards above the strip of planking on its stilts above the riverbank. If I dove I could have hit the water.

Something glinted.

I looked down, to where a few reeds stuck up obstinately from the water in front of the wooden pilings. Blinking, I waited for the sun to catch it again.

Yes.

Something silver lay down there, safe from the tide thanks to its budding green guardians. I looked over my shoulder into the room. Harry had had the sense to close the door when he'd left. Ahead, wherries moved up and down, some close, some farther towards Lambeth. Gripping the lintel with both palms, I eased myself down. My arms shook with the strain; my belly danced wildly.

I thudded to the wooden planking, hunched forward, nearly fell down into the water, and then managed to regain my balance. My back slammed into the honey wall of the palace, and I almost lay against it, screwing my eyes shut, silently offering up a prayer of thanks. Only then did my whole body begin to tremble. Laughter threatened. When I had a rein on it, I bent down to the reeds – carefully, as carefully as I could – and felt around for the thing that had been glinting. Bracing one leg on the pilings, I took hold of something smooth and lifted it.

It glinted brightly in my hand.

A thin, silver ewer – the kind used for washing of a morning.

It was empty now – whatever it had held had been washed away by the Thames.

A valuable thing, I thought. Whoever had been searching Rowlet's room had not been looking to steal good household stuff.

Why throw this out?

I returned to the firmness of the wall, regarding my find. I was so intent on it that I didn't hear the voice at first.

'I said, what's all this?'

I looked up. A wherryman on his craft. He'd come from the water gallery, over to my right, and bobbed ahead of me, resting on his oars and staring back. His expression was too distant to read. 'Can you fetch me?' I shouted over the water. Some little birds took chirruping flight from the reeds farther downriver.

'What's that? Hold.' He took an oar and began manoeuvring himself towards me. I stood patiently, wondering if I had to explain myself to a wherryman. I must, I realised, have appeared a thief, livery or not. His next words caught me by surprise. 'Another one?' he asked. 'Is this the new means outta yonder fine house?'

'What?' He was close enough now that I could leap into the wherry if I chose.

'Oh, you're for coming, are you? Well, come, then.'

I looked down at the ewer, still gripped in my hand, and reluctantly placed it firmly up on the planking by the wall. Bracing myself again, I hopped over the reeds and landed, wobbling, on the wherry. The whole thing rocked, drawing delighted laughter from the fellow. 'Well done of you, lad,' he said. 'Good sport, heh?'

I flopped down gratefully. When I caught my breath, I said, 'Thank you. Thank you. What you said – "another one"? Has someone come down out of the windows before?'

He gave me another look of amusement, before jabbing a finger at his frieze coat. 'Saw it myself, yesterday.'

My heart skipped. 'You did – who – when?'

The wherryman shook his head slowly, smiling to himself. 'You palace men . . .'

'Please,' I said. 'It's important. I'll – I'll pay you.'

His smile faded. 'You pay to gets where you're going.'

I'd offended him, I realised. I held up my palms. 'I'm sorry. It's. . .' I grasped around in my mind. 'A robbery. His Grace was robbed yesterday. We think the fellow stole down from yonder window.'

This yielded a result. Robbery was no small matter, especially of Wolsey's house. 'I seen him,' he said. 'If it'll helps His Grace. My name's Andrew, you tells him. I've worked this path, ups and downs, for ten year, you tells him.'

'I will, Andrew. What did you see?'

He looked beyond me, frowning up at the palace. 'Yesterday – afternoon it was, I was coming up from London. That's where I lives. No fare – coming up to see if there was any messenger or the like needing a boat. Good business, that.' I nodded him to go on. 'I was passing here – just where I saw you just now. And I sees a man climbing down from that window. Just there.' He pointed to the same window I'd come from. 'His back to me, came down careful. Moved all stiff.'

'What did he look like?' I asked.

Andrew considered this for a moment, his jaw working. 'Didn't gets me a good look.'

Of course you didn't.

'Beardless fellow, like yourself, young sir.' He clutched at his own sparsely bearded chin. 'Only not so dark as you are, not foreign-looking, like.' He said this without a trace of insult. 'I shouts to him, as I did to you, but he didn't hails me. Just moved off, all stiff.'

'To where?' I asked.

He jerked his chin east, away from the water gallery. 'That way. Cheap, some folk. Or up to no good.'

I followed his chin, looking eastward down the long southern wing of York Place. A fellow could, easily enough, return around the outside of the building and enter by the postern, or else disappear into the town at Westminster and through the fields and woods to London beyond.

'I didn't know he was no thief,' said Andrew. 'Else I'd haves reported him.'

'And you saw nothing before him? He – he threw nothing? You saw nothing – uh – sinking? In the tide?'

'Threw? No, I only caughts a sight of himself – himself, climbing down. Ignored me, he did. Cried what ails you, sir, and can I helps? And ignores me, he does.'

I said nothing for a moment. And then I gave him a

smile. 'You've been a help, sir.' He seemed pleased with his promotion. 'I'll tell the cardinal.' I meant it. Andrew the wherryman would, I hoped, find his fares increasing. 'Would you row me just over to the gallery?'

'With pleasure, sir. With pleasure.'

It took only a few minutes to row over towards the marble steps leading up between the columns. But it was all the time I needed. In my mind, I was beginning to see the connections now, though I could scarcely credit them.

'Thank you,' I said. I had my purse at my belt, and I paid him a whole penny for the minuscule journey.

'Andrew, remember,' he said, as I stepped out of the wherry. I raised a hand to him without turning, tapping my way up to the gallery. I gathered speed as I made my way along it, passing the porter with a nod and entering the palace proper.

With my head up, with ideas now jostling for position, I barely paid attention to where I was going: through the White Hall with its groups of men, through halls, past a blur of tapestries and arrases, until I reached the stairs up to Wolsey's privy lodgings. I was halfway up them when the sounds of the palace changed.

Conversation, which had been everywhere, low and murmuring, rose into something else – something excited – ahead of me.

The doors to the first of the cardinal's rooms stood open.

I paused, sinking into the carpet, and turned, looking down. Whatever was going on up ahead, news of it hadn't yet reached the lower chambers. I stood for a moment, irresolute, and then ascended.

Harry met me at the door, his face flushed. 'Anthony,' he

said, taking my hand in both of his. 'You are free, my friend.'

'What?' I asked, my mouth hanging.

'The search – Mr Audley began the search, without warning. We have found him! We have found the vile murderer!'

23

'Mr Deacon, a secret follower of Luther!' barked Wolsey.
With Harry at my side, I'd been shown through
the magnificence of the cardinal's private rooms – the privy
chamber, hung not just with tapestries, but the spotted hides
of strange creatures, their eyes replaced with glittering jewels;
the withdrawing chamber, decorated in reds and pinks; the
vast long gallery, with windows overlooking the orchards
and gardens – all the way to his secret study. These rooms
beyond the privy chamber: these were the secret lodgings
usually fit only for his closest friends and attendants, where
he lived out whatever passed for private life for a public man.
The little closeted study was a room I hadn't even known
existed – a chamber covered, every inch, in carved oak, with
a velvet-topped desk at its centre. But, strangely enough,
only the panelling and the desk spoke of luxury in the heart
of Wolsey's private spaces. There were no jewels in the
room, no plate, no heavy candlesticks or arrases. The only
decoration was a single, plain, white crucifix hanging on the
wall.

I stood there, feeling out of place, feeling lost, whilst
Audley poured Wolsey wine. The cardinal held it up. 'We
toast you, young Anthony Blanke, French fashion. To your
very good health. We understand that you were the very
begetter and deviser of this search of our own people. Yes.'

He drank deeply, before settling himself more firmly on the plain chair behind the desk.

I looked at Audley for permission to speak. He gave a very slight lift of his brows. 'What, sir, was found?'

'Found?' Wolsey snorted derision. 'Filth. The *Disputation on the Power and Efficacy of Indulgences*.' He leaned forward, his eyes gleaming. '*Contra Henricum Regem Anglie*.'

I don't know what that means.

Harry, at my side, said, sotto voce, '*Against Henry, king of the English*. A work by the wicked Luther.'

'One of our own ushers,' said Wolsey, holding up his cup to be refilled. As Audley did so, the cardinal said to him, 'We marvel not a little that you did not suspect the man hitherto.'

'He had us all well blinded,' said Audley, without missing a beat or spilling the wine.

'Yes,' said Wolsey. 'Yes.'

I watched the column of red die to a trickle and then cease.

Mute, dumb, my mind wandered out of the study and into the gallery, swimming past the marble statues and the arrases, past shelves and cabinets buckling under silver and gold plate studded with precious stones, and in search of Mr Deacon. It tried to follow him about this palace and Richmond, to peep over his shoulder, to match with his own mind and grope about there.

Fruitless.

Books, I thought. Lutheran books. Deacon the usher had been a secret follower of Luther, the German devil and enemy to the cardinal and all of our faith. 'Where is he?' I asked.

'Mr Deacon is being conveyed to a place of greater safety

and security,' said Audley, fixing me with a glare, as though it was none of my concern.

'Crying his denials, like a wounded pup. The filth was found secreted amongst his own things. A bosom serpent.' The wine brought a bloom to Wolsey's cheeks. He seemed not annoyed but delighted. 'All is well,' he said, taking a sip. 'I regret only that I must concede the ground to Sir Thomas. He suspected the hand of Luther's apes in this matter.' He gave a short laugh. 'Yes.' His gaze returned to me. 'Yet we perceive – we see – no danger attaching to us. These late outrages – committed by our servant – yes . . . yes . . . that is regrettable. But evidently he was our secret enemy, working against us. Beguiled and bedevilled by the false and heretical teachings of Luther. We shall tell the king. Yes. We shall tell His Majesty that this horror in our own house proves only that the infection of Luther must be checked.'

'He killed . . . Rowlet?' It had started off as a statement. Somewhere on its journey out, it became a question.

'I informed Mr Audley,' said Harry brightly.

Wolsey fetched a sigh. 'Yes. We understand the spy Rowlet has been murdered. Thrown in the river, yes? That shall be hard news for Sir Thomas, even if he was right.'

'A terrible thing,' said Audley. 'Rowlet, Cosyn, Mordaunt, the aged friar. All persuaded and beguiled by a Lutheran. It seems they refused to fall in line with his deeper heresies and were slain for their adherence to the true faith.'

'Hm,' said Wolsey, setting down his cup. 'Yes. Yes. Fools. To have involved themselves with such a creature at all.'

But what about Rob the prentice and Mistress Cotes?

I swallowed. 'Could . . . but could Mr Deacon have left

your household, Your Grace? Gone to London to kill there? Without being seen?'

'Could he? Could he? He did,' said Wolsey. 'It is plain. The man found the first body. He was present in my own rooms when that damned physician was poisoned. It is plain.'

I hurried on. 'A good wherryman – I've just come from him – Andrew – saw a fellow climb down from Rowl – from Mr Rowlet's window. Yesterday, when we were away at Blackfriars. A beardless fellow who moved stiffly and – uh – went along the riverbank.'

'Andrew?' barked Wolsey. 'Then he misjudged of the time. An easy thing.' Doubt crossed his face, drawing lines. He shook it away. 'Unless Deacon had some confederate.' He turned to Audley. 'Has anything else been discovered?'

Audley said, 'Some . . . bawdy books. Drawings of women's parts. One of the other ushers – Cavendish – some scribblings of his life in service. Your Grace appears rather well in them.'

'Bah.'

'Nothing,' said Audley, 'as wicked as that which we discovered amongst the defunct usher's things.' I shuddered at his use of the word. Deacon had become a former person, an unperson.

'If there is some murderous confederate. . .' said Wolsey. 'I think it unlikely. Yet he will be found. These great searches – a marvellous thing.'

I looked at Harry, who seemed as satisfied as the other two.

Silence ticked over. Eventually, Wolsey reached again for his cup. 'You have done well, Anthony Blanke. You are free. This is a great day for us. A follower of Luther uncovered and manifestly the author of these terrible crimes. Meant to strike against us.' He thumped a fist on the velvet. 'We are not deceived. From the first, this foul serpent has sought to make us and ours – I mean you, boy – the doer and begetter of these murders. To blacken our name.'

'Yes, Your Grace,' I said.

His tone softened. 'You are free, lad. You might rest easy tonight. We give you leave not to attend on the opening of our parliament on the morrow.'

I was dismissed. My cap was already off, and so I gave a bow and began backing across the carpet towards the door. I threw a look at Harry; I wanted to speak with him privately.

'You might remain with us, young Mr Gainsford,' said Audley, seeing my look. Harry glanced at me, a pained expression on his face. I frowned but managed a slight nod.

'If it please Your Grace,' I said, looking directly at him, 'I would like to attend tomorrow. If I may. I'll go early – I'll take a wherry and pay myself. I . . . I should like to see the great display.'

'Mm? Yes. Yes, if it please you. All England – all the world – will be watching on the morrow. Looking to see these degenerate knights of the hedgerows and burgesses bow before His Majesty's will. Yes.' He didn't bother to look back at me; he waved a hand in the air. He felt he'd done his part, I thought, showing me favour as his thanks for suggesting what sounded like it would be a regular purging of the household.

Turning, I left the room, ringing again with Wolsey's ebullient voice.

I was shown out of the gallery and the vast secret lodgings by the silent Cavendish – evidently, silence was now to be the preferred stance amongst the ushers. He left me at the staircase leading downwards. I descended into the buzz of conversation of dozens of men. The news had evidently reached them: the murderer had been discovered.

You might rest easy tonight.

I gnawed on my bottom lip, as I wound my way about the palace aimlessly.

I wouldn't rest easy, of that I was sure.

Something didn't fit. Something was wrong.

Voices echoed in my head.

The eyes of the world are upon us.

All England – all the world – will be watching on the morrow.

He said . . . something about the world having the scales wiped from its eyes – when it's forced to look.

Yes, I thought. And I, too, would be watching.

24

The April morning brought a lover's promise of summer – meant well, but unlikely to last. I stood, amidst the hubbub of friars and lower servants running to and fro, feeling the tension in the air – that sense that something was about to happen.

Something was, of course.

I'd specially sought out Andrew the wherryman, not because I thought he could tell me anything, but because I felt I owed him some little token of favour; he'd rowed me over to Blackfriars when the household had still been rising. All the hushed talk, as I'd washed and dressed in my livery, had still been of Deacon being discovered to be a murderous follower of Luther.

I'd spoken to Mark the evening before, after I'd come down from Wolsey's secret lodgings and given an account of their richness. He'd listened but seemed untroubled by my doubts. Like Wolsey, like Audley, like Harry, like everyone, he seemed content to accept that a murderer had been at work, a murderer had been found, and the theory Sir Thomas More had advanced had been correct. He didn't say it, but he seemed to think it some perversity in my nature that I wasn't content. 'You're free,' was his succinct assessment. 'So fuck it.' From what I'd heard, Deacon had been rowed away to be imprisoned somewhere, pleading that the books had been a gift – then falsely hidden on him – then that he was sorry; he had read out of curiosity but never thought nor known anything of murder.

Let it go.

No.

The path up from the water stairs had been covered over with assorted lengths of parti-coloured carpet. I didn't tread on it; instead, I kept to the grass at the side, as I wandered up past the lodging houses where I'd spent the night. Others had had the same idea; men were already sitting about the grass, staking out spots as close as possible to the carpeted path. On the opposite side, between the cedars, more milled, enjoying the shade. As I moved northwards, in the direction of the parliament hall, I scanned as many faces as I could. I recognised no one. These were, I judged from their dress, servants of the burgesses and provincial knights who would form part of the procession. They chewed on lengths of grass and passed around wineskins, chatting amongst themselves in a rainbow of accents.

When the cottages were behind me, I moved towards the windowed parliament hall. It was a vast barn of a building, its slate roof still damp, either from dew, some night rain, or some unfortunate servants sent up with buckets. Great oak doors opened into its western side, facing the path which snaked around it; they were shut tight, though. A pair of yeomen in white and green were already stationed on either side of them, their beribboned halberds resting against the stone wall at their backs. I took a look behind me and then marched towards them, my head down.

'Expecting trouble?' I asked, padding over the carpet.

One of them looked at me and spat. 'Won't have trouble

from these outland country squires.'

The other, who had neater, more serious features, said, 'If it's trouble your master looks for – he'll find it inside. In the arguments.'

Inside.

'Has the place been searched?' I asked, addressing the second yeoman, who seemed more pleasant.

He stood a little straighter. 'Top to bottom. Under every bench for concealed weapons.' He thinks I'm spying ahead for Wolsey, I realised. 'We have men at this entrance and at His Majesty the king's privy entrance from Bridewell. The hall has been cleared of servants, the woolsacks have been felt most carefully for concealed needles, the—'

'Thank you,' I said. And then, because I felt I ought to, I added, 'I'll assure His Grace that you've all . . . that all's as it should be.'

The first yeoman spat again, whilst his colleague straightened so that he nearly fell back on his halberd.

The parliament hall was empty, clear of people.

Still, I felt uneasy. I continued on, right up the length of the huge building, looking down towards the grey ribbon of the Fleet, over which a covered bridge led from the new Bridewell Palace: a frothy, double-courted place of red brick, with gleaming roofs rich in cupolas, vanes, and chimneys. At the northern end of the parliament hall, another pair of yeomen were already guarding the privy entrance, which itself was connected by a golden canopy to a network of galleries leading from the king's private bridge.

Well-guarded. All well-guarded.

When I returned again to the western length of the hall, I looked Thamesward and could see that the crowds on either side of the path had already thickened. Only the presence of the yeomen seemed to keep folk away from crowding the entrance directly.

The sound of trumpets rose in the clear, crystal air.

He's here.

I began moving south, clinging to the sides of the cottages, darting looks at the backs of the men who had risen to attention. As I drew closer to the water stairs and gatehouse, I could see that the cardinal's barge had arrived and docked. It stood, looking stately and grand, as though the dead Brother Gervaise had never been near it.

A cheerful tolling of bells rang out from the church to the north. Trumpets blew again, from the gatehouse this time, and I stood on tiptoes. I immediately rocked back down. Singing filled the air – the *Te Deum* again – as a procession of monks began making their stately way up the path in pairs. They passed on, not taking the route around to enter the parliament hall but bearing right towards their own spaces. Murmurs of approval rose around me as they disappeared. And then, as one, caps, bonnets, and feathered hats came off, making it easier to see.

Mark!

There he was, looking serious, walking in lockstep with one of the household musicians. Both had spotless white surcoats of lawn over their liveries. As soon as they'd stepped from the gatehouse onto the carpet, they paused and blew again. A cheer went up from the men ahead of me. I raised my own hand, not to be seen, but to join in the general cry, to be part of it.

As they began the procession, I started at a familiar figure. Hal Percy followed them, his face a slate, carrying the red, round cardinal's hat. He walked with a modified slouch. Wolsey, I supposed, meant to show him favour; or, perhaps, he enjoyed advertising his humiliation, which had surely reached beyond York Place. Percy followed Mark and his fellow trumpeter, and behind him came four black-clad priests, the first two bearing enormous, solid-silver crosses which winked in the bright morning sunlight, and the pair behind them each carrying silver pillars. A collective gasp of appreciation – or awe – went up at the sight.

It rose in pitch. Wolsey's herald advanced, holding aloft a sparkling gold and silver mace.

Eager cheers broke out.

The cardinal himself, folded onto a mule – which must have been sent over in advance and dressed in crimson velvet and golden stirrups – rode sedately, his back straight. Around his broad, scarlet-clad shoulders glinted the heavy, golden chain of Ss which marked his office as lord chancellor.

I'd seen similar processions before, many times. They always amazed me. Wolsey always amazed me. It wasn't the trappings that did it; it was his bearing, his calm, dignified features, his straightness of back.

Majesty, I thought.

My master had true Majesty.

Dangerous thought.

He rode on, his mule keeping its head down, heedless of the footmen who marched just behind it, their poleaxes – lightweight, gilt things – turned upwards so that their tips caught the sun. There began to pour after them the officers of the household.

Minus one.

As usual, the ushers began a singing chorus: 'On, my

lords and masters, on. Make way before His Grace.' For show, of course. The path was clear. Before the gentlemen of the household could follow, I began moving back up the path, parallel to the cardinal on his mule. As he reached each cluster of men, the cries and shouts went up in unison, each man apparently hoping that a glance might be cast his way, the cardinal's eye caught, a face remembered and marked out for favour.

As Wolsey – and me with him – neared the parliament hall, I heard similar cries of acclamation rising from those who had opted to go northward, to see if they might catch a view of the king instead. More trumpet blasts roared out. I considered going to see him myself but thought better of it. Not only was King Henry the most guarded man in England, but his way from Bridewell was covered on all sides by the bridge and the walls of the privy galleries leading to the hall.

How he must hate that.

Mark and his colleague's trumpets again fought with those coming from the northern end of the building, as Wolsey reached the entrance, and his gentlemen rushed to help him dismount. The two yeoman made a great show of opening the doors, and the cardinal was gone in a whirl of red.

The rest of the procession – no end of a procession – caught up. Those of the cardinal's household stood back, making way, as the men of the parliament who'd lodged with Wolsey made their hesitant way up the path. Their faces each wore nervous, out-of-place looks. That, I supposed, was the point of the great cavalcade – to cow these country squires with the pomp and glory of their betters. It would be a brave man from the arse-end of nowhere who defied either king or cardinal in refusing to vote in favour of raising money in the shires.

The crowd thickened around me – I lost any hope of trying to spot a face – any dangerous face – in it. Some enterprising men had brought tabors and pipes and added their own noise – more well meant than pleasant – to the din of hurrahs. For what seemed like hours, burgesses and obscure knights were disgorged from wherries and made their way up the path. I recognised, amongst them, the hard features and lumpen figure of Sir Thomas More. Someone – his wife, I suppose – had ensured that his gown was unrumpled, and his face shaved close. Still, his hat was the same battered thing I knew well enough. He didn't, as most of the parliament men did, keep his head down in a show of ignoring the crowds, but raised a hand occasionally and called back to men who shouted greetings.

The sun was rising fast. Heat came with it, for once, raising sweat on my brow.

The torrent of men reduced to a trickle.

I wasn't the only one to notice it. The men – and some women – watching from the sides of the path began to settle back. Some drifted off. Others collapsed on the grass. The spectacle of the day had been Wolsey's procession – as the cardinal had known – and he had delivered it. I looked around for Mark, hoping to speak with him, but he had apparently gone inside the hall with Wolsey, likely to blow him on waves of music up to wherever his place was inside. The rest of the household had melted away too, likely for refreshments as they awaited the day's business being concluded.

At a loss, I sidled through the retreating crowd and made my way towards the huge doors. They remained open.

Though I knew little about parliaments, I understood that the idea was that they were public things. It was supposed to be that any man might stick his head in and listen to the affairs of the realm being debated. In truth, of course, only a brave one would dare to presume upon the goodwill of the yeomen.

I puffed my chest out, to ensure that they could see my badge – though I felt sure they'd remember my face.

'Cardinal forgot something?' asked the friendlier one as I hopped from grass to carpet.

'No, I . . . I wished to look.'

'To peep at the king?' snorted the other. He knew better than to spit now, though.

I said nothing, assuming I had leave. Stepping between them, I stood in the doorway of the parliament hall.

The vast space yawned before me. I gasped. It was the height that threw me – it somehow seemed far higher inside than out – three storeys, possibly four. The ceiling was hammerbeam, and banners displaying England's arms hung in profusion from between its carved rafters. A huge chessboard of a floor spread ahead, sparkling white and black. To my right, scaffold-like seating, as you'd find at a tournament, held clouds of hatless men: all the fellows who had traipsed up the path and were now lit from behind by oriel windows. Directly in front of me, on the floor itself, single rows of benches faced one another, these awash in the rich reds and whites of the noblemen who must have come in via the northern entrance. A little to my left, more men in red sat on the woolsacks, which were arranged roughly in a square.

But farther left, at the far end of the hall, was the greatest sight.

A shallow flight of steps, covered in fringed blue silk and golden fleurs-de-lis, led up to a dais that ran almost the width of the chamber. It was dominated by a white throne, its armrests two richly carved, crowned lions covered in gold leaf. This stood at the centre of the dais, below a shimmering, creamy canopy. Fighting for attention, however, was the still form of Wolsey, whose redness stood out against the vibrant sea-blue. He was sitting on a low stool at the foot of the throne, some lesser prelates in red and white a step down from him.

Trumpets blared from somewhere I couldn't see.

The noise – a low hum – silenced. The vastness of the hall amplified the sudden cessation of noise, so that there was something emphatic in the quietness.

From some secret entrance to the right of the throne stepped King Henry, made smaller not only by distance but by the vastness of the room. He was dressed as I'd never seen him: a cloth-of-gold suit was almost hidden under similarly bright robes, all lined in ermine. His reddish blonde hair was covered by his crown, and clutched in one hand, lying across his broad chest, was the sceptre of state.

The king took one step forward and surveyed his people. His expression was solemn, impossibly handsome. And then he turned, so that we could see his profile – his long, strong, straight nose, the fringe of his golden beard. He moved forwards, seeming almost to float, until he was before the throne, before turning back to face us. From nowhere – no one was looking for them – a pair of attendants appeared at his side and lifted his robes so that he could settle securely onto the throne. Wolsey and the other prelates settled back on their stools, as another attendant materialised, carrying a velvet cushion bearing an ermine-lined cap. Only then did I realise that the rest of the men in the room, whether the red-robed noblemen, the clerks half-hidden on the giant chessboard, and the men up on the benches, had all stood. With whispers of cloth, they began to take their seats again.

'Christ, another one.'

The voice tugged at my back. It took me a second to place it, so lost was I in the strange spectacle of the parliament assembling before me.

The yeoman.

I turned, reluctantly.

'In black. Commons man? Bloody countrified dolt.'

'Hush, it's a friar. Must be bearing a message. Better let him pass.'

I followed their gaze, frowning.

Up the deserted path, unwatched by the few people who had remained standing on the grass beside it, tottered a figure in a black cope. It nearly fell, regained its feet, and stumbled forward again.

'Christ, what's wrong with the man?' asked the unfriendly yeoman.

'Get your weapons,' I said.

'What?' asked the first guard.

'Get your weapons!'

25

I threw myself forward, away from the doors into the parliament hall, my palms up. The figure looked at me without recognition. Sweat shone over skin an unhealthy shade of yellowish white.

'Good morrow, Mr Rowlet,' I said. It had taken me a moment to recognise him without the beard.

He leapt forward, clutching at me. There was, I felt, no strength behind him. Yet he managed to hook his fingers into the front of my doublet, and he clung there, whimpering.

'I am murder – murdered,' he gasped.

The more active yeoman had got behind me, his halberd before him. 'What is this?' he asked.

'The man is wounded,' I said, feeling my heart begin to race. 'Ill.'

'It's a sick man,' said the guard. I sensed him turning away from us. 'Sore sick, by the look of him.'

'Murd-ered,' choked Rowlet.

And then, with a sudden show of force I wouldn't have thought possible, he lurched forward, sending me sprawling on my back. Cries of surprise from the yeomen sounded over me. I rolled onto my side, winded. 'Stop him!' I gasped. 'Stop him! Don't let him pass!'

Both men stood, frozen, as Rowlet staggered into the doorway and gave a long, low, plaintive wail. I could hear the chorus of cries from within, echoing up to the rafters.

'I am murdered,' he screamed, 'by the cardinal's—'

He was cut off, as the rougher yeoman seized the back of his cope in his bunch of a fist and nearly lifted him off his feet. 'Get them fucking doors shut!'

His fellow did as he was bid, offering nothing to the vast sea of men within the hall.

I regained my feet, trembling all over. Rowlet hung limp in the guard's grasp. It appeared his final spurt had robbed him of the last of his power. 'What the bloody hell is this?' barked his captor.

Before I could answer, a commotion behind me sounded. I spun, in time to see a friar pounding up the carpet. The people who'd been watching began to gather again, as though the sense of something odd happening had infected them.

'Brother Alfred,' I said, exhaling relief as I recognised the stone-faced master of the friars' household.

'You,' he said. His gaze darted between me, the sagging Rowlet, and the yeomen. 'Begging your pardon. He – got out. We thought him too far gone. He awoke this morning and begged to be let out.'

'Do you know him?' My voice came out hard.

Good.

'Know? He came upon us yesterday. Grievous wounded. We've been tending him in the infirmary. Christian duty. He gave no name. Thought he'd come from the city.'

No. Just from York Place.

'His name is Rowlet,' I said.

'Says he's been murdered,' said the yeoman who was still free. 'He tried to break in upon the king.'

The friar whitened. 'Please . . . help me return him to the infirmary. He has been sore wounded – don't know how.'

'Give him to me,' I said. 'Brother Alfred and I will – we'll get him back to his bed.'

The yeoman launched Rowlet at me and, before he could collapse to the ground, I gripped him under an arm. The friar did the same. When he was securely between us, some animation crept into him. 'I am . . . murdered.' His head lolled. It rose again and seemed to see me. 'You! Murderer!'

'Ignore him,' I said, heaving. 'He raves. Madness.'

Together, we dragged the fellow onto the grass and made as inconspicuous a journey as we could eastward through the grounds of the Blackfriars, not pausing until we reached the low square of the infirmary building. Alfred let go, transferring the weight of Rowlet to me as he opened the door.

'In here,' he said.

I heaved him in, as the friar indicated a featherbed – and then I threw him down on it and stared around the room. It was a large one, with only a pair of good beds but plenty of low, unfurnished pallets. Shelves of medicines stood on one wall, and by the door we'd come through were nailed wooden pegs, each bearing copes. I returned my attention to the stricken man and nudged the bed with my foot, none too gently.

'Have a care,' said Alfred.

I didn't reply. Instead, I looked down at the fallen figure, at the waxy pallor of his skin, at the carefully shaven beard; he hadn't even begun to show red stubble.

Beardless fellow, like yourself, young sir.

That explained the silver ewer. An attempt at disguise in case he was seen.

'What ails him?' I asked. 'Show me the wounds.' I was being rude, I knew, brusque – but Brother Alfred seemed the type to respond better to that. He did as I asked, bending down.

'He's taken this cope from here,' he said, prising it apart. Underneath, Rowlet was clad only in a white nightshirt. The friar loosened it, to reveal a criss-cross of careful, thin cuts. 'He has been cut severely. Here. Upper arms. At the ankle.'

'With care,' I said. 'Expertly, would you say?'

The question seemed to throw him. 'I couldn't . . . Yes. Well pierced. As in bleedings.'

I sniffed. 'He arrived yesterday, you said?' The friar nodded. 'And he'd tried to bind his wounds, hadn't he? In linen, perhaps? Strips of painted cloth?'

Alfred frowned. 'Yes. We put them to be laundered, to be put to some better purpose. Bloodied. We've tried to treat him . . . but see here? The raising of the skin? He's lost much blood. Infection . . . I fear corruption.'

'I think,' I said, 'he tried to treat the wounds himself.'

'Yes. Or someone did. The bindings he came in – they were . . .'

'Stinking?' I knew the smell, from the phials left in Rowlet's chamber. It was the same rotten stuff I'd once been given to treat my scars: the foul concoction of clay and shellfish and assorted detritus which I'd been led to believe was sovereign against open wounds.

'Has he said anything?' I asked. 'Other than begging to be released from the place today?'

Alfred gave me a long, hard look, and then his gaze fell to

my badge. 'He has . . . cried out for forgiveness.'

I looked down at the man. 'Forgiveness? For what?'

'I couldn't . . .' He looked towards the door of the large, plain room. 'For the two lives.'

'Two lives he'd taken?' I asked.

This time he met my gaze. 'I couldn't say. He was raving. Corruption, as I said.'

I nodded. I had enough, I thought. Still, I leant down and took a grip of Rowlet's clothes, ignoring the weak murmurs from the friar. 'The boy,' I said. 'The London lad. You slew him.'

The name roused him, though he didn't open his eyes. His hands, claw-like and white, flailed up towards where I had a grip of him. 'Ungodly. Wicked ruffian. He would . . . a noose . . . would have met a noose. Wicked. God forgive me.'

'Met a noose,' I echoed. 'Perhaps. He might have slain me, eh? Was that what you promised him – the joy of that? Only to murder him first.' Phlegm or blood rattled in his chest, but he said nothing. 'And the woman?' I asked. 'Cotes?'

Again, a name seemed to work some weak magic. 'Not part,' he croaked. 'Not . . . no woman. She had no part. Her part only to cry out.' Then his eyes opened, red-rimmed and seemingly sightless as they were. 'Not my fault. Not. She aped her brave master. Womanish.'

I released him and drew back. 'Oh? You did not use your smooth tongue to steady her purpose, then?'

Rowlet continued gazing upwards, fearfully, at nothing. 'Not of our company. Not of our fellowship. No woman.'

'No,' I said. 'Yet your fellowship left her with nothing. Her blood is on your hands, and you shall burn in Hell for it.'

At this, he cried out, 'No! No! God – God forgive me!

Fri – friar – God forgive me! Godly design, *Deus prop –
propi* . . . forgive me!'

After a moment, I said, 'He might. I won't.'

I turned to the friar, who was gazing at the scene with his
brow furrowed. I said nothing to him, offered no explanation.
The rest, I had just about worked out to my satisfaction – if
satisfaction is the right word for an ugly truth. 'Will he live?'

'I cannot say. He's lost a lot of blood. We might . . . continue
to treat him.' His eyes slid from the stricken man to me.

'I don't care,' I said. 'You'll be saving him only for the
hangman to finish the job.'

26

I waited in an anteroom in the prior's lodgings in the Blackfriars, following the lines of a tapestry that depicted Solomon delivering judgement. He sat enthroned, one arm raised as he pointed down at the scene before him. The only nods to antiquity were the loose, flowing robes; otherwise, Solomon looked very much like our King Henry, perpetually youthful and full-blooded.

A door clicked open, making me step back.

'His Grace will speak with you now,' said Cavendish. I slid off my cap and moved towards the door. It was late, the sun already beginning its descent. I'd had to wait until the opening of the parliament was over. The king had returned over his private bridge to Bridewell to be re-dressed for the evening's festivities. Wolsey and Sir Thomas More had retired to the prior's palace tucked away next to the church, and it had been all I could do to get a message to them.

But it was a message they needed to hear, as long as a man was falsely imprisoned for murders he didn't commit.

I stepped into the room – a fair place, well-furnished, but without the glitter and shine of those hidden rooms in York Place. Wolsey reclined on a couch, stripped down to his white robes, a wooden cup on the floor beside him, whilst More sat on a stool beside him, clutching his in both hands. The scholar-lawyer looked rumpled enough now. Already, a darkening of stubble shadowed his cheeks.

'Anthony Blanke,' purred the cardinal. He made no effort to straighten himself. 'You come upon us at rest. You must be quick. We must cross the river for supper with His Majesty.' He yawned, as though the thought bored him. 'Yet we must banquet. To toast Sir Thomas. He, we think, will be elected our very good Speaker this term.'

More turned a smile towards me – a shy smile; it made him look younger. 'It is possible,' he said.

'It will be,' said Wolsey. 'We would have it, my friend.'

'Yet all things, you must own, remain merely possible until they happen.'

I bowed to them both, eager to cut off the flow of their banter. When I rose, I said, 'Your Grace must release Mr Deacon.'

This raised him to a sitting position, and caused More to turn sharply to me, the smile frozen on his face. 'Must?' asked Wolsey, seeming more offended by that word than anything else.

'Your Grace might,' I said. 'I . . . have discovered what occurred.'

'Is this,' asked More, 'to do with the madman who attempted to come upon as we sat?'

'Yes,' I said. 'It was Mr Rowlet.'

'What?' More stood, nearly knocking over his stool. He turned, baffled, to Wolsey. 'Your Grace told me my friend was dead. Murdered.' He looked at me. 'What is this? Some jape – some trickery, I think.'

I took a deep breath. I had had the rest of the day to work out what had happened – to see how it fit together. The reality of it, though, the truth: that was laced with wrongness. 'Mr

Rowlet lies wounded in the infirmary here. Dying, perhaps. He wounded himself. He drew blood. From his chest, his ankles.' I'd known it, from the moment I'd found no body, only blood – and when the wherryman had acknowledged no sight of one, it had been clear enough: the last outrage, Rowlet's supposed murder, had felt wrong, had felt like a feint of some kind.

I lifted my own foot from the ground and pointed. I'd been bled myself, for the good of my health. It was an unpleasant thing, but, though I didn't admit it, in the past I'd found that it tended to make me paler, for a day or two at least. 'He was a physician's assistant,' I said. 'He knew how to do it without . . . causing sudden death. But I understand infection has come upon him since, and he's made himself too weak to fight it.'

Wolsey, all traces of tiredness gone, got to his feet and began balling and releasing his fists. 'What is this madness, boy? It is plain you think you have some discovery that absolves the heretic Deacon of these late crimes. What is it?'

I looked at More rather than Wolsey; he seemed less imposing. 'It's . . . it began with Mr Cosyn.'

'Yes, yes,' said Wolsey. 'In our house, awaiting our presence. The wicked Deacon killed him, to blacken our name.'

'No,' I said. I blinked, feeling my mouth dry.
Don't say it.
Say it. Face it.
'Mr Cosyn killed himself.'

Wolsey stopped moving. More lifted his hand to cover his mouth, as though I'd just sworn some impossibly evil oath, and sat back down. Taking advantage of their shock, I plunged on. 'He was – when he came to us at Richmond, he was nervous. He kept glancing at the door. I thought at first, perhaps he suspected someone would come to arrest him. Or worse. But . . . but no. He intended to die in your house, sir. He was dying anyway. He took a great lot of pain medicines – hoping to make the feat easier, I think. He wished . . . to make it appear to be a terrible murder. His last act against you. To bring Your Grace down.'

I was certain of it. I'd gone over it in my mind many times now, thinking again and again of the beginning of this whole gruesome affair: the frightened old man, his shallow, inexpert wounds. It would have taken great courage, great will, to pierce his own flesh with a poker. But it would have taken little physical effort to free his wasted, failing body from pain. I could recall Dr Mordaunt's shock on discovering him. Evidently, though he was part of the plot, he'd had no idea of the brutal means by which his old friend would stage his own murder.

'No,' said More. 'It cannot be. Mr Cosyn was. . .'

But Wolsey was staring at me, his face suddenly soft. Gently, he said, 'Cosyn was a man of extremes.'

'He gave away everything he had to this house. Blackfriars. He had a friend here.'

'That friar – Gervaise?' asked Wolsey.

'Who?' asked More. 'A friar was amongst Mr Cosyn's company indeed?'

Wolsey shook his head. 'Go on, boy. You have our ear.'

I nodded, trying to rearrange my thoughts after the interruption. 'It was a plot.'

'A complot,' blurted Wolsey, before holding up his palms.

'A complot,' I said. 'Arranged between a group of men in

a tavern. The sign of the Bottle. Mr Cosyn, Dr Mordaunt, Mr Rowlet, and that Brother Gervaise. Most of them very old. Ill.'

'Dr Mordaunt too?' asked More. 'I knew he was . . . growing loud in his. . .' He stared at the floor before looking up, sharply, at me. 'Are you saying, Anthony, that Mr Rowlet killed the doctor? His own master?'

'No,' I said. 'Dr Mordaunt killed himself too.' More slumped, clearly disbelieving. 'This was their design. He took a draught of a poison he carried himself. When he was in audience with Your Grace,' I said, looking at Wolsey, who had begun pacing the rush matting of the room, 'he was wet with sweat. He might have drunk the stuff before coming to see you. He threw the bottle down – perhaps as he fled. Perhaps before.' I shifted my gaze to More, my jaw set. 'That's how I found it, sir.'

'But . . . but this is monstrous. If true, this is monstrous. Unspeakable.'

And I'm sure it shan't be spoken of, I thought.

'An aberration,' said Wolsey. Even he, man of the world that he was, seemed taken aback, his arms falling still. 'An abomination in the sight of God. If true.'

I swallowed. I'd gone too far now, in accusing dead men of an unforgiveable sin – too far to turn back. And I was right – I knew it. 'Sir Thomas spoke to me of a murder that was dressed to look like a . . . self-killing.' Wolsey cast a sharp, silent glance at More, who remained without expression. 'Yet – you see – it might work the other way. It did – it was supposed to. That should have been the end of it. You should have been ruined, Your Grace, brought low by the scandal. But you weren't.'

'The king was displeased,' said Wolsey, almost to himself.

'But nothing happened. Save Sir Thomas was charged with investigating what looked like crimes.'

'But Mr Rowlet is my friend,' said More. He shook his head at me. His expression had changed from disbelief to something approaching disgust, though at what I couldn't say.

'Go on, boy,' said Wolsey.

'It. . . Mr Rowlet must have had the idea to – to lay the blame elsewhere. At someone in your household. And I fit well enough. He. . .' I looked down at the rushes myself. One stick of them had stuck to my shoe and I scraped it off. 'He knew I might be . . . suspect. And so he followed me to London. You recall, Sir Thomas? When I returned from London, after Dr Mordaunt was killed, you said that Mr Rowlet had brought you books from the city? He was there, then, when I was?'

'Is this true?' asked Wolsey.

More sagged on his stool, regarded his big hands, and then clasped them between the folds of his black gown. 'Yes, but . . . yes.'

'He was free to go to London again, when I did. He'd followed me about – saw me with the prentice boy. He slew that boy. And the old woman – she was as hot against my master as her own had been.' This was the part of the tale I couldn't see clearly – it was all beyond my vision. 'He visited with her, after I first met her. I knew someone had gone into the yard – I heard the dog. But I . . . I didn't go back.' I hurried on. 'He took a knife from her table then – or after – and used it to kill the prentice.'

'He didn't – he didn't kill her too?' asked More. Then,

more certainly, 'Impossible! He was by my side before she
. . .'

Yes.

'. . . *kill her* too.'

He was beginning to see it. He was beginning to believe
me. That, I knew, was key in persuading people of the truth:
to lay it before them, like a painted cloth or a picture. When
they could see it, they could accept it. 'No.' I was, I felt, on
firmer ground again. 'You recall, sir – you saw that her throat
was cut and that Mark and I were innocent.' He inclined his
head. 'She cried out that a cardinal's man was about her. She
cried it out. She wasn't crying for help, as we thought. She
wished someone to hear – anyone. And then . . .' I swallowed.
'She cut her own throat.'

'Another!' barked Wolsey. 'Another mad old monster.'

More opened his mouth to speak and I cut in, as smoothly
as I could. 'I noticed – in her chamber, there was no way a
bloodied murderer could have escaped without leaving a
trace.'

'Nor was there a knife,' said More. 'Nor did poor Mistress
Cotes have any bloody weapon in her hand.'

'No. No, I wondered about that. And I thought – her
table – you recall, the board on a barrel?' He said nothing
but stared evenly at me. 'It was cracked, broken. It wasn't,
from what I remember, when I first saw it.' I knew that was
flimsier than the board itself had been, and so rushed on.
'When Mark and I left, his dog – the dog we took – it was
sniffing at some sharp piece of dirty wood. I threw it away. I
didn't think of it then.'

'Well?' asked Wolsey. But before I could answer, a strange
smile crossed his face. 'This old wench cried murder, cut her

own throat with her edge of sharp wood, and threw it out as you rushed in on her.'

'Yes,' I said. The memory of it all prevented me from smiling. 'I don't know – but I suspect Rowlet had warned her that cardinal's men might visit her again. She must have known what Cosyn and Mordaunt had done. She elected to play her part too. "Aped her master," he said. She and Rowlet might have had much traffic when he was in town. Sir Thomas – you sent him into my lord cardinal's household after . . . after I was freed from the gaol. But he was with you in the city.'

'In London, yes,' said More, gruffly.

'Persuading you, sir, to follow me. To be suspicious of me.' He didn't answer or look at me. 'And then persuading you to have him take up a place in York House. Where he wrote to the Blackfriars and bid the old friar come to him, to make his end on the cardinal's great barge.'

A little strength returned to More's voice. 'This is too terrible. I cannot conceive of any . . . I just cannot. . .'

'He should have had to go no further. It should have ended with his murder of the prentice. I should've been hanged for it, and it should all have come out – how my lord bid a murderous servant to kill his enemies. But it didn't. I was freed. And Mistress Cotes's—' I nearly said *sacrifice* – 'self-murder failed too.

'And so the rest of the plotters – this friar – he decided to give up his own life. Another old man. He went willingly to his death. I believe he came to York Place in the night and awaited Mr Rowlet. The bast—, the varlet crept out to the landing stairs from his chamber window – along the outer walls of the palace. I've done it myself, now. He met that old friar and . . . and killed him swiftly – well, you might say. An easy death. As he'd murdered the prentice after luring him up to meet me in the city. And when that, too, failed to cause a great ruffle . . . then, there was only Rowlet left. He didn't mean to die, I don't think. He meant to wound himself. He'd the skill to do it, as a physician's assistant. He meant to wound himself, only, I think. After turning his chamber all about to make it look like he'd been truly attacked by someone who wished to silence him. Then he intended to reappear – to cause a mischief and upset the parliament.'

I stopped. I'd run out of breath, but I thought I'd included everything as I'd tried, in various ways, to thread it together since my trip to the infirmary.

No one spoke for a moment.

At length, More said, 'But I . . . I set Mr Rowlet to sp—' He turned to Wolsey, his face blanching. 'I asked him to aid Your Grace in the discovery of these crimes.'

Another silence fell, this one more tense.

'Yes,' I said, breaking it. 'That put him in York Place. He'd failed to have me kept in gaol, blamed. Yet he could still make it look like he'd been attacked himself. By anyone he wished to blame. Would you have believed him, sir? If he'd appeared, all wounded and bloodless, at the parliament – if he'd come tearing in and said an attempt had been made on his life in the cardinal's house, would you have believed him? Would all those men of the parliament? Would the king?'

Wolsey took a shuddering breath. 'Well,' he said. 'Well, Thomas? Would you have believed such a cunning slander?' More didn't answer, and the cardinal gave a snorting, humourless laugh. 'My dear Thomas. It appears you set a plotter to investigate wicked crimes of which he was. . .

What is it – that old saw the Scotch have – of which he was *art and part.*'

More's head hung, shaking a little, frowning. He seemed to have gone numb, as if the thought of his old friends deciding that God had marked them for death – but that they might choose the means of it – had sent his mind somewhere else, somewhere beyond reach. His gaze was unfixed. In a whisper, he mumbled, 'If this is known . . . if this becomes known . . . no man will trust to the wisdom of scholars.'

It won't become known, though. . .

Wolsey moved to the horn window, opened it, and let in a wave of cool, twilit air. It carried the scent of the river on it – not sour, as it usually was in the heart of London, but refreshing, mingled with the scents of small meadows and herb gardens. He began working at the thing, easing it open and closed on its hinges, as though needing something to do and enjoying the fan. At length, he turned. 'What you have said, lad – these accusations – they are monstrous. These men formed a confused – a monstrous – an accursed and iniquitous. . .' Eloquence failed him and insult provided. '*Sect!* A damned *sect!* Monstrous.'

'Yes, Your Grace.'

'Self-murder,' mumbled More, still on his stool, still not looking at either of us. 'I cannot believe it. I knew these men had grown hot in their passions, but . . . self-murder.'

'I think,' I chanced, 'that they saw it as a . . . form of sacrifice. The friar had been reading the lives of martyrs who chose death for their faith – who let themselves be killed for it. He cast images of pelicans. They might have seen themselves as pelicans, giving up their lives for . . . something else.'

'Pelicans?' spat Wolsey, as though I might have believed

in their strange cause. 'Rather a flock of ageing, unpuissant roosters. Pecking with impotent rage, ay, about the feet of the great cock. I mean,' he added, with a gracious incline of his head, 'our true Church. Fighting us, in all ignorance of the ravening wolf which prowls without. I mean the poisonous body of Luther's dupes. Any little reformation in our universal Church shall proceed from our wit and will. Ay, and wisdom.'

To my surprise – my horror – I saw that tears had begun to flow from More's eyes. He looked to the plain wooden ceiling. 'Can I have been so deceived in a man? In *men*? Is my judgement so weakened – can I have been so deceived?'

'Peace, Thomas,' said Wolsey. '*Creo quia absurdum est*. If true, this was an enterprise drawn with all the cunning of devilry.'

'If true,' echoed More. Something like hope bloomed in his watery eyes – faint, but there. 'If true. . . Have you proof of these wild claims, Anthony?'

I looked first at him and then at the cardinal. 'Rowlet lies sick. Dying. Bloodless. In the infirmary here.' I swallowed. 'You said, Your Grace, that the men here were loyal.'

'And so they are.'

'If he's a man of faith – if he believes himself a man of faith – might he not . . . be induced to confess before he dies?'

'The confessional is sacred,' said More, his own voice passionless.

But Wolsey grasped my inference. 'You cunning young . . . yes, I think, we have friends enough here that might . . . reap our favour. If this man should confess his wickedness openly, in the sight of God.'

More threw his head back again and rubbed the sides of

his stubbled face with both hands. When he spoke, his voice sounded rusty, distant again. 'Let it be done, if it must be done. The light of truth must be shone. Yet it could never be produced as evidence in court.'

Wolsey turned again to the window. 'If he confesses to such evil, he shall never see a court.' He returned to us. 'He is dying, after all. From this – this loss of blood. By God, what shall I say to the king?'

'It yet seems so . . . impossible,' said More.

'All things,' I said, 'seem only possible. Until they happen.'

'Well said, young Anthony,' smiled Wolsey. 'We shall send Mr Audley down to speak with our loyal friends the friars. We shall have the truth of this. You may go. My people are lodging here tonight.'

I bowed my thanks. And then I remembered what had driven me. I cleared my throat. 'And Mr Deacon, Your Grace? If his innocence is proven. . .'

More answered, rising and cuffing away the dampness on his weathered cheeks. 'Mr Deacon is not to be arraigned for murder,' he said, 'but to be examined for heresy.'

'Quite,' said Wolsey. 'The wretched serpent shall remain where he is. The king's mercy does not extend to heretics, by God. Sir Thomas is even now writing to refute the book that the foul creature had in his possession.' As though as a sop, he offered, 'We are not overeager with the flames.'

Seeming to bristle at the last, More said, 'The king's justice will be done him. Do not trouble yourself. The least of the king's subjects has justice.'

'Yes. You may go now, Anthony. You have done well –

your service pleases us, even if the news is strange. Now, Thomas, to frame this to His Majesty. . .'

Dumbfounded, I backed from the room.

* * *

The grass outside the row of cottages had become a blaze of light. Bonfires had been lit, and we of the cardinal's household passed around wineskins, bottles, and tankards. Some of the household musicians had got up a consort and were singing and playing Italian tunes. The sky above was a deep blue, peppered with stars, and the air was thick with the rich smell of smoke.

'He shall be buried outside,' said Harry. 'Mr Audley says that it counts as self-murder, even if it was not . . . immediate.'

I nodded. I'd been unsurprised when news came from the infirmary, warping and bending through the household, that the raving madman there had been shriven but had died. No one seemed to know of what. Privately, I suspected he'd been given something to ease him out of the world he was teetering on the edge of. Infirmarians, so I'd heard, did that often enough, as a means of alleviating suffering.

And at whose order this time?

'Good,' I said. He would have seen me hang as a murderer, for no other reason than he thought my face fit the crime and I happened to be a servant of his and his friends' imagined great enemy – one of the baubles of a great court he thought shouldn't be.

Yet . . . yet . . . there had been honesty in his madness. There had even been some fair observations, not that I'd ever admit to them. He and his mad old friends had aimed at something. Every man, I thought, was in pursuit of *something* – riches, love, place, a quiet life, or some greater policy. Some were just wilder and more passionate in their pursuit than others. My unjust execution would have been one small death in his great design – a worthy sacrifice.

Tough.

My life mattered more than one man and his friends' hatred of my master.

'Here,' said Mark, coming towards us, the reflected flames of a bonfire dancing up one side of him. He held out a bottle. 'French wine.' His white coat, so pristine earlier, was spotted with dark stains. 'You should have some, sir,' he said, addressing Harry. 'And maybe you'll be loosened enough to tell us about this lady what ye're hopin' to court. And your good friends'll be honest enough to tell you if we think you're good enough for her.' He held out the bottle, but Harry only pursed his lips.

'Envy is not to be borne,' he said. '*Ut ameris, amabilis esto.*'

'What?' snorted Mark, one eyebrow crinkling his brow. He had, I noticed, kept his hat on: a general sense of license, fuelled by the wine, had descended. Rebuffed, he offered the bottle to me.

'No thanks,' I said, thinking of the wine cellar at Richmond, and of blood pooling on an old woman's floor. My mind was turning on Deacon, wherever the poor wretch had been taken. I had no particular liking for him – he was another household officer, like any other. But it was me who'd suggested a search. It was me who'd had him taken up.

For owning evil books.

He was guilty of that – or would be found so.

In the eyes of the law.

The least of the king's subjects has justice.

'I'm . . . I can't believe there's such madness in the world,' I said, unsure if I meant Rowlet and his group of madmen or the blind, waving, horribly sharp sword of justice, which seemed to cut down men it wasn't even aimed at.

'See it,' said Mark, offering a burp. 'Believe it.'

'I agree,' said Harry, drawing a grin from Mark. 'With Anthony.' The smile faded. 'Mr Audley says that as long as these sects spring up to attack the Church, His Grace must stand firmer and mightier than ever.'

'It's the standing firm and mighty as makes folks want to strike at him,' said Mark, before taking a swig.

'Just so. If we allow fighting amongst ourselves, we will be weaker prey to any other attacker. It is as well that enemies within remain in ward, where they cannot attack our master in thought or deed.'

'Enough,' I said. 'Enough.'

'I agree,' said Mark, mimicking Harry's voice with quite some accuracy. 'With Anthony.'

'Is that an attempt at mockery, sirrah?' asked Harry.

Mark shrugged, making a face. 'I make a foolish noise better than any man.'

'Yes,' countered Harry. 'I know. I have heard you play the trumpet.'

Mark barked laughter. 'Well played. For a gentleman. *Sir.*'

'Another attempt at wit? I ask only because I would hear sharper from your flea-farm of a dog.'

Mark jerked back, as though struck. 'Are you going to let him talk about little Blackjack like that, Anthony? Our own little Blackjack?'

'*Blackjack?* Who the hell is Blackjack?' I asked.

Our arguments and laughter rose up and blew away with the smoke.

AUTHOR'S NOTE

In 1523, Cardinal Wolsey sat at the height of his powers. The state papers of the year indicate this, showing him busy at work, operating as a king in all but name. Indeed, when Henry visited the fortifications at Portsmouth in March, Wolsey was left behind to continue seeing to affairs of state. Common also to this period are voluminous letters and papers covering the saga of the Turks' attacks on Rhodes, and the attempts of cardinal and king to raise money for their ongoing war with France via the first parliament called in eight years. This war would, in the end, peter out ingloriously; Surrey and Suffolk would campaign without much success on the continent, and Wolsey's unpopularity would grow as he sought various means to fill the English war chest. In addition to the state papers, useful in writing this book were Diarmaid MacCulloch's *The Reign of Henry VIII: Politics, Policy and Piety* (1995: Macmillan) and Carolly Erickon's *Great Harry: The Extravagant Life of Henry VIII* (1995: Robson). It was from the latter that I drew such interesting details as the ways in which towels were folded over the arms of various household officers, and the perennial problem of young men scrawling phalluses on the walls of palaces.

The state papers do not make clear when Henry returned from Portsmouth; having him intrude on the Maundy ritual (which really was the queen's day – Mary I would continue it) is my own invention. He had obviously returned prior to the parliament, however, which assembled on Wednesday the

15th of April. There, he gave a speech on justice as part of the opening. More would be elected as Speaker of the parliament on the following Saturday.

In writing Sir Thomas More, I drew primarily on Peter Ackroyd's *The Life of Thomas More* (1991: Chatto & Windus). This book is marvellous in conveying just how rich and colourful the city of London was in its late-mediaeval/early renaissance years. It is commonly thought that Wolsey and More were enemies, based on the latter's eventual disassociation from the cardinal. In 1523, however, they were still friends and colleagues; Wolsey, in fact, was almost certainly behind getting More elected as Speaker at the parliament. Sir Thomas More was, at this early stage, in high favour as a counsellor – but so too had he long harboured doubts about the princely way in which Wolsey (and others of his rank in the Roman Church) lived. These were far from Lutheran beliefs; More and his circle were very much in favour of reform *within* the Church, and in time the scholar would come to refute, emphatically, attempts from without to make doctrinal changes. He was, throughout his life, a man wedded to institutions and their permanence. Less permanent and trickier to draw a bead on, were his living quarters.

Numerous printed sources date the move to his famous house at Chelsea to as early as 1520. Bucklersbury was More's first London home. According to Ackroyd, the Mores came to Chelsea only in late 1525 or early 1526. He was certainly a man interested in property; he had acquired also a house in Bishopsgate – Crosby Place – once owned by Catherine of Aragon (and probably less charmingly, Richard III). The lease on Crosby Place was finally purchased in June 1523, and then sold to Antonio Bonvisi six months later – in what appears to have been some elaborate, early modern house flip. Confusingly, Bonvisi later leased it to More's son-in-law, William Roper. E.E. Reynolds' book on Margaret Roper claims that, about the time of the Bonvisi house flip, More began buying land in Chelsea with a view to building. The Mores certainly also owned a property in Butclose (near the present Royal Albert Hall) which he leased to his daughter and son-in-law after they wed in 1521, and he appears to have leased Bucklersbury to his ward, Margaret Giggs, when she married John Clements in 1526. I have thus chosen to locate him at Bucklersbury in the novel, as this is the only home which sources are unanimous in identifying as a place he most certainly (still) owned in 1523. I do, however, disagree with Ackroyd in imagining that, in the 1520s, London was quite as waterlogged and canal-filled as he suggests – and thus I've altered the visibility of the Walbrook to only a few dozen feet inland.

The events of the novel, and the men in More's 'Greek' circle (a term used to denote those interested in 'new learning', or 'humanism'), are fictional. However, I based the suicide of Lancelot Cosyn on a bizarre, real-life death, albeit one from a later century. In the coroner's records for Victorian Devon is a haunting tale of 'frightful self-mutilation'. One James Woodgate, blacksmith, was found dying, and it was recorded that 'there were four wounds in his abdomen which had been made by a red-hot poker. Mr Boddy [in a marvellous piece of nominative determinism], surgeon, was sent for; and he advised his removal to the Devon and Exeter Hospital, where he was removed the same evening; and died on Thursday night from the injuries he had inflicted. When asked why he did it, he said, "For the want of the grace of God."' I'd advise anyone with a penchant for the ghoulish to delve into the coroner's records.

The murders recounted by More in the novel – of the 'suicide – or was it?' and the strangling of a man and the roasting of his corpse in an oven – are both real Tudor-era events (the first being the notorious Richard Hunne fiasco). You can find them in John G. Bellamy's *Strange, Inhuman Deaths: Murder in Tudor England* (2006: Praeger). This book is also invaluable in demonstrating how murders in the period were commonly investigated (or not).

On the subject of early modern medical men, it is worth noting that 'doctor' in the period more often denoted a divine rather than a physician. Wolsey did have his own physician – the mysterious Dr Augustine – who was briefly dismissed for bribery before returning to service and greater favour. This fellow seems, however, to have been busier in spying activities than in administering to the cardinal's aches and pains. For all things medical, I'd recommend Sylvia Barbara Soberton's *Medical Downfall of the Tudors: Sex, Reproduction, and Succession* (2020). Soberton provides not only a thrilling account of the dynasty's ailments but also traces the development of the field of medicine in the period. She must also be commended for shedding light on less well-known (and less flattering) images of Catherine of Aragon, which indicate that she had the stout, prominent lower jaw and underbite more commonly associated with her relatives, the Habsburgs.

Another event depicted in the novel is the famous dressing-down delivered by Wolsey to Lord Henry Percy, heir to the earldom of Northumberland. This is recounted in Wolsey's usher George Cavendish's *The Life of Cardinal Wolsey*. It is supposed to have taken place in 1523, though the specific date is unknown (and therefore as mysterious as so much of Anne Boleyn's early life at court). I have placed it in April. In her *The Rise and Fall of Anne Boleyn* (1989: Cambridge University Press), Retha Warnicke suggests that a letter written by Northumberland in June, complaining that he had to return to London despite having just been there for the parliament, might relate to his being recalled by Wolsey over the Boleyn affair. However, she notes that the letter does not explicitly state this, and so his reasons for being recalled on this occasion remain conjecture. At any rate, it is clear that some form of relationship between Anne and Percy existed, and was broken off at Wolsey's – and Henry VIII's – command during this year. As always, fans of Anne are best served by Eric Ives's seminal study: *The Life and Death of Anne Boleyn* (2004: Wiley).

I hope you enjoyed this book and hope equally that Anthony will return to life in a future story. Whether you did or didn't like his latest experiences in service, I'd love to hear from you. You can get in touch with me on Twitter @ScrutinEye or on Instagram @steven.veerapen.3. Thanks for reading!